MORRIS AUTOMATED INFORMATION NETWORK
P9-EMF-415

LEOPARDS KILL

LEOPARDS KILL

Jim DeFelice

A TOM DOHERTY ASSOCIATES BOOK
NEW YORK

This is a work of fiction. All of the characters, organizations, and events portrayed in this novel are either products of the author's imagination or are used fictitiously.

LEOPARDS KILL

This book is printed on acid-free paper.

A Forge Book
Published by Tom Doherty Associates, LLC
175 Fifth Avenue
New York, NY 10010

www.tor-forge.com

Forge® is a registered trademark of Tom Doherty Associates, LLC.

Library of Congress Cataloging-in-Publication Data

DeFelice, James.
Leopards kill / Jim DeFelice.—1st hardcover ed.
p. cm.
"A Tom Doherty Associates book."
ISBN-13: 978-0-7653-1436-9
ISBN-10: 0-7653-1436-3
1. Security consultants—Fiction. 2. Missing persons—Fiction. 3. Afghanistan—Fiction. I. Title.
PS3554.E357L46 2007
813'.54—dc22

2007004514

First Edition: May 2007

Printed in the United States of America

0 9 8 7 6 5 4 3 2 1

Leopards kill; it's what they do. . . .
—proverb

Note: This is all fiction. It's not supposed to be real. Even the things that are real have been changed, like the mass in Kabul, which is really at 1700, not 0800.

Half along life's road
I lost my way in a dark wood,
Savage and fierce, its
Shadows more desolate than death.

I do not know how I got myself there,
But this is how I came back.

—DANTE ALIGHIERI,
The Divine Comedy

PAGANS

1

VEGAS

YOU expect more things out of life as you get older, and you come to think of your expectations as natural. You start to think that the things you get are things that you're entitled to. You forget about the way luck plays its hand, about the little tricks of fate that take you to a certain place and time. You have what you deserve, then you are what you deserve, then the things that surround you become your identity. You start thinking of yourself as the man with the big house overlooking the hills, the guy with the well-kept lawn and the gunite swimming pool. You start measuring yourself by the vacations you take, and the car you drive, and the shade of granite your wife wants for the perfect kitchen counter. These become who you are, and you stop measuring yourself against the things that lie deep within your heart—the rage, the anger, the insatiable hunger.

You go on like that, unconsciously lulling yourself into thinking there is nothing else until you stand in a fancy hotel in Las Vegas, running your hand on the marble of the bureau top, gazing across the open room at your wife lying naked on the bed: you think, this is what I am, the Italian pants and loafers, the bespoke sport coat, the Cuban cigars waiting on the table. This is what I expect out of life and this is what I am.

"I'm going now," you tell your wife. "I'll be back."

She murmurs something. You tell her you love her. The voice comes not from your heart, not from that dark deep place where hunger and pain live, but from the surface, from the silk shirt and the gel that smooths your hair. You remember how she felt beneath you an hour before. You tell her you love her again, vaguely uneasy, and you go, you leave, because it's business, and it's what you've come to expect.

WHEN I left the room that night it was a little past eleven, Vegas time. My wife Sharon and I had come in from New York only a few hours before and our bodies were still on East Coast time. Most of my adult life has been spent changing time zones, and I'm used to the switches, but Sharon wanted to sleep. Which was fine with me, because I'd arranged to meet with the people who'd invited us here, security types who'd hired my firm to help review security at the Palatine, where I was staying, and another hotel farther up the Strip. They were interested in beefing up their coverage for high rollers and other VIPs, which was one of our specialties. My partner and I had dozens of specialties; we used to tell our clients that our company Iron Rock would do anything for them from mow the grass to kill their competitors, though not for the same price.

Some people laughed when I told them that. Others asked how much contract killings cost.

The head of security at the Palatine was a man named Johnny B. McCann—Johnny or Johnny B to his friends, Mr. B to employees. Johnny had started out as a Teamster in New York. Judging from the stories he told, his main job had been to grab stuff off trucks and walk picket lines when locals needed to strike. From there he got into restaurants, working as a front manager. This was back in the late sixties and early seventies when the Mob in New York had a heavy Teamster connection and ran about fifty percent of the restaurants, usually into the ground. I'm guessing that when Johnny went from trucks to tablecloths, he was simply moving from one division in the "company" to another, but Johnny would never be so indiscreet as to mention the Mob, especially in Vegas.

Johnny's big chance came one afternoon when a fire broke out at the restaurant. He jumped behind the counter, grabbed the cash register, and hustled it outside—protecting it from the firemen, he says. The bosses noticed; in a couple of months he moved to a restaurant with a shortage problem and took over as manager. The restaurant's medical insurance skyrocketed, but the shortage stopped. After that, Johnny's employers sent him to Chicago, and there he got involved with the Playboy Clubs, and then somewhere along the way, he got to Vegas and went legit, or at least as legit as anyone in corporate gambling can be.

Johnny B was waiting in the hotel lobby when I came down. He had one of his brighter lieutenants with him, a man called Peanut. Peanut had been in the U.S. Air Force and had left as a chief master sergeant. He'd had something to do with security on nuclear-missile bases, which sounds damn impressive unless you happen to have visited them.

Peanut was a hulk of a guy, looming over me and I'm a good six three. He wasn't in any sort of shape, but he was big, and size can cover a lot of mistakes. Unlike Johnny, who flashed a gold chain and exotic rings along with his black silk shirt and white jacket, Peanut was turned out in a sedate black suit, fitted so perfectly to his frame that you couldn't tell he carried a good-sized breadbasket with him. Where Johnny flashed a Rolex and a huge turquoise ring, Peanut's watch was tucked well up his sleeve. But it was a Patek Philippe, probably more expensive than Johnny's.

"The man himself," said Johnny as I got off the elevator. He walked toward me, pointing his finger like a gun. Johnny was a short guy, and though well into his sixties, he still moved with lithe grace, a boxer skating across the ring at the start of a fight. The strains of Hell's Kitchen played in his voice, and he had a way of tugging at your jacket and poking you when he said hello that suggested something beyond intimacy. The first time you met him you came away thinking he knew you all his life. You could go for months without seeing him, and there he'd be in the hotel lobby, pulling you along, asking where your cigar was, demanding whether you were finally ready to give up drinking that crap bourbon and move up to Scotch.

We shook hands, I said hello to Peanut, and we walked outside. A limo was waiting. All the doormen—there were a dozen—snapped to attention when we came out. My first drill sergeant in the army would have thought he'd found heaven.

"We'll pick up Freslevan and have a little fun," said Johnny. "You know Chris?"

Freslevan was the vice president for security at the Kingdom Casino, the other hotel I'd come to look over.

"I talked to him on the phone. That's it."

"You'll like him. Great friend of mine. Real character."

In Johnny's world, you were a player, a character, or a jerk. Most people were the latter.

The Kingdom was just as big as Johnny's casino and, while they were owned by the same conglomerate, in many ways a bitter rival. But the security staffs often worked together, sharing data and techniques; keeping the scumbags out was in everybody's interests. And getting along with other people when it was in his interest was Johnny B's style. His ego didn't get in his way, and he seemed not to be particularly jealous or competitive—at least not in the ways that most of us are. He could stand apart from things, above them, really. That was what I admired about him. That and the fact that he knew his business pretty damn well. He came off like a backslapping politician, and he was that, a throwback to the old-school gladhander, the hustlers he'd grown up with in New York City. But his eyes saw a hell of a lot, and his ears caught what his eyes missed. The fancy suit and jewelry were a costume, camouflage for something very hard, very ferocious if it needed to be, but also very controlled. I had no doubt that if I ever got into a fight with him, even a fistfight, it would be a close thing. And that's the highest compliment I can give a man.

After we picked up Freslevan, we went over to a small club a few blocks off the Strip. It wasn't a casino or even a bar; it was a shooting gallery. Johnny had arranged for us all to bust up some paper with vintage tommy guns. The Thompson is the weapon that gangsters made famous back in the 1920s and '30s. Most times in movies you see it with the drum in front of the trigger. There's a belt of bullets there; fifty or a hundred bullets can spurt up through the gun in only a few seconds. It's a real rush the first time you use the gun, mostly because of the romance from the movies. The design's outdated now—the Thompson can't really compare to something like an H&K MP-5N, the submachine gun of choice for most counterterror and SWAT teams. But it can still get the job done and it's got a hell of a roar when it lets loose.

People think I'm a gun nut because I had a marksman's badge and was a weapons sergeant in the army. I'm not that into guns, though, no more than a carpenter is into hammers or saws. They're tools. I like good tools, but I don't make a fetish of them. I did the best at the range but it didn't mean anything special to me, not nearly as much as it did to Peanut and Freslevan especially. He would have liked to have beaten me. He had a competitive glint in his eye and that locked-jaw frown some people get when they block the rest of the world out and really concentrate on an objective. But he had a little trouble with the gun's initial kick and couldn't keep it steady enough through the burst to do as well as I did, even after a few turns.

"Winner buys," laughed Johnny B after our hour was up.

They all thought that was funny. I even laughed, and when we reached the bar on the observation deck at Stratosphere I laid down my credit card. The bartender glanced at Johnny, then pushed the card away.

"Mr. B's friends don't pay in this town," he said.

I put away the card and took out a hundred bill to leave for a tip. Such largesse deserved to be rewarded.

"Here's to Paradise," said Freslevan, holding up his drink.

"Vegas is more like the desert where Jesus was tempted," said Johnny. "Forty days and forty nights, then taken to a mountaintop and shown the universe. That's Vegas—the mirage at the bottom of the peak."

I smiled, even as I was thinking it wasn't any of those. Metaphors are easy. A thing is what it is, a place is itself. You could get anything here, true, but it wasn't a fall from grace as Johnny implied. At least not for me.

"If it's not Paradise, it's close," said Freslevan. "Hell on you if you gamble, though, huh, Jack?"

"I guess," I told him.

"How's Merc?" Johnny asked. "Getting along?"

Merc Conrad was my partner.

"Merc's Merc," I said.

"Not around, huh?"

"Overseas."

Merc spent a lot of time overseas, mostly on projects for the government. "Something for Uncle," we called them. We had things going in Iraq, Afghanistan, Morocco, and Italy. I hadn't seen Merc since back around New Year's or maybe just after, but that wasn't unusual. We handled different parts of the company and were busy as hell. A lot of our time was spent traveling in opposite directions. We used satellite and cell phones, e-mail, and instant messages when we had to communicate, depending on the circumstances.

"You were in the army like Merc?" Freslevan asked as my glass was refilled.

"That's where I met him, yeah."

"Special Forces?"

I gave him my standard reply: "If I tell you, I'm supposed to kill you."

Lame, yeah, but everybody laughs. And they generally move on, getting the idea that you don't talk about it.

"Why'd you leave?" Freslevan asked.

Sometimes I say that my hitch was up, that it wouldn't have made sense to stay much longer because with the pension, I'd be working for half pay. Sometimes I say I got bored. Sometimes I say I thought I'd get out and get rich. Each has some truth to it. Even better, each one is the sort of thing people like to hear. Ties things into knots for them, makes them think they know something about me.

Tonight I just shrugged.

I took out one of the cigars I'd had in my pocket and cut it, aiming carefully with the double-edged razor and pushing hard against the tobacco so the tip snapped off with a loud click. I leaned my elbows against the bartop and took out my Zippo to light it.

"Nice lighter," said Johnny. "Old one?"

"Actually it's not," I said. "Hard to get the right fluid for the old ones." I finished lighting the end of my cigar and handed him the lighter. Then I took out a cigar for him. It was a Cohiba Esplendidos—a Cuban cigar that cost nearly fifty dollars American. It tasted fantastic—but let's face it; I didn't buy it for the taste. I bought it because Cohiba Esplendidos are outlawed in America, and are therefore very expensive to get here. And because Johnny would know what it was.

"You have good taste, Jacky," he told me as he slid his fingers up and down the cigar, turning it over as if it were a jewel to be examined. "Very good taste."

He lit it and then took a long, slow taste, staring at the glow at the end pensively. Then he started telling some of his stories.

I'd met Johnny four years before when I first came out to Vegas with Merc; I'd seen him at least twice a year since then and he always told stories. I'd never heard the same one twice.

Tonight he talked about growing up on the Lower West Side of New York—aka Hell's Kitchen. The Irish gangs there were tougher than the Italians, he said. The Italians would try to get their money out of you if you were late; they might beat you up, but they'd let you live, figuring that was the best way to get you to pay. The Irish would just kill you, and get the money from your relatives.

We drank for a while more. Freslevan was from the Midwest and had been an FBI agent. He'd worked on some pretty big cases, he claimed, and told us one about a politician who'd accepted a bribe in exchange for awarding contracts to build a sewer system in a local town.

Johnny B smiled through the story. "That's nothing," he said. "Show me a town where the mayor, the highway superintendent, and the building inspector aren't on the take, and I'll show you a ghost town. You think anybody in the world's honest?"

"Most are," said Freslevan. "Most."

Johnny turned to Peanut, who was silently sipping his rum and Coke. "Most people honest?" he asked him.

"I'm surprised how many are," said Peanut. "Truly surprised."

"Are you honest, Jack?" Freslevan asked me, leaning down across the bar.

"Jacky's an exception," said Johnny quickly. "He doesn't count."

"I'm honest," I said. But Johnny had already launched into another story and the others weren't listening to me.

At some point four very good-looking women wearing pretty silk dresses descended on us. They wore a light veil of perfume, each one subtly different, each the clean scent of someone who'd just stepped from a bath. Johnny bought them all drinks. He looked at me. I shook my head slightly. The girls stayed for a drink and then they left.

We hung around until it was nearly five A.M. I smoked two cigars, and had several drinks, though not nearly as many as the others. I didn't offer any stories. I'm not a talker and, besides, the best stories I have are ones I can't tell.

As we walked to the elevator Freslevan mentioned something about Central America and what a shithole it was. He'd been there for a month on an FBI assignment and came away convinced it was the armpit of the world. I disagreed. I said the jungles there were beautiful, or they had been when I was there.

"You were there?" asked Freslevan. "In the jungles?"

I explained that I had helped train some government troops to deal with rebels in Guatemala. I'd also spent a little time in Nicaragua and Peru. All of that came before Afghanistan, my last assignment before leaving the service.

As we were talking, another guy got into the elevator with us. Johnny and the others didn't notice him, but I did. He stared at me with bloodshot eyes. They didn't go with the rest of his face, or the rest of his body. If you took those eyes away, he'd have looked like a normal working-class guy, maybe a truck driver or a factory hand who'd managed to put a little money away for a few days off. But his eyes—they were locked into something that wasn't middle class. They weren't the eyes of a driver or a carpenter or a clerk who worked nine to five and dreamed of winning his retirement stake on the roulette wheel. These were eyes I'd seen before, though not in a Vegas elevator, not in a real fancy hotel. They were violent eyes, the kind that sizes you up a split second before striking. They radiated anger. Taken by surprise, I could feel my heartbeat jump.

"You were in Guatemala?" said the stranger.

"Yeah." I snapped the word out, quick and flat, without any emotion—certainly without an invitation to talk.

He didn't get the message.

"You were in the army, right? I heard you talking. You were in Special Forces."

"Nah."

"You're not that tough."

"Hey, now." Johnny B pointed at the guy. "Leave my friend alone. Don't be a jerk."

The idea of an older, shorter guy sticking up for someone obviously stronger and younger than himself baffled the man. He probably was insulted at being called a jerk, but he didn't know what to say. The elevator stopped, we got out. As we walked, I took my last cigar out of my pocket, turned back to see if Johnny wanted it.

The man in the elevator had pulled out a gun. It was a small pistol, an old one, snub-nosed, a revolver. He stood maybe eight feet from me, and only four or five from Johnny. No one spoke.

"Put that away," I told the guy. "Or you're going to regret it."

He didn't move.

"If you don't put it away," I said, "you're going to be damaged very badly."

Thinking back, it may have been Johnny who moved first. It would be very much like him. Even at sixty-something he was still a fifteen-year-old at heart; even in Vegas he acted like he was on the streets of Hell's Kitchen. All I know is that the man started to bring the pistol up, extending his arm to fire. I pushed down with my left foot, took two steps and launched my right foot into his arm. It was a straightforward move, something I'd practiced many times in Krav Maga, an Israeli self-defense discipline originally designed for just such situations: unarmed defenders facing people with guns. The gun went off, but by then my foot had pushed the man's arm away and the bullet flew toward the ceiling. In the next moment I had the bastard pinned on the ground with both knees on his arms.

And then I started hitting him. I don't know how many times. I lost control of myself somewhere after the kick. It wasn't the way I had been trained, neither in Krav Maga nor in Special Forces, nor anywhere else. You train always to be in control. It wasn't the bourbon, or the jet lag. It wasn't anything chemical or external. It was me.

Johnny B finally stopped me. He put his hand on my shoulder and gripped it, hard.

"You want to back off now, Jacky. These fellows will take it from here."

I looked up as if I'd been woken from a dream. Two of the hotel's security people were standing there. I rose, and they grabbed the man off the floor. Another had already retrieved the gun.

"I appreciate what you did for me there," Johnny B told me, straightening his collar. "That son of a bitch would have gut-shot me. I appreciate it. You're a real player."

My hands were red and raw. I looked over at the guy I'd been hitting as the security people got him up, finally aware of how hard I'd been pummeling him. I worried for a second that I'd killed him. He was coughing and moaning, and as the security people prodded him forward he walked on his own power. Barely.

"I think maybe Jacky oughta go get cleaned up and get some rest," Johnny told Peanut. The Stratosphere's security supervisor had appeared and was standing nearby. "Why don't you take our friend back over to the hotel? Make sure the woman he sleeps with tonight is his wife." He grinned, and then pointed at me. "I owe you one. That's a good thing."

A good thing.

I walked out of the hotel, still slightly dazed. I was thirsty, but I knew better than to stop for a drink. The car had been parked in a

VIP slot on the front drive and the valets brought it forward instantly. One of them opened the door for me and I slid in. Peanut got in and put it in gear, and we went out onto the Strip.

My cell phone began to vibrate.

"Jack," I said, pulling the phone open. I expected it was my wife, asking where I was, or maybe Johnny telling me the security people or police needed to talk. But instead it was a male voice I didn't recognize.

"Is this Jack Pilgrim?"

"Yeah. Who is this?"

"I'm calling for Jason," said the man. "You're needed right away."

Jason wasn't a person; it was a program we were running for Uncle in Afghanistan. It was Merc's deal; I didn't know much about it.

"I'll have Merc get to you as soon he can," I said. "He's really the expert."

"You're going to have to be here by noon. It's about your partner."

"He's not dead, is he?"

I don't know why I said that.

"It's about your partner."

"Noon's impossible," I told him.

"I thought your business was to do the impossible."

The phone clicked dead. I stared at it for a second, then folded it up and put it in my pocket and turned to Peanut. "I think you better take me to the airport."

2

D.C.

THEY called the company "Genius Imports." Whoever says the CIA doesn't have a sense of humor has never dealt with them. Or maybe they dealt with Cody Unsel.

Unsel's face looks like one of those fancy fossil rocks they put inside boardrooms to impress visiting VIPs. It's possible he'd had acne as a kid, but more likely that his personality ate its way through his skin. By the time I met him, he was on the dark side of forty and wore his pants high under a dark suit hoping to disguise the basketball he carried around where his stomach should have been.

The CIA literally had hundreds of agents with experience in Afghanistan, stretching back to the 1980s when the Russians tried to rub out dissension in the Muslim workers' paradise once and for all. Unsel wasn't one of them. I'm not even sure he had ever even been there. He was well qualified for his job, though, since the main requirement was that he be a prick to deal with.

Unsel was an officer from the covert side in charge of coordinating what Uncle called "external projects" in Afghanistan. He had a business card claiming he was executive vice president of Genius Imports; according to the company's Web site, it imported clothing from "exotic Asia." It was a front, of course, and a damn elaborate one—you could buy everything from Iranian rugs to Afghan hats off the Web site. I was tempted once to see what would happen if I ordered an Iranian rug, which supposedly were illegal to import.

Genius Imports was set up so the CIA could hire companies like mine to do jobs that were too petty or too nasty or too important for the government to do, without making it too obvious who hired us. It was a very small part of the overall Afghanistan program, and the amount of money Genius Imports doled out was nothing compared to the overt aid projects that brought food and other supplies into the country. Genius Imports also didn't deal with the big security and contractor firms like Blackwater and Halliburton. It was simply for small fry like us, who could stay below the radar.

Contractors have gotten a lot of ink, most of it bad, because of Iraq, but all most of them do is what they are hired to do. They're not really replacement armies, even if in some cases they've been pushed into that role. Armies are trained to fight wars, not fix electric grids or build schools, or even provide security for local officials. I'll grant you that in a lot of cases it'd be cheaper for the government to invest the time, money, and lives to do the job itself. But you could say the same thing of anyone who hires a lawn company to take care of the grass.

Jason was one of those special jobs Genius Imports handled, something that had to be kept quiet and confidential—not for security reasons, but because of international politics. It called for us to provide a number of different training sessions for police officers and officials from around Afghanistan, everything from first aid to hostage negotiation. Most of the sessions were in Kabul, the capital. While we ran some of the classes ourselves, mostly what we did was arrange classroom space and instructors, made sure there were refreshments, then sat back and collected the money.

Thirty years ago, the State Department would have handled Jason itself. But the penchant for outsourcing of government functions made outside coordinators necessary, if only because the government no longer had the expertise in-house to run the programs—and yes, the sort of expertise I'm talking about mostly involved picking up the telephone and offering people money.

There was a twist in Jason's case, which was the reason we were selected in the first place. The UN mandate for "nation building" in Afghanistan called for funds from private groups, rather than governments. To keep the UN happy, the paperwork was arranged to make it look as if nonprofits—not Uncle—had hired Genius Imports to hire us. We'd done that sort of thing before, most importantly in a project to count poppy production in the eastern provinces. A UN-designated group did the counting while we provided security, ostensibly funded by a grant from an antidrug group. But the dollars came to us directly from the CIA.

Not so coincidentally, arrangements like this were perfect for getting money to people in the outer provinces whose support for the central government was shaky. The money was virtually untraceable by GSA auditors. No embarrassing questions, no unworthy answers. That had happened during the poppy program, where Unsel gave us a list of people who were to be given "expense money" prior to the start of the operation. This was in addition to the "rental payments," which were essentially bribes to local warlords to keep the UN surveyors alive in the southern provinces. As far as I knew, those sorts of arrangements weren't part of Jason.

Genius Imports' office building looked about as fancy as a rental storage unit. There were plenty of names on the directory in the reception area, but I didn't see anybody else in the building except for the two bored security guards at the front desk. They didn't bother asking my name when I came in, and I didn't give it. I'd been watched by security cameras from the moment I drove into the parking lot, and no doubt Unsel had already told them to let me through. I took the elevator to the second floor and stepped out into the dimly lit hallway. Steel-gray doors lined the corridor, the occupants identified mostly by numbers and letters, though here and there a small plaque next to the door gave a name: FIRST CENTRAL SECURITY, INFRA-CIRCUITS, ACME TESTING. Front companies all, I'm sure.

Genius Imports was at the end of the line. The door buzzed open as I reached for the knob.

"You look like hell, Jack," said Unsel, sitting behind the steel desk at the center of the room.

"Yeah, well, I blew off an appointment with my hairdresser to get here."

"You could have at least taken a shower."

"Is Merc in trouble?"

"Don't you know?"

"I'm not his babysitter."

"Where is he?"

"In Afghanistan, last time I checked."

"Where in Afghanistan, Jack?"

"Kabul, I think. The capital."

"I know what the capital is." Unsel's tone, not particularly pleasant to begin with, got two or three degrees nastier. "He's not there, Jack. Where the hell is he?"

"I don't know."

"Why not?"

"Because I'm not his babysitter. Is this about Jason, or what?"

I wasn't trying to be uncooperative. At this point, I figured Merc was in trouble—serious trouble—and the fact that neither I nor our office coordinator Cynthia Munson had heard about it only made it seem more dire. I'd had Cynthia send several text messages to our Kabul office, a rented desk in an office we shared with several other foreign firms. She hadn't gotten an answer.

Unsel frowned. "When was the last time you saw your partner?"

"Saw him? I don't know. A few weeks back."

"Weeks or months?"

"You know, Unsel, I'm starting to feel like I'm under an inquisition here. Or like maybe you have the mistaken notion that I'm back in the army and you're a colonel and I'm a punk private."

"You should be so lucky." Unsel got up and grabbed a small briefcase that had been propped against the empty bookshelf at the side of the room. "You know what's going on in Afghanistan, right, Jack? The media says the UN is taking over, but really we're bugging out. In two weeks, Jack."

"Two weeks? I thought it was by the end of the year."

"Two weeks. All military units will be out, except for token forces."

"How does that affect us?"

The official line was that our guys and the NATO people were no longer needed, and Afghan troops were taking over, with the UN people there more or less as window dressing. I had a natural prejudice against most of the Afghan units—based on bitter experience—but the bottom line was, we couldn't stay in the damn country forever.

Unsel slapped the briefcase flat on the desk and opened it; he fished out a photograph and slid it across to me. "Is that Merc?"

The man in the picture had a beard and wore an Afghan greatcoat over nondescript pants and shirt; the photo was so grainy I couldn't tell whether the pants were gray, green, or maybe even brown. He wore a traditional wool *pakol,* an Afghan hat that can be rolled down for warmth, or, maybe in this case, to help hide some of the face.

The man in the picture could have been just about anyone—except for the thick, lightning-shaped scar that ran from the corner of his right eye down his cheek and into his beard. It was dark, the most distinct feature in the photo. I knew that scar as well as I knew any of the wounds on my own body, including the three healed bullet holes. Merc got it saving my life.

"Looks like Merc when we were there in the army," I said.

"It was taken a month ago. Look at the date."

"Is that when it was taken, or did you just have the computer stamp it like that?"

"Stop playing games, Jacky. Where the hell is your partner? He took off with the money for Leopard. We want it back."

"What's Leopard?"

UNSEL didn't explain what Leopard was. He didn't believe I didn't know. I don't blame him.

I didn't know what Leopard was, but obviously it involved money that the CIA hadn't gotten back. Pleading ignorance didn't get me very far, and I just shut up when he wouldn't explain. Maybe it was the influence of lawyers, or maybe it was just plain old common sense finally kicking in.

Combat sense, really—recce the situation before committing your forces.

Unsel told me I had a week to account for the money, which meant, get it back to the CIA. If I'd been in a better mood I would have laughed. Nothing happens in Afghanistan in a week. A week there is like an hour here.

Or an eternity, depending on the circumstances.

"Two million dollars, Jack. We want it back and accounted for. You got it?"

"Listen—"

"No, you listen. I don't care about Afghanistan, I don't care about the Taliban, I don't care about you, and I sure don't care about Mercury Conrad. That money comes back and is accounted for in a week. If it's not, you're going to prison. And it won't be a cushy place like Danbury, I guarantee."

3

NEW YORK

We called our firm Iron Rock Solutions, and usually shortened it to Iron Rock. The name came from the road where Merc's aunt lived in Pennsylvania; when we first got out of the service, he crashed there for a bit. We liked the name because it was simple and didn't really give away what we did. Which meant we could do anything.

Mercury Conrad and I met in the army when we were both trying to get into Special Forces. I don't know what it's like now, but at the time the training was considered so tough that the army offered pre-training for it. I call it training, but it was really a kind of selection process, designed to winnow out guys who couldn't take the pressure, physically first, then, and much more importantly, mentally.

Real training didn't begin until you were actually selected. At the time, the army liked to say that Special Forces guys selected themselves. I guess that was true to an extent, but I think the instructors were pretty good at subtly convincing people that they were not cut out for the job. Sometimes they weren't so subtle at all, but those were the obvious cases, crazoids usually, though I remember this guy who had to weigh close to three hundred pounds and looked like he was going to have a heart attack just kitting up.

For me, the worst part of the selection process wasn't the combat drills or the survival stuff or even the marches, which were brutally boring and went on forever, slog after sleep-inducing slog. The worst part was having to trust someone else, time and again, with your life. I never felt that in basic training or anywhere else in the army, not even in airborne school, where you *are* putting yourself in the rigger's hands and the aircrew's. Maybe that was a defect. I know guys say combat is really all about your buddies, trusting them and fighting for them. I just never felt it until I got to Special Forces. And Merc was the first guy I learned to trust. In a lot of ways, he was the only guy I ever really depended on.

There's a certain mystique attached to Special Forces. Like most guys, I guess, I got sucked into it a bit, especially at first; my head got swelled. I'd be lying if I said I didn't buy the macho take-no-prisoners crap. I did. I still do. But I got into Special Forces for a lot of other reasons. Boredom was one. I couldn't stand doing the same old, same old, different day, same shit.

Money was another. Not a lot of money in the vast scheme of things—sure as hell not even pocket change compared to what we did with Iron Rock—but a little extra here and there, which when you're an enlisted man, even a sergeant, adds up. The army is a lot like a big corporation, and enlisted grunts like me are blue-collar workers. You get extra pay for different job qualifications and tougher working conditions. A little bit for this training, a bonus for gritting your teeth in that situation. Special Forces was one way—not the only way, but one way—to do a little better by yourself.

Merc, though, joined the army with the plan of getting into Special Forces; it just took him a heck of a lot longer than he originally planned. He had trouble making sergeant, which at the time was a requirement. This has changed a bit, but at the time you couldn't enlist and go straight into any of the Special Operations Commands; you had to work your way there, put in your dues and climb up the ranks. Merc had a bit of a problem interfacing with officers, and that black mark held him back until finally he managed to work himself into a situation where that was considered a plus.

We met during a three- or four-week course designed to toughen up volunteers before they went for the selection program. I was in good shape before I went, but Merc was better. If I did five hundred push-ups in a physical training session—and yeah, I'm bragging—he could do a thousand. If I hiked twenty miles with a full combat load, he ran it. The only place where we were even was after selection, out in the field, when we had to come up with solutions to problems that didn't involve physical strength or endurance. Merc was good, don't get me wrong—he always saw angles and exits and work-arounds. But sometimes he was just too clever for his own good. Sometimes he ignored the obvious, charge-ahead solution in favor of some Rube Goldberg approach that showed how sharp he was.

Merc also had a tendency to piss people off. They didn't know how to take him. A lot of times they thought he was bragging when really he wasn't. A lot of officers couldn't stand him. I don't know how it is now, but at the time officers were assigned to Special Forces for pretty short periods; you could have a captain with an A team, the main building block of Special Forces units, for maybe six months. A lot of these officers didn't have anywhere near the military experience that the men they were commanding had. That's not to say that they weren't good soldiers or good officers. But.

At a minimum, most didn't have anywhere near the same dedication to Special Forces as the soldiers they commanded did. They saw it more as one more important ticket to punch en route to generaldom. We saw it as our life's ambition.

And there were a fair amount of officers, not a majority, but a number, who were just shit-ass dumb. That's just the way it was. Merc's problem was that he let them know it.

By the time we left, Merc had worn out his welcome in a variety of places. He'd received a bunch of commendations and two bronze stars for valor under combat, but his reputation as being hard to work with had gotten him shunted to what was basically a clerical position at Special Operations Command. He could have stayed there another eight or nine years, playing golf most afternoons then retiring. Instead, he talked me into forming Iron Rock with him. I'd just come back from southeastern Afghanistan, and frankly, a job hauling abandoned cars to junkyards would have sounded like a good idea.

This was in early 2002, when we had al Qaeda on the run, before the invasion of Iraq. Security was a hot ticket then; everybody wanted more of it, corporations especially. They had big bucks to spend showing their board of directors that they weren't going to let another 9/11 take them down. A company owned by two ex-Special Forces guys had instant credibility in the security field. It was kind of silly, really; I don't think more than a tenth of what we'd spent our time doing in the field had any application back home. But I guess SF did prove that we could deal with the harshest crap going and come up smiling, so maybe they weren't that far off.

We had more than job credibility, though. We were treated like rock stars, celebrities, because we'd been on the front line in the "war on terror." Afghanistan was on the other side of the world, but in New York City especially, people knew what the war was all about. They could still smell its first casualties in the air. Shaking hands with a guy who'd been hunting the Taliban for months was the next best thing to having been out there doing it yourself.

We set up our office in a Midtown tower, one of the ones you crane your neck at and still can't quite see the top. The reception area had fancy glass-block and gnarled walnut walls. There was an Italian marble floor, and the restrooms had more gold in them than Fort Knox. The entire floor had belonged to an ad agency that went belly-up after 9/11; we leased what had been the agency's front office. They'd designed it to impress their clients, and it sure worked for ours. Within a few weeks, we were running security checks and training bodyguards for several international banks. Each contract was worth several times more money than I'd been paid in my entire life. It wasn't all profit, of course, but a heck of a lot of it was. We hired old friends, then old friends of friends, then friends of friends of friends we never even knew we had, and still there was plenty of money left over for us.

Seven or eight months after we started, things began to slow down. We still had plenty of commitments, but since most of the contracts we'd signed were front-loaded, we didn't have that much cash coming in. We started worrying about making payroll. The realities of running a business set in.

Merc and I beat the bushes for new clients. Iraq tarnished a bit of the SF mystique, and at the same time the boutique banks and hedge funds that had been our best customers began cutting back to save the bottom line. Selling security's a lot like selling flood insurance—you can write plenty of policies after a big storm, but when the sun's shining the money dries up.

That's when I stumbled onto casinos as a specialty. I began with an Indian casino that was owned by a tribe a good friend of mine belonged to; I had to learn on the job, hiring an old pro and a reformed con man to teach me. The con man was a piss and a genius, and obviously not to be trusted. I picked up enough things on the fly so that within a year we had a gig in Atlantic City. A few months after that, we got into Vegas.

Meanwhile, Merc was hooking up with Uncle. Our first contract was to train Iraqi air traffic controllers in self-defense. I can't say how good a job we did, because all six controllers disappeared after our classes in Cairo. Rumor has it they decided being out of work in Egypt was better than holding any sort of job in Iraq. But that hardly mattered to us; we'd done our job and were paid for it. Things grew from there.

OUR New York office was mostly for show. We set up operations with as little overhead as possible. We dealt personally with jobs we wanted to deal with personally, and farmed out the rest. Most of what we did at the office was meet customers there before taking them out to be wined and dined.

Cynthia Munson was part of the show, a big part. She was our secretary/receptionist; she looked and dressed as if she'd just stepped out of a *Vogue* magazine. If there's such a thing as too beautiful, Cynthia was it. Her creamy skin and straight brown hair made her look like an angel some days, and the skirts she wore always seemed as if they were a skin itching to be peeled away. She wasn't dumb either, though like a lot of very pretty women she tended to be treated that way.

Besides sitting behind a large desk and looking good when we had clients in, Cynthia's job was to coordinate communications between our different "interests," as we called the contractors who worked for us. To do that, she had to know where everybody was, Merc and I especially. So I didn't believe her that afternoon when I got in from D.C. and she told me she didn't know where Merc was.

"Honestly, I don't know, Mr. Pilgrim. I don't."

She always called me "Mr. Pilgrim" when things weren't going well.

"He's in Afghanistan, I know that," I told her. "But where?"

"I don't know. Kabul, I would think."

"Then why hasn't he answered the IMs? Or the phone calls? Or the e-mails. You sent them, right?"

"I did."

"How long has he been there?"

"I—" She looked a little bit like she was going to cry, and for the first time it occurred to me that Merc might have been shagging her. "Let me see."

She punched up one of her programs.

"I'd say about three months. Sometimes he's a little vague. You are, too."

"He's been in Afghanistan a lot the past year, hasn't he?"

She nodded. Her eyes were just about welling over now.

"Let's go get a drink down the street," I told her. "Relax a little bit."

"It's four-thirty, Mr. Pilgrim."

Four-thirty was her quitting time.

"Yeah, all right. You're still on the clock, okay? We'll pay you. Or you leave early tomorrow. Your option."

We went down to a small restaurant and bar a block away on the cross street. Back before they outlawed smoking in New York City, the place had been an unofficial cigar bar, a hangout for bankers and financial types who liked to puff on their stogies and sip the latest single-blend whisky in from Scotland. The Scotch was still there, but the smoke was gone, as were most of the place's customers. We got a booth and ordered drinks; she had a martini, I went to double bourbons.

"You look a little beat, Jack," she said.

"I haven't slept. I'll look better tomorrow."

The first sip of bourbon lit a fire in my mouth and throat. I took a deep breath, and when I exhaled, my head felt as if it were encased in a helmet made of pins and needles.

The second sip tore off the helmet. The third sip calmed the fire in my throat.

"Tell me everything you know about what Merc has been up to in Afghanistan," I told Cynthia.

"Is he in bad trouble?"

"I don't know. He may not be in any trouble. Or he might be in a lot. Until I find him and talk to him, I don't know."

Her hand trembled as she put the martini to her lips. It steadied her, but it didn't loosen her tongue much. Probably she didn't know all that much more than I did. Merc was handling Jason, which supposedly had been taking more and more of his time lately; whenever she asked what he was doing, Jason was the answer. She couldn't remember the last time she talked to him on the phone. The last instant messages she had from him were almost four weeks old. They were routine notes, and they didn't say where he was. Cynthia just assumed Kabul, because that's where our operations were.

Our secure messaging system gave you the option of saving the messages sent to and from our computers, but when I asked her if she'd saved them, she narrowed her eyes and looked at me as if I were wearing a mask.

"I wasn't supposed to save them. Save no IMs. That's company policy."

"Since when?"

"Like a year at least. Mr. Conrad was very clear on that."

Had I signed off on that policy? I couldn't remember.

"When was the last time you saw Merc?" I asked her. "Face-to-face."

She glanced away, as if she were looking up the memory in a book whose pages were written on the nearby wall. The soft light of the bar made her look even more beautiful than usual, and the slight puffiness around her eyes from her sadness made her more alluring. Every man has an innate protective instinct. Call it the damsel-in-distress syndrome. We can't help feeling sorry for a woman who's hurting, and from feeling sorry it's a short leap to feeling something else.

I'd never been interested in Cynthia sexually—too consciously pretty, too delicate, and besides, she was part of our "team" and therefore too important to screw up with a casual affair—but at that moment lust rushed through the crack opened by her tears. I drained my bourbon and pushed the glass toward the edge of the table for a refill.

"I don't think I've seen him since December," said Cynthia. "Winter. Now it's spring."

I hadn't seen him since just after New Year's, five months now. It didn't seem that unusual until I thought about it. With cell phones and sat phones and e-mail and IMs and faxes, I lost track of how I communicated with people. More than that, Merc and I had been steadily moving into our own separate spheres. Not just with work, either. We used to hang around a fair amount when we started Iron Rock. Then, after I met Sharon, that happened less and less.

"What else was Merc up to in Afghanistan?" I asked her as the waiter set down a new drink. "Besides Jason?"

She squinted at me again. This time, the squint was more attractive—a prelude, I thought.

"Jason was the only thing that I know."

"Nothing else?"

"Wouldn't you know?" she asked.

"Yeah, you'd think. Did Merc ever refer to something called 'Leopard'?"

"Leopard, no." She put her hand on mine. Her warm fingers sent a shock through me. "Is he all right, Jack? Really all right?"

"You know Merc. He's always all right," I told her.

Her eyes held mine, then hardened. She took her hand away.

"Sharon," she whispered.

"My wife went with Merc?"

Impossible. For a long moment, though, it was all I could think.

But that wasn't what Cynthia meant at all.

"What the *hell* are you doing?"

SHARON'S voice was like the growl of a dog, warning an intruder away. It wasn't addressed to Cynthia, though; when I turned she was staring at me, hands on her hips, chin set. "Why the hell didn't you tell me you were leaving Vegas?"

"I explained."

"Bullshit. All you said was, 'I have to go to D.C. I'll explain.' That's not an explanation."

"I think that qualifies."

"No it doesn't. You didn't tell me anything. You left me cold. You didn't even tell me when you'd be back."

"I didn't know."

"Merc's missing, Sharon," said Cynthia.

She meant it as an excuse, I guess, but it didn't mollify Sharon. If anything, it did the opposite.

"I have a taxi waiting outside," Sharon said. "I need cash to pay him."

Sharon always had plenty of cash, not to mention credit and bank cards. She was showing Cynthia—and me—exactly who had claims where. I pulled out my wallet, took out two twenties.

"I took it from Kennedy."

"A hundred, two hundred?" I fished out more bills, threw them on the table. I saw the gold bracelets on her wrist. They seemed to glow in the dim light. "Take it all," I told her. "Get yourself some more bling while you're at it. Buy out the store."

Sharon's eyes narrowed to slits, miniature ice picks aimed at my face. "You can't buy me off, Jack."

"Right."

"Do you need me anymore?" asked Cynthia.

I'd forgotten she was there. "No. Go on, hit the road. I'll talk to you tomorrow."

Cynthia slipped from the booth and left. Her martini was still three-quarters full. Sharon took another twenty and left the rest of the bills.

"How'd you know where to find me?" I asked her.

"It was easy, Jack. You're always in a bar."

"What do you want to drink?" I asked her as she turned toward the door. "I'll order it for you."

"Nothing."

The way she said it, I knew she wasn't coming back.

I STAYED through two more drinks, long enough for the bankers and lawyers and upper exec types to filter in. A couple of guys in their thirties sat at a table behind me, talking about how bad the property taxes were in New Jersey where they'd just bought their houses. They sounded like they were complaining, but what they were really doing was bragging. They couldn't say outright that they liked the fancy Italian marble around the fireplace in the two-story study, or that the custom-designed stained glass in the atrium turned them on, but they could talk about taxes without seeming like sissy boys.

What they really wanted to say was something along the lines of: I just dropped three mil on a piece of property that was a cow farm two years ago, and in two or three years I'm going to move up to one that was a chicken farm for five times that. But if they did it that baldly their friends would think they were materialistic blowhards, which was even worse than being a sissy boy. Not that they *weren't* materialistic blowhards, but being one and acting like one were two different things.

I knew exactly the kind of house they were talking about because

Sharon was headed toward ours. We'd bought it two years ago, moving from Hoboken; she'd tell anyone who asked that we moved out there because it was a better place to raise kids, which changed the subject because we didn't have any yet. I'd say we moved there because Sharon wanted to. But the truth was I moved there because a $3.2-million-dollar-house—and the mortgage that went with it—meant I was someone.

And then I saw the $4.5-million and $8-million places two towns away, and I readjusted my perspective. Suddenly a house whose living room was bigger than the entire Cape Cod I'd grown up in seemed a little dingy. The fact that we had more bathrooms than the cleaning lady who came Tuesdays and Thursdays could count meant nothing anymore. And every time I wrote out the check for the mortgage—more money than I made the first year I enlisted—I felt like I deserved much more. Especially the months I let other things go to pay it.

Sharon was different. Sharon took money and position for granted. Sitting in the bar, listening to the men bragging, I could easily picture her waiting for one of them at home. Not waiting actually—expecting them. Just like she expected me. And if the money dried up, she'd stop expecting.

EVENTUALLY I went back to the office. I sat behind Cynthia's desk and stared at the empty leather couches. The last thing I wanted to do was go to Afghanistan, but I already knew that was what I was going to have to do. I could deal with that. Afghanistan was just a place—a real crappy hellhole, but I'd been in crappy hellholes before. The thing I wasn't sure I could do was confront my partner about lying. I wasn't even sure I had the guts to figure out what the lies were.

If I didn't straighten this out, Uncle wouldn't stop at pulling our contracts. The CIA has its problems, but piss them off enough, and they pull together like a college hoop team in the Final Four. Iron Rock would be finished, and I'd be wiped out.

But I wasn't worried about the money or my future, my house or even my wife. I was worried about Merc.

Merc had saved my life three times. That didn't necessarily give him a hold on me. Saving somebody else's life is what you're supposed to do in combat, and the fact that I would have done the same thing for him evened out the debt, at least a little. Being there in the first place, and getting through it, that was the bond. I owed him if he was in trouble, just like he owed me.

But now it seemed like he was holding out on me, taking gigs I didn't know about. If that was true, could I really trust him?

Thinking like that was like looking out an airplane the first time you jumped out at night. You couldn't see where you were going but you had to go. And with that step there was no going back.

Once I didn't trust Merc, where would it take me? If I didn't trust Merc, who could I trust? Not even myself.

Eventually I turned on Cynthia's computer and started going through her files. I went into her documents and correspondence; everything was routine, there was no mention of Leopard and no hint of trouble. There were answers to bids, contracts attached, that sort of thing. I realized as I looked through the files that I recognized less than half of the projects we had. And a good many of them were projects that I must have initiated myself. Amnesia? Mental overload? I told myself they didn't seem familiar because I was tired and needed a rest. So maybe I did know about Leopard, or had heard about it, and just couldn't pull the connection back into my brain.

Merc's office was to the left of the reception area. It was a little bigger than mine—I'd lost the coin toss—but its view of the city was almost identical. You could see all the way downtown, right to where the World Trade Towers used to be. The night glowed in the distance, the city's lights radiating off the sides of the skyline, foaming up in a surge to crown the island. Lights blinked to warn planes away; a spotlight strobed the sky for an event at Battery Park.

I might have stared at the sky for the rest of the night, mesmerized, but the phone rang. I went to Merc's desk and picked it up.

"Iron Rock. Jack Pilgrim."

"Jesus, Jack, where the hell have you been?"

It was our business manager, Terrence Deroucher. Somewhere along the way he'd gotten the nickname Leo because of the famous baseball manager Leo Durocher, though he was no relation, and that's what everybody called him. In fact it was a bit of a shock the first time I looked at his signature and realized that wasn't his name at all; we'd always put Leo on the checks.

"I was in Vegas and D.C. and now I'm here, Leo. You could've called on my cell. What's up?"

"We have to talk about payroll, Jack. It's in two days."

"Okay." I sat down in Merc's chair, not really understanding what he meant.

"So?"

"Leo, you're talking in riddles. What's up?"

"We need to make payroll. There's no money in the checking account."

Rather than putting him on hold and going to my office, I leaned over and flipped Merc's computer on. It was password protected but that was no big deal—I knew his password already, and could have guessed it if I didn't: MercRules.

The company books were kept in a proprietary accounting program that could handle the complicated system of contracts and billings we needed to use with the government and some of our larger clients. It was a little trickier than your basic Quicken or Money program, but the modules that showed cash accounts were easy to use.

"Plenty of money," I said. "I'm looking at the books right now."

"You better check with the bank, Jack."

"Hold on."

I pulled up the browser and connected. We had one of those one-stop-shopping setups with Chase where you could see all of your balances at a glance. Leo was right—the payroll checking account had a little less than thirty bucks in it. Our other checking account, which we used for general operations, had exactly nineteen.

"What's going on, Jack?" asked Leo.

"I'm just looking at our accounts," I told him.

Large transfers—the equivalent of three pay periods, and we paid by the month—had been taken from both accounts two weeks before.

"We'll use the Key Bank money market," I told him, logging out of Chase and calling up the bookmark.

"You don't have the money in there, Jack."

"You sure?"

"You don't have the money anywhere, Jack."

I didn't bother checking. "We can use the HSBC account."

"That's for your payroll taxes, Jack. You touch that money and I quit. Besides, that check's due, too."

We used the account to hold money we withheld from paychecks for Social Security and taxes. Technically, it didn't belong to us, though companies used similar funds all the time. Leo gave us a big lecture on how bad an idea that was when we first took him on as comptroller, threatening to quit if we ever suggested using the money.

"Look, I'm kind of in the middle of a minefield right now that I have to get straightened out," I told him. "I'll cover it myself until I get it figured out."

"How?"

"Cynthia will call you tomorrow with the details. Or Sharon, maybe. We'll wire it in and get it straightened out when I get back. Okay?"

"You sure about this, Jack?"

"Nah, I'm talking out my ass," I told him. I laughed as if it were a joke and hung up.

LEO was right about the Key Bank account. A large withdrawal—a *really* large withdrawal—had been made by wire the same day as the other withdrawals. I printed out the account detail, figuring to use it to trace the withdrawal. I logged out and started going through Merc's files.

Or I would have, if there had been any there. Our computers were networked, with a local hard drive and a common network drive. Usually you'd keep your personal stuff, work files, e-mails, what have you, on the local drive. The accounting program and a few things we used for planning and presentations were on the common drive. Merc's personal files had been deleted. Even the history folder on his Web browser was clean.

I felt a powerful need for a drink. I got up from the computer and went into my office, where I poured myself a couple of fingers' worth of bourbon and stood by the window, looking out at the city. After about ten minutes it occurred to me that I hadn't tried getting a hold of Merc in a while, and so put the glass down and turned on my computer and sent him an instant message: *Hey, where are you?*

Then I opened up the e-mail program and sent him an e-mail that said the same thing. I called his cell phone and left a message telling him to call my cell, then I quick-dialed his sat phone. The system claimed the account was no longer active.

I called our computer guy, an expert who ran a security firm and did a lot of subcontracting for us, as well as mundane stuff like maintaining our little network. I told him we had a couple of discs that needed to be checked for deleted files, and arranged to drop them off on my way home. I snapped open the computer cases and had them out in a few minutes. I ended up packing the network drive as well. Then I stood staring out the window, the cell phone in one hand, my drink in the other, expecting Merc might call me back any minute. I waited until the city's reflected light had burned into a soft haze and the night was more than half gone, then I left.

SHARON lay at the edge of our bed, all the way over on my side. Her arm stretched out to the edge of the pillow, grasping it as if she were climbing up a rock and it was a rope she could use to pull herself up. The covers were off, and her long smooth gown had hiked halfway up her legs, showing the curve of her calves and the bottom of her thighs. Her long hair splayed over her face; I was tempted to move it away, but she looked too perfect there, too much like a vision or an angel, something unworldly that I wasn't worthy even to touch.

I'd felt the same thing the first day I saw her, sitting on a bench in Central Park. I was taking a walk—blowing off steam, actually, trying to force myself back into a rational head so I could deal with one of our subcontractors. I forget exactly what I was mad at now, or how I'd found my way from my office to the park, a good twenty or thirty blocks away. The only thing I remember from that day is Sharon, who in my memory materializes on the bench across from me. She's wearing an old-fashioned cotton dress, a long flowing summer dress that comes down to her ankles. Her hair, a blond shading slightly toward brown, flows over her shoulders. In my memory of the day, I look up and find myself locked in her gaze. Her eyes, blue, are aimed in my direction, but they have a certain glaze to them, as if she's seeing beyond me or maybe through me.

Then she starts to cry. And when that happens, I feel as if I've been shot in the chest. Adrenaline pumps through my veins and I leap up and go across to her.

"Are you okay?" I ask. "Are you all right?"

She looks up at me, starts to say something, then shakes her head. I sit down on the bench and go to hold her, but I'm afraid to touch her. It's not that I think I'm going to hurt her. I think if I touch her, whatever spell has fallen over me will be broken, and I'll realize this is a dream I'm in.

Eventually, I manage to push away the hair from the side of her face.

"You shouldn't cry," I tell her. "I'm sure he's a jackass."

She starts to laugh. She's not crying over a boyfriend, she told me; she'd just blown a part in a play at an audition downtown.

"I never cry," she says. "I never do. I didn't even want the damn part. How dumb is that?"

She's an actress, and has a boyfriend. Or *was* an actress—she'd given it up nearly two years before, working as a secretary, but then heard about this role, this perfect role, and decided to try out for it. Doing so meant blowing off work, which probably—might, maybe, hard to tell—meant her job would no longer be there. But the role was perfect, and for the first time since she'd given up she felt no, this was it, this was her life right in front of her.

Except she was wrong. And so everything else was wrong. And that's why she was crying.

Which she didn't ever do. She wasn't a crier.

Within an hour we both knew we were soul mates. We spent the afternoon walking through the park, talking. I didn't hold her hand or touch her; I was afraid it would break whatever spell we were under. We went into the Metropolitan Museum, and for the first time in my life I actually enjoyed looking at paintings.

More than that, I understood what the painters were trying to capture on their canvas.

Six months later, we were married. That day, too, is a blur, except for one shining moment when our lips touched, as if for the first time, at the end of the ceremony. I've felt that kiss, over and over again, in good times and bad, just like you're supposed to.

I even felt it that early morning when I got home from dropping the hard drives off to be scanned. I felt it and it scared me, because it was the only thing in the world that could keep me from going to Afghanistan and finding Merc, maybe saving him, maybe just bringing his body back, and getting this mess straightened out.

I HAD to force myself out of the room. I walked downstairs, through the kitchen and family room, across the living room to my study at the far end of the house. I poured myself a drink, and took a cigar from my humidor—not one of the Cubans, but a more dependable Dominican.

The tobacco tasted stale in my mouth. I didn't really want it, but I smoked it anyway. I turned my computer on and checked my IM account; Merc hadn't responded.

"Where have you been?" Sharon asked.

"I'm sorry I woke you up."

"Where have you been?"

"I was at the office."

I put the cigar down and got up to kiss her. She turned her head away, but I pressed in anyway, forcing my lips against the corner of her mouth.

"Leave me the hell alone, Jack," she said, pushing away.

"Hey. Don't do that."

"Leave me alone."

I wasn't angry until I let go of her. The idea I'd had at the restaurant—that she'd run off with Merc—flashed back in my mind. As absurd and ridiculous as it was, the emotion of it, the combination of anger and jealousy and fear that had grabbed me that second, flooded back now.

"What's going on?" I snapped.

"You're asking me what's going on? What's going on with you?"

"Merc is missing and I'm trying to figure out why. The CIA claims there's money missing."

"Merc took it?"

"No. He didn't take it." My voice was so vehement she took a step backward. She'd put a silk robe on over her long gown and drawn it tight; her nipples poked through the fabric. I saw them and couldn't say anything more. Most of my anger slipped away; I felt even more drained than before.

"Where is he?" asked Sharon finally.

"Afghanistan, I think. Kabul."

"You're not going there, are you?"

"Yeah, I am. I got to."

"You said you'd never go back there."

"I was wrong." I went back around the desk. "I need you to do something for me," I told her. "I have some Treasury bills and stocks I need you to sell. Tomorrow. Then you have to wire the money to Leo."

"Wire the money to Leo?"

"We have a cash-flow problem. I need to cover it."

"*Jack!* Jack, no. What Treasury bills? The ones with the money from our wedding?"

It wasn't all money from our wedding; some, most, was profit from our first year in business that we'd never spent. Maybe two-thirds of it was mine outright, but I knew what she meant. It was "our" money, not "mine" and certainly not the company's.

"We have to make payroll," I said. "The money will be replaced. With interest."

"You're not taking it, Jack. You're not."

"Now that you have your claws on it, right? It's my money, too, Sharon. It's all mine, you greedy bitch."

"Greedy? Me? I'm greedy?"

"Damn straight. All you think about is money."

"Bullshit, Jack."

"We need that money to survive. If the company goes under, we go under. Then you'll have nothing. Not the house, not your jewelry, not the car, nothing."

"I don't care about any of that."

"Give me a break. You care. Money's all you care about."

I kept talking, faster and faster. I told her what would happen if Iron Rock went bankrupt, if our contract employees and subcontractors and contacts and foreign vendors and everyone else in the world we owed money to weren't paid.

It wasn't really about that. It was about how I needed her to back me up now, to trust me. That was the one thing I didn't say in the whole speech. It was the most important thing to say, and the only thing I couldn't have forced from my mouth with a crowbar.

I only stopped talking when she said, "I'm leaving, Jack."

She walked from the room. I wanted to believe that she meant she was leaving the argument and going back to bed, but I wasn't sure.

I sat down at the desk and figured out what had to be done to cover the payroll. Some of it would be my salary and Merc's; we could lop that off without a problem. Still, I'd have to sell quite a bit of the Treasuries to keep afloat the next few months. We had some contract payments due before the end of next month, but my head was too foggy to work out the details. I made a note of what I had to sell—I could do it myself over the computer tomorrow, then tell Leo to make the transfer when the sales came through.

When I was done, I poured myself another drink, then went to the kitchen to get some ice. I plopped a few cubes in, then leaned against the counter. I took a sip, but the bourbon suddenly tasted strange, as if the ice cubes had spoiled it. So I just stood there, running my finger over the top of the glass.

What sort of threat was that? She was going to leave?

She couldn't leave me. Going to Afghanistan was just a temporary thing. I'd be back.

Sharon was just afraid for me. I could understand that. She wanted me to stay.

I couldn't stay, though.

"Did you hear *anything* I said?" Sharon asked.

I looked up. She was standing a few feet from me. In all honesty, I hadn't even realized she was there.

I could see her eyes welling up and knew she was going to cry. For the first time in my life, I wanted her to. All of a sudden I hated her—I hated everything and everyone. I realized I'd been suckered into thinking I was someone, that I was part of the big time, when in reality I was just a puny grunt, doomed to trek through the mud.

And Sharon was pulling out exactly at the moment when things were tough, when I needed her. I wanted to smash the glass and hurl the bottle of bourbon against the wall and throw over the chairs. The only reason I didn't was that I knew that if I started I'd never stop. I'd trash the house and burn it down. I'd destroy everything. I'd destroy the world if I weren't stopped.

Maybe Sharon sensed it. I looked down at the glass and then back at her and saw that she had the edge of her teeth against her lip; she looked like someone looking at a man who's fallen from a building but hasn't hit the pavement yet.

"Don't leave yet," I told her, tapping my finger on the glass. "Because if I die, you'll get everything. The insurance at least will be there. And estate lawyers are cheaper than divorce lawyers."

With that, her eyes flooded and she turned and ran upstairs. Now finally I felt I could release some of what I felt. I smacked the glass against the Allmilmo cabinets. The pieces rebounded against the refrigerator, the bottom thick enough to dent the brushed-aluminum skin.

THE SULLEN & WRATHFUL

4

KABUL

KABUL: everything you've heard, and worse.

It's a brown city. The streets are brown, the buildings are brown, the air is brown. The people are gray.

The streets are surprisingly wide, at least in the central part of the city, what you'd call a business district in any other urban area. The place is spread out, with suburbs like spiderwebs radiating at odd angles from the older settlements. It'd be more like Long Island than Manhattan, if you could figure out a way to translate that into Pashto, or any of the other half-dozen languages spoken here.

Getting to Kabul wasn't all that difficult, but it was expensive. My tickets cost fifteen grand. And all five legs were coach.

Afghanistan isn't Iraq, and Kabul isn't Baghdad. The airport is primitive compared to most of the rest of the world, but you don't have to hop in an M1A1 for the ride to the center of town. The last time I'd been here, Afghan soldiers—I use the term "soldier" loosely—manned the customs stations and patrolled the runway. A few were barefoot, and the Kalashnikovs they carried were older than they were. Now, the customs people wore civilian clothes, a mix of what looked like eastern European hand-me-downs and native dress. The soldiers had boots and uniforms. Only their AK-47s and bloodshot eyes looked old.

It took almost forty-eight hours to get from New York to Kabul; I made stops in Iran as well as Pakistan. Unsel had not offered to arrange government transportation for me and I wouldn't have accepted it if he had. I planned on operating on my own, flying below the bureaucratic radar. I realized that was a naïve notion as soon as I hit the tarmac and saw two people noting my every move. For all I knew, I'd been followed the whole way, handed off stop by stop. I wasn't paying enough attention. My head was back in the States somewhere, out of the game. That was going to have to change if I expected to stay here for very long.

Springtime in Kabul. A light crust of snow covered the mountains in the distance. My feet, sheathed in the latest Gore-Tex boots, went numb from the cold in the ninety seconds or so it took to walk inside.

Or maybe it was just an allergic reaction.

Most times when you get off a flight, there are teary scenes of people greeting long-lost relatives and dearly missed family members. Passengers walk with a spring in their step, nervously anticipating the reunion, looking forward to that first rush of joy. Everything may go to hell for them out in the parking lot, arguing over which highway to take home, but for that moment at least they know they're in heaven.

There was none of that anticipation at Kabul, not among the people I landed with. I guess you don't go home to Kabul these days; the people who want to have already been. The most optimistic travelers, I guess, would have been the business people trying to sell something—toilets, medical supplies, paper. They were all frowning, though, already resigned to returning with only token sales.

Then came the aid workers, newbies mostly, who had got the first taste of what they were in for with the onerous security check in Pakistan, which included strip searches for any female looking halfway decent. They were here on a quest, modern knights of the Round Table, and they were about to find out the Holy Grail was just a mirage in the mountains. A few would face that and keep going; most would leave as soon as they could.

Then there were people like me, here because they had to be. Most of us had been here before and knew exactly what we were getting into. Most were here for the money, whether it was a contract that paid ten times what they could make back home, or because they'd heard rumors that if you made the right connection here you could get rich. There were a lot of dreamers among us, but they kept their fancies hidden behind the grimmest faces, showing their hearts to no one.

I got through customs easily enough, which may have been the work of the CIA shadow who picked me up inside the terminal. She was an Asian-looking woman, probably Japanese, in American clothes; to say she stood out in a crowd of mostly Afghan men is to understate the case by a mile. The CIA was always pretty good about fitting its important people into the background, so I guess that said a lot about the woman's position on the totem pole—and mine.

People did crowd around the gates as you passed through customs, but they were hawking things or looking for work, selling rides and for all I know their little sisters. My Pashto had never been particularly extensive, and I was so rusty it would take a few days at least before I got used to even the most basic phrases. Nor was I in much of a mood to push my interpretative powers—my head hurt, and I needed a drink badly.

I'd sent two messages to our office in the city, telling our best operative, Verge Maro, to meet me at the airport. Even so, I wasn't surprised when I didn't spot him. We called him Verge—I can't remember what his real name was, or even if he had one—because he was always on the *verge* of doing what he was supposed to. Verge had been an Italian working with NATO peacekeepers in some sort of vague NGA post when we took him on as a general roustabout and office manager. He had two qualities that were extremely useful in Afghanistan—he could speak Pashto, the most common local tongue, and Dari or Afghan Persian fluently; he could fake Uzbek and Turkmen, as well.

The second quality that made him invaluable was his ability to fade into the background. That's a much underappreciated art, but an essential one if you want to stay alive.

Verge had been in Afghanistan for almost five years and knew just about everybody who was important to know, and most of the people who weren't. That was useful, too. That's why we put up with him, or I should say why Merc put up with him. I knew Verge only by reputation from what Merc had told me about him, most often through complaints.

NGA stands for "nongovernmental agency." It covers a whole range of sinners, from the Red Crescent to Doctors Without Borders to charities you never heard of and wouldn't accept help from if you were about to be flushed down a sewer hole. I've had some bad experiences with a few of the latter, including a couple that were clients. More than a few so-called church groups are fronts for the Devil, judging by the people who work for them. I guess if you can tell yourself that you work for God, you can justify just about anything you do.

I'd just concluded that Verge wasn't around when a short, stocky American with a Muslim-style beard and an Arab headdress came up to me and asked in English if I needed a driver. He had an Eastern-seaboard accent, maybe Baltimore, maybe Virginia. His gaze wandered, poking around the airport behind me, then suddenly coming back and focusing on my face. His look was intense, and he had a desperate air about him. It wouldn't have taken too much for an artist to change his face into John Brown's, bulging forehead and eyes ready to pop out.

"Twenty bucks and gas to the center of town," he told me. "Better than you'll do anywhere else."

"All right."

"I don't carry your bag. I ain't a coolie."

I followed him past a line of people queuing for the official taxis into the city, and another for a bus. The bus was new and shiny, as nice as you'd see in New York or another big city. Its white and blue sides gleamed, though the afternoon was overcast and dull.

The American led me to a Russian-made jeep, a UAZ 469. It was at least a decade old, probably much more. The side panels had rusted out and been partly replaced with screwed-on sheet metal. The fabric top had a blanket secured with duct tape about a third of the way back. I didn't dare look at the tires.

"I need the gas money before we start," said the driver, stopping next to the jeep.

"Fill it up and I'll pay."

He frowned, like I was ripping him off, then pulled open the door.

"I'm Ken," he told me after the first crank failed to start the engine. "I'm an American. Private citizen."

"Jack. I'm private, too."

"Yeah, I could tell. You had a spook following you."

"Maybe she'll give us a jump if your jeep doesn't start."

It took three attempts before the motor was running. He revved it once it caught; the truck vibrated so badly I thought it would fall apart. The motor sputtered when he took his foot off the gas and he pushed back gingerly, working it through a set of hiccups as if it were a baby that'd had too much formula.

I'd figured Ken for the silent, taciturn type, but either that was wishful thinking or my character judgment abilities hadn't adjusted to Afghanistan. Once we filled up—the gas tank had been nearly bone dry—he started unloading his life story, or rather his favorite version of it. According to Ken, he'd worked in SpecOps for a number of years, got out of the army, bounced around, owned a gun store and a diner, then came to Afghanistan to do what he called "bit work" for the CIA.

He kind of fit the profile of a burned-out Special Forces soldier—takes one to know one—but the way he told his story made it clear that most of what I was hearing was bs. I didn't really care. What I wanted was a ride into Kabul, and if listening to some crackpot's fantasies about who he was and what he'd done was part of the price, so be it.

The only concession to his story that I made was asking to be dropped off at the hotel rather than our office; I figured it'd be a hell of a lot easier to duck him there if it ever came to that, and I wouldn't have to worry about him bugging our people.

The streets of the city where we drove were busier and better paved than I remembered, but otherwise the city hadn't changed much in five years. Fewer armed men standing around doing nothing, more decay on the buildings. Barbed wire and cement car-bomb barriers roped off the compounds on either side of the wide boulevard we took to the hotel. Dust rose everywhere.

"Taliban's back," said Ken. "People thought they were gone, but they're back."

"Yeah, I heard something like that."

"You can't trust the news. That's all bull. Taliban—they're everywhere in Kabul. Probably half the people you meet. They'll slit your throat for Allah if you turn your back on them."

"I'll try to remember that."

"U.S. is getting out, UN is coming in. In—out. UN in charge, Taliban comes back."

"Sounds like a mathematical formula."

"It is. Yeah. Like one and one. Equals three."

Whether that was supposed to be a joke or some profound piece of wisdom, I had no idea. The Taliban—followers of a very strict form of Islam who'd welcomed Osama bin Laden and supporters of al Qaeda into the country—had never really left Afghanistan; I knew that. When we helped the Northern Alliance to victory, only the diehards ran away. Most of the Taliban just shaved off their beards and went on with their business.

Half of Kabul? No way. Most of the people in the capital were refugees, outsiders who couldn't make a living in the provinces, which had been damaged by years of drought and war. They weren't Taliban. And most of the city natives hated the Taliban worse than Americans did.

The Taliban wasn't even in half the provinces down south where they'd come from originally. There were plenty of people who'd slit your throat, though, if the price were right, or if they thought they could get ahead by doing it. That wasn't a religious thing at all. It was basic instinct.

"This is it," said Ken, stopping in front of the driveway to the hotel. He was in the middle of the road, and expected me to hop out. I wasn't sure whether that was accepted local custom or just his way. I handed him the twenty bucks we'd agreed on.

"You want to have a drink?" he asked.

I did, but not with him. I begged off and took my bags, lugging them to the side of the road.

Car bombings had not been a big thing in Afghanistan when I'd been there last, certainly not in Kabul. But there'd apparently been a few over the past several months, and the Afghan army had a checkpoint out in front of the hotel. This was a real checkpoint, with an officer who made me turn on my laptop and phones to show they worked.

Two more security types stood at the front door of the hotel, beyond the stone wall and fence that had been erected in case a terrorist and his Toyota managed to make it past the fat cement barrels in the driveway. They did the search again, then frisked me for a weapon. This may have been designed to impress guests as they checked in, but the frisk was professional, quick, and would have found all but one of the guns I normally would have carried hidden on my body.

Until recently, Kabul had had only three or four hotels of any size; the Centennial where I was staying was the fourth or fifth largest, depending on how you counted. Its main competition were the Intercontinental and the Moustafa hotels, both of which were larger though not necessarily nicer. The four-story building had been damaged by a bomb right before the Taliban was chased from power; what was unusual about this was the fact that it was impossible to tell where the damage had been. Not only had the building been repaired, it had been painted and impressively outfitted with new beds and mattresses, plumbing that worked consistently, and even backup generators to deal with the chronic power failures. The generators kept the hotel's vital operations—the reception desk and the bar—dimly lit at all times.

I doubt Michelin would be coming around any time soon to hand out three stars for the accommodations. The place had been some sort of bureaucratic building under the Russians, abandoned and left to rot for years until being resurrected as a hotel within the past year. The old offices, small to begin with, had been sliced down further. If you opened the door all the way it hit the bed or the small dresser bolted to the wall. The bathrooms were all in the hallways.

I dumped my clothes in the room, stopped at the bar for a drink, and then made my first mistake in Kabul—I set out for our office instead of going to bed.

5

KABUL

YOU won't find guides to Kabul or Afghanistan in the travel section of the local Barnes & Noble. I guess it was a beautiful place once, but that once must've been thousands of years ago, when Alexander the Great came through.

Afghanistan has 250,775 square miles. That makes it just a little smaller than Texas; slice off the Texas Panhandle and turn the state on the side, step on it, and you get roughly the shape of Afghanistan. There's a huge desert in the southeast, one of the most barren places in the world, though plenty of people manage to live there. The center and eastern edge of the country are a mass of mountains. Kabul, the capital and largest city in the country, sits at eighteen hundred meters above sea level, about even with Denver, Colorado. The Himalayas aren't all that far away.

Because Afghanistan has been linked so closely to Muslim wackos over the past two decades, a lot of Americans think of it as an extension of the Middle East. It's not. Its politics have nothing to do with Palestine or Israel, with the caveat that because Palestinians are fellow Muslims, Afghans tend to feel their pain and voice their resentments, even if it's usually just for form's sake. Afghanistan is to the east of Iran, tucked in between Pakistan and what used to be the Soviet Union. It borders on China, not Egypt or Saudi Arabia. And the people who live there aren't Arabs.

Then again, they're not Afghans, either. Technically, there's no such thing. Most of the people who live in the country are Aryans of different tribes with mostly separate histories. There are also a good number of Mongols, the people who conquered China and gave meaning to the words "barbaric horde."

The Persians and Greeks, or reasonable facsimiles, ruled what is now Afghanistan from the sixth to the second century B.C., when a bunch of nomadic tribes swept in, including one called the Kushān, which rose to preeminence. The tribes apparently decided to call Afghanistan their home, but that was just so they'd have a place to hang their spears at the end of the day. They conquered a good bit of the surrounding areas, pushing down into central India and up into China. For a while, the Kushān were among the most powerful and wealthy people on earth, made rich by the Silk Route, which ran through Afghanistan. But the center didn't hold, and a succession of nomads, seminomads, and foreign armies have fought for domination ever since. Islam came in A.D. 642; Genghis Khan rolled through in 1219.

Tribes—another way of talking about ethnic and racial identity—are still very important in Afghanistan. The largest ethnic group is Pashtun. Technically, the Pashtun people constitute a couple of different tribes, but they tend to be lumped together. All speak Pashto, and they all look more or less alike to outsiders, the way Caucasians do to them. Unlike other Afghans, Pashtuns tend to be light skinned and have light features.

The tribes near Iran on the east and north include the Tajik and the Hazara; they speak Dari, which is the official language of the country. (Dari is a dialect of Farsi or Persian, the main language of Iran. Pashto is sometimes spelled Pashtu, and is also spoken in Pakistan, mostly up near the Afghan border.) The Turkmen and the Uzbek tribes, which are related to the Tajik, are also important in the northern areas of the country.

The country's geography promotes the separation of the tribes and the different languages. In the areas where they come together, like the cities, there has always been conflict. In Kabul, for example, the Pashtun looked down on the Hazara; traditionally the former were the teachers and leaders, the latter servants.

But you can't understand recent Afghan history without factoring in the Russians, who in all honesty probably wish they'd never heard of the place.

The Soviet Union didn't have a huge amount to do with Afghanistan until the end of the 1950s, when conflicts between Afghanistan and Pakistan led to the closing of the border between the two countries. The prime minister—he was actually a general who'd taken power in a coup—turned to what was then the Soviet Union for economic and military aid. By the seventies, the Soviets were looking at Afghanistan as a province—and a wayward one at that. They marched in after a series of coups and revolts in 1979. At that point, the United States began one of the biggest covert operations of all time, designed to kick the Russians out. Ronald Reagan gets most of the credit, but the policy was actually started by Jimmy Carter, so the Democrats and Republicans can take equal credit and blame for everything that followed.

The guerrilla war the Soviets fought in Afghanistan helped bring down the curtain on Communism as a world force. It also bred the radical form of Islamic separatism bin Laden and al Qaeda have come to represent.

The Taliban were a subset of Pashtuns who were influenced by a puritanical strain of Sunni Islam that flourishs in Saudi Arabia known as Wahhabism. Wahhabism started as a reaction to the British occupation; like a lot of reactionary movements, it linked itself to a distant, ideal past. Strictly limiting what women can wear and do is one of its features. It also takes a rather dim view of western "infidels," Jews, and most especially other Muslims who aren't pure or strict enough by Wahhabism's lights. Osama bin Laden didn't introduce it to the region, but he sure helped it grow.

The Taliban were just one of the different mujahideen, or "warriors of God" guerrilla groups, during the war against the Soviets. The CIA helped them, and a bunch of others, figuring in good ol' American style that any enemy of my enemy is a friend of mine. While bin Laden et al. were never big fans of capitalism, it was only when Sadaam Hussein invaded Kuwait and the U.S. sent half a million barbarian Christians close to the holy lands of Mecca and Medina that they decided things had gone beyond the pale and called for the crusaders to be eliminated. Osama was a Saudi (technically, his family comes from Yemen, but it's close enough for us heathens), and a rich one at that, but after conflicts with the Saudi government he eventually fled back to Afghanistan, where he and like-minded crazies formed al Qaeda. The Taliban, meanwhile, had essentially won the civil war that followed the Soviet withdrawal and were imposing their style of stability on the country, taking it from wrack and ruin to something more like Armageddon.

Then came 9/11. We helped the Northern Alliance—think of them as any tribe that's not Taliban or Pashtun, depending on how discriminating you are. The Taliban ran to the mountains bordering Pakistan, where they died with their prayer caps on.

End of story.

Except of course it's not.

OUR office was in a two-story building about a mile outside of the city proper. NGAs and liaisons for various agencies and the occasional exporter had crammed into the place, attracted by good phone lines, space for satellite dishes, and generators that guaranteed a semireliable electric flow. Most of them, like us, shared a cubicle with two or three other businesses, sometimes using the same desk or cramming a bunch together so the workers had to rub elbows as they worked. Generally, though, this wasn't a problem, as actually showing up for the workday on a consistent basis was considered a very Russian thing to do, and most people in Kabul still hated the Russians.

In our case, we shared a secretary with a company that had been hired by the U.N. to bring grain into the country; he also did some freelancing on the side, taking calls and passing messages for businesses that had even less of a presence in the capital than we did. He was a local, and despite the fact that he was working now as a secretary, he supposedly had some training to become a doctor. His name was Sim, shortened from something much longer and less pronounceable. Why he was working as a secretary in a country that was desperate for medical professionals probably had a lot to do with money, but I never asked.

I waited for him to get off the phone. He glanced at me a couple of times but kept jabbering, maybe hoping I'd leave. Finally I leaned over the desk and put my face near his. He got the message and hung up.

"You are?" he asked, in an accusing tone.

"Jack Pilgrim. Your boss. You got my messages?"

He smiled nervously, then held out his hand. "Boss. I have not seen Mr. Maro many days."

"You might have mentioned that in a message back."

"I thought he show up."

"Next time, send somebody else, Okay? I'm looking for Merc. Do you know where he is?"

"Mr. Conrad? No."

Fear flooded his eyes, real fear.

"You haven't seen him?"

"No."

"When was the last time he was here?"

The phone rang. He started to answer it. I put my hand on the receiver so he couldn't pick it up.

"I know Merc's in trouble," I said. "I'm here to get him out of it. Tell me what's going on."

He glanced over at the other side of the office, where another man had his eyes pasted on the desktop.

"Let's start by going somewhere we can talk, all right?" I told him.

Reluctantly, he got up and led me outside.

"Unwise to talk in front of anyone," said Sim after we'd walked down the road a ways. "You never know."

"Unwise to talk period, or just about this?"

"Not smart to say anything. Information is always worth money."

"About Merc?"

He shrugged.

"Where's he staying?"

He held out his hands in a shrug. "Dunno. Haven't seen him in two months."

"Two months?"

Another shrug.

"He was in Kabul two and a half weeks ago to make transfers," I told him.

That was news to Sim, and I could tell. So was the fact that his sat phone account had been closed.

"You haven't tried calling him?" I asked.

He shook his head.

"Where does he stay?"

"The Inter-Continental."

"You see him there?"

"Mr. Conrad did not talk to me. He said I was to do what I was told, and that's it."

"What about Verge?"

He gave me the kind of look you'd get if you asked a kid why the dog ate his homework.

"If you want, I can pull your fingernails off one by one until I get an answer," I told him.

Sim shook his head, but still didn't say anything.

"What's the story, Sim? I don't want to hurt you."

By now my head was pounding. And even though it was spring and I was wearing a heavy winter coat, the cold had seeped into my bones. My lungs felt as if they were filled with ice cubes.

"Ask at the Intercontinental," Sim said finally. "In the meantime, I ask around."

THE Intercontinental Hotel was Kabul's largest hotel. After the Taliban left town, the interim government moved in, holding court on the lower floors. Some officials had left for the nearby villas or government buildings, but there were still plenty when I arrived, along with reporters and business visitors, execs from NGAs and the odd "entrepreneur" who figured he could make a killing here—just the kind of mix Merc would have been drawn to.

It took a while to find someone at the reception desk who would actually listen to my questions, but once I did that, a guide was found to lead me to Merc's room. He'd paid for a full year, and his "lease" still had three months to go. But no one could remember seeing him recently, and the manager didn't know whether he was in or not; I'd have to knock on the door and find out myself. Which was just fine by me.

Calling the place a hotel really doesn't describe what it looked like. It felt more like a frat house, where all the brothers were armed and holding meetings on the upcoming rushes, or maybe a dorm that had been taken over by rival Mafia dons. The corridors were lined with guards and small knots of people waiting to get in to see someone. And some of the corridors weren't hallways at all, but paths through cordoned-off spaces. The man showing me to Merc's room took me through a hotel kitchen, out to a fire escape, and through a room that had been partitioned into a narrow passage.

Walking through the place, I began to feel a little nervous at being unarmed. I hadn't brought any guns with me on the airplane, obviously, nor had I stopped to buy any. I realized now that had been a mistake. Most of the guards were in their late twenties or thirties and while they looked tough, they at least seemed like they'd have enough professional judgment not to fire indiscriminately. But it only takes one person to lose his temper, or to be a little rash. Having a gun in your belt here was a token of power, a sign to even the least experienced that you were not to be shot at lightly.

The upper floors of the hotel had been damaged during the war, but had recently been reopened. Merc's room was near the top and close to a stairwell, apparently a sign of status, at least in the eyes of the man who led me there. He lingered long enough for me to realize he was expecting a tip; I gave him a twenty-dollar bill and he left smiling.

They'd led me to the door, but had declined to give me a key; just because I said I was a friend of Merc's was no guarantee that I actually was one. They'd leave it for him to decide.

I knocked twice. When there was no answer, I knelt down and examined the lock, trying to figure out what I needed to do to get it open. The only lock picking I'd done in the army involved a large dose of explosives, but I had some experience jimmying open simple locks on my apartment door with a credit card. I took out the corporate Visa and put it to good use.

Belatedly, I wondered if I should have worried about a booby trap. It was too late by then, of course, and I stood there like a jerk, half in the hallway and half in the room.

"Merc," I said finally, pushing myself back into motion. "Merc, what the hell's going on?"

There were no booby traps, and there was no one in the room. In fact there was nothing in the room, except a lone mattress on the floor. If Merc had ever even been here, he was long gone.

I was tired from the flight and jet lag, and inevitably when I sat down on the mattress my eyes grew heavy and I fell off to sleep. How long I slept I have no idea; I woke to a sharp rap on the door.

"Yeah?" I said, pulling myself up.

"Mr. Pilgrim?"

The voice was a woman's, faint, with a British accent.

"Yeah?"

"I have information."

I pulled open the door. A woman dressed in a long burka with a full headpiece stood in the hall. She was under five feet tall, a wisp of a thing, and the little I could see of her face was cream colored. Two men, not much bigger than she was, stood behind her with AK-47s.

"Mr. Pilgrim, you need information. Mr. Saruj Muhammed sent me."

Sim.

"Good."

I followed the woman down the steps, through the labyrinth on the lower floors, and out to a white Toyota Land Cruiser. There was a Red Crescent on the truck.

The woman's name was Hariti Kedar, and she was Indian, not Afghan or even Muslim. Hariti actually worked for a different relief organization and was only borrowing the truck and its bodyguards, a common arrangement, she said. Neither the guards nor she looked threatening enough to be kidnappers, which really stoked my paranoia. With every turn I tensed, ready to grab the nearest gun and make a lunge for the door.

We drove through the city and then out toward the suburbs, passing quickly through an area of houses that were still rubble, years after the war here had officially ended. Here and there I could see people moving, and I realized there were lean-tos and shelters amid the debris.

We drove a few miles out of the city center, winding through neighborhoods of walled-off compounds and overgrown lots.

Hariti asked me if I'd just arrived. I guess the stunned look on my face must've given me away.

"A few hours ago," I said. "It's been a while since I've been here. Five years."

"I see."

"It's not that different," I told her. "That's what's so confusing."

I laughed, trying to make it sound like it was a joke. She didn't laugh back.

Hariti's organization ran a clinic in a suburb on the northeastern side of the city. Even though it was late afternoon by the time we got there, people were lined up out to the road. They swarmed the Toyota when we pulled in, hands out, beseeching us for anything we could give. Hariti set her face just as the truck halted. She looked like she was on her way to kill her mother. The bodyguards got out first, but it was Hariti who cut the path through the crowd, walking slowly but steadily toward the building and ignoring the cries of "sister, sister" from the people around us.

The line continued inside the front hallway of the building. People were being examined there by women about the size of Hariti, looking at tongues and poking chests with stethoscopes. We passed them and walked down a narrow, unlit corridor lined by open rooms where the seriously ill and injured lay in beds.

"There are only a few hours more of light," said Hariti. "Everyone is desperate to be seen before then, because once night falls, the clinic closes."

There was no electricity. Private generators at a few places provide power for phones and some lighting, but for much of the city electricity is a luxury that comes a few times a week or month. Hariti's organization didn't have the funds for a generator; if they'd had any spare money, she told me, they would have spent it on more security.

Hariti gestured toward a door at the end of the hall. It turned out to be the entrance to the basement. I descended a few feet into pitch-black darkness, then stopped, waiting as Hariti retrieved a flashlight from a shelf at the side of the steps near the door and descended behind me.

The place smelled like a wet garbage dump where something big had died. Tables were crammed around the foot of the steps, each covered by one or two large plastic bags.

Body bags.

Hariti came down the stairs and turned left, leading the way through a narrow aisle. She turned to the right and stopped, checked some notation on the table or bag I couldn't see, then reached over and unzipped it. The halo of her flashlight illuminated a bearded face between the claws of zipper.

"It's not Merc," I whispered to myself.

Then I realized it was Verge. He looked almost beatific in the bag, more at peace than in the e-mailed photo I'd seen when he was first hired.

"You know him?" Hariti asked.

"I may. I haven't actually met the person I think he is, though."

"This was with him." She reached inside the bag and pulled out an ID card.

It was Verge.

"He worked for me, for Iron Rock," I told her.

"Vincenzo Maro?" she asked, a perfect Italian popping through her Hindi accent.

"Yeah."

"We have papers upstairs."

"Sure."

But she didn't lead me upstairs. She led me to the next table. I closed my eyes, knowing that when I opened them I was going to see the man who'd been my best friend in the world lying dead before me.

Except I didn't. It was another man, a European I didn't recognize.

"Him?" asked Hariti.

"I don't recognize him."

She dug into the bag. I don't know what sort of morgue keeps IDs in temporary coffins. Maybe they made it up as they went along, like we all do.

"Balfour?" she asked, showing me the card.

The name didn't sound familiar.

"Mr. Saruj says he worked with Vincenzo Maro," added Hariti.

"All right," I told her. "If he says so."

I braced myself, but she didn't show me another bag.

The bodies had been found by the local police force or the Afghan army or an informal militia—it was hard even in Kabul to keep them straight—the day before. They had ID cards from Iron Rock, pictures, even some local money. Holding the bills in my hand, it amazed me that the corpses hadn't been robbed, but of course for all I knew they very likely had been carrying a lot more money, or maybe American money, or even credit cards. And weapons would have been the really valuable thing anyway; they didn't have any when they were brought into the clinic's makeshift morgue.

Hariti said both men had been shot by assault rifles; their torsos were riddled with bullets. That was the extent of any coroner's report they were going to get. Interesting someone in their deaths would be a waste of money as well as time. Truth was, if I paid enough, I could "solve" their murders any way I wanted. I could even exact "justice" from an alleged murderer of my choosing, so long as I chose with discretion.

Guessing from what little I knew of him and his resume, I

doubted Verge had any immediate family. I didn't know about Balfour, but even if I had managed to find someone, what would they have done? Flown in from Wales, where he'd come from, according to the papers found on him? Order the body shipped back? That would cost some poor relative tens of thousands of dollars. If you were military and you died here, the services took care of getting you home in however many pieces they found you. Civilians had a harder time. It wasn't just the cost of preparing the body and the flight; the paperwork—a fancy way of saying "bribes"—was murder.

It took a bit before I realized that what Hariti really wanted from me was money to bury the bodies. She was squeamish about bringing it up herself, just kept hinting about costs and formalities, until finally I got the message.

"The company has a death benefit," I told her, lying though it was obviously the right thing to say. "We'd like to take care of the arrangements."

The amount she wanted was pathetically small, the equivalent of a few dollars, but it had to be paid in local currency. And she wanted to have them cremated as soon as possible—now, as a matter of fact. They'd need the space by morning.

So my first day in Afghanistan included a funeral. Two, actually, side by side, the bodies surrounded by a pile of junk wood and some sort of pitch that gave off a black odor as it burned. Verge and his companion were seen off to the afterlife by a small Indian nurse, two men who would bury their ashes in a field that had once held almond trees, and an American who barely knew their names and who kept checking behind him, hoping that at any moment his best friend would show up, and ask him what he was doing in this hellhole.

The man in charge held up his torch and looked at me, and I realized he and the others were expecting me to say something before they set the bodies on fire. All I could think of was "dust to dust." I said it in a reverent tone as everyone bowed their heads. But as I stared at the flames I thought we aren't dust or ashes even, but fire, waiting to burn.

6

KABUL

HARITI turned out to be much more informative than Sim. Because she needed money to pay the men for the cremation and burial, she took me to a money changer who could be trusted not to cheat me too badly. She also gave me innumerable tips, many of which I already knew, like don't drink the water, don't trust strangers, and always have a return ticket and a bag packed for the airport.

She said she didn't know Merc, but gave me some advice on where to look for him. Some were obvious, some less so. I tried the obvious places first—the bars at the Intercontinental and the Moustafa Hotel. Then I started wandering in the not so obvious places, guesthouses that catered to Europeans. These were private homes that had been turned into Kabul's version of a bed-and-breakfast. Most often the guests were relief workers and people from UN agencies visiting the capital for a few days. In a couple of cases, the places were favored by journalists on low budgets, and therefore likely spots to pick up gossip. Hariti sent me to a place called "Yellow House," not far from the Dilkusha Palace, one of the government buildings in the town center.

The king lived in Dilkusha Palace back in the days when there was still a king. In 1933, King Nadir Shah was shot by a student he was honoring for his achievements. That's Afghanistan.

Yellow House was too small to have a formal bar. What it had instead was a common room, kind of an oversized living room, where guests and visitors sat around in clumps and drank tea, juice, and booze—a lot of booze. The chairs were a wild collection ranging from fancy antiques covered in elaborate fabric, with intricate beads and finely carved wooden legs, to frayed lawn chairs that looked as if they'd been pulled from a town dump.

I found a seat near a group of Germans and sat down; within a minute a silver-haired man appeared and inquired what I might want to drink. I asked if they had bourbon. When he didn't seem to know what exactly I meant, I ordered whisky and got a Scotch.

It didn't take much to get other people talking to you in a place like Yellow House. You started out with something benign—you could talk about the weather if you wanted, especially since it was on the cold side for late spring. Within a few minutes people would be telling you their life stories. I'm not sure whether the surroundings made them feel as if they needed as many connections to the outside world as possible, or if the people who came to Kabul were somehow self-selected to tell a stranger their most intimate secrets. Most conversations began in English; it was the one language everyone knew a little bit of.

I talked to the Germans just long enough to realize that they had only been in the country for a few days, then leaned back in my seat, sipping my drink, while I decided if it was worth talking to anyone else here. A tall, skinny man sat at the opposite end of the room. He had a clear glass in his hand; it could have been water but I figured it was vodka. While I was watching, a woman about twenty-five, with skin so white it seemed to have been bleached, came over and sat down beside him. In contrast to her skin, she had raven-black hair, and eyes so green they were like lights in her skull. She wore a long, flowered skirt, and a blouse so stiff and ill-fitting that it might have just come out of a box.

She kissed the man on the cheek, and sat down next to him. I got up and sat down across from them while the waiter took her order for green tea.

The man glared at me.

"My name's Jack," I said. "I just got into town."

He continued to stare as the girl turned toward me and gave me a beam of a smile

"Mary," she said.

"You're American." I held my glass up for the waiter, who turned out later to actually be the owner of the place. "Are you new here?"

"I've been here two weeks. Going back home tomorrow."

"Where's that?"

"Arkansas."

"I thought so," I lied. "You have a pretty accent."

She blushed a little, but any color would have shown up on that face.

"I'm Jack," I said to the man, holding out my hand.

He stared at it, but didn't take it. "Khattak," he said finally.

"Really," I said. "Interesting name."

He continued to stare. Khattak is an Afghan name, and the guy sitting in front of me wasn't an Afghan. He had a very thin stubble and close-cropped hair that didn't quite hide the fact that his hairline was receding prematurely. He wore jeans and a pair of thick shirts.

"What do you do, Jack?" asked the woman.

"I'm with a security firm," I told her. "I'm looking for a friend of mine. He's somewhere in Kabul, but I don't know where. His name's Mercury Conrad."

"Merc," said Khattak. "Too bad."

KHATTAK's real name was Gerald Greene, but he never used it. He was a Brit, and he'd been in the war as a combat air controller, probably as part of a commando team, though he never told me. Those guys do a lot of things, but in his case his job was to work with the locals and call in air strikes on Taliban positions. He was vague on dates, but at some point he left the country, left the British army, and came back as a helicopter pilot. He owned his own chopper, an old Russian ship that looked fierce as hell from the distance. Up close, you'd wonder how it managed to get airborne. It was one of the few nonmilitary or nongovernment-owned helos in the country.

Khattak didn't volunteer any of this that night, although the girl told me about the helicopter. His background came out later, in dribs and drabs, the way backgrounds usually do.

"WHY do you say 'too bad'?" I asked Khattak.

He shrugged.

"You know Merc?"

"Met him," he said.

"Where?" When he didn't answer, I added, "Have you seen him recently?"

He shrugged again. I couldn't tell if he was being a wise guy or what.

Part of me wanted to jump up and grab him, squeeze the collar of his thick shirt and ask what he was talking about, what he meant. But part of me was starting to realize that if I wanted to survive here, I had to think about the long haul.

And another part of me was just too tired to grab anyone, let alone punch them. Especially when there was a real good chance they were armed.

"Listen, I'd really like to find Merc," I told him. "I could definitely use help. You'll be paid."

Now the shrug turned to a smirk. Progress, I guess. "How much?"

"The going rate."

"Finding people is very expensive," he said. "Make sure you can afford it before you offer it."

"Let me buy you another drink."

"It's water," he said.

"That's not free, right?" I turned to Mary. "You want more tea?"

"We're busy tonight," said Khattak, who clearly didn't want me bothering her. "Talk to me tomorrow."

"That sounds very fair. When and where?"

"Whenever. I'm at the airport. Ask for me."

I said good-bye to Mary, then made small talk with another group before retrieving my driver and going back to the hotel. There I had the most inexplicable experience of the day: I slept soundly, without waking, and without a single nightmare.

7

KABUL

THE master of Kabul was a short, pug-type guy whose arms were as thick as his neck, which itself was thicker than most people's thighs. His shaved head made him look a little like Caesar, an effect he undoubtedly aimed at. Well into his fifties, he spoke with the quick staccato of someone who had grown up in Washington or maybe New York, but looking at him you'd be hard-pressed to think of him as a child at all. His deeply tanned face and arms—he wore a short-sleeved shirt even though his office was cold—had the leathery look of a turtle's tail. His name was Charles "Pitch" Black, and he was the CIA station chief.

"I don't like Leopard. It's not my program," he told me after having someone fetch me from my hotel the next morning. "But I like thieves even less."

"That's good, because neither Merc nor I are thieves."

I pulled out a chair and sat down. He squirreled his face into a frown, as if I'd broken some sort of protocol by sitting before I'd been given permission to.

"So where's the money?" he asked.

"I'm sure it's around."

He made one of those derisive sounds with his mouth that amount to controlled spitting.

"Right now, I'm more concerned about finding my partner," I told him. "Merc—"

"Yeah, that's a damn good idea," said Pitch. "Where is he?"

"I just said I was trying to find him, right? Two of my employees were found dead yesterday, outside the city."

"Day before yesterday," said Pitch. "You buried them yesterday."

Well, if you're so damn smart, I thought, then why don't you just cut to the chase and tell me where Merc is. But I kept my mouth shut.

Pitch got up and started walking around his office, stalking like a cat getting ready to strike wounded prey. I didn't have a lot of experience with CIA station chiefs, and from what I've heard, Pitch was unusual in a lot of ways. He was older, maybe physically tougher; his personal style ran to the dirtbag police detective instead of the refined diplomat.

It turned out that Pitch was one of those people irked by silence. I guess he figured if I wasn't talking, I must be thinking of ways to kill him.

Which I guess I was.

"I don't like Merc, and I don't like you," he said as he paced. "Just so you know."

"Good. Are you going to help me find him?"

"You know anything about Paktika?"

"Province in eastern Afghanistan, on the border with Pakistan. I served there during the war. So did Merc."

"You got a week. Go."

I SAT there for five minutes, maybe more, waiting for him to explain. He never did. First he stared at me, then he frowned, then he stared again, then finally he picked up the phone and started talking.

When he hung up, I asked if Merc was in Paktika, but he didn't answer. I asked if the agency was going to help me get down there. That got a little curl of a smile at the edge of his lips, but nothing else. I could have asked what Leopard was, but figured I'd get the same response. When he picked up the phone again I remembered that coming here hadn't been my idea in the first place. I got up and left.

SIM, our maybe-doctor secretary, had not reported to his desk when I arrived at our office. Which was just fine with me, since it gave me a chance to look through all our files and the computer without him standing nervously behind me.

There wasn't much there. The files contained no reference to Leopard at all, which obviously didn't surprise me. But there was scant reference to Jason, either, or any of the programs we'd run here. It wasn't until I started analyzing where we'd spent our money—or at least where the records indicated that we'd spent our money—that I started to get a handle on what was really going on.

The classes and programs that were part of Jason had a bunch of fancy names that didn't lend themselves to acronyms, like Indigenous Force Training Certification, each of which had their own separate line codes clearly designated as subaccounts of the master project. The classes ran in different cycles in tune with things going on in Afghanistan. But they'd stopped about a month and a half before, with no new classes scheduled until the transition from the U.S. and NATO to UN forces was complete.

Which meant, or should have meant, that Merc had nothing to do here.

Leopard didn't exist on the books or in the files at all. But there were a subset of Jason expenses that clearly had nothing to do with training programs in Kabul—like medical supplies from Poland and meals ready-to-eat. These had no class or program code attached, and were relatively easy to spot.

There were also transport charges to Paktika, the eastern province on the border of Pakistan that the CIA station chief had mentioned earlier.

As I went through the invoices and pay registers for earlier programs, I realized that many of the vendors we'd used in connection with the UN poppy survey had been paid under Jason, and in the same manner as the medical supplies and transportation. While there was always the possibility of *some* overlap, the programs were utterly different, starting with the fact that the poppy count took place out in the eastern provinces, not Kabul. The more I looked at the charges, the more I saw a connection, especially in Paktika.

You don't need trucks, or fuel, or extensive medical supplies bought from Poland if you're teaching police chiefs how to question suspects. You might think that you don't need medical supplies to count poppy fields, either, but in fact you do. Medicine, even aspirin, could be pretty valuable; a solid stock of penicillin could buy off a good hunk of a province, at least for a few weeks. Not that you'd give it to the clinics or doctors yourself; you'd give it to the warlord you wanted support from, the one best able to profit from doling them out.

Warlords, government leaders, tribal elders—these are just different words for describing the people in charge. Calling them warlords makes them seem less legitimate, because it emphasizes the fact that they are willing to use firepower to enforce their will, but they have a lot of the same concerns as the mayor of a small town in the States. It's just that rather than having to pick up the phone to call the police force, they *are* the police force. And instead of reading people Miranda rights, they shoot them.

The warlords who hadn't been elected—and a lot had—would have won an election anyway. Of course, they might have done so with a fair mix of propaganda and intimidation. Then again, that might be said of a number of American small towns and big cities, as well.

JASON, or most of it, was legit. Courses *had* been held in Kabul, at least according to the Kabul police instruction coordinator, whom I met later that day. He plied me with tea and sugar cubes, extolling the classes' virtues. He was on the payroll for the equivalent of a thousand dollars a week, a rich man's salary in Afghanistan, so his enthusiasm was not surprising.

I managed to tease some useful information out of him, though admittedly it was slight—Merc had mentioned that he was going east to set up training programs with provincial police officers.

"Out in Paktika?" I asked.

The man smiled broadly and agreed—which in Afghanistan could mean anything from "yes, of course" to "beats the shit out of me."

After the police department, I went over to the airport to look up Khattak. I stopped at the bazaar on the way and bought a pair of AKs and twenty clips. The Kalashnikov AK-47 comes in a mind-boggling variety of configurations. The ones I got had folding metal butts that made them a little easier to carry and, if the need arose, to conceal. Though the guns were old, they had two things to recommend them: they shot good-sized bullets, which made large holes at close range, a good thing, and ammunition was readily available throughout the country.

It didn't surprise me particularly that Khattak wasn't at the airport. He did definitely have a place there, though. People rolled their eyes when I asked about him. They thought he was a bit of joke; not only had he adopted an Afghan name, but he often dressed as if he were a tribesman. This was considered a serious eccentricity in a place known for eccentricity.

Nobody could say where he was or when he'd back. I hung around until the sun started to set and my driver rolled out a little mat in front of his beat-up Toyota sedan to say his prayers. His car was big enough to carry two or three bodyguards, but I hadn't decided yet whether I'd need them. The problem wasn't money, or even finding people—finding the right people, though, *that* tended to be difficult.

I went to the Intercontinental. Not only was the bar there one of the best places to pick up information on what was going on, the food was decent and I hadn't eaten much all day. I went up to Merc's room, used my "key" and let myself in. Then I took out the sat phone and called home.

Sharon didn't answer. Maybe it was the time difference; I couldn't remember whether it was morning or evening there. I left a message on the machine, telling her I loved her, that I was okay, and that this was all going to work out in a couple of days. For some reason, I even gave her a corny kiss before I killed the transmission.

SHARON and I started living together two weeks after we slept together for the first time. It wasn't a planned thing. I'd just moved to Hoboken, New Jersey, a few blocks from the train station and ferries, which made it easy to get into Manhattan. She stayed over on a Friday night, then Saturday, then Sunday. Somewhere in the following week, she started looking for furniture with me.

Buying a couch with her was an experience. Until then I'd thought of couches as benches covered with something soft. She saw it as part of a whole style, knew the fabrics and the colors. When she saw the right one—and it took a few stores until she did—she knew it instantly. What was really impressive was simply the way she made up her mind, the way she sized it up. It was like she possessed some hidden knowledge foreign to me. The sofa cost thousands of dollars—I think twelve or thirteen—but you knew looking at it that it was worth it.

Twelve thousand bucks for something to sit on.

The money had just started to roll in. It was like play money, zeroes where decimals should be.

Two or three weeks after we got the couch, Iron Rock got a contract to do a security review for a hedge fund company. Merc and I took bonuses, and I blew half of mine on a diamond bracelet for Sharon. She liked it—oh, she liked it all right. She saw it and she smiled and she touched it and modeled it and hugged me, and making love that night blew my mind.

My wife wasn't born into millionaire money, but she was always well off. Her father was a cardiologist and her mother a corporate lawyer who went back to work when Sharon was nine. They lived in a big house in the Connecticut suburbs and took trips to Europe; she had a tutor even though she had good grades in school. I don't know if she was spoiled but she was used to certain things—used to money, unlike me.

One night we were having dinner in a restaurant in Manhattan, a fancy-ass place, the sort where you make reservations a month in advance and you end up next to the kitchen if your name isn't in *Who's Who.* But we got a good table with no hassle because we'd done some work for the owners. Halfway through the meal I realized Sharon was stealing glances at one of our neighbors, an older guy in a nice suit with a gold watch on his wrist and a fancy black opal ring on his pinkie. He was eating with a woman maybe half his age.

"You know him?" I asked.

"Who?"

"Guy you're staring at."

"*Jack—*"

"Just stating the obvious."

I dropped it for the rest of dinner. I didn't want him to realize I was jealous of him—and that's what I was—but I brought it up later back at my place, our place by then.

"What did you see in him?" I asked.

"Who?"

"The rich guy in the restaurant."

"What? Nothing."

"He had a real fancy watch. Nice suit. Is it money that turns you on?"

She pressed her lips together and folded her arms. Her face got red. She didn't say anything. Finally, I went to make some drinks and changed the subject.

I was right, though. I know I was right. She was impressed by the fact that the guy was rich. It was an aphrodisiac, a turn-on. And it pissed me off.

I bought my Rolex a few weeks after that, and found a guy to make me suits.

IN retrospect, I probably should have been more suspicious or at least less surprised when Captain Race Mulligan walked into the bar at the Intercontinental and did a double take when he saw me. Race had been my captain when I was in Afghanistan. He wasn't in the army anymore, but what he was in he didn't say. So I should've figured it was some sort of setup right from the get-go.

Race did have a way of showing up at times when you'd least expect it when we were in the army. He'd also been a pretty good captain, a decent leader, especially under fire. He led from the front, not from under a desk. He also figured out pretty early that being successful in combat was as much about keeping the bureaucracy off your butt as about dealing with the enemy.

This is how screwy things were after the first phase of combat, when U.S. troops were conducting missions: if you were fired on at your camp or base, you needed permission to go and chase the motherfuckers down. Even when you got it, that could take more than an hour, by which time the bad guys were on the other side of the mountain. Race prefiled patrol plans every stinking day, and did a dozen other little things with the red tape to make sure the leaves and birds above him would be satisfied if the shit hit the fan. Nobody above him ever caught on.

"What are you doing in Kabul?" he said, pulling out a chair at the small table I was sitting at. Race emphasized each word, so that there was a bit of a gap between them; talking to him sometimes was like talking to one of those computerized phone systems.

"Came for my health."

"Oh, ho, that's a good one, Jack. Ha! Yeah. Never. Heard that before."

"What are you doing here?"

"Love. Jack. Love." And he broke into a verse from an Irish drinking song, "Brown Jug." When he was done, he pulled out a picture of an Afghan woman, I guess so I'd know he was lusting for a female, not booze.

"You stayed because of her?"

"Came back, Jack. Came back. Why are you here?"

"Looking for Merc."

"Merc? Mercury Conrad? The one and only. Saw him a couple of months ago, Jack. How come you're friends with him?"

I shrugged. Then, because it felt like I had to say something, I added, "He saved my life a couple of times."

"You saved my life. I'm not your friend." He grinned. "Just kiddin', Jack. Brothers. For life."

"Where'd you see him?"

"This very hotel. Over there." He turned and stared across the room, as if Merc might materialize if he looked long enough.

"He tell you what he was up to?" I asked.

"Merc? You know Merc. Tells you everything but the truth."

"Merc's always been pretty honest with me." The words came out of my mouth without the slightest bit of irony or sarcasm. I guess some habits of thought are hard to break.

"Want another of those, Jacky?" said Race, pointing to my drink.

8

SOUTHEASTERN AFGHANISTAN, SIX YEARS BEFORE

MERCURY Conrad grew up as a poor-shit white kid in East St. Louis. I've never been to East St. Louis, but from everything I've heard, it rates as one of the worst ghettos in the country, a little slice of the Third World in our own backyard. Merc's mother was white and so was he; she moved to East St. Louis and married a black man there after he was born. The man wasn't much of a father—he spent a lot of time in jail—but Merc didn't blame him; he wasn't his father anyway.

"Didn't beat me, so that must've meant he loved me," was Merc's description of "Old Sugar," which was his stepdad's nickname. Merc's mother died when he was seven or eight—probably of a drug overdose, though he was hazy on the details. From there he stayed with an aunt of his stepfather's, and went into the army as soon as he could, getting a GED rather than a regular diploma, probably because he'd never have passed the attendance requirements.

The army made him sharper. Merc must've been a pretty good talker when he was growing up, but the army made him into a master. He could talk his way into a lot of things, and out of even more—when he wanted to. He could also back the talk up with action. Not just in the sense that he was willing to fight. As a matter of fact, I can't think of Merc ever getting into a fistfight or even a shoving match. What I mean is that he could figure out what needed to be done and make sure it was accomplished—or at least have it appear to be, which in the army a lot of times was even better.

In combat, he shone. Everything he learned in the various military schools jelled with the street smarts he'd grown up with. You could plop him down in the middle of a jungle or a desert; he'd figure out where he was and how to get out of it. He could spot two Taliban guerrillas on a ridgeline and know exactly where the rest of their troop would be, and how to ambush them. He could pick up a grenade that had fallen on the ground and toss it away before it blew up. I know he could do all those things, because I was there when he did.

But there was more to Merc than that. There was an indescribable sense about him, a sort of intuition about what to do. That's what made us close.

Merc was the team leader on a three-man recce or reconnaissance mission our first or second week in Afghanistan. They flew us into the middle of nowhere with maps that the Russians had cursed more than a decade before for their inaccuracies. We were supposed to scout a group of Taliban militia, sending back intel to a Northern Alliance unit and-or calling in air strikes, depending on what we saw. The helicopter put us down in the middle of the night a half mile from the highway we had to watch. We dug into the side of the hill, made a little hide that would blend into the hill, and took turns watching and pretending to sleep.

Much of Afghanistan *is* desolate and empty; you could throw a thousand darts at the 1:100,000 map we'd been given and never come close to a house. But our dart was the thousand and first. I don't know whether the helicopter pilots screwed up or the intel boys just plain got it wrong, but it turned out we'd camped on the side of some farmer's field. When dawn came, a couple of kids came with it, kicking a soccer ball just below the entrance to our little hooch.

Chuck Priest, the third guy on the team, was on watch. I woke up hearing him and Merc whispering about what they should do.

Chuck was thinking that we could grab the two kids and tough it out. Merc said we weren't going to do that.

There are regulations about dealing with civilians and taking hostages like that in a war zone, but I guarantee none of us thought about them. We were operating on a much more primitive level, reacting to the situation. We didn't want to shoot the kids—*we weren't going to shoot the kids.*

Certainly not once Merc said we weren't.

For a minute, it looked like they were going to go away without seeing us, or at least without making it obvious that they had seen us. Then the soccer ball bounded up and hit the tarp we'd used to camouflage the top of the hide.

In all my time in Afghanistan after that, I never saw another stinkin' soccer ball. That may have been the only damn ball in the country, and it bounced right on the one spot that would clearly give us away.

I popped out of the hole and grabbed the ball. The two kids stopped at the foot of the hill, staring at me like I was an alien. And probably as far as they were concerned I was. If I'd put on my helmet I'd definitely have looked like one.

I stared back at them. They were the first Afghan kids I'd seen up close. They looked like scruffy kids everywhere, probably a lot like me when I was little, except for the shoes—they didn't have any.

I punted their soccer ball into a high arc over their heads and into the field beyond. Dumb thing to do, but that's what I did. They kept staring. Finally, I did a bogeyman yell and they leaped away.

Merc, meanwhile, got on the SatCom radio and called for an emergency extraction. We gathered our gear and got into a defensive position, which basically meant hunkering down with as much ammo near our fingertips as possible.

An hour passed. Two. The helicopter was on the way.

Three hours. Afghanistan can be maddeningly hot at times, and this was one of those times—even though it was winter. We were kitted up with helmets and flak vests and sweat poured down our faces and backs like we were sitting in a shower.

Chuck Priest was a black guy who came from somewhere in

Louisiana. He was a Catholic, and after we'd been hunched there for three and a half hours he took out a set of rosary beads and draped them around his neck.

"We need all the help we can get," he said.

Just then we saw two people come up around the bend at the far end of the hill. These weren't kids, but they didn't look like Taliban militia, either. They didn't have guns that we could see, and they weren't doing anything to protect themselves or sneak up on us. My guess is that they were the kids' fathers or maybe older brothers, who'd heard their wild stories and didn't believe them. We watched them come toward us, until finally they saw us and stopped. They stared for a couple of minutes, then took a few steps up the hill.

"Git!" yelled Merc. He jumped up from his crouch and waved his gun at them. *"Go!"*

They turned and ran back down the hill.

Twenty minutes later, another group of men came toward us. This time there were six of them. One or two had rifles, but they were toward the rear of the group. The weapons were pointed toward the ground, as if they were part of an unenthusiastic hunting party returning from a day of tramping in the woods.

Priest yelled at them. They stopped and stared at us, a bit like people do at the monkey house in the zoo.

Merc stood up and fired a few warning rounds up in the air, well away from them; they scattered.

I was on the radio, screaming at whoever was on the other end that we needed those sumbitchin' helicopters and we needed them sumbitchin' now.

"I'm not hearing them," I told him. "Get off your butt and find out where they are. *Now!*"

When I finally got off the radio Merc pointed down the hill. There were dozens of people there now, women as well as men, staring at us. There was a group of kids, a big group of kids, kind of off to the side looking.

"We should tell them we're here to save them," said Priest. "We're on their side. They don't like the Taliban, right?"

Priest had the right idea, but between us we knew maybe a dozen words in Pashto, and we weren't even sure we could pronounce them correctly. Finally Merc stood up and gave it a try. He told them we were friends, here to help them, and wouldn't hurt them. Then he switched to English. It was kind of like what you might see in a really old Western: "Me friend. No hurt. Friend. No shoot friends."

Maybe a third of the men in the crowd had guns, but to get them we'd have had to take down a good number of the unarmed people around them. And there was a good chance we'd never get all of them before having to reload.

"I'm gonna fire another burst and see what happens," I said.

"Hang on." Merc took another step toward them and repeated his speech. The crowd had continued to grow; there were maybe a hundred people there now, and more were slipping in.

They made no sign to indicate whether they understood what he was saying or not. They just stood there looking at us.

Finally, we heard the low beat of helicopters in the distance.

"Better tell them what the hell's going on here," Merc said.

I grabbed the radio, managed to get on with the lead chopper pilot, and, as best I could, described the situation. I don't think he believed me until his bird came over the hill line and saw us surrounded by a mob. He said later it looked like we were rock stars or something.

We were a long way from being in the clear. The helicopters couldn't land on the hill, and there were people between us and the flat field. The choppers were Special Forces versions of the Black Hawk, flown by crack crews who trained with us all the time. They had machine guns mounted in the cargo area, but I don't think the gunners would have been any more enthusiastic than we were about the prospect of shooting their way in or out. Killing some guy with a gun who's taking shots at you is one thing; "popping a woman holding a baby is a whole 'nother thing," as Priest put it when the choppers began circling around our little piece of heaven.

Priest and I wanted to try scattering them with a few bursts, then make a run for it. Merc said no.

"What we need to do is walk out real calm," Merc told us. "Get to the middle of that field, and let the helicopters grab us."

"You're on drugs," I said.

"No, no. Trust me on this. Come on."

Priest and I looked at each other. I don't know what was in my eyes but doubt was in his. It was too late to talk Merc out of it, though—he was already walking down the hill. We scrambled after him, guns ready. We weren't just locked and loaded; our fingers were hovering just over the triggers. I had to struggle to breathe. But Merc, he just walked calmly toward where he wanted to go, just walked.

The crowd parted like he was Moses and they were the Red Sea. He reached a spot maybe thirty yards from the base of the hill and stopped. Then he made kind of a shooing sign with his hands, pushing them back so the chopper could land.

The next thing I remember is that I was on the helicopter and we were miles away. We could see gunfire in the distance, a black ribbon of 22.3-millimeter antiaircraft shells spitting up several hills away. Probably it was aimed at us, but it was impotent.

Nobody in the chopper said anything until we landed. It had nothing to do with the loud chatter of the engines. What had happened was all too surreal, too strange to process.

That was my introduction to Afghanistan. And even though Merc and I had been friends for a long while before then, it was the first time I really understood what he was capable of. The fact that he saved my life a bunch of times after that never came as a surprise.

9

KABUL

RACE, my old captain, bought me a bunch of drinks that night. He gave me a few tidbits of information, naming people who were movers and shakers that might help me, either because I'd been in the army or because I was a friend of a friend, or, mostly, because I'd be likely to show my gratitude in a tangible way. In the course of the conversation he told me about a colonel who commanded an airborne unit whose operational area included Paktika. He also gave me some advice on where to get better weapons if I needed them.

In retrospect, I should have realized from the beginning that Race had been sent by the CIA station chief to make sure I was headed in the right direction. But I was slow on the uptake, my senses dulled from jet lag and the shock of being back in Afghanistan.

In exchange for Race's largesse, I listened to him detail his puppy-dog love. He kept throwing little bits of Irish drinking tunes into laments about the how the woman he loved had him under her spell. He made her sound like some sort of witch, even as he said he was in love with her. She apparently worked for the UN, and was committed—his word—to saving Afghanistan from itself.

"I came back for the money, but I'm staying for her," said my old captain. "I'll end up with neither. Drink up, Jack."

"How were you going to make money?"

"Drink up, Jack. Drink up, boy. Some tales can never be told." He winked, and ordered another round.

I DIDN'T sleep well that night. I didn't much sleep at all. The adrenaline that had brought me here was starting to wear off, but it left me jittery. I guess I was only starting to understand how deep a hole I was in, and how hard it was going to be to get out.

As I lay in bed, I started thinking about Sharon. Not about her now, not about how bad things had become, but about how we had started.

Being with Sharon the first few months was like living in a pornographic movie. We made love over and over. She was voracious, and so was I. It was as if I had to make up for years of being deprived. Not that I'd been a virgin, of course, but I'd never had sex like this—insatiable longing and an unimaginable high. We were like aliens who'd suddenly stepped into bodies and had to experience every possible sensation. We made love at home, in hotels, in any place where we could lock the door, and in a few where we couldn't.

Once I got a call on my cell while I was having dinner with a client at the Algonquin in Midtown New York. I pulled the phone out of my pocket, looked at the number; it was Sharon's cell. The guy I was with owned an armed-car business that wanted us to run security protocol checks for them; the contract was good money for little work. He was one of these guys who needed a lot of hand-holding and suck-up; he needed your undivided attention while he pontificated about the variations of color in vintage Tiffany glass. All I needed to do to nail the contract was nod and keep drinking the expensive-as-hell wine he'd ordered for us.

So I shouldn't have taken the call. But I flipped the phone up anyway.

"I need you," whispered Sharon.

"And?"

"Downstairs."

"Huh?"

"I'm downstairs. Come and get me."

I flipped the phone closed. There was no conscience or superego or whatever it is that keeps you from doing something you know you shouldn't—I was just going to see her, to make love to her; I could feel my heart pumping already, and I probably already had a hard-on.

"I have an emergency I have to take care of right away," I told my client. "I'm going to make a call and be right back."

He kind of gaped at me, as if I'd called him a big fat worthless fuck. I smiled and walked around to the lobby, then down the steps.

Sharon pulled me into the men's room. There wasn't a lock or anything, but we didn't care. We went at it in one of the stalls. Somehow the thin scent of ammonia and the vague aroma of waste just added to our frenzy. I have no idea if anyone came in while we were screwing or how long we were there. I don't really remember any of the specifics except how it felt—a total immersion in this racing high.

When I got back to the table, my client was gone, and so was the contract. I didn't care. At least he'd paid for dinner.

SIM remained MIA the next day. I suspected that some of the entries in the books were bogus, and that he thought I'd figured out which ones and was going to take it out of his hide.

No one else had called in or e-mailed or left a message, either. I started tracking down people on the list I had from our records. Most were impossible to find. Deciphering who the local reps were for some of the vendors proved impossible. The few people I found appeared reluctant to even admit they knew Merc, let alone give me anything approaching useful information about where he might be.

I visited two warehouses on the outskirts of western Kabul where we rented space and found some meager supplies there—toilet paper was the most useful, and I took a box and threw it in the back of my driver's car. I also found some old medical supplies—bandages, baby diapers, formula, and a small box of medicines—and took them, as well.

By the afternoon I'd toured a lot of the area, but didn't know much more than I'd known when I started. My head hurt. The cold snap was starting to break and I felt hot and sticky though the temperature was barely fifty.

Around three o'clock, I went up to the clinic where Verge's body had been taken, to give Hariti Kedar the medical stuff. She seemed surprised to see me, and almost scolded me for giving her the supplies.

"I just thought I'd say thank you. If you don't want it—"

"I take, yes. I take."

We stood talking in the small foyer of the clinic, in front of a line that was at least as long as the one from the other day. Many of the same people may even have been on it.

"But in Afghanistan, thank you is not necessary," she insisted.

"Maybe then you can tell me more about my friend Verge," I said. "Mr. Maro."

"No more to say."

"You don't have any idea why they brought him here?"

She shook her head.

"Who brought him here exactly?"

Hariti turned to one of the men who'd picked up a box of the supplies. She said something quickly in Pashto and he responded with an equally quick and incomprehensible answer.

"Someone dropped them off, rolled from the back of a truck, and left," said Hariti.

"Is that common?"

"Very."

"But he stayed long enough to say they'd been found near the creek, right?" I was just repeating, more or less, what she'd said to me the other day.

"Yes," said Hariti.

"Maybe you should ask him if he knows anything else."

"He doesn't," said Hariti. She turned to him and nodded; he left.

"One thing I noticed, sister. My company paid your clinic in connection with a UN operation a year ago. I was surprised by that."

Her guard slipped for a moment, but her stone face quickly returned. "At one time, we could afford regular security but now it is less necessary."

"No, we paid you. This operation was to count poppies. So I don't quite understand what we were paying for."

"You'd better go."

"I don't think so."

I glanced across the room at the lone bodyguard. He had a pistol tucked into his pants. I could run over and flatten him before he'd ever get it out to shoot me. Or I could simply raise the AK-47 from my shoulder and slice his head in two.

"I'd really appreciate some information," I said. "I'm not going to make trouble. I'm trying to find Merc."

"We do good work here," said Hariti. And she burst into tears.

THE money did not go to the clinic. It went to a man named Raz Omar, who had a small rug shop outside Kabul, in a suburb on the south side of the city that had once been very fashionable but was now overrun by refugees. The small bazaar and business district remained, however, and Omar's shop was only one of a number of stores. The area had gone from tony to tired, but he found it convenient to stay for a number of reasons.

Rugs weren't Omar's main source of profit. He was a facilitator in several different lines of business—a smuggler in other words—who had connections in a number of southern and eastern provinces. The money we had paid was a payoff, protection money so that our people wouldn't be hurt while conducting the survey. The clinic had provided a thin cover, a way for us to give Omar the money without it looking bad. If anyone ever checked, they'd figure it was for some sort of medical services, or at worst a donation to help the clinic stay on its feet.

Kind of ironic, paying off a drug smuggler so you could count the poppies he was going to be transporting in a few months.

"Merc suggested this to you?" I asked Hariti. "Mr. Conrad?"

"He is a very good man."

"Where is he?"

She shook her head. Hariti was vague about when she'd last seen him, and she swore she knew nothing more about my two dead employees.

"All right," I told her finally. "All right. I'll send you more medicine in the morning."

OMAR'S shop would have looked like a junk kiosk anywhere else, and even for greater Kabul it looked a bit divey. It was about half a block from an open-air bazaar. You couldn't drive down that half-block; you had to walk there, which meant you were completely surrounded and covered at all times by Omar's lookouts. They were up on the roofs of the nearby buildings and in the windows across the way and for all I knew hiding under the stones at the side of the street. I took one look at the setup and knew it wasn't going to work. But pulling a quick U-turn wasn't a solution, either; the next time I came back the lookouts were sure to recognize me, and maybe they'd just shoot rather than find out what I was up to.

So I walked down the half-block to the open shack, walked inside, and asked the man standing next to a small pile of rugs where Omar was.

The man pretended not to know what I was saying.

"Omar," I repeated. "I'm a friend of Merc Conrad. I need to talk to Omar."

Merc's name brought the slightest flutter of recognition in the man's eyes. But he didn't say anything.

"Where do I find Omar?" I slipped my hand against the AK–47. There were probably three or four guys with guns across the way who had me in their sights, so there was no way in the world I'd've gotten a shot off. But the gesture made him take me seriously.

"At tea," said the man.

"Where's that?"

"Kabul Cafe," he said. He told me how to get there; it was two blocks away.

Two blocks is a long way in Kabul. These two were part of an open-air bazaar where sellers squatted on the ground with their wares, or stood behind flimsy tables and displays that looked as if the next good gust of wind would take them away. I passed through a row of vendors selling cards of Indian women. The women were fully clothed, but the pictures passed as pornography in a country where something like ninety-five percent of the female population covered themselves head to toe. The cards were traded and bartered for things; real porn probably was worth a fortune, but it could get you arrested if not killed. Under the Taliban, even these cards would have been prohibited, so I guess there'd been some progress.

The Kabul Cafe had a dozen tables on an outside dirt patio next to the building. It being a beautiful spring day by local standards, the area was packed. I didn't have to puzzle out who Raz Omar was, though; I just scanned the place until I saw a couple of large Afghans with sunglasses and baseball caps, and figured he must be the guy they were standing behind.

The maître d' stopped me as I headed in that direction. Guns weren't allowed in the cafe, he told me in English, and mine were rather conspicuous. There was a set of cubbies to the side where I could leave my weapons. He assured me no one would steal them.

"That's Raz Omar, right?" I asked, pointing toward the table.

The maître d' shrugged, which was all the answer I needed. I slid the rifles into an empty box. Clearly no one would steal them; they were the rattiest looking weapons there.

The most evil men in the world are often the most nondescript. Think of Himmler, who ran the Nazi SS and death camps; he looked like an underfed store clerk. Even Hitler—take away his rants and trim his moustache, and he's just a lousy painter scurrying from attic to gutter, trying to make a living.

Raz Omar had them all beat. He looked like an accountant's clerk, the guy whose white shirt is just a little stained around the cuffs, who no matter how he tries can't seem to get that cowlick to lie down flat at the back of his head. He was Pashtun, light skinned and slightly chubby. I would guess that his family had long been part of the country's privileged class—not leaders, and not wealthy, but assured that no matter what else happened they were better than their neighbors who weren't Pashtun. And for most of us, that's what privileged means.

He was holding court with some business associates when I came over. Two of his bodyguards got in my face, blocking me a few yards from the table.

"I want to talk to Mr. Omar," I said loudly. "I'm from Iron Rock and I have to straighten out an old bookkeeping problem involving a clinic on the other side of town. I know he's very good with math."

My explanation seemed to amuse Omar, who smiled and signaled for his men to let me through. Obviously, my friend at the rug shop had called ahead.

"You are a friend of Merc's, I understand," said Omar, gesturing for me to sit.

"That's right."

A waiter brought a glass for tea over. Afghan tea is strong and green. It has a taste all its own—one that takes a lot of getting used to. But you don't refuse it when it's offered, especially not in a situation where you're trying to get information and you're surrounded by guys whose pistols are barely hidden beneath their bulky shirts and jackets.

"I have not seen Mr. Conrad in months," said Omar. "A pity. He was very good to do business with."

"Actually, I'm looking for him. I was hoping you might be able to help."

"Oh?" He pretended to be perplexed. "I thought he was in America?"

"He's here."

"Kabul?"

"No, I don't think Kabul. Or anywhere nearby."

"Oh." He nodded solemnly. "I don't think so, either."

"Where do you think he is?"

Another perplexed look, but this time no answer.

"I know you were very helpful to my company in the past," I said. "Maybe you could help us again."

"You do not know much about what is going on here, do you, Mister—"

"Pilgrim. Jack Pilgrim."

"You seem an ignorant man, forgive me for saying so."

I admitted I was ignorant. I've been called worse things.

"In Afghanistan today, ignorance can get you killed," Omar said. He might have been scolding a child.

"I'd like to remedy that. I don't want to stay ignorant forever."

"Maybe if you find Mr. Conrad."

"Sure. Help me."

The perplexed look returned once again, only this time it seemed genuine, as if he really couldn't fathom the possibility that I needed help.

"You lost two men the other day, two employees," said Omar.

"Yeah, I did. How'd you know?"

"Kabul is a very small place. A very small place. Do you know why they died?"

"No, and I'd like to find out."

"When commitments are not met, every contract has a penalty clause."

"Okay, so let's stop talking in riddles," I told him. "What did they do?"

Omar waved his hand, dismissing me. Before I could say anything else, two of his bodyguards grabbed me by the arms and hauled me to my feet. I started to react, but saw that the two men behind him had their hands on their stomachs, ready to pull their pistols out.

"I'm just looking for information," I told Omar. "We can work together."

He snickered. The two thugs tugged me backward. I pushed them away, more for form than anything else. I'd already lost my self-respect, practically pleading with their boss to help me.

THERE are situations where showing weakness, any weakness, is tantamount to slitting your own throat. Someone like Omar saw weakness as something to be eradicated. People who were weak were his enemies. If I really wanted him to help me, I'd've had to come on strong, very, very strong—I'd have to have left no doubt that I didn't need his help, that I considered him puny, and that I would sooner crush him than ask him for the slightest favor. What I'd done at the Kabul Cafe was the exact opposite of that. I'd told him I deserved to be crushed like an ant.

It took him about two hours to take a shot at doing just that.

10

KABUL

IN celebration of my day of utter failure, I decided to have dinner at one of Kabul's two Japanese restaurants. I don't know exactly how he got to Afghanistan, but the proprietor of the restaurant where I ate was in fact Japanese. He even made and served sushi, though knowing how many thousands of miles Kabul was from a sizable body of water I went with the teriyaki steak.

Oshu House was another place with the "no weapons in the dining room" policy; you left your gun on the long table at the other side of the room.

It may have actually been against the law to openly carry firearms unless you had some sort of permit or military status in Kabul. But not having a weapon was not only dangerous, it put you in a decidedly small minority.

My AKs were sitting on the table about thirty feet from me when the two men came into the dining room. One of them was wearing an American-style baseball cap, its brim facing backward. The hat was blue, and that's what tipped me off—Omar's men had been wearing hats of the very same color, with New York Mets insignias on them.

Not much to go on, but more than enough.

By the time I got my table up and dove to the floor, both of the men had pulled automatic rifles from under their long coats. Big rifles. They were AR15s, civilian versions of the M16, and they were set to automatic fire. The first man pressed the trigger on his and blew his entire wad of bullets, obliterating what had been my table and chair.

Fortunately, by then I'd rolled a good five feet away. By the time he realized I'd moved, it was too late—I'd pulled up the .45 I'd kept beneath my napkin in my lap and put two bullets into his Mets cap.

The other guy was a real bozo. He hadn't even started to shoot when I nailed him. My bullet caught him at the top of his forehead. His body compressed slightly, as if I'd hit him with a hammer or something. Then the rifle dropped from his hands and he fell forward.

The three or four other patrons in the place were so stunned and this had taken place so quickly that they were all still at their tables when the gunfire stopped. The owner came running out from the back kitchen, dropped the tray he had in his hands, then retreated.

I took some American bills from my pocket, threw them on the ground where my table had been, and left.

IF I'd been thinking, really thinking, I might have checked the men for IDs or, more usefully, money; maybe I would have taken their guns, which were much better than mine. But I was still a couple of steps behind the curve, still not up to Afghanistan speed. At least I moved quickly. Moving is always better than standing still.

I had no doubt who'd sent them. A black Land Rover, probably armored, sped off as I ran outside. I'd seen one near the cafe when I talked to Omar that afternoon.

So now I set out to make amends.

TO get the sort of weapons I needed to deal with Omar properly, I had to go to Sorobi. Sorobi is a district south of Kabul known for its gemstone dealers and hidden ammunition dumps. Every few months, the police would announce a major raid, discovering machine guns and mortars and rocket-launched grenades. They'd say that the district was now clear of heavy weapons. Coincidentally, they'd never make an actual arrest of a person connected to the weapons they found. What the actual deal with the police was I can only guess, but I knew from our payments that the man I had to talk to was a police officer in the district.

Traveling at night cost me the equivalent of fifty bucks over the fee I had already paid my driver. Curfews had officially ended in the city about a year after the interim government took over, but there were still sporadic arrests. Those really didn't bother him; they were just opportunities for bribes, and you would be released at the roadside if you paid a small fee.

But some people who worked at night weren't interested in bribes; they wanted your ride. So driving out at night cost extra to begin with, and on top of that I had to agree to pay for any damage to the vehicle. Cosmetic stuff was cheap—five bucks a bullet hole. But replace glass or a tire or an engine, and you were talking serious money.

We drove without stopping to the address in my file, ending up at a regional police station a little before midnight. The man I was looking for turned out to be sleeping in the back room. For the first time since I'd come to Afghanistan, when I mentioned Merc's name, I got a smile and a nod. Within a half hour, I was on my way back to Kabul with an RPG launcher and six grenades.

"RPG" stands for rocket-propelled grenade. The initials are used for a number of different weapons, but in this case they applied to a Russian RPG-7 launcher. The oval-shaped grenade sits at the front of the weapon, which is targeted using a very simple optical sight and fired from the shoulder. I won't give you all the technical details because frankly I don't know them. I know the projectile is accurate enough in skilled hands to take out a helicopter at over two hundred yards.

MY target was stationary, and I aimed to get a lot closer than two hundred yards before firing. I had my driver drop me off about a half mile from Omar's shop and dismissed him for the night. He had a relieved look on his face, and told me he'd look for me in the morning.

Getting onto the roof of the building across from Omar's shop wasn't hard—I found a ladder right down the street, and set it against the side wall. The hard part was sticking my head over the side of the roof. When nobody kicked me in the face, I pushed myself up and over. The roof gave a little bit, but held. I crouched at the edge, getting my hearings. I didn't have night goggles, but there was just enough light for me to make out where one of the guards was sitting against a narrow metal chimney, three buildings away. I moved across the roof as quietly as I could, settling each footstep as gently as possible.

Something happened to me on that roof that I can't explain. With each step, I felt as if I lost a little weight. My footfalls became so light they didn't exist. By the time I reached the guard, I was a ghost, silent, dark, invisible.

I was finally back to my old self, back to the warrior I'd had to be to survive Afghanistan. Not that I had completely shucked the weight of the intervening years, literally and figuratively, the extra pounds or the mental flabbiness. But I was better, a lot better—no more would I be behind the curve.

The guard was sleeping. I slit his throat with a straight, hard pull. I could feel his life drain into my hands.

The feeling made me drunker than I'd've been if I'd consumed two whole bottles of bourbon. It was beyond drunk, beyond a rush—I can't describe it, let alone deny it.

From the outside, from the distance, you can dress an act of killing up with different things. You can justify it, consider it righteous, call it a crime. But inside at the moment, your heart pumps like an animal heart. Your body careens through the moment, not taking stock, not making categories, counting sins, or bestowing blessings. You move to the next thing you do. You're an animal, human certainly, but an animal, all reaction and instinct. No judgment, no analysis, no context intrudes; you're just quick breaths and the will to keep moving. It's total freedom, untethered from the things that hold you to society, to the place where right and wrong actually matter.

Something came toward me at the far end of the roof. I threw myself down. There were bullets, or there must have been bullets; I don't remember precisely. All I know is that in another few moments I was standing over another dead body, my AK in my hand.

And the rug shop had started to burn. Somewhere along the way I'd pulled the launcher off my back and fired the grenade into the shop. Before I killed the second guard? After?

It must have been before, though I have no memory of it. As I looked down at the small shop a curdle of flames spun from the metal grate and turned the most spectacular red, leaping upward as they strove voraciously for fuel.

By the time I jumped off the roof, there were shouts in the street. The rest of the guard force, which had probably been sleeping in the building below me, realized they had screwed up big time and were now in serious shit. As they ran toward the fire I went in the opposite direction, hauling down the block and up a cross street, running full out until I reached the spot where I'd stashed my other rifle beneath a pile of crates at the side of a half-demolished building. I didn't figure to need the launcher or the grenades anymore, so I left them there, caught my breath, then circled around to a spot where I could watch what was going on.

A lone police car responded as I crept up through the darkened bazaar. Two armed men met it, blocking the way; I wasn't close enough to hear what was going on and wouldn't have understood the words anyway, but within a few seconds the driver threw the car into reverse and sped away.

A few minutes later, there was a secondary explosion and flames catapulted skyward. I watched as the men Raz Omar had hired scattered in all directions. I could tell from the way they ran most weren't coming back.

The burst of flames brought the local fire department. A fresh contingent of policemen and Afghan troops came with them. People from the neighborhood milled around as well, chattering about what was going on; by the time the flames started to die down, it looked like half the town was there.

The one person who wasn't there was the one person I wanted to see: Raz Omar. Eventually I concluded that he was too smart to show up, and that there were too many people with guns around for me to grab him anyway. I slunk down the street and made my way to one of the warehouses where we'd taken storage space about a mile away, thinking I could get a little sleep. But I was too exhausted; I worried that if I actually let myself sleep I'd fall into a stupor so complete I'd never wake up. So I moved ahead with Plan B.

HOSPITALS are the scariest place on earth at night. The moans and sobs of the helpless ripple up your spine. The labored huff of the desperate breaths down the hall overwhelm your own, and the light beep of machines keeping people alive gradually replaces your own heartbeat. A single cry of pain can unravel all the knots you've tied your muscles into for defense. The sounds are echoes of your own vulnerability, reminders that no matter how brave, how prepared, how strong, there is a point where you, too, will break.

It's the kind of knowledge there is no defense against. You can cover your ears, but then the shadows begin to play in front of your eyes, the shadows of nurses with syringes, of gurneys being pushed in desperation to a corner where the death gurgle can't be heard by the living. And if you close your eyes, there's the smell, not of blood, not of feces or pee, but of medicine, a cold metallic stink that rises above the animal and antiseptic, the scent that reminds you your lone capsule of a body can never be enough to keep you alive. You're there, and you can't escape, and so you just hang on until morning comes.

When Hariti arrived at the clinic an hour before dawn, I'd already been there an hour and a half, my nerves chiseled bare. She walked into the room without switching on the light, and was only a few feet from her desk, and my rifle, when she caught sight of me and stopped.

"I brought the medicine I promised," I told her.

She didn't answer.

"It's by the door." I got up. "I'm sorry I surprised you. I wanted to be here first thing, so I wouldn't interrupt your patients."

"It's okay." She walked to the side of the room where the lamp was and turned it on. The room snapped yellow, poking my eyes. Even her tan face seemed washed out by the light.

"I was wondering if you could do me a favor," I told her, moving so she could sit at her desk. "I need to talk to Omar. I need to arrange a meeting."

"Omar?"

"Raz Omar. He tried to have me killed yesterday. He and I have to discuss that. I have to find out why."

I was playing for her sympathy, but it didn't work. It was dumb, really; Hariti would be the sort who'd save her sympathy for people who actually needed it.

"I don't think I can help you," she told me.

"I'll make it worth your while, the clinic's while. More medicine."

Tell me that wasn't a good deal—medicine that would save a dozen, two dozen lives, kids maybe, innocent people, certainly compared to Omar, whose business brought death disguised as bliss to thousands of people, and who probably killed another dozen every month in the course of things. But Hariti wouldn't take it. I could tell in her eyes.

"Unfortunately, you can't say no," I told her, raising my gun.

Even then, she had to calculate, and hesitated before picking up the phone.

I stood against the wall, watching as she dialed the number. She got an operator or maybe some sort of assistant, hung up, and waited for a call back.

Phone service in Kabul is not exactly on par with phone service in Washington, D.C. It works better than the electricity—as far as I know, there are no rolling blackouts—but there's a very limited number of places that actually have phones, or wires that connect to them. Sat phones are the communication form of choice, and even they can be very unreliable, more because they depend on batteries that can't always be recharged than because of the vagaries of satellite coverage. But the clinic had a real phone, and apparently Omar did, too.

"Someone will call back." She got up.

"Where are you going?"

"I have work to do."

"We'll wait here."

"I have work to do," she insisted. Then she walked past me, into the clinic, calling my bluff.

I'd gotten in by bribing the guard, who not only remembered me but saw the medicine and figured I was a friend. Hariti gave him a stern look when she saw him in the hall, but didn't explain. I thought the poor kid was going to cry. I followed her into the clinic, walking behind as she stopped at the beds. It may have been my imagination, but the sobs and moans seemed to stop the moment she walked in; even the labored breathing calmed.

"Why are you here?" I asked her as she went among the beds. "Why did you come to this hellhole?"

She looked at me as if I were pathetically stupid. "What else to do, Mr. Pilgrim?"

What else to do. The only thing I could think of was that she had committed some awful sin and had to make up for it. But what sort of sin could possibly bring you here?

She stopped in front of the bed of a boy who was four or five. He was sleeping peacefully; he even had a smile on his face. I thought the kid had the flu or measles or something and was just getting over it until she patted the bed where his right leg should have been.

"A mine," she said, and walked on to the next patient.

It took a half hour before the phone rang in her office; in that time Hariti had stopped at every patient in the large open room, and visited about half of the smaller rooms in the nearby wing. The ailments and injuries were as varied as the letters of the alphabet. Two people had died during the night; she pulled the sheets over their heads, a signal to the orderlies to prepare a plastic bag and take them to the basement. Their beds would be filled as soon as the clinic opened.

When the phone rang it was like an alarm clock, shaking me from a stupor; I walked quickly behind her to the office, standing over her desk as she picked up the phone and began speaking in rapid Pashto to the person on the other side of the line.

"Well?" I said when she put the phone down.

"Omar died last night," she told me with the same flat voice she had used to describe what was wrong with the boy. "Someone firebombed his shop where he sleeps."

HERETICS

11

KABUL

JACK, Jack, Jack. You are a busy lad. And industrious." Race Mulligan sat down beside me in the Intercontinental Bar, where I'd spent most of the day after leaving the clinic. I'd told myself I was working up a Plan C, but I was really taking a break from reality, numbing myself with bourbon.

"Hey, Cap," I told him. "Pull up a stool."

"Don't mind. If I do." He signaled to the bartender, who brought him a vodka in short order. After a gulp that drained the glass halfway, he turned to me and said again, "Jack, Jack, Jack."

"That's my name."

"You are one tricky devil."

"How's that, Race?"

"I heard you were in the market for rugs. But didn't like the price."

"You can't believe everything you hear." I crossed my arms and leaned back, looking at him.

"Oh, I don't, Jack. If I did. Well, I can't entirely say what would happen. If I did."

"You were a good officer, Race. I have to give you that."

"Flattery will get you everywhere, Jacky. Everywhere." He drained his vodka and pushed the glass back for another. Suddenly, I didn't feel like drinking anymore. I got up.

"Something I said?" asked Race.

"Just going to the WC," I told him. "You're welcome to join me."

Race took it as an actual invitation, rather than the sarcastic remark I'd intended. He followed me to the bathroom, sidling right up next to me at the urinal.

"Raz Omar. Was the slime of the earth," he said. "Nobody's going to cry. That he's gone."

"That's nice."

"Still, there's a certain order to things. That has to be followed. A certain progression."

"Uh-huh. Look, Cap, I kind of have trouble with the plumbing when somebody's breathing down my chest, you know what I mean?"

"Sorry." Race took a half-step back. There was someone in one of the stalls, but he didn't lower his voice or make any attempt to hide what he was talking about. "The authorities have problems with people blowing things up. In the middle of the night. It's not good for public relations. Even if what blows up deserves to be blown up."

"Yeah."

"I heard. Someone tried to give you food poisoning yesterday," he said. "And that they met with unfortunate accidents. Oddly. They seem to have worked for Mr. Omar."

I flushed and went to wash my hands.

"Have you seen the colonel yet, Jack? Colonel Armstrong? The one I told you about yesterday."

"Haven't had a chance."

"I'd make it a priority. Jack. Jack. You're going to Paktika?"

"I don't know where I'm going, Cap. Maybe to bed."

"I heard you guys had an operation. Going out there."

"The operation we had was in Kabul."

"We're not talking about Jason, Jacky."

"What are we talking about?"

"Leopard."

"I don't know anything about Leopard."

Race gave me a sour scowl.

"I'd see the colonel, and I'd get a ride out to Paktika," Race told me. "And I'd be careful. Really careful. Any more accidents or coincidences in Kabul. They really might get you serious trouble."

I looked up from the sink. "You don't think I'm in trouble now, huh, Race?"

"You were a good soldier, Jack. You said I was a good officer, but you were a better soldier. But we're not in the army anymore. I can't help you."

He left while I dried my hands.

The door to the commode opened. I figured it would be some sort of backup guy for him, a CIA paramilitary or something—obviously Race was working for the spooks, either directly or indirectly—but instead it was a short, wiry Afghan. Given the fact that Race hadn't worried too much about being overheard, I figured that he was somehow in with him, so I ignored him and dried my hands.

"You killed Raz Omar?" he said as I turned to leave.

"What difference would it make to you?" I said. "You a cop?"

The man shook his head violently. I left the restroom and went back to the bar. Race was gone, but he'd left a stack of bills on the table next to my drink. What the hell, I figured; better that I spend some of the money than the bartender grabbed it all. I ordered a fresh one.

"I'm a businessman," said the man who'd been in the restroom, taking Race's seat. He nodded to the bartender and ordered a green tea.

"Race sent you, huh?"

"No."

"Right."

"Your friend is CIA?"

"I don't know what he is."

"You shouldn't drink too much. Bad for your soul."

I laughed. It was kind of funny to hear someone worried about my soul here.

"What do you want?" I asked.

"My name is Khan." He extended a hand. "And I'm a businessman. I have interests in Paktika."

"You do, huh?"

Khan was maybe five four, weighed one ten, if that. His eyes looked as if they'd been drilled into his skull. They were green pinpoints in dark holes, and they bounced back and forth in their sockets. His age—that was impossible to tell. He looked twenty-five, say, even younger. His beard was thick but trimmed low to his face, and what was covered by hair was smooth. But his voice was an old man's voice, seventy at least, with a weariness to it.

"What kind of interests?" I asked.

"Business."

"Like Omar, huh? I don't buy drugs."

"I do not sell drugs."

"Or rugs."

"No rugs. You don't have to buy anything. We can work together, I am thinking."

"This is like Hansel and Gretel, right? The CIA drops out these little crumbs and I'm supposed to follow along?"

I was talking too loud and I knew it. I shut myself up by taking another slug from the bourbon.

"Our interests may coincide. I don't work for the Americans. I would like to go to Paktika." Khan slipped a business card out onto the bartop. "Usually, I am at Kane's. Today was just a coincidence that I was here. My sat phone is on the card."

A coincidence. I was going to ask him if he'd heard what Race had said about them, but when I turned to do so, Khan had left.

SOMEWHERE, the urgency between Sharon and me faded out. I don't know if it was time or sheer repetition.

I couldn't say where, exactly, the point was when sex with her became . . . not routine, not boring, because it was never either of those, but less urgent, less overwhelmingly necessary. That's what I missed now, in Afghanistan—not the sex itself, not the delicious softness of her breasts against my chest, or the wet lick of her tongue against my neck, but the rush of desire, the need that filled every blood vessel: that's what I wanted. Sitting in the bar finishing my drink, I longed for the adrenaline rush that came from gazing across at her and knowing we were minutes away from making love.

Until I left, I hadn't even realized I'd lost it. I knew it wasn't the same, but I hadn't thought about it. Now it felt like something physical, like the sliver of ice melting in my throat.

My first reaction was to push it away. It was gone, utterly gone, buried under everything else that had happened between us. Wallowing in the past was dangerous, especially in Afghanistan.

Sex—it was always a diversion, wasn't it? A temptation, something to pull you away from what was really important.

Especially if it was only sex.

COLONEL Armstrong presided over a special task force that had been formed about six months ago to chase the resurgent Taliban in the provinces along the Pakistani border. The fact that he ran that task force from a base in Kabul, a couple of hundred miles away, said a lot about what he was up against—not in the field, but at CentCom and back in Washington.

CentCom—Central Command, in charge of prosecuting the war—and more accurately the Pentagon, which had its thumbs into everything CentCom did—didn't want any high-profile disasters out in the field, especially now that the final orders had all been cut and everyone was homeward bound. But even before that, they didn't want to spend any sort of serious resources to eradicate guerrillas who supposedly had been exterminated five or six years before. Colonel Armstrong was expected to be a wizard, vanquishing the enemy with press conferences and press releases suitable for publication back home, while all the while holding the forts with as many Afghans as he could muster and a few American units to bolster their courage.

To be fair, Armstrong had been given half a lemon and some sand, and managed to make something approaching lemonade. But the first time we met, I took a pretty instant dislike to him. He looked like he was about twenty. Given the way the army works, he had to be a lot older, but he was still young for the rank, helped along by all the right staff jobs and the West Point ring on his finger. He had a pink face, the famous fluorescent-light tan, and the scent of Irish Spring soap nearly knocked me over when I walked into his office.

"Pilgrim, I've been expecting you." He didn't bother getting up from his desk, as if I were some punk clerk who'd finally retrieved the morning coffee. "Your reputation precedes you."

He might have meant that sarcastically, but it never pays to play anything an officer says less than straight.

"Thank you, sir."

"You were a sergeant in the army, right?"

I nodded and a smug look appeared on his face. "Yes, sir." The sirs came to me reflexively, part of my accent.

"I like sergeants," he told me. "Sergeants are the blue-collar backbone of the army."

I resisted the impulse to tell him this ex-backbone of the army now made six or seven times what he did. Instead, I started playing with my Rolex, taking it off my wrist, folding and smoothing the band as he went on about how he'd always thought sergeants carried the weight of the universe on their shoulders, and how he always made it a point to *listen* to them, because by God they were the backbone of the army and they knew, just for crissake *knew,* what they were talking about, and if they didn't know then at least they felt like they knew, and feelings were important. You listen to a sergeant and he'll bust his butt for you, step and fetch and carry you home until dawn, yessir mastah, your bath is ready now.

If he noticed the watch he didn't let on. I looked at it and realized I was back in a place where a watch was just a watch. The only thing that mattered about it was that it told the time. And no matter how much money I made last year or next year or this, I was still just plain old Jack Pilgrim in this office, and beyond this office, in all Afghanistan.

Jack Pilgrim—no exclamation point, no capital letters, not one iota of status that a Rolex or a Mercedes could supply. Maybe I just wasn't rich enough, I thought; maybe if I had a private jet, well then maybe this asshole of a colonel wouldn't have been talking to me like I was his trusty white Uncle Tom.

Then I thought maybe it was the fact that I was back in the army's world, which was probably close to the truth as far as the colonel was concerned: a sergeant is a sergeant is a sergeant, especially to a colonel. If I'd had a star on my collar, well, that would be a *Crissake* different conversation.

But it was more than that. As long as I was in Afghanistan, I was worth only what I could do for the person looking at me, and sometimes not even that. The CIA wanted their money, but only to the point where it became easier to rewrite a budget line and lie about what had happened.

Worse than that. In this room and in most of the country, I was a nonentity, worthless to everyone, of value only to the extent that I might scare them. That was true of everyone here, except that most people, especially people like the boy colonel, didn't realize it. They just walked on blithely, assuming that because they got a good lather out of their soap in the shower that morning, the world would never smell their shit.

"I hear you have to get out to Paktika," said Colonel Armstrong finally.

"So it seems."

He got up and walked to the side of his office, where a large map of some of the southeastern provinces hung. I recognized the map; it was one of the same pieces of inaccurate fantasy we'd used when I was here.

"The provincial capital over at Sharan?"

"For starters."

Westerners use a lot of different names for the capital of Paktika: Sharan, Zareh Sharan, Sharon Woluswali, Sharana, Sharen, Shiran. It's in the northwestern part of the province, a little over a hundred miles south of Kabul.

"Where do you go from there? East? I can get you out to Camp

Harriman." Harriman was a forward operating base near Urgun or Orgun as the army usually spelled it.

"I don't know where I'm going, exactly," I told him. "Sharan definitely. Beyond that, I don't know."

"I heard you wanted to go east, Gayan, Barmal, out there."

"Maybe I do."

Gayan and Barmal were districts in Paktika right on the border of Pakistan. The poppy-counting project had called for heavy payoffs in that area.

And not coincidentally, Merc and I had spent considerable time there during the war.

"We have choppers running out to Harriman every Tuesday and Thursday," said the colonel. "We can get you to the capital, and then over to the base. I'll reserve you a space."

The colonel would have known as well as I did that running helicopters on a predictable schedule like that was foolhardy, so I didn't point it out. On that score I'll give him a break: more than likely he had no control over it. The choppers were probably fed to him by some scheduling geek from another outfit entirely, a guy who was into symmetry.

"I'm not sure when I'm going out there," I told him. "I have some work to do around here first."

He looked disappointed, as if I'd just turned down an invitation to join him at the officers' club. But he recovered quickly.

"If you need anything, Pilgrim, use my card. You show it to one of my men, doors will open." He pointed to a stack of them on the edge of the desk, aligned in a fancy holder. His name and insignia were embossed, and the card itself was thick and substantial—almost as impressive as mine.

"Take a few. You may need them," he told me.

"Thanks," I told him. But I left it at one.

THEY say the world's a small place, but in my experience it's huge, and getting larger every day. The bigger it is, the more people there are, and somehow, the way statistics work, it's easier to run into at least one person you know.

In this case, it was two—Bill Bozzone and Michael Blitz.

Bozzone and Blitz had just joined Special Forces when I'd last seen them. They'd been prize pupils in one of the classes I taught in my last few weeks as a member of the U.S. Army; if I remember correctly, they'd both been specialists at the time.

I wasn't surprised they'd been assigned to Afghanistan. Both were good soldiers, smart, no-bs kind of guys, and you'd expect them to be where the action was. The only knock against them the army had was the no-bs bit; it can be tough to move ahead if you voice your opinion about the state of things too freely, which was a special problem for Blitz. I don't think there was one officer in the entire military he thought did a decent job. Bozzone might have had the same opinion, but he didn't feel it necessary to share it with most of them.

Seeing them in a way was like seeing me and Merc, five years removed.

"What the hell are you doing in Afghanistan?" shouted Blitz, pointing to me as I walked out of the headquarters building.

"The army sent me to tell you there was a mistake at the recruiting center," I told him. "You flunked the tests. You only qualify for the Coast Guard."

"Since when did the Coast Guard lower its standards?" said Bozzone.

We did the usual things guys do when they haven't seen each other, mixing insults with snatches of news and catching up. I wanted to pick their brains about Afghanistan, but they didn't have time to talk. They'd just gotten back from a mission, and besides the paperwork they'd come to square away, a thousand little details had to be seen to. We arranged to meet that night at the bar of my hotel.

I asked them if they were sure they could do that. They said absolutely not and told me to have the beer cold and waiting.

WHEN I was done, I drove over to the civilian side of the airport, where Khattak had his hangar. A Russian Hind helicopter sat out on the tarmac in front of it, its overhead blades drooping toward the ground like tired arms. A red and white shark's mouth had been painted on the front years before; the paint was faded and the metal dented. Pale green camo dressed the rest of the body.

The color scheme made the aircraft look as if it were disintegrating before my eyes. Up close, it was worse. The fuselage was pockmarked with bullet holes and dents, and there were cracks in most of the windows.

The Hind—officially, the Mi24—is a Russian-made helicopter that combines the firepower of an American Apache with the troop-carrying capability of an American Black Hawk. There are a slew of different versions, but all have a pretty fierce cannon in their nose and a pair of wings capable of holding missiles, rockets, and bombs. Besides the pilot and gunner, the chopper can carry eight guys and their gear.

The Hind was a staple of the Russian occupation force during their war here. The bird was a fierce fighter, but like all helicopters it could be vulnerable to antiaircraft fire, especially shoulder-launched missiles like the American Stinger, which the CIA doled out like candy.

"It flies," said Khattak when he came out of the hangar and saw me staring at the aircraft.

"I didn't think it didn't."

"What do you want?" He was wearing a *chapan,* which is a loose-fitting Afghan coat with large sleeves. He wore it over other Afghan tribal clothes, which look a lot like oversized pajamas to American eyes, or at least to mine.

"I'm Jack Pilgrim, remember?" I stuck out my hand. "I'm a friend of Merc Conrad's. You and I met the other night."

He looked at my hand.

"You told me to look you up, remember?"

"No." He turned and walked back into the hangar. The place

smelled like a car shop, with maybe a little more metal and less exhaust. There was no office, just a desk pushed to the side of the wall near the main door. He went over to it and began sorting through a pile of small pieces of paper.

"I was wondering if you could tell me what you know about Merc Conrad," I told him.

"I don't know anything."

"Sure you do. We paid you quite a bit to fly him around the country."

"Who's we?"

"Iron Rock. I'm Merc's partner."

He gave me a scowl. "You're CIA?"

"Do I look like CIA?"

He eyed me top to bottom. "Yes, you do."

"Well, I'm not."

Another scowl, this one twice as severe. "You're really with Merc?"

"He's my partner."

Khattak started digging through some papers on his desk. Finally he pulled one out. "You guys owe me three thousand dollars, American."

"All right." I reached for the paper, thinking it was an invoice, but he didn't give it to me. "What do we owe it for?"

"Extra fuel."

"Okay."

"My flare dispenser and some of the hydraulics got shot to bloody hell," he added. "I have to replace them."

"How much is that going to cost?"

He smirked, but he wasn't holding me up. He was explaining why it was important for me to pay what we owed him.

"I can fly without the flare dispenser for a while, depending on the destination," he said. "Some of the infrared warning gear is gone, so it doesn't make a difference. Radio's out, I need some backup tires, another extra drop tank, odds and ends. I'd get what I need from Poland, except I can't order them from here. I can't use my name, either. I'm on some sort of shit list."

"Maybe we can work something out. I've been on a few of those myself."

Khattak and I didn't exactly become bosom buddies right then, but we started a working relationship. I checked the time, then called Cynthia at home, where by some miracle she was already awake even though it was only six-thirty in the morning. It took about an hour, all sat-phone minutes at ridiculous monopoly rates, but we managed to give her a list of the parts he needed and all the details to order them.

While we were waiting for her to get confirmations from the people in Poland—fortunately it was in the early afternoon there—he made some tea on a small butane stove. It was strong stuff, as strong as you'd get out in the countryside. He didn't offer any sugar, either.

"You flew Merc out to Paktika?" I asked.

"Yeah."

"When?"

"Bunch of times."

"When was the last time?"

"Two or three weeks ago. Maybe more." Khattak didn't have much of a sense of time, though I didn't realize it yet.

"Where'd you take him?"

"Sharan, I think. The capital."

"You ever take him anyplace else?"

Khattak shrugged. "Farther east. Near the border. No towns, though—just GPS coordinates. Middle of nowhere."

That may have been a sign that Merc didn't trust Khattak, or at least didn't trust him completely, but I didn't mention it.

"What was he doing out there?" I asked.

"The reason people hire me is that I don't ask questions like that." Khattak got a funny a little smile on his face. "I heard Raz Omar met an untimely death," he said, putting down his tea. "You had something to do with that?"

This time it was my turn to shrug.

"Bloody slime owed me ten grand. Wasn't likely to pay, though."

"Was Merc running drugs?"

"You'd know better than I, wouldn't you?"

Most likely not, but I dropped it. I was thinking that the back of Khattak's chopper would hold quite a bit of opium. On the other hand, his rates were high, and drug trafficking here was a low-overhead business. And I just couldn't see Merc involved in it.

"Where are you going in Paktika?" he asked.

"The capital. Then maybe east. Gayan or Barmal."

"I can't take you there until I get my flares. The capital, I can do."

I could travel overland from the capital, though that was admittedly my second choice. The real problem was getting out in a hurry if I had to.

The tea was starting to taste almost normal. "What if it were an emergency?" I asked, putting down the glass.

"Flying that close to the border is very expensive. It could be arranged, for an emergency."

"Once you get the gear, does the price go down?"

"No." Khattak scratched the back of his neck. "Do you have a guide?"

"I've been out there before."

"You would do better with a guide. Things have changed."

"Because the U.S. is withdrawing?"

"Because time moves on."

"I met this guy named Khan the other night."

Half of Afghanistan's named Khan, so I described him. Khattak shrugged and said he didn't know him.

"I thought maybe he was some sort of drug dealer," I told him. "Or a CIA plant."

"Drugs, maybe. Small time. If he came up to you he's not with the interior ministry or their spy service, that's one thing."

"How do you know?"

"Because they can sit on their arses all day in the safest bunker they can find. And CIA? No. The locals are backing off—no more dealing with the CIA now that the U.S. is pulling out."

"No way."

"The *good* locals. What's his name again?"

Khattak pulled out a sat phone from beneath the papers on his desk and made a call. He spoke to someone in Dari; five minutes later he told me that Khan was not a CIA operative, but might or might not be one of a half-dozen small-time drug dealers or smugglers with ties to the border area.

"The name may be a fake, but the description, the place where he hangs out," Khattak explained, "that narrows it down."

"You'd trust him?"

"Only as far as I could throw him from my bloody helicopter."

That turned out to be high praise from Khattak, who in the space of the next fifteen minutes proceeded to run down just about everyone in the country, foreigner and native.

"Your CIA is all screwed up. I don't work for them under any circumstances."

You just take their money indirectly, like everybody else, I thought. But I didn't say it.

He told me the kid who'd been answering the phone for us was a thief, which wasn't big news. Before I left he told me about a few "freelancers" who might be available and trustworthy as backups to take with me. The problem, he said, would be finding them.

"Finding anything in this country is a matter of luck," said Khattak. "Most of it bad."

As it turned out, I had the opposite problem. People kept finding me the rest of the day.

12

KABUL

KEN, the American with the Russian jeep who'd given me a lift when I'd arrived, was waiting outside the hangar when I finished talking with Khattak.

"I heard you gunned down Raz Omar," he said as I walked toward the car. "Good going. I been after that slime for weeks."

"Is that a fact?"

"I saw your car in front of the hangar."

"How'd you know it was my car?"

He waved his hand as if I were joking. "I got something to show you."

"I'm kinda busy today, Ken."

"My name's really not Ken. It's Anastasias Disney. Disney, like the movies, you know? People call me Diss. It's like a nickname, 'cause I *diss* people, you know? I diss the enemy big time. And because of my last name."

"Yeah, well, see you around, all right?"

"You really gotta take a look at this. Take only a second."

I'm generally a pretty good judge of character, and I knew this guy was nuts. Still, if I was so desperate that I needed someone, Diss might end up my only choice.

God help me.

"Where is this thing you're going to show me?"

"In town. Well, almost. You won't be going ten minutes out of your way."

"How do you know?"

"Follow me."

I got into the car. The driver gave me a look when I told him to follow Diss, but he put the truck in gear and we went back toward Kabul, circling around the north side of the city to a compound surrounded by a tall cement wall. A lone guard stood behind the gate. Diss jammed on the horn but he didn't open up until Diss got out and yelled at him.

"Open up!"

"Password," said the man. He looked to be about thirty, with a thick beard. From his accent I knew he was American.

"Screw the password. Can't you see it's me?"

"You said—"

"Just open up, okay?"

"Is this a test?"

Diss glanced back in my direction—we'd pulled off the road right behind him—then back at the guard.

"Alexander the Great," he said.

"Advance and be recognized," said the guard, gleefully pulling open the gate.

I debated whether I'd be better off leaving the car and driver near the road. It was a tough call, but finally we went through the gate.

The house was a small one-level stucco building, with a four-sided roof. There'd been other buildings, but they'd been cleared away; bits and pieces of old foundations and walls littered the compound. There was a large patch of dirt about ten yards to the right of the house where we parked.

"Perfect for a helipad, huh?" said Diss as he led me toward the house. "Used to be three different properties. We took them all over."

"Nice," I said, not because it was but because I figured that's what he wanted me to say. I'd taken my AK with me. The driver, who usually didn't even let on that he was armed, had a sawed-off shotgun in his lap back at the car.

"What is it you're showing me, Diss?"

"It's in the house. You'll have to check your weapon with the guard. Those are our rules."

"The only way I'm going to check it is to see if it's loaded. And I do that by pulling the trigger."

He blinked, but he got the message. "You're special. You don't need to worry about that. Come on."

Another guard met us at the door. He was tall, but with a belly that made him look like he was pregnant. He had long, wild hair, and eyes that were almost as fired up as Diss's. But his face had a slack quality to it, like he wasn't entirely with the program. Kind of Baby Louie, without the diaper.

"I got Sergeant Pilgrim," Diss told him. "Let us in."

The man stood aside immediately. If I'd gotten half that much respect when I was in the army, I might not have left.

The front room had no furniture except for two kitchen chairs, whose padded seats were covered by ill-fitting and stained oilcloth. Candy wrappers were strewn on the floor. A case of Gatorade sat in the corner.

"This way, this way," said Diss, leading me to the door at the back of the room.

I tensed up and stopped before the threshold. I couldn't see Raz Omar having anything to do with someone like Diss, so I didn't figure this was a setup for revenge or something like that. But I didn't know what it was, exactly.

"Come on," Diss said, beckoning me from the other side of the threshold.

Baby Louie in the front room was watching near the door. He was armed only with a pistol, and it was holstered. Diss didn't have a weapon showing.

But once paranoia takes hold, it's hard to shake it. I could see the wall to the left of the other room, but nothing to the right. That's where the ambush would be.

I sprang into the room, gun on my hip, ready.

Something moved and I dropped, rolling back to fire.

I'm not sure how I kept myself from actually shooting, but I didn't. Two men were in that corner, all right, but they were chained to the wall, blindfolded and gagged.

"Jesus, Sarge, relax," said Diss. "We got them under control."

I got to my knees. The two men were Afghans. One of them had a stain on his pants where he'd peed himself.

"What the hell is this?" I asked.

"Prisoners, Sarge. Taliban. We grabbed them yesterday."

I went over and looked at them. The men were both in their forties or maybe early fifties, disheveled, and scared. They smelled like they hadn't had baths in a month. It was obvious they were weak—the chains were anchored by thin bolts that could barely hold their weight; it wouldn't have taken very much to pull them straight out of the wall.

"How do you know they're Taliban?"

"Smell 'em, Sarge. You can tell."

"Why are they here?"

"I'm going to turn them over to the authorities, once we get some information out of them."

"I don't think it's a real good idea to be grabbing Afghans in the middle of Kabul."

"They're bad, Sarge. Real bad."

I glanced around the room. The back window had been boarded over; there was no other exit. I motioned to Diss to follow me back to the front room.

"First of all, don't call me 'Sarge,' okay? I haven't been a sergeant in a long time, and you weren't in the Army with me, right?"

"I've been thinking about it, and I think I was," said Diss. "I was a rigger for a while. I'm sure we met."

I doubted it.

"Second of all," I told him, "you have to release these guys. You have no authority here. You're kidnapping them."

And probably torturing them.

Diss's eyes narrowed and his expression, which looked pretty crazy when he was calm, got wilder.

"These are Taliban, Sarge."

"Release them, Diss."

"Taliban, Mr. Pilgrim. Taliban. I should just slit their throats and be done with them."

"That is not a good idea, Anastasias. Let them go."

I didn't want to turn my back on him, so I kind of sidled toward the door. The guard there had a confused look on his face.

"You, you killed Raz Omar," sputtered Diss. "You did that."

His voice had an off-key pleading note to it. I decided I'd been far too indulgent until now, dangerously indulgent, and had to take immediate steps to correct any misperceptions before they became dangerous.

I had him up against the wall in about a second and a half.

I'll give him this, though, he wasn't weak; I might have had to struggle more if I hadn't taken him by surprise and hadn't been able to put the AK right against his temple.

"Listen, what did and didn't happen to Raz Omar is none of your business, you understand?"

"Hey, no sweat, man, no sweat. I get it. Yeah, no sweat, Sarge."

"You release these men now, or turn them over to the authorities. Got it?"

"Oh, yeah. Anything you say."

I let go of him.

"I didn't mean anything by it, Jack. I didn't realize you were so sensitive."

Baby Louie had come into the room, but still had his gun holstered. I gave him a look and he took a step back against the wall.

"I'll talk to you another time, Jack," said Diss, following me as I walked outside. "I can call you Jack, right? That's better than Sarge."

"Let them go," I told him, getting into the car.

SIM was still AWOL at our office. Frankly, it would have been surprising to find him. The company we shared him with had called Cynthia, trying to see if we had any information about where he was.

"What'd you tell them?" I asked her when I checked in from our desk.

"That you'd get back to them."

"Good. Listen, did the accountant call?"

"Was he supposed to?"

I assumed the fact that he hadn't meant Sharon hadn't interfered with the transactions. I also assumed that it meant we'd made payroll. On that score, the fact that I was talking to Cynthia was probably a better indicator—I'm sure she would have walked if we hadn't.

I told her that I needed her to put some more money into an HSBC account I could access here. I figured that Sim or someone I didn't know might have access to the other accounts, which had only token amounts in them anyway.

I was just about to hang up when the door flew open and a man about six ten filled my doorframe. I pointed my AK at him. He stopped, which was a good thing—I'm not sure the bullets would have done more than slow him down if he'd charged at me.

"I gotta go," I told Cynthia. "Talk to you soon."

I dropped the phone on the desk. The bear who'd burst into the cubicle was trying to figure out who the hell I was.

"You have some business here?" I asked.

"You Iron Rock?" The bear spoke English with a thick foreign accent.

"More or less."

Wrong answer. His face turned beet red. "You owe me money," he said, taking a step inside.

"Slow down, brown bear." I raised my gun. "I don't want to shoot you."

"You're a thief!"

"Look, if I owe you money, you'll be paid. We pay our debts. Who the hell are you?"

"You owe me money!" His roar rattled the office's thin partition.

"I need a name for the check, right?" I said.

"No check!" He took a step forward. "Cash. On barrel top."

"Your name is?"

He frowned. But he also glanced at the rifle.

"I'm not paying you anything unless I know who you are. That'd be pretty damn stupid, right?"

"Ivan Perkorski."

Perkorski. The name sounded familiar even before I looked through the files of the contractors. It came to me after I found it on the list for Jason—Ivan was one of the freelancers Khattak had told me about.

"They call you Hokum, right?" I said. He was down for five grand for "personal services," whatever that was. There was no indication that we owed him anything else, but then again there was nothing saying we didn't either. "A friend of mine told me about you. You're pretty handy with weapons."

His brow furrowed into a ridge. "Two thousand you owe me," he said, thinking I was trying to butter him up so I could rip him off. "Euros. Not rubles, not Afghan money for play. I taught how to handle weapons, now you owe me."

"Did they learn what you taught them?"

"Ah. Afghans. Take notes and forget. Pay in euros. Not play money."

"Euros aren't that easy to get here," I told him. "But dollars I can manage."

"Dollars okay."

"It happens that I'm going over to the bank right now," I told him, getting up. "Come with me."

HOKUM in Russian means werewolf, and while no one, least of all Ivan himself, explained how he came to be called that, it did seem a pretty obvious nickname once you met him in person. Not only did Hokum tower over everyone here, including me, he looked a lot more animal than man. His fingers curled into pointed nails; you got the idea when he looked at someone that he was contemplating how to rip them to shreds.

But there were things about Hokum that weren't obvious on first glance, things that took a while to figure out. Those nails were pointy because he nibbled at them fairly regularly. He wasn't so much scared of things as just jumpy. He told me later that he hadn't slept more than two or three hours at a stretch since he was nine or ten. While his face looked more menacing than intelligent, as a rule he thought before he acted, and if he didn't always make the right choices he at least had a plan and a reason for what he did.

Hokum also hated to be cheated, and considered people who would cheat him lower than pond scum.

But that wasn't the reason he refused to get in my car to go to the bank.

"Why not?"

"Everyone knows cars are American big shots," he said. "Not safe."

Actually, I thought all the big shots drove white Toyota SUVs; at least to my eye the car looked innocuous.

"Not safe," said Hokum. The driver, leaning against the car, stiffened. "Not even armored."

"I need an armored Mercedes in Kabul?"

"That worse. We take mine."

"If I drive, sure."

Hokum nodded reluctantly.

He had a van so old and battered I had no idea what make it was. The key had been lost long before—assuming Hokum ever had it. To start the engine you touched two different sets of wires together; once it caught you pulled one of the sets apart. You had to time it just right. Otherwise the engine would sputter to a stop or the starter would grind furiously. The sound alone was fierce enough to crush bones.

It took three tries for me to get it. Hokum chiseled at his nails the whole time.

Khattak had told me that Hokum had been a Russian paratrooper during the war here, which made him a few years older than I'd've guessed, though to be honest his face was so ugly it was pretty near ageless. I asked how long he'd been here as we drove.

"Long enough."

"You like Afghanistan?"

"Hellhole."

"Why don't you go back to Russia?"

"Worse."

"I'm here in Kabul looking for Merc Conrad. You wouldn't happen to know where he is, would you?"

"If I know, I get money from him."

"You hear any rumors about where he might be?"

"Rumors bullshit."

I couldn't argue with him there.

Things went smoothly at the bank, maybe because the manager saw Hokum come in with me. He even found enough Euros to pay Hokum what he said I owed him.

"Come out to a bar and let me buy you a drink," I told him after we counted out the money in the bank lobby.

"Ivan doesn't drink."

"You don't drink?"

He shook his head.

"Well, let me get you a tea or dinner or something. I have a job you might be interested in."

He said something in Russian. I don't speak the language, but I could guess pretty easily what it meant: it'll be a cold day in hell before I work for you again.

But Kabul had touched freezing just a few mornings ago.

"Double what we paid you last time. And half up front," I told him.

That interested him enough for him to use English when he told me to go to hell.

13

KABUL

DRINKING real drinks now, Sarge?" Bozzone said when he saw me at the bar. "You must be doing all right for yourself."

"Thinks he's an officer," growled Blitz, sitting on the other side of me. "Nice watch, Jack."

He looked at me like I was some sort of traitor.

"Yeah, it's nice. I got jobs for you guys when you want them."

Blitz snorted in derision. Bozzone put up his hand to call the waiter over.

"So what the hell are you doing here?" Blitz asked.

"I'm looking for Merc Conrad. I don't know if you guys ever met him. He was a sergeant in my unit. We went out right around the same time."

"Oh," said Blitz, with a tone that implied he should have known that all along.

"Merc and I have a security firm," I added. "We do a little business over here."

"Yeah, we heard a little about it," said Bozzone. "Iron Mountain."

"Iron Rock," I said. "We lost touch with Merc last week. I'm trying to find him."

"Last week?" said Blitz.

"No one's sure when, I guess. When do you think?"

"I don't think anything, Sarge. You know me."

Five years ago, if he'd said that, it'd have been a joke. Now it sounded more like an insult.

The beers came.

"So where you guys been?" I asked.

"If we told you, we'd have to shoot you," said Blitz.

"I only meant—"

"Down in Zabul," said Bozzone. "We put together a small team of guys and did a little job down there for a few days."

Zabul was the next province south of Paktika. A "little job" could be anything, but in my day I would have used the phrase if I meant we were "extracting" someone of interest, "extracting" being the preferred euphemism for "kidnapping" at the time.

"How'd it go?" I asked.

"*Così, così,*" said Bozzone, using an expression that meant, roughly, so-so. "We didn't lose anybody."

"That's better than so-so," I said.

"Depends on who's doing the grading," said Blitz.

"Merc went out to Paktika," I said when they didn't explain. "I was thinking of going there myself."

"You gotta do what you gotta do," said Blitz.

"Things've changed since you were here last, Sarge," said Bozzone. "We're leaving. Taliban's coming back."

"You guys didn't do a good enough job kicking them out," said Blitz.

"Guess not."

I took a sip from my drink, parceling it out now because I thought I was close to getting a little light-headed, and I wanted to stay as sober as possible. I didn't take what Blitz said personally; he hadn't been through what we'd been through, so all he knew about what Afghanistan had been like was what he'd heard from other people. Experiences varied quite a bit.

"Over the last six, seven months, they've been making pushes all along the border," Bozzone told me. "Alliances."

"In Paktika?"

"Everywhere."

"They working with the drug dealers?" I asked.

"Not usually," said Bozzone. "They would, I think, but most of the dealers don't trust them because they burned the fields when they were in control."

"What do you think about Paktika?" I asked.

Bozzone shrugged. "Haven't been."

"A hellhole like the rest of Afghanistan," Blitz said. "That's where Conrad is, huh?"

"A lot of people seem to think so."

"And he's got his own army there?"

"I don't know about that," I said. That was as close to seeming nonplussed as I could manage.

Blitz smirked a little, kind of like: anything you say, Jack.

"Why do you think he's got an army?"

Blitz didn't answer me. Bozzone concentrated on his beer.

"Come on, guys—what've you heard?"

"I heard there was an American who went crazy, thinks he's going to find bin Laden," said Bozzone. "I don't know if that's your friend, though. Probably not."

"There's a lot of crazy Americans around Afghanistan. But Merc's not crazy."

Bozzone shrugged. I turned to Blitz.

"Mike?"

"I heard what Billy heard," said Blitz. "I'm just putting two and two together."

We batted that around a little more, but they didn't give me any real information. I wasn't sure whether it was because they simply didn't have any, or because I was an outsider now, and worse, a guy who drank drinks in glasses rather than beer from cans.

They gave me some opinions about the officers in their unit, the Afghan troops, and the contract agencies they'd come in contact with. Not a word of what they said was important. I could've predicted their opinions word for word before we talked. Around nine o'clock they said they had to get back, which was fine with me.

The problem was, they needed a lift. I called up my driver, who told me I was welcome to use his car—as long as I paid as if he were along. He wouldn't venture out himself, aside from driving over and leaving it for me; apparently our trip to the arms dealer the other night had been a bit more than he could handle.

Or maybe he'd heard what Diss had been up to. In any event, I figured his deal was about the best I was going to do.

"Take care of yourself, guys," I told Bozzone and Blitz as they got out of the car at their base. "I'll see you around."

"Not if we see you first," said Blitz.

It didn't sound all that much like a joke the way he said it.

BEING new to Afghanistan, I didn't know all the nuances associated with roadblocks and petty bribes. So when I saw the truck in the road on the way back to the city, I didn't know to analyze the situation. I reacted instinctually, slowing down as if I were going to stop, then jamming the gas pedal as I drew close to the truck. I punched the wheel to the left. There was just room enough between the truck and the guardrail to get by, or there would have been if I hadn't pushed the wheel a little too sharply.

I hit the guardrail and bounded off. The rear end of the car smacked against the hood of the truck. I kept my foot on the gas, struggling to keep the car headed in a straight direction. Something popped behind me as I took a curve. I thought it was a tire but the car stayed under control. It wasn't until I looked back that I realized the rear window had been shot out.

I could see headlights behind me in the distance. I took the first turn I could find, my heart pumping. Within a few minutes I'd lost whoever was following me.

But I was lost myself. It took nearly an hour to get back to a part of the city that I recognized, and even then I headed in the wrong direction and had to double back.

Finally I found the Intercontinental. The guards didn't say anything about the window being shot out. I went inside to a restroom and picked the pellets of glass out of my clothes, neck, and back of my head.

"Every time I see you. You're the worse for wear," said Race, appearing behind me while I daubed my neck with wet toilet paper. "Kabul. It does that to people."

"Funny I should meet you here. You're exactly the person I wanted to talk to."

"You know what I think. About coincidences, Jack. What is it you want?"

"Tell me about Merc's army."

"Sergeant Conrad has an army?"

Race's smirk was the tipping point. I spun and pushed him up against one of the stalls. I held him by the neck of his shirt, pressing my fist against his Adam's apple.

There's a huge taboo in the military about hitting a superior officer. Crossing that threshold releases an enormous amount of energy, so much force that it's difficult to control.

On the other hand, there are the consequences.

"Jack, you're getting very excited," squeaked Race.

"I'm tired of being played for a fool. Tell me what Merc is doing out there. What was Leopard?"

"Leopard? You don't know?"

"Do I look like I fuckin' know?"

The door to the lavatory opened. Two military types in civilian clothes came in, standing shoulder to shoulder between me and the door.

"It's under control," Race said, his voice almost normal.

"Yeah. Go outside now," I told them. "Or when I'm done with him I'll flush both your faces down the toilet."

"You'll get yours, Pilgrim," said one of the men before leaving. Something about certain people makes it difficult for them to resist cheap exit lines.

"You're really letting Kabul get to you, Jack," Race told me when they were gone. "You have to take things. Calmer."

"Maybe you're right." I tightened my grip. "Tell me about Leopard and what Merc is really doing."

"This isn't the place. Let's go outside and have a drink."

"This is just fine."

"It's safer outside, Jack. The walls have ears here." He glanced up at the ceiling.

I don't know if the restroom really was bugged or not. It could have been, I guess. Then again, Race could have been wired. His shadows had appeared awful quick.

I let him go. He straightened himself out in the mirror, then led me outside and into the bar. By the time a waiter came over, the color had returned to his face.

"I heard you spoke to the colonel today," Race told me. "A very good step."

"Just tell me about Leopard and Merc."

"I'm surprised. You don't know this, Jack. I just assumed you knew. What was going on. Being a partner. I'm not even involved. I'm just doing a friend a favor."

"Which friend?"

"You." He grinned.

Coming back outside was a mistake. Race was more comfortable here, more sure of himself; he'd say what he wanted to, nothing more. But it was too late to haul him back inside.

"Leopard was a recruitment program. To get people on our side. Help the tribal authorities maintain order." He put up his finger as the waiter returned with our drinks; we remained silent until the man had left. "You guys had the connections out in the countryside because. Of the past. And. You were trustworthy. Merc said he'd handle it himself. I guess everyone assumed. You were in, too."

"I wasn't."

"You're partners?"

"Partners." I took a long slug from my drink.

"This was beyond Urgun. Out in Gayan, Barmal, Gomal. Places you loved during your tour here. You were the perfect choice. Perfect."

"The money was for projects?"

"Inefficient. The government needs support there, Jacky. The UN's coming in. We don't want chaos. We want loyalty."

Two million dollars might not sound like much, but they were talking about spreading it around in the equivalent of three small counties. Maybe there were forty thousand people in the mountains out there. You might—might—have a thousand officials, police officers, and useless brothers-in-law to bribe. A grand would be more money than most of them would see in a lifetime. Two would set them and their families up for life.

"Where's Merc's army come in?" I asked.

"You tell me, Jack." Race took a sip from his Scotch, savoring it before continuing. "I heard he went a little. Crazy in the bush. But that's all I know."

Race leaned forward like he was going to give me some critical piece of information, but all he was doing was trying to excuse himself.

"Leopard wasn't my project, Jack. Between you and me. I don't think buying people is a good idea long-term. But it wasn't my call. And now that you messed up. Someone has to straighten it out."

"How do you know Merc didn't give the money to the people who were supposed to get it?"

"We know."

I couldn't figure out whether Race was working for the CIA or the army or the Defense Intelligence Agency or was somehow on his own as a private contractor. Any of those things was possible.

"Who are you working for, Race? Spooks? DIA?"

"I'm irrelevant. My bosses." He waved his hand. "Irrelevant."

In a way I guess he was right; ultimately everyone here had the same faceless masters, giving orders from somewhere back home.

"Does the CIA want its money back, or do they want Merc?"

"They want the money. You know how these things are. Some bureaucrat. Needs to cover his fanny. So the cash has to reappear."

But that wasn't the whole story, not if Merc was running around with an army.

"How big is this army Merc has?" I asked.

"Who did you talk to in Washington?"

"Unsel."

"Did he mention an army?"

"No."

"That's your answer, Jack. Go find Merc. Armstrong's waiting for you. He's a good officer. He can be trusted."

"Just like you, right?"

"I'm your friend, Jack. Don't forget that."

14

CENTRAL AMERICA, SEVEN YEARS BEFORE

THE first time Merc saved my life we were in the jungle in southeastern Colombia, near the border with Venezuela in the Amazon highlands, where we were helping train the Colombian military to deal with narcotics smugglers. At least that's what the orders said we were doing. In real life, we were going out on patrols with small teams, telling them what to do, and liaisoning with a pair of spotter planes rented by the CIA. The drug operations were small potatoes compared to what was going on to the east and the north, where the Medellín cartels ran things. Our targets were just as nasty, though, and since they were tied up with guerrilla groups out there, it was just as important to stamp them out.

The colonel who sent us found it funny that drug smugglers and revolutionaries would work together. I always thought of it this way: they were basically in the same business. Marx said religion was the opiate of the masses. As Merc put it, politics got everybody else.

We were out on a patrol one night along a deep stream that the smugglers used to move their product. The mission was supposed to be a reconnaissance only, without any engagement. The unit was brand-new, first time in the field. Merc and I had been there only two days, and we were still trying to figure out exactly how bad our Spanish was. This was just a shakedown cruise to learn how to roll our *r*'s.

We'd split a platoon in half and were working both sides of the stream. This was fine when the stream was just a trickle two feet wide, which it was when we started out. But about a mile into what we'd planned as a three-mile hike, the gap grew to about thirty yards—twenty-eight more than the map claimed. The water was very shallow, no more than two and a half feet, but the bottom was silty, a murky kind of quicksand that would suck a soldier's boot right off him—if he was lucky. Rather than joining back up, which was the right thing to do, we let the local commander call the shots and continue with his team in two groups. In our defense, the airplane with infrared hadn't seen anything, and contradicting *el comandante* in front of his men the first night out wasn't the best way to make friends.

Around mile two the creek started to narrow again, funneling gradually toward twenty yards. We went a little way farther and the commander decided it was time to call it a night. As we passed the order to turn around, the jungle on the eastern side of the creek lit up with gunfire.

It was impossible to figure out exactly what was going on right away. Everybody had night gear, but even if it had been daylight the jungle would have been hard to see in. Bullets started whizzing in every direction.

The NCOs, without prompting, began screaming at their men to stop firing. There was a brief lull, the sort of pause that makes you think you've got it all under control, and that even though you've screwed up and lumbered into a bad situation, it's going to be one you learn from rather than simply regret.

Then someone screamed. In the next second, the thirty-odd guys on patrol with us panicked as one, and ran.

Every single one of them, private to captain.

A few threw down their weapons. A couple of others were hit by bullets. But most just ran like hell in the direction they'd come from.

Merc and I were on opposite sides of the stream. I can't speak for what he did but I know my first reaction was to curse like all hell.

In the movies when something like this happens, some brave officer or sergeant stands up and threatens to shoot the whole lot of cowards if they don't stop. That saves the day. I might have tried something like that if I saw anybody to shoot. The only thing in front of my eyes were tracers and shadows. Some of the tracers were huge balls that seemed to have been spit out of a volcano. Whoever was firing at us had a 12.7 cannon, good enough to take down an airplane.

"Where are you, Jack?" yelled Merc. We didn't have personal radios, a shortcoming we hadn't had time to remedy.

"Stay down!" I yelled back.

"No shit."

"Let's move back to that set of rocks a quarter of a mile downstream. Maybe I can cross."

"Go. I'll cover you."

He unleashed a few rounds from his M4. This got him attention and I hopped up and started back down the trail. When I reached a large tree that had fallen roughly parallel to the path, I stopped and fired on my own, returning his favor. Then I got as close to the ground as I could, bullets ripping through the jungle all around me.

It took about a half hour for us to work our way back to the rocks. The big gun wasn't following us, but plenty of little ones were. I was on the side with the enemy; my idea was that I would go across the stream and join up with Merc. From there we'd have a lot more options.

I started right across as soon as I reach the rocks. They were slippery and it was dark; worse, they only extended about halfway across the stream. But I didn't realize it until I was staring at twelve yards of open water.

Telling myself it didn't make sense to go back, I pushed off the rocks, trying to make my movements slow but deliberate. My left leg sank in but I pulled it up. Three or four steps later I slipped and fell on my side into the water with a splash. The current pulled at my pack, pushing me to the side so fiercely I lost my rifle. I tried to stand myself but something hit the side of my leg and I pirouetted down. I pushed back up, only to find one of my feet cemented to the streambed.

The gunfire, which had been sporadic a moment ago, picked up with a vengeance. Bullets began flying off the rocks. Desperate to get away, I pulled off my pack, threw off my goggles, and pushed toward the other shore. One leg got unstuck and the other was trapped, this time in something that felt like a bear claw.

I learned then that there's a moment just before you die when you become resigned to your fate, when you accept it, no matter how unfair or unfortunate it may be. It doesn't bring peace, and it doesn't feel very good, because you know you're going to die. But it's there, waiting for you as you slide toward your end—a hollow place just big enough to fit your head.

In my case, something else was in that space. I felt myself pulled up out of the stream, out of the muck, my foot wrenching against whatever it had fallen against, then suddenly free. Before I could catch a breath, I was on dry land again.

"Stay the hell down, Jacky," hissed Merc in my ear. "Those bullets have eyes."

WHOEVER was following us made only one attempt to cross the water. Three guys got out onto the rocks before Merc opened up with his M4; he got them all. He thought later he should have waited, maybe gotten more guys, maybe not even have wasted bullets. Odds are the water would have grabbed them like it had grabbed me.

My ankle, wrenched somewhere between a strain and a sprain, hurt like hell. I tied it up with strips of cloth I ripped from the back of my shirt—I'd lost the medical kit—while Merc found a tree branch strong enough to use as a crutch. After about twenty yards I threw the branch away, figuring the speed I gained was worth the added pain.

The gunfire continued from the other side, but it was more generic harassing now than actually dangerous. Since we couldn't trust the map and knew the creek would help us cut down the pursuers, we stayed close to the water.

My foot swelled up as we went. Eventually I had to accept the fact that I couldn't walk on my own. Merc helped me hobble for a while, then finally carried me about a half mile on his back.

The Colombians had gone into hiding at their base when we returned; we went straight to our little hooch, broke out some tape and advanced painkiller—Dewar's—and holed up until the next morning, when *el comandante* came around and asked if we were all right.

My foot felt a lot better by the time the Colombians got up the balls to go back, five days later. This time we went during the day, with helicopters above us and three times as many men. Three soldiers were lying where they'd been killed, their boots and weapons gone but other personal effects intact. There was no trace of the guerrillas or whatever they were that had fired on us.

On the way back, I stopped at the spot where Merc had pulled me out. In the daylight, I realized I'd picked probably the worst spot along the whole damn stream to try and cross.

"How'd you know to come get me in the water?" I asked Merc. Looking at the spot in the daytime, it seemed even wider than it had that night. "You must've left before I even started."

"I'm your friend, Jack." He said it like it explained everything. "Don't forget that."

15

KABUL

RACE left the bar with his goon patrol and I finished my drink. Then I got in the shot-up Toyota and went out to find Khan at the hotel bar where he'd said he usually hung out.

Drinking alcohol is considered a sin in Islam, and while more than a few Muslims will sneak a drink every so often, in general you don't find them doing so in public, at least not ostentatiously in a place like Afghanistan where there's a strongly puritan influence. Khan was a notable exception. He not only hung out at Kane's Foreigners Exclusive Bar, but he did so with a large bottle of sweet vermouth in front of him.

The Foreigners Exclusive Bar was on the second floor of the Kabul Luxury Hotel. The walls between four or five rooms had been partially torn down to make the bar, so the bar was full of hidden spaces and dark corners, just the sort of thing someone in Khan's line would find conducive to business. The hotel itself had been converted from a dormitory or temporary residential building erected in the 1970s by the Soviets. The architecture might have been boring, but the walls were of thick concrete, a highly desirable feature in Kabul.

"You came," said Khan when he spotted me approaching his table. "Mr. Pilgrim, sit down."

Two Frenchmen were sitting at the table as well. Khan said something to them in French which I didn't understand, and the men nodded at me.

"You don't speak French, do you?" said Khan.

"No, I'm sorry I don't. If you have business, I'll come back."

"We were just concluding." He said something to his guests, maybe translating. By the time the waiter came over to see what I was drinking, they were gone.

"I hope I didn't scare your friends off," I told him.

"Not friends. Business. Friends are different."

"Yeah."

"So, you've decided to go to Paktika?" Khan got a big grin on his face.

"Yeah, it looks that way. I need a guide and a translator, though."

"Then I come with you. No charge."

The "no charge" thing was a red light, flashing in front of my face.

"What is it that you get out of it, then?" I said.

"What?"

"What's your motivation? Because we're not friends. And as far as I can tell, I don't owe you any money."

"I have interests that it would be helpful to see," said Khan. "I need to go to Paktika, and going with others would be useful."

"Why don't you go by yourself?"

"I could. Yes. But."

He picked up the bottle of vermouth and refilled his glass, adding perhaps a sip's worth to it. Then he picked up the drink, twirled the glass slowly around in his hand, staring at the way the velvety liquor coated the sides.

"But to go with someone else would be more convenient," he said finally.

I guessed that if he went out with an American, it would seem as if he had more juice behind him—protection from the authorities. People would want to deal with him. That's what he was getting.

Maybe.

"You smuggle drugs?" I asked.

"No, no, no." Khan shook his head quickly. "I am more like an equipment supplier."

"Weapons?"

"Equipment." Khan gave me a half blink, intended to imply confidence, then changed the subject. "Our interests coincide in many ways. I am familiar with the area, you are not. I speak Pashto, you do not."

"I've been there before. And I can speak a little."

He rattled off a phrase. I told him, in Pashto, to speak a little slower.

"It is an advantage that you have been to the area before," he said in English. Then he started telling me that Paktika was a big place and having a good guide was essential. He started saying this in Pashto, then somewhere along the way segued into Dari, though he spoke too quickly for me to do anything but realize that's what he was using, and then only just. Finally he switched back to English and told me, "It's a curse, really. I hear the different languages in my head, like the Tower of Babel. Sometimes I forget myself and speak in the entirely wrong tongue."

"I see."

"It is not the same there now. You will do better with a good translator."

"That's why I'm here."

"Which part of Paktika are you going to?"

"Sharan, then Urgun. From there I'm not sure. Maybe Gayan and Barmal. Beyond that, who knows."

"Sharan is easy to get to," said Khan. "But Urgun is another story. And beyond that—"

"If you're not interested, that's fine."

He put his hand on my arm as I rose. "I am definitely interested. That is where I wish to go. I was only stating the obvious. It's a bad habit."

I sat back down. Khan's reluctance was an encouraging sign. Urgun was maybe sixty kilometers from Sharan, but it was a hard sixty kilometers. I'd be starting on one mountain and ending on another. In between there was a lot of rocks and scrub, with pockmarked roads that were difficult to find let alone navigate. And while the road ran through the calmest area of Paktika, that wasn't saying much at all.

"I need two trucks when I get out to Sharan," I told him. "I can bring gas, water."

"Mules would be better."

"If I need them, I can get some in Urgun."

Khan shook his head. "I would not count on that. Things have changed."

"There's no mules there?"

"Well, if we were talking camels—"

"Camels won't work farther east or south."

"True."

"I don't want to ride mules all the way from Sharan."

"No."

We talked about the logistics for a while. Khan clearly had his own agenda out there; maybe it was drugs, maybe it was weapons. Maybe Uncle had secretly hired him to watch out for me, despite what Khattak said. Whatever, he had a good handle on the situation, knew what things cost and where they would be easiest to obtain—and openly admitted that he didn't know things, rare in Afghanistan, and the rest of the world, for that matter. He said he could arrange for the trucks and some other supplies at Sharan; I'd cover that cost, and he'd provide his services for free.

So maybe he was picking up a bit of a vig there, too. The possibility reassured me.

"I stay with you until you find your friend," he told me. "Whatever it takes."

I figured that was a line of bull, but I drank to it anyway.

16

KABUL

THE next day, I did something I hadn't done probably in twenty years: I went to mass.

Afghanistan being a Muslim country and not particularly tolerant of other religions, there are no churches anywhere in Kabul. But there's a small chapel in the Italian embassy, and Sunday masses there have been a regular event at least since the Russian occupation. One of the men Khattak had recommended was a regular. So I put on a fresh set of clothes and went there first thing in the morning.

The altar looked like a white computer desk with a bleached cloth over it. But there was a surprisingly reverent feel to the place. I left my AK and pistol at the back and got into a pew near the side. Maybe three dozen people had come to the mass. All were male except for the three Italian nuns in the first row near the pulpit.

The guy I was looking for was an American contract worker named Jimmy DiMarco whose contract had recently expired. He had a bald, almost round head with a bright red mark near the crown; supposedly the mark was a souvenir from a rocket attack. I saw him up in the front, second row back, hands over his face in prayer.

Before I could change my seat, the priest came out from the side and the mass began. He was Italian, but he sprinkled English and German into the liturgy, obviously a nod to his multinational audience. The mixture made the service familiar and impenetrable at the same time.

I'd been raised Catholic but hadn't been to church since my confirmation at age twelve. It wasn't that I lost my faith; it was more like I never understood what it had to do with church in the first place.

My father made me go to mass when I was little. He and I would stand by the door at the back, ready to book as soon as communion was over. The sermons tended to follow certain predictable patterns. About half were about the people who weren't there, with the priest complaining that their souls were going to rot in hell. I guess that was his way of reassuring us that we hadn't wasted our time. Most of the rest were about abortion and how evil it was. He might start out talking about Easter or Christmas, the Good Samaritan or the prodigal son, but abortion snuck in there by the end.

The unborn were a big deal at our church. They had crosses and even empty caskets. Every mass we prayed for them, sometimes twice. My father said once this was because the church eliminated limbo and there was no place for them to go.

One day my dad wasn't there to insist I go to church anymore. That was just fine with me. My mom only went to watch me or my sister receive communion or confirmation, so it was fine with her, too.

Still, I'd gone enough that I knew when to stand and when to kneel, even in Italian and German. When it came time to receive communion, I walked up with the rest of the congregation. That was probably wrong—I should have gone to confession first—but it seemed more a sin not to join in.

"Jimmy, wait up," I said to DiMarco as he started out when mass was over. He'd already picked up his gun from the back and pulled his shades on. "I wanted to talk to you."

"Yeah?" His voice was noncommittal, but he slowed his pace as we walked out into the small garden outside the chapel.

"Friend of mine says you're looking for a job," I told him.

"What friend?"

"Khattak. My name's Jack Pilgrim. I own Iron Rock."

"That's Merc Conrad's operation."

"Merc's my partner. Actually, he's why I'm here. I haven't heard from him in a few weeks and—"

"He's a nut. I'm not getting involved with him." DiMarco started to walk away.

"Whoa, whoa, wait up," I told him. "We can work something out."

"Fat chance. Conrad thinks he's God, doesn't he? Pulling all the ragheads out in the field together. No thanks."

"You know where he is?"

"Down south. You don't?"

"I heard Paktika."

"There you go."

"Listen—"

But he wouldn't listen, he wouldn't even slow down. I decided I wasn't going to run after him and stopped.

Fuck him.

The people who'd been nearby for the mass pretended they hadn't heard as they passed me. Most of them looked the other way. I was just starting to walk again when a large hand pounded me on the back.

"I'll go," said a voice in English with a Russian accent.

Hokum.

"I go," he said. "When?"

Suddenly I was suspicious. "You mind if I ask first why you changed your mind?"

"You're a holy man. Go to mass."

I laughed. I guess one misconception was as good as another.

UNLIKE Khan, Hokum wouldn't be going for free—five hundred per day, plus expenses. I considered it a pretty good deal, especially since it didn't come with death benefits.

We spent the rest of the day picking up supplies. Hokum insisted on using his van, which was fine with me; it had plenty more capacity than the Toyota. I decided to pay off my driver, giving him enough money to fix the damage I'd done and throwing in a couple of extra days' pay for his trouble. He wasn't sorry to see our relationship end, even if it had been profitable for him.

Most likely, he wasn't going to bother fixing the car, or at least he'd wait to do so. Bullet holes and missing glass were as common in Kabul as low-profile tires in L.A.

We got new rifles—HK 416s, M4 look-alikes that came equipped with grenade launchers and night scopes. Besides the attachments, the guns were a lot lighter than the AKs, and shorter, which made them easier to handle. We also found two old British L7 General Purpose Machine Guns, with a dozen belts of 7.62 rounds. The "Gimpy" is a British take on the Belgian FN MAG, a post–World War II gun that was the basic squad-level machine gun in the 1960s.

The Gimpies were supplements to Hokum's "personal" machine gun—a DShKM heavy machine gun. Hokum had obtained the "Dushka" in payment of a debt from some mujahideen; it was a large and heavy gun, weighing about eighty pounds when empty. The bullets it fired were similar to the fifty-caliber jobs spit out by a "Ma Deuce" American Browning M2. Here we had a little trouble locating the right ammunition, and ended up paying twice what Hokum said was the going rate for eight fifty-bullet belts. I called it the "Kabul tax" and paid up after fifteen minutes of hemming and hawing failed to lower the price. I'd've given in earlier, but with less time haggling, I'd've been considered an untrustworthy customer.

We bought grenades to go with the rifles, another handgun, and as much extra ammo as I thought we'd be able to carry. If there's one thing you don't skimp on in Afghanistan, it's firepower.

Another thing you don't skimp on is water. Drinking the local water can bring serious consequences for someone whose gut hasn't incubated Afghan germs since they were born. In the army, I was taught to plan on four gallons of water per man per day. Clearly that's excessive, but if I thought we could have carried anywhere near that much with us, we would've. I ended up buying roughly eighty gallons, split between four five-gallon jugs and a bunch of smaller liter and half-liter bottles. I was counting on it lasting three people for two weeks, with plenty of stretch time and an allowance for "shrinkage."

A case of Jack Daniel's in Kabul went for three grand. That's thirty-three cents a milliliter, between a dollar and a dollar and a half a sip. But I would have paid considerably more. I transferred the whiskey to plastic bottles and two steel flasks, and split it among the rest of the gear.

I thought Armstrong might object or find some way to make trouble if he saw us leaving, so I arranged with Khattak to fly us from a field near one of the warehouses Merc had leased outside of Kabul, with kickoff scheduled for the following morning. It took a few hours to shop and ferry the supplies there. Stashing the gear involved a certain amount of risk, and we kept as much water and ammunition with us as we could. Surprisingly, theft is not a big problem in Kabul, but it's not considered theft if you take from your enemy, and by definition an American is the enemy to a lot of people in town.

By late afternoon we were good to go. I had a plan: Khattak would fly Khan, Hokum, and myself to Sharan. I'd check with the local authorities there, then drive on to Urgun and beyond. Khattak would check in at various points to see if I needed emergency transport. His just being available cost a ton of money, but every ship needs a lifeboat, especially one as leaky as mine.

As a contingency, I'd have to sign a blank invoice to be used in case I didn't make it back. Of course, Khattak probably realized it wouldn't be worth shit in that case, because there'd be no one left to pay it, but he didn't mention it and I didn't bring it up.

What would I do when I found Merc?

That was the one part of the plan that I hadn't really figured out. Ask him what the hell was going on, basically. Ask him why—if maybe—he was cheating me. Ask him about rumors that he was nuts and might have an army. Talk to him. Look him in the eye.

Hopefully that part of the plan would take care of itself when I got to it.

WITH everything ready to go, I probably should've tried to get a few extra hours of sleep. But that's the sort of thing only wise men do, and I hadn't come to Afghanistan because I was wise.

Rather than trying to call my wife again, I went to an Internet cafe and wrote her a long e-mail. It started out pretty generic, with the usual stuff you write when you're missing someone and you've been away long enough to forget the things you don't miss about them. At some point, I started writing about our wedding day. I told her how I'd felt more sexual that day than any other time in my life. Then I erased it, realizing it sounded stupid, more pornographic than anything else. It'd give her the wrong idea, like sex was the reason I'd married her, when it was the last thing.

In the end, the message I sent consisted of two sentences:

> I'm fine. Miss you a lot.

Even at that, half of it was a lie.

I ENDED the night at the Moustafa Hotel, in their lounge, listening to a British Pakistani tell me how he got rich. He'd been a doctor in the north of England, Yorkshire, I think, just south of Scotland. Apparently being a doctor in Great Britain wasn't the status thing he thought it would be, for he complained bitterly of how the patients looked down on him, treating him worse than they treated the nurse. He thought it had something to do with his accent rather than his skin, but the two probably went together. Though he'd spoken English his whole life, it had an Asian tint to it, and his skin was a light mauve. And yet with all his resentment and frustration, he had volunteered as a do-gooder with a church group going over to Afghanistan soon after the Taliban were overthrown.

"I couldn't believe how grateful these people were." The wonder was still fresh in his voice, undiminished by all that had followed. "I signed on to stay three months instead of the two weeks I'd agreed to. And then, indefinitely. I gave my notice, I worked hard, I saved lives. I saved many lives.

"Supplies were always short. One day we needed aspirin. This was in Balkh, in the far north. I took matters into my own hands and ordered a case from some people I knew in Pakistan. People wanted to pay me. I took only the reimbursement; even the fare of the man who drove me to pick it up I paid from my own pocket. I was going there anyway and what did it matter? A few weeks later they needed bandages, and yellow pads to write on. Coffee for an American nurse. Some tins of treats. The administrator urged me to charge a little extra for my trouble. Finally, I took ten pounds to keep him happy, and when I was paid I donated it to the clinic for the food fund. It was a little money we would get together to buy items for a food bank, for people who had been too sick to work, so they would have something when they went home. Ten pounds could buy a family food for a month at the time.

"The winter was cold, and some of our volunteers needed sweaters. There were many ways to get these things, even for free, but they involved a terrible amount of red tape. So they came to me. This was not the same as medicine, of course, and I did not know all of the charges in advance, so I added a little extra.

"And then it occurred to me—if there was a need for these things here, there was a need throughout the rest of the country."

From that start, the doctor had turned himself into a major importer. He had a number of contracts with the government, and owned several planes. His voice had a self-satisfied wonder to it as he spoke, as if he couldn't believe he had done all this himself. Lately, he'd begun investing his profits in property both in London and Pakistan; he admitted to being a rich man. He regularly traveled back forth between Kabul and Karachi in Pakistan, as well as England, France, and China; he knew all of the important government officials here, and had met with the American secretary of state as well as the British foreign secretary.

I couldn't figure out why he was telling me his story. Maybe I was a fresh face to impress. Or maybe he was looking for some sign from me that he'd done the right thing—that it was okay be rich, okay to be considered important, to do something other than being a doctor and saving lives.

He never asked what I did, but it was probably obvious that I wasn't a journalist. I was dressed far too well for that, and I was older besides. Not being a journalist, I must have been a contractor, so maybe he guessed that I shared some of his wonder, if not his guilt.

A WEEK after Merc and I started our company, we had our first big interview for a contract. It was with a financial company on Wall Street that needed to protect couriers moving paper and electronic backup files to different countries.

The first clue that this world was utterly different than anything else we'd ever known was the suggestion by one of the partners that he'd send a car to pick us up. The second was his advice that we discuss the pitch over drinks, not in the boardroom.

"Feels more like a date than an interview," I told Merc, and it was.

They paid for everything—drinks, cigars in a private club, a baseball game, and dinner afterward. They treated us like minor celebrities. We'd just come back from Afghanistan, and everybody in uniform was riding high then, heroes for kicking the Taliban out of the country and getting a little revenge for 9/11.

The attacks weren't just something they'd seen on TV. The ruins at the World Trade Center were down the block from their office; they were still being raked for body parts. All three partners had watched the first tower fall before realizing they better get the hell out of there. They knew more than a hundred people who'd died in the attacks, people they dealt with in business, people they bought newspapers from, people they sat next to on the ferry and train into work every day. From their point of view, we'd made the dead rest a little easier, and they were more than a little grateful for the peace of mind.

Even so, showing us around town that night was pretty much business as usual for them. They had corporate accounts and memberships everywhere, from the bar to the car service to the MVP Championship Club tickets at Yankee Stadium. A waiter lugging drinks to the seats near the dugout was part of their everyday existence; if we weren't with them, someone else would have been.

It was the first time in my life I smoked a Cuban cigar. In fact, it was the first time I ever smoked a hand-rolled cigar at all; until then I'd probably had a total of three machine-made White Owls, handed out by buddies who'd had a kid and whom I didn't want to disappoint by not lighting up. The Cuban, a Monte Cristo, gave me more of a buzz than the single-malt Scotch they bought me.

Doors opened for us all night. The Lincoln Town Car whisked us from Manhattan to the Bronx, cut through the traffic and deposited us right in front of the Stadium gate. There were more drinks inside, then down at our seats. With the Yanks leading 7–1, we cruised out after the seventh. The maître d' at Ron's Steakhouse recognized our hosts and showed them immediately to what looked like the best table in the house. Drinks appeared, hors d'oeuvres, extremely thick, buttery steaks—it all flew by.

We spent eight or nine hours with those guys that night, and while we talked about a lot of things, the job they wanted us to do wasn't one of them. I tried bringing it up once, but I let it slide when Merc gave me a back-off stare.

"It's a whole new world for us," Merc told me when the night was over. "This is a world with money. This is what serious money does. You have to take it all for granted, like it's all natural."

And I guess it was, because we got the job. The contract ran for a year, and when we signed it we got an advance ten times what Merc and I had made, combined, our last year in service. I must've stared at all those zeroes for a good hour and a half.

17

KABUL

I DIDN'T sleep much my last night in Kabul. The funny thing is, I dropped right off as soon as I got to the room, just went deep out. But maybe twenty minutes later a muffled explosion in the distance pulled me halfway back to consciousness, enough to wrench me from whatever odd shapes I'd been dreaming, but not quite enough to shake me entirely from sleep. I stared at the ceiling, unsure where I was for a moment. Then I was on a couch—I was sure I was on a couch—back in New York, in a loft where Sharon and I had gone for a Christmas party a year and a half before.

Sharon was there, and someone else, in another part of the room. I could hear them moving around behind me in the dark. Moving, then making love.

I jumped up in the bed, shaking. I was sure it was real. I didn't want to look around the rest of the room. I was afraid I'd see them, or see something that told me it wasn't a dream.

Merc.

Had he been the one with Sharon in the dream?

No. I was thinking of him because I was here to find him, to bring him back, to save him like he'd saved me. I'd just confused him in my mind with everything else.

But maybe it *was* him with my wife. In the dream, if not in real life.

The idea just kept coming back and back.

A siren wailed in the distance. Another joined it, and another, like wolves serenading the moon.

I looked at my door, expecting that someone would knock and tell me the city was under attack. But no one came. It was just another night in Kabul.

I got a dose of paranoia about leaving so much of my supplies guarded only by the rental people at the warehouse, so I went down to the desk and arranged for a ride over. I spent what was left of the night huddled in front of the gate to my stuff.

Hokum met me around five and we got ready to leave, packing as much as we could fit of the supplies into the van and then heading over to the field where Khattak was supposed to put down. I'd planned to take off at 0700; Khan was supposed to meet me here at six-thirty. He didn't show until about half past seven, but Khattak and his helicopter hadn't come by then, either.

Khan presented me with another complication—he drove up with four guys he wanted to have come with us.

"We don't have room," I told him. That wasn't technically true; I just didn't want to be outnumbered.

"Where you want to go is not a good place," said Khan. "A few more men would be handy."

"You scared, Khan?" I asked.

"A wise man is always scared."

Which I guess was meant to imply that he was both. In the end, I agreed one of his men could come along with us. He picked a skinny kid named Muhammad Bajaar who didn't seem to speak any English. The others appeared relieved by the choice and lost no time leaving.

An hour later, Khattak still hadn't arrived. I called him on the sat phone, but got no answer. So we sat down and waited. By now Kabul was about as awake as it ever gets, and while curiosity isn't a highly prized character trait in Afghanistan, we were getting more than our share of glances from passers-by.

I was thinking of sending Khan's kid over to the airport to find out what the hell was going on when I heard the heavy whomp of chopper blades approaching. The big Hind circled once over the warehouse complex, then came in for a landing about thirty yards from where we were with the truck, kicking up a heavy cloud of dirt and rocks.

"You're late," I told Khattak.

He shrugged.

Just as we started loading the chopper a white four-door pickup drove past the field and over to the warehouse area. The back of the truck was filled with men. I didn't think all that much about it when I saw it go by; I was too busy getting stuff out of the van so I could go back over to the warehouse and get the rest. But when Khan's kid Bajaar and I drove up to the main door, I saw that the pickup was sitting around the corner, empty.

The building had a large garage-type door which opened into an aisle that ran down the center of the building. I backed in, driving slowly past the steel-wired cribs that ran down both sides of the aisle. When you rented your space, you had to supply your own lock; that was the warehouse's basic security feature. Security guards might keep the most obvious looters away, but only if they weren't in league with them.

The guards were nowhere to be seen as I backed down the long, wide space in the middle of the building. Bajaar hopped out as soon as I stopped, an eager kid, or maybe just a scared one, wanting to get the hell out of here quick. Lights blazed from the rafters but the place was still dark and claustrophobic. I undid the lock and pulled the gate back. Bajaar grabbed some boxes of water and started humping them to the truck.

We were just about done when I heard the murmur of voices approaching. It wasn't a conversation; clipped, quick phrases were being exchanged.

"Into the truck," I told Bajaar.

He didn't get the words, but the way I swung up the 416 put him in motion.

I got the door open just as the gunfire started. The first few rounds smacked into the concrete floor a few yards from the front of the van, spraying rock chips into the windshield. I lifted the rifle and fired back in the general direction, then dove into the truck. Bajaar scrunched down between the seat and the dashboard; as soon as I saw he was with me I pulled off the brake and jammed the gas, holding the wheel straight as the van bolted ahead. A fresh shower of bullets struck the windshield and the glass disintegrated into pellets and dust.

We were maybe two hundred feet from the entrance. But that was a long way. I held the 416 up and fired blind, more to do something than in any hope of actually hitting anything. Just as the sunlight hit the front of the van the wheel jerked hard to the left. I pulled it back and gave more gas as the truck smacked against the side of the building and careened to the right, spinning around in a one-eighty. I saw someone running in front of me and punched the gas; the truck lurched forward, then stopped; I'd stalled it out. And there was no way I was going to get it going again without dealing with the welcome wagon outside.

"You stay down!" I yelled to Bajaar, jumping out.

The van had stopped at a ninety-degree angle from the entrance. I couldn't see any of the gunmen near the building. Everything was quiet, and for a few seconds I thought maybe my friends had left. But that was just wishful thinking—a long steady burst from around the corner of the building took out the last two tires on the truck. When I fired back in that direction, two gunmen came charging from the building itself, their rifles barking. I spun and emptied the 416's mag, putting bullet after bullet into the bastards but barely slowing them down. Finally, the first one dropped, pitching to the right in slow motion. The other dropped his gun and ran past me, as if he were being pushed from behind by an unseen wind. Finally his legs slipped out from under him and he crumpled to the ground.

I pulled the empty box from the gun and slapped in the backup I'd taped to its side.

If the guys who'd been firing from the corner of the building were smart or maybe a little braver, they could have rushed the truck and pinned me. But they stayed put around the corner, not even firing. They might have been trying to flank me, sending some of the team around the building to try and get me from both sides. Whatever, they gave me enough breathing room to lean back into the truck and fiddle with the wires to get it going again.

Bajaar was still crouched in the space between the seat and dashboard, but he had his pistol out. It was a revolver, a big ugly thing that looked like a .357 and probably was a Yugoslavian Crvena Zastava older than he was.

"We'll be out of here in a second," I told him as the engine caught. I pulled myself up behind the wheel and stepped on the gas. The van jerked forward unsteadily, rocking but moving on the shot-out wheels. Another burst of gunfire hit the back, and seemed to push us forward; we spurted ahead ten or fifteen yards, twenty.

Then I made the mistake of trying to turn. The van tipped sharply to the right, balancing on what was left of the tires and wheels. It started to fall back, but something in the back shifted or maybe my luck finally ran out—we slapped down hard on the passenger's side. I fell against Bajaar, practically headfirst. My ears ringing, I pushed against him to get up and get out through the windshield. My head spun as I hit the pavement. I reached back for my rifle but all I could find was Bajaar's revolver. I grabbed it as rounds began peppering the truck again.

The pistol practically flew out of my hand on the first shot; the bullet flew far from the mark. I gripped the gun with both hands and fired again, this time striking one of the gunmen as he came around the corner. Unlike the rifle's bullets, this slug tore into him and he fell, his gun flying away.

Bajaar, meanwhile, had regained his senses and pushed out of the truck, my rifle with him.

The road was another fifty feet away; there was a ditch there, which would give us a little cover. I grabbed the back of Bajaar's jacket and pulled him in that direction. We'd taken maybe a dozen steps when one of the gunmen's bullets finally found the van's gas tank and it exploded. The blast knocked us both off our feet, but we managed to crawl and scramble to the ditch.

We traded guns and caught our breath. The kid looked a little dazed, but not completely out of it. For a first time in combat, he was doing okay.

Not great, but you can never expect great.

Flames shot off the van, and a thick curl of black smoke furled in a semicircle to its right, dragged there by the wind. I got up, figuring we could use the smoke as cover to get away. The helicopter was only a few hundred yards away, on the other side of another set of buildings; thirty seconds of running our butts off and we'd be okay.

I got up. Bullets ripped through the air, inches away. The barrage was so heavy I dropped back down.

A car raced up on the highway and skidded to a stop. I jerked around, saw a guy with a gun emerge from the front. I pulled my rifle up to fire, then realized he was shooting at the men who'd attacked us.

"Get in the car!" the man yelled. "Come on!" Then he shouted something in Pashto.

My first thought was that this was one of Khan's men. Then I thought it might be an Afghan policeman, since many of them used their own vehicles. It took me a few more seconds to realize I'd seen the truck before—it was a Russian jeep, and the driver was Diss, the psycho American who'd given me a ride from the airport and had a private prison in his home.

You don't get to choose your savior. Bajaar and I retreated under his covering fire. He hopped back in and started moving before we got there. The kid and I ran along the other side, using it for cover while alternately firing back and trying to jump in.

"I got a chopper over there," I told Diss.

"Yeah—the Afghan army has people on the way."

I threw myself into the backseat and he floored the old truck toward the field.

"How do you know what the Afghans are doing?" I asked.

"Radio, dude." He pointed at the scanners and other gear under the front dash. "Remember?"

I didn't, actually.

"You pissed some pretty important people," he said, veering across the field. "Those guys work for Raz Omar's brother. He's in the defense ministry. When you took Raz Omar out, he swore vengeance. It's all over town," he added, throwing his arm over the seat and turning back to look at me. "You really oughta learn who you can piss off and who you can't."

"Watch where you're driving."

"I wanna come with you," he added. "Take me."

"No way."

"I just saved your life. Come on—I know where you're goin'."

"Where's that?"

"Pakistan, right? To get the Taliban."

"I'm not going to Pakistan, Diss. I'm going out to Paktika. That's this side of the border."

"But you're hunting the devil, and I want to go with you."

"Watch where the hell you're driving."

I DECIDED to take him with me. A pair of Afghan army trucks appeared at the edge of the field as we pulled up next to the helicopter, and I'm sure they would have been competent enough to kill him if I left him, but the truth is I'd already made the decision. It was a gut thing. I didn't trust him—I half suspected that he had somehow been involved in tipping Omar's people off, though in retrospect the fault there probably lies with me, since I'd gone about my business fairly openly. But Diss had a crazy aura about him, the sort of maniacal energy you need when you're in a life-threatening situation. You sure wouldn't want him with you for a backyard barbecue, but his insanity could be put to good use where I was going.

Plus, he came with two massive crates of AK ammo. We packed them into the chopper and took off as the Afghan troop trucks closed in. Khattak passed so close to one of the trucks I thought the Hind's chin would clip the windshield.

It didn't. And within a few minutes Kabul was far behind us. Mountains and high desert lay ahead as far as I could see. We were six, half the number of an A Team, half the number of Christ's apostles, setting off for the wilderness in search of my wayward messiah. I gripped one of the rails near the door and watched the mountains grow, amazed that I'd fallen so far back in so short a time.

THE VIOLENT

18

SHARAN

THE idea that Sharon cheated on me stayed with me the rest of the day. I tried to think of other things, tried staring at the landscape, the mountains that rose toward us, the cold grayness we were racing toward, but inevitably the idea snuck back into my head, poking at the fringes of everything I saw or thought. It was like the taste of something that had gotten stuck at the back of my throat, a hint of bile I couldn't get rid of. I told myself I didn't care, but I guess that wasn't true.

Glimpses of parties and events we'd been at filtered through my mind, whispers in another room. This rich French guy we'd done business with, a kid out of college whose father was on the Forbes list—I remembered looks she'd given them.

Just looks, nothing else.

Had they really been there? They hadn't registered with me at the time.

I couldn't believe I would have missed them, if they really had happened. But I couldn't really trust myself, could I? I'd completely missed whatever Merc had been up to. I'd been oblivious to everything.

Not oblivious, maybe. Distracted.

I bought Sharon a diamond bracelet for our first anniversary. It cost thousands; I don't even remember how many now. Many. What I wanted to see was the glow in her eyes when she opened the box.

We went out to dinner at an exclusive place in the city, ridiculously expensive. I ordered champagne and gave her the box.

Her right eyebrow raised ever so slightly. She had a blank expression for a moment, then a smile came to her lips.

"Oh, Jack."

Oh, Jack.

Yeah.

I sipped the three-hundred-dollar champagne, basking in that smile. The smile was almost better than the sex.

Had her eyes wandered that night? Had they wandered before that—was that why I needed the bracelet, or the smile?

I tried to remember the night, tried to see it again in my head. The harder I tried, the fuzzier it became, until all I could remember were the most insignificant details, and all I could see were the diamonds on her wrist.

Was being here, being away from her—was it all twisting me into something I wasn't?

Or was it stripping away what I wasn't, and revealing what I truly was?

FACTS without context rarely convey much information, but this one may: Paktika's governor during the time I was there had served the Taliban as their police chief in the next district over.

The U.S. has had a huge impact on Afghanistan, most of it for the better. Life expectancy is up, there are schools that teach more than how to kill people, hospitals, roads—the tangible signs of progress are pretty obvious if you've been here before. Not all of this has been the military's doing. A lot of humanitarian groups, which weren't allowed under the Taliban and were barely tolerated by the Russians, have had an impact. And enough Afghan Alger Hisses have pulled themselves up by their own bootstraps to spawn a cottage industry printing heartwarming true-life success stories.

But there are a lot of places where the West's impact has been blunted by nature first of all, and man second. Eastern Paktika falls in that category.

Much of it's inaccessible by any vehicle that doesn't have legs. It's not just a matter of terrain, though the mountains and rocks—and in some cases, the high forests—make driving difficult. Everybody here is related to everybody else, and it's instantly obvious whether you belong or not. If the people don't want you here, there's not a lot you can do about it. They may not shoot you—as a rule the people who live here are very much of the don't-kill-me-and-I-won't-kill-you philosophy. But they won't help you, either. And without their help, a lot of the border area is uninhabitable for more than a few hours.

But Paktika is a relatively big place, the equivalent of a small state back in the U.S. Sharan is in the western part of the province, and with a major U.S. base on its outskirts it's pretty stable.

The colonel in charge of the base wanted it to stay that way for the next two weeks. After that, he really couldn't care less—he was going home, his unit was going home, the whole damn American army was going home, and the Kenyans or whoever the UN sent to replace them could bulldoze the place for all he cared.

He told me this after two of his men picked me up at the small field where Khattak landed us a few miles outside of the village. Khan's trucks were already waiting, a good sign, I thought, and we were about halfway through loading them when an up-armored Humvee stopped near the road. A captain got out of the vehicle and strolled over, about as relaxed and comfortable as if he were at a college homecoming game.

"Y'all wouldn't happen to be Mr. Jack Pilgrim, wouldya?" he said in an Arkansas twang.

So much for the virtues of traveling unannounced. Then again, we'd made such a racket leaving, all Afghanistan probably knew where I was.

"My colonel would like to invite you to lunch," the captain told me when I introduced myself. "As soon as it's convenient, sir."

"For him or for me?"

"It's very convenient for him right now," said the captain, with only the faintest hint that this was one of those invitations that couldn't be refused.

I put Hokum in charge of the gear and told him I'd meet them at the house Khan had arranged for us to stay at. Then I climbed into the Hummer and rode over to the base, which was just east of the city.

The colonel was being hospitable by inviting me to lunch, but he wasn't trying to snow me or impress me; lunch was some grilled meat and canned potatoes, same as what everybody else was eating. I considered this a good sign, since it made it clear where I stood.

"You were a sergeant during the war against the Taliban?" he asked, digging into his canned potatoes the way a kid goes after ice cream.

"That's right."

"Things have changed since then, I bet."

"This camp is bigger. Rest of the place looks about the same."

"World of change, son. For one thing, we're leaving in just thirteen days. You'd best remember that."

It was kind of funny that he called me "son," since we were about the same age, but I didn't point that out.

"I wouldn't go driving off just anywhere," added the colonel. "The farther east you go, the less likely people are to be friendly. And south."

"I'm not really counting on making many friends out here," I told him. "I'm just here to find Merc Conrad."

He took that in stride. I assume that Armstrong or Race or someone else in the chain of spooks had given him a complete dossier.

"Mr. Conrad is an interesting man," the colonel told me. "What are you going to do if he doesn't want to be found?"

"I'll talk to him and figure it out from there."

"I meant, if he doesn't want to be found at all."

"I'll find him."

It occurred to me, though, that maybe the colonel was speaking from experience, so I asked if he'd been looking for him.

"Why would I do that?" he asked.

"You seem to know him."

"According to what I've heard, your friend Conrad's a real problem. He goes around firing up tribespeople, telling them to fight the Taliban to the death. Riles 'em up, like one of those guys in the fancy clothes at a bullfight before the matador comes out."

"Fighting the Taliban doesn't sound like much of a problem to me. Isn't that what we want?"

"What we want here, Pilgrim, is peace."

"Aren't the Taliban trying to destroy that peace?"

"Not necessarily. It depends on where you're talking."

"Out east?"

"Not a good place," admitted the colonel. By now he'd wiped the plate clean of his potatoes and was working methodically on the steak, cutting it into miniature parallelograms, divvying it all up before even tasting a piece.

"I think that may be where Merc is," I told him. "Out beyond Urgun."

"I wouldn't be very surprised."

"The Taliban there?"

"Not necessarily. But maybe."

We talked for a while about the area, then the colonel circled back to Merc.

"I have heard rumors that he was trying to raise his own army," said the colonel. "That wouldn't be good."

"I don't see how that would be possible out here," I told him. "They're all Pashtuns. Why would they trust him?"

"I don't think they would," said the colonel.

"So what do you think the real story is?"

"I think he has a few men with him. I think he believes he's going to find bin Laden and take home the fifty million. But bin Laden's not out there. If you want my opinion, he died in Tora Bora."

THE colonel was probably sincere, but the opinion that bin Laden had died was decidedly a minority opinion. Bin Laden *should* have died at Tora Bora, and maybe he would have if we hadn't insisted on fighting the war mostly by proxy, using the Northern Alliance to go after the Taliban government and their devoted mujahideen.

The problem was that the Northern Alliance's agenda and our agenda weren't entirely the same. They wanted control of the government and the Taliban out; we wanted the Taliban eliminated. Wishful thinking made that seem like the same thing.

When the going turned against the Taliban, bin Laden ran to Tora Bora, located in the Spin Mountains in eastern Afghanistan. The caves there had been reinforced and made into a network of natural bunkers. These weren't the caves Huck Finn and Tom Sawyer chased pirates in; they were more like the Maginot Line that protected France before the start of World War II, without the guns. You could outflank them easily, but getting inside was a son of a bitch. Bin Laden had spent years at Tora Bora and knew by heart the cave network and the surrounding area, with its footpaths into Pakistan, its windswept mountain valleys, and its rock towers. He had three to four thousand soldiers sworn to protect him with their lives.

We sent twelve Americans against him. They were Special Forces guys, very possibly the best fighters in the world, but even the Magnificent Seven had the townspeople behind them. The locals here were, at best, neutral.

The leader of the Afghan forces attacking Tora Bora negotiated a deal that made a lot of sense to him—bin Laden leaves, he wouldn't follow. The American public didn't read about that in the newspapers or see that on TV, but that's what the deal was. They also didn't read or hear or see that we knew damn well where bin Laden was and that he was getting away.

But the fact that we sent a relatively small contingent of SpecOps and air force guys to the country was pretty plain, and there weren't many loud protests about that—or at least none claiming we were sending too small a force. Logically, a few hundred, a few thousand men on the ground aren't about to take control of Texas, which is about Afghanistan's size. Forget the Alamo—when Mexico and the United States slugged it out over Texas, President Polk sent more than half the U.S. Army to settle things. The army didn't stop until it held Mexico City.

Were we scared of big body counts and body bags? Or was the real truth that bin Laden and the so-called War on Terror weren't really that important?

It seems like sacrilege to even ask the question, but when you stand back and look at what the situation was and is, it gets hard to answer. If you're a person who lived in New York or New Jersey and you lost your father or your mother or a son or a friend or a lover in the World Trade Center, if your business tanked, if your life was wrecked, getting bin Laden and the rest of his crew might make a real difference to you. If you were at the Pentagon or knew someone there, nailing the murderers once and for all would be a pretty high priority. But if you're an average guy in Des Moines or Indianapolis or Charleston or wherever, maybe it doesn't compare with what you need to do to pay the rent every day. You want to feel good about your country and yourself, but beyond that, what happens in Tora Bora or anywhere in Afghanistan isn't going to affect you, no way, no how.

If it had been my decision to make, I'd've leveled the country literally with every nuke we had. I'd've sent a lot more troops, more and more and more, until I ground the SOB's bones into dust. I'd've wanted his skull on my desk so I could smash it with my very own hammer. I would have stopped with nothing—because in bin Laden's world, out in Tora Bora and beyond, anything else, anything even a fraction of a fraction of half a centimeter less, is weakness, and weakness will be despised and revenged. Anything less will prove that the attacks were warranted and should be repeated. Anything less is victory for the people we want to defeat. Anything less is a guarantee that we will never win.

LUNCH ended. The colonel asked what my plans were. I told him I was going east and looking for Merc as soon as possible.

"If he's a nut, why don't you just leave him be?" asked the colonel.

"I don't think he's a nut," I told him.

The colonel gave me an indulgent smile and then slipped into lecture mode, as if he were an old uncle and I was a kid bound for college. His main concern seemed to be that I was going to get stuck somewhere and then have to rely on his people to get me out. He kept saying they were going to be gone in two weeks, and that he intended having every single member of his "family" out and safe.

"Not even a bug bite."

I told him that I had no intention of getting stuck, that all I was doing was looking for my partner, and that if it became obvious he was in areas where it was too dangerous to go, I'd bag it all and go back to Kabul.

"If he's out east in Gayan, he's not in a good place," added the colonel, getting up from the table.

"Then maybe he needs help."

"Don't get in a bad place yourself."

Kind of an odd thing to say to someone in Afghanistan, but I let it go.

19

NYAZI, NEAR SHARAN

ONE of the people Khan had come to meet was an important regional official in the NSD, which is the national security service, kind of like the FBI, though it's a little hard to picture a G-man sharing pistachios with a gun dealer. I went along because I wanted to see what he knew about Merc.

Khan and the official talked for a while in Pashto. I couldn't tell whether Khan was selling him supplies, which is what he claimed, or negotiating to buy some. Maybe he was doing both. When they were done, they both switched to English. The official had one of his sons bring us more tea, and offered some dates to go with the pistachios.

I asked about Merc, but he claimed not to have heard anything about him. Then I asked about the Taliban, how strong they were in the province.

"No Taliban here."

"In this part of Paktika, or the whole province?"

"Nowhere."

"None?"

He shook his head and said something in Pashto which didn't sound particularly flattering.

"No Taliban," said Khan.

"Yeah, right." I got up. "I'm kind of tired. I think we should be getting back."

Khan frowned but got up.

"What the hell was that about no Taliban?" I asked him as we bounced on the road back to the house.

"You have to be careful about insulting people," he told me.

"What, for leaving?"

"You should share food and talk. To leave abruptly can be considered insulting."

"So can lying."

"Our host was with the Taliban before the war. Afghanistan is a complicated place," Khan added. "You must be more careful."

"He was in the Taliban and he's in the NSD?"

"He at least is a man who can be trusted."

"How do you figure that?"

"He could have lied and told you what you wanted to hear."

"Instead he lied and told me nothing."

"That is a sign of honesty."

SHARON and I were lying in bed, on a warm summer morning, in our house in New Jersey. She was wearing a silk chemise, pulled up over her hip. We'd made love the night before and her panties were under the covers somewhere, tangled in the sheets. I moved my hand up her leg and across her belly, lingering at the edge of her nightdress, circling the lace hem. I cupped her breast with my hand, and though she was still sleeping, I felt her nipple grow erect against my palm.

I slid close and began kissing the back of her ear, my lips catching on the earring she'd left on. I rose over to kiss her face.

She turned to face me.

It wasn't Sharon.

It was Cynthia, our secretary.

Cynthia.

I tried to jerk myself away from the dream, but it hung with me as I got up to pee, following me into the cold night as I went behind the house to relieve myself.

I'd never slept with Cynthia. Never. I knew it. But the dream clung on, more real than any memory I could replace it with.

Standing beneath the stars, I began to shiver.

WE spent the next day rounding up supplies to replace what I'd lost when I'd been ambushed at the warehouse, visiting Sharan and the small settlements around it. In the distant past, the area had been heavily farmed, and there had been an initiative recently to refurbish or extend the irrigation system. Green plants dotted the landscape—wheat, I guess, which had been brought in by the U.S. and the UN. It wasn't like in America, where the fields would be vast stretches of plants—those amber waves of grain in "America the Beautiful." The Afghan fields looked more like stubborn spots in a sandy lawn where grass was just starting to come back, or maybe the forehead of a guy who'd just had a hair transplant. But it was better than the yellow and brown collections of rock I'd seen my last trip through.

The farmers, or at least the ones I saw, did their work either by hand or with the help of oxen. Their faces were wrinkled by the sun, and they had the tangled toughness of people who were close to the land. There were more motorbikes and trucks now than there had been a few years before, but the real difference was the satellite dishes. I don't know where they got the electricity to run the TVs and radios they were connected to; there were power lines around, but they were pretty haphazard and I can't imagine that electricity was more reliable way out here than in Kabul.

I wanted to talk to the police chief in Sharan, but I kept getting different stories about where he was every time I went into his office. Finally, with Khan's help, I figured out where his house was and went there. The place was empty, the door missing. The simple furniture in the front room was covered with dust.

Hokum, standing behind me, crossed himself and started mumbling in Russian.

"You sure you got the address right?" I asked Khan.

"The town is not that big a place," said Khan.

We went across the street to ask the neighbor if he knew anything. The old man who came to the door put his finger across his chin, as if he were sawing against his beard to find the answer.

"Not many weeks," he said. He insisted on speaking English,

even though Khan had addressed him in Pashto, and he addressed me, not him, apparently put off by something I missed entirely. "Gone."

"Did he say where he was going?"

"Gone."

THE attack at the warehouse cost me three-quarters of my bourbon ration; I still had my two flasks and the equivalent of another quart split between two containers. That wasn't much in the scheme of things, and I tried rationing myself. It was a losing battle.

"You like the whiskey," said Khan as I sipped from one of the flasks before hitting the sack that night.

"It has its benefits."

"No energy drink?" His accent made the words sound funny—"en-erk-gy dink."

"For some reason I was always more worried about calming myself down than revving myself up," I told him. I probably lost him with the slang but he nodded anyway.

Khan's question was on the mark. For most guys in Afghanistan—I would almost assume this was true everywhere, really—the problem was staying revved, doing without more than a quick nap every two or three days. The longer you go, the harder it is to keep your edge, and keeping your edge is damn important out here.

For some reason I didn't have that problem, not when I was in the army, and not now. I drank coffee to wake up, two cups if I could, but generally no more than that. Two-hour naps, for days on end—not ideal, but doable.

The problem I had was laying back. Maybe not so much in the field, I think—you walk for a whole day, or go without sleep for a couple, and your body finds a way to shut you down. But back at the base, back home, to get off the train, something to drop me down a notch or two came in handy.

Bourbon was part of the scene at work, especially when I was working at the casinos and taking clients out. And I was always meeting with clients, taking them out to impress them—to show them that I really didn't need their business, which for some reason made them want to give it to me all the more.

Lubricate deals, make talking easier: there were a lot of reasons to drink. On some level alcohol might have been armor, though I'm not sure exactly what from. From racing too fast? Or from focusing on where I was and how I'd gotten there?

You don't ask these sorts of questions when you're in the middle of it. You just move on. It's a habit, and it was a habit now, the soft sting of the bourbon in my throat.

Sitting in the room before going to bed, I glanced up and realized Khan was still waiting for me to answer.

"You want some?" I asked, holding the flask toward him.

He shook his head. "Not here."

"Suit yourself," I said, taking another swig.

WE left Sharan the next morning, starting out when it was still dark. The road we took was comparatively easy to follow, a deep rut in the side of the mountains for the most part. We went up and across a hillside, then down a ridge, paralleling a riverbed. A few weeks before, water would have been coursing down, the last of the spring thaw bubbling through the rocks. Now there was the barest trickle, with pools here and there.

The route from Sharan to Urgun went from one set of mountain ridges to another, crossing a rippling plain in between. About three hours out of Sharan, we stopped the trucks to take a leak, have something to eat, and get our bearings. We'd gone about thirty kilometers, not quite halfway.

"Bad dirt," said Hokum, staring at the parched ground all around us. "Not enough rain or snow."

I told him the lack of rain wasn't a problem as far as I was concerned; it meant we'd be able to use dry streambeds to travel on if we had to.

"This should all be a farm," continued Hokum. "If there were water, there could be more food. If they have food, the people don't fight."

"You sure, Hokum?"

"Common sense."

There was plenty of evidence to the contrary, but I decided to change the subject.

"You a farmer, Hokum?"

"My grandfather. Communists ruined Russia for farming. Here, at least, it was the rain. America is a land of farms," continued Hokum. "That is why your country is great. Family work hard. Real work."

"A lot of corporate farms now. Not quite the same thing."

"What corporate farm?"

I tried explaining it to him, but he couldn't quite get it. The truth is, I didn't understand agriculture well enough to explain it, either. The thing I did know was that the connection to the land Hokum idealized didn't exist for most Americans, and hadn't for a hundred years, if then. Out of frustration, I finally told him it had nothing to do with agriculture—factories had made the U.S. great.

"Russia has factories," he told me solemnly. It was supposed to be some sort of answer, but I didn't quite get the point.

"Everything's made in China now anyway," I said, and went to check on the others.

LOADED with gear and tarped for protection, the pickups looked more like amphibious boats than trucks. Gear hung off the sides like the reactive armor on a tank. Hokum had spent considerable time setting up his machine gun in the rear of the lead truck, wedging gear beneath and around the tripod so that he had a semiprotected firing position. We'd divided our guns and grenades between the cabs, with some backup weapons and ammo in the beds and on the outsides of the trucks.

We started out again, Hokum in the truck bed and Bajaar and me in the first truck. Khan took the wheel in the second, with Diss riding shotgun. Our path cut between Ju TurKhona, the district capital of Sar Hawza on the left to our north, and a string of settlements along the seasonal river on our right. There were a few clusters of houses scattered along the rutted road ahead but no big villages in the valley.

I'd driven the first leg so I let Bajaar drive; the kid turned out to be fairly adept at following the road, not a skill to be undervalued here. After an hour I climbed out the window and got up on the back to take a look around. The sun was intense, but it was relatively cool, in the lower seventies if that. I wore a baseball cap and ballistic sunglasses—goggles that keep all manner of crap out of your eyes, critical in Afghanistan.

A settlement sat about two miles ahead, and the road curved in a way that made it difficult to see what might be in our path.

"We should go across to the plain," suggested Hokum, pointing to the right. "Cut across."

"We'll get stuck in the dirt."

"Better than being shot in village."

"That's not going to happen here."

He said something in Russian which I didn't understand. I explained that as bad as the roads were, they were at least packed down.

"Roads always disaster," said Hokum, and without bidding he began telling the story of a Russian assault team that had been flying in an open valley just like the one we were coming through.

THERE had been six helicopters, unarmed, moving back north after an operation against gun smugglers near the Pakistan border. One of the helicopters began lagging behind the others, apparently because of mechanical problems. Finally, the pilot radioed that he was going to have to set down. He did so, right next to a road in a wide open area, kilometers from the nearest village. The distance from the settlements was a plus; the Russians would have found little help there.

Night came on. For some reason, the relief flight was delayed and didn't arrive until the next afternoon. When they got there, the Russians discovered that the helicopter had been stripped and the eight soldiers and four crewmen who'd been in it were missing.

An intensive operation was mounted to recover them. Five days later, two of the paratroopers who'd been on the helicopter were found on a hillside ten kilometers away. They'd died of dehydration and maybe sunstroke; their clothes had been taken and the tendons in their legs slit so they couldn't walk. According to the doctor, it had taken them three days to die.

"THOSE are the people who live here," said Hokum. "They don't know God."

"If you hate them so much, why do you stay?"

He frowned at me, like it was a stupid question.

The horn from the other truck ended any further discussion. I turned around and saw Khan, who was behind the wheel, waving wildly at me. I pounded on the roof for the kid to stop, then jumped off and ran over to the other truck.

"Never. No." Khan opened the door and hopped out of the truck.

"What the hell's going on?"

"I will not ride with him. No. Never."

"What'd I do?" asked Diss from inside.

I turned to Khan for an explanation, but he was too angry to talk coherently, spewing something in Pashto or Farsi or Martian—it was too rapid to decipher.

The general meaning was pretty clear, though.

"What the hell did you do?" I asked Diss.

He shook his head, genuinely confused.

It took a while, but eventually I figured out that Diss had been talking about food, and going on about a pig roast. Khan thought he was trying to provoke him—as a Muslim, pork was unclean meat.

I couldn't tell whether Diss had purposely pissed him off or not. We switched places and drove on.

20

BUNDI

GETTING through the small hamlets took a lot longer than driving on the open road. The main drag—the *only* drag—would inevitably be studded with people and animals, a vendor or two, sometimes a truck or car, with or without tires. As soon as you slowed down, kids would appear from nowhere, looking for candy or some other handout. I'd stocked up on the sweets and would hop from the cab to hand them out. Some of the tribespeople judged you by the way you dealt with their kids, during the war candy had been a cheap way of buying goodwill, or at least indifference. Now, though, people eyed us suspiciously no matter what. When I stopped to say hello or had Khan say something friendly, they held back, reserved. It might have been because they couldn't figure out who the hell we were. We obviously weren't soldiers, and just as clearly we weren't NGAs or journalists. If you couldn't figure out a man's agenda here, you had to be suspicious of him.

As we snaked uphill toward Urgun and the American forward base there, my own paranoia grew. The road was in shadows by now, the sun behind the mountains. Urgun was only a few klicks away, but it felt as if something were waiting for us up the road, waiting to spring at us in the dark. It was irrational—the American base made this a pretty safe area. But I couldn't shake the feeling. I'd gone back to riding with Khan and Hokum; Bajaar rode shotgun with Diss. When Khan suggested we stop a few miles outside the city for the night, I agreed.

We found a place to stay near a few brick huts about a half mile from the road. Two kids were playing soccer near a barbed-wire fence with a red triangle warning that there were mines beyond it. Every so often the ball would skitter under the fence and one of the kids would run in to grab it. I yelled at them, but they didn't stop. I grabbed Khan and made him tell them there were mines in the field.

"They know already."

"Tell them!"

He did.

"No problem, Joe," they said, addressing me, not him. Then they went back to kicking the ball.

The only way to keep them from the stinking minefield was to play with them, so I did for a while, booting the ball as hard as I could in the opposite direction. By now it was so dark it was impossible to see more than a few feet away. But the kids kept playing. They were pretty good, able to navigate the wildly uneven yard, twirling the ball in all different directions, possibly using the rocks that were strewn all around to their advantage.

The others set up a campsite next to the two trucks. Khan sent Bajaar up the road to buy some chickens, and we got a pair of scrawny, dusty birds for about three times the price locals would pay—an excellent deal, all things considered. Hokum plucked them, then Khan played chef, gutting them and stuffing them with some vegetables the chicken seller threw in. He grilled them over the propane fire, tending them with the care of a practiced kebob vendor. As they roasted, locals began to gather around, looking for a taste. We shared with them, but that didn't seem to chase off the suspicious glances, and as soon as the chicken was gone the crowd was, too. Still hungry, we broke out some of the rations we'd brought with us.

My stomach felt empty. I was still trying to pace myself, adjust to eating less. One meal in the U.S. was practically the equivalent of half a week's rations in Afghanistan, and my stomach hadn't had time to tighten.

But what really bothered me was the lack of drink. I knew I had to pace myself, since replenishing the bourbon at this point was out of the question. The thirst built, unquenched by the sips I rationed out, or even the ones I "snuck" over the quota. My head had started to hurt somewhere during the day, a sneaking kind of headache that moved up from the back of my neck and began gripping the sides of my skull behind my ears. I thought it was the heat, and wrapped a soaked bandanna around my head. The day wasn't that hot, though, and at night after dinner when the pounding didn't slip away I realized it was a kind of reverse hangover.

My first impulse was to grab the flask. But as my fingers touched the metal I stopped myself. Was I really drinking so much that my body went through withdrawal when I slowed down? I didn't think it was possible, and to prove it, I suffered through the headache for another hour, before giving in and taking a couple of hard swigs.

The headache went away, which made me feel even worse.

HOKUM and I divided the night between us, four-hour shifts—he'd relieve me at one. I took Diss as my backup, Hokum got Bajaar. I didn't figure Khan to be much of a shot, so I left him out of the mix, which was just fine with him. We set up a watch area, moving around it at irregular intervals.

I gave Diss one of the HK 416s, and he played with the night scope like it was a toy, scanning back and forth adjusting and readjusting the unit for over an hour. I had a set of generation-three night glasses. They were American-issue, bought at the bazaar. I hadn't asked how they'd come to be for sale; it's one thing to be lied to, and quite another to ask for someone to do it.

"You better be careful with that gun," I told Diss as he aimed it at an imaginary enemy. "You're going to shoot something accidentally. Probably yourself."

"Just bein' ready." He had his finger looped in front of the trigger, rather than pointing straight so the gun couldn't be accidentally fired.

"Didn't anybody ever teach you what to do with your trigger finger?" I asked. It was supposed to be the setup for a joke—it involved insertion in another body part—but Diss got defensive before I got to the punch line.

"I know what the hell I'm doing. I was in Special Forces."

"Hey, you know what, Diss?" I told him, "Stop playing with the gun, start acting serious, all right?"

"I got it, Sarge. I got it." He made a show of securing the rifle. "I was in Special Forces. I know what I'm doing."

"You were a rigger."

"That, too. I was on an A Team, Sarge. Same as you."

"You don't have to bullshit me, all right?"

"Whatdaya mean?"

"I know you weren't in Special Forces."

"Shit, yeah I was. C Company, Third Battalion, Twentieth SFGA."

The unit he named was part of the National Guard. I knew they'd been called into Afghanistan during the war, but I could tell he was bluffing. And for some reason I was feeling just ornery enough to call him on it.

"What'd you do?" I asked.

"Eighteen. Medic."

Well, he had the designation right. Finally I realized it made no sense to keep poking him—all he was going to do was spin out more fantasies. At this point, I was stuck with him anyway, so why keep kicking him?

I let it drop—but he didn't.

"Why don't you believe me?" Diss insisted. He put his face practically in mine.

"Who says I don't believe you?"

"Sarge, I can tell by your voice."

"You don't seem like someone who was in Afghanistan during the war."

"I didn't say I was here during the war. Did I say that? I wasn't. I was sitting on my rump back home, twiddling my thumbs. I should've been here. I should've been in Iraq, too."

"Careful what you're doing with that gun."

He looked at it a second, then put it down on the ground.

"All right, Diss. Relax. Pick up the gun. Just be serious, okay?"

"I'm sorry, Sarge. I'm sorry."

"Call me Jack, okay?"

"Sorry."

He stooped down and picked up the rifle, his manner subdued, almost humble. When he spoke again, the wildness was gone from his voice; he spoke calmly, like a normal person, like a person who wasn't in Paktika, out on the edge.

"You know what I was doing before I came over here?" he asked. "You know what I was doing?"

I shook my head.

"I was working as a janitor in the local school. Nights. I used to have a gun shop, but it went bust."

"Why don't you use your medical training, get a job as a paramedic?"

"I don't want to be a nurse."

"Be a paramedic then. Physician's assistant."

"Fancy words for a nurse."

I shrugged, and went to walk the perimeter. I still didn't believe him, of course, but it really didn't make any difference what I believed. My head was pounding, and it was two long hours before Hokum's shift.

"I know what you're thinking," said Diss when I got back. "You're thinking I should save people, right? I don't want to save people. It ain't worth it."

"I don't think you should do anything, except watch what the hell's going on around here. We don't want anybody sneaking up on us, right?"

I could see the whiteness of his eyes, staring at me.

"Right, Sarge, you're right," he said. "Nothin' gonna get close while I'm here."

NOTHING did, but that was probably because anyone interested in checking us out already had.

I woke Hokum and Bajaar a little after one o'clock and tried to sleep for a while. Things drifted in and out of my head, good stuff like Sharon, the day we got married, bad stuff, like the bad-ass drug dealer's friends who tried to avenge him back in Kabul. And then there was the weird dream, or fragment of a dream: I was playing football, receiving a kickoff. I took the ball to the right and started running, and in two steps I was in the middle of a poppy field. The purple flowers had miniature heads on them—people wearing cloths wrapped around their heads, like some of the Afghans we'd met during the day. I kept running for the goalposts, but they stayed in the distance.

At least I didn't dream about playing soccer in the minefield.

THE forward operating base near Urgun was manned by a few hundred American troops, along with a smaller contingent of the Afghan army. When I'd last been here, it had only just been established, but the key features remained: mud huts and camels that marched by every morning.

The base commander's office was in one of the wattle huts, about the size of a toolshed back home. He had an AC and running water. He offered me a shower as soon as we met.

"I smell that bad?"

"You do, actually."

"Maybe later."

"My colonel back at Sharan says you're looking for Mercury Conrad."

"That's right. He had a contract to teach some of the police forces south and east of here. We had a contract," I said, correcting myself. "But he was handling it."

"How well do you know Mercury Conrad?" He leaned back in his chair, his hands behind his neck and his arms extended. The commander was a major. Ordinarily an FOB of this size and importance would have a lieutenant colonel at the helm. There were a lot of ways to interpret this; I decided the major was particularly effective, earning the extra responsibility and headaches because he was the best man for the job, regardless of rank.

"I know Merc pretty well," I told him. "We served together."

"Good soldier?"

"Damn good one."

The major got up. "Take a walk with me."

We went out into the base, walking along one of the walls. He kept stopping to talk to his men, and I couldn't figure out what he was up to. Then we went to a lookout post, basically a guard tower built of prefab concrete that stood at the edge of the compound and looked out over the valley below. I followed as he climbed up the metal steps to the observation deck. The thing reminded me of a backyard fort my cousin's father built for him when we were kids, except that had been built of wood.

"Hey, Gerry, how's it hanging?" the major said to the soldier manning the post.

"Not bad, sir. Real quiet."

"Go grab a smoke," said the major. "Be back in five minutes."

The private scrambled down the steps.

The major pointed eastward. "Those mountains are Pakistan."

"I'm pretty familiar with the territory."

"There could be an entire army out there, the Pakistanis would never see it."

True enough.

"Is there an army out there?" I asked.

"The Taliban are waiting until we leave. They're counting the days."

"How many of them are there?"

"Couple of hundred. We sweep through Gayan, they disappear. Why are you smiling? Doesn't sound like that much?"

"No," I told him. Here, a few hundred men could have a big impact, if they were well led and disciplined, qualities that Taliban troops sometimes, though not always, displayed. "Just that they disappear. They used to do the same to us."

"Why change what works, right?"

"Is Merc out there?" I asked.

"I don't know where your friend is. He *was* here. He had his training programs, setting them up with the locals. They didn't do much, though."

"Why not?"

"Police weren't being paid. Central government didn't think it was a priority."

"I thought those sorts of problems were long gone."

"Can't believe everything you read."

"When was this?"

"Couple of months ago. But your friend knew they weren't going to work. He was recruiting."

"For his army?"

"If it were an army, I'd have had to do something to stop it."

I was quiet for a minute, not so much because I was trying to figure out how to get him to tell me more, but because I wasn't sure how much more he actually knew.

"So Merc's in Pakistan?" I asked finally.

"I don't know where he is," said the major. And he turned and went down, ending the tour, and our conversation.

21

URGUN

That afternoon, Khan and I went to the bazaar in town to talk to some of the camel traders. We weren't interested in their animals; I hoped to pick up something useful about Merc. They knew who I was talking about—the "dark beard American" they called him. They claimed he was south, or east, or in Kabul. No one had done business with him, or so they said.

The local police chief claimed to know Merc well. He said he'd even taken a class with him. As far as I knew, Merc hadn't taught any of the classes himself, but the chief had the buzz words down, peppering his Pashto with "overwhelming force" and "preemptive intelligence," straight from Merc's PowerPoint presentations to security chiefs at big-buck conventions.

He was as impressed as any corporate Pooh-Bah. "Mistuh Conrad" was a great leader, an inspiration to anyone who aspired to be a true Afghan, declared the chief.

"Why?"

The chief clenched his right fist and pounded it into his left palm. Khan had trouble getting the sense of the words that followed.

"Straight," he said finally.

Merc spoke Pashto maybe a little better than I did—basic concepts and needs only. He could do a class in basic security techniques, but for anything complicated he'd need an interpreter—or at least I thought he would.

The police chief told us he'd grown up fighting the Russians and had seen many wars, but Merc was the first man who'd truly inspired him. I didn't doubt it was true from the way he spoke, but how Merc had pulled it off I wasn't sure.

WE left Urgun the next morning, driving along the ridge south. The road was well packed, comparatively free of pockmarks, and easy to see—a regular interstate highway.

Settlements were scattered on either side, hamlets and the occasional village tucked in crevices and shallow valleys on either side of the ridge. Within an hour the population had started to thin and the road became rockier. South of the district capital of Sarobi—a village with maybe fifteen hundred people—the mud huts thinned even further. Poppies grew in some of the fields not far from the main road.

We were about two hours south of Sarobi, working our way down a washboard section of the road toward Gomal when Diss hit the horn behind us. I jerked my head out the window in time to see the other truck skid sideways across the road, bound up and then spin against a pair of large rocks before sliding to a halt in the ditch next to the roadbed.

Khan had the good sense not to stop our truck until we were well out of the way. I jumped out and ran back. Bajaar sat white-faced in his seat, his knuckles white as they gripped the door.

Diss was laughing his ass off.

"Tire blew," he managed finally. "Tire blew and I lost it!"

"You think that's funny?"

"It sure felt like it. What a ride. Wooo-houu."

Actually, he'd blown two tires, both on the left side. Before we could change them we had to get the truck onto halfway level ground, which meant pulling it out from the ditch. Since the truck had wedged itself into the rocks, that took nearly two hours. By the time we had the new wheels on we had less than an hour of daylight left. I decided we'd stay nearby for the night.

While Hokum and Diss finished up with the truck I took Khan

and Bajaar down the road to scout around. We found an open space on the side of a cliff about a half mile away, far enough off the road that we couldn't be seen easily. It had a good view of the surrounding countryside and, while not completely inaccessible from below, anyone coming up toward us would be exposed for a good hundred yards at least.

I sent the kid down the hill to scout while I went down the other side of the road to see if there was anyone nearby who'd spot us. I found a cluster of huts about a mile and half to the west, gathered around a narrow streambed. Smoke curled from one of the buildings, probably a dinner fire. I couldn't see anyone in the fields near the house.

I was walking back when I heard Bajaar scream. I bolted up the hill to the road and ran to the trucks, gun ready. Khan was standing there with the kid, a hand on each shoulder, trying to calm him down. Bajaar was shaking his head violently, talking loudly and, I gathered, incoherently. Finally, he just stopped talking.

"What's wrong?" I asked Khan.

"He wants us to see something down below the cliff. He claims he can't describe it. We have to see it for ourselves."

"Let's go then."

I touched Bajaar's shoulder, to have him lead the way. He jerked up, then wouldn't move.

"Stay with him," I told Khan. "I'll check in by radio every ten minutes."

Radios in Afghanistan, even good ones, can be notoriously fickle. The cliffs and canyons seem to eat the radio waves rather than deflect them. Our radios were middle-of-the-road German models, not quite as good as the gear we used when I was in Special Forces, so it wasn't surprising that I lost contact with Khan and the others when I reached the foot of the hill. I adjusted the headset, figuring that eventually I'd be back in range.

What had looked like an open field from above was actually the top of another cliff; the shadows had simply blurred the edges. I walked across it gingerly, gun ready. When I got near the edge I dropped to my hands and knees and peered downward.

I was on the roof of a large overhang, maybe a hundred yards long. Hanging over the edge, I thought I saw a roof. At first I thought it was some sort of optical illusion, but as I worked my way to the right, gradually another building came into view, and then another. A small village had been built into the cavern below the hills.

At the far end of the ledge I was on, water or perhaps the wind had eroded a V-shaped wedge downward, a kind of natural staircase that was easy to get down after the first few feet. It turned away from the buildings I'd seen, and met what looked like a manmade path, with chiseled stones in a few spots. When I finally reached level ground I had to turn a sharp corner to get back to the cavern.

When I reached the corner I realized what had frightened Bajaar. A human skull lay wedged in a crevice, right at the spot where he might have put his hand out for a handhold to ease around the bend. It had been there for some time; the bone had a bleached look to it, grayish brown rather than white or black.

The settlement looked like the pueblos in New Mexico and Arizona, though on a much smaller scale. The building walls were the color of the surrounding dirt; here and there a section had crumbled away, but most were intact. The doorways were open; whatever wood had once guarded them was long gone.

I stopped in front of the first house and tried the radio again. Still didn't work. The area had to be checked out, but I would have preferred not doing it alone. On the other hand, by the time I went all the way back and got Hokum or Diss, the light would be completely gone.

Leaning in the door of the first house, I saw what looked like a pair of sticks on the floor at the right. I froze, then gradually leaned in farther.

The sticks were leg bones. They belonged to a full skeleton, who sat intact against the wall. Two other skeletons sat to his left, mouths open in death grins.

There was another room beyond. I walked across the dirt floor, rifle pressed against my hip. I had to duck down to get through the doorway. Five more skeletons, smaller than the others, sat against the far wall.

As I backed out, I heard something outside, a rock maybe, falling down the hillside. I went to the door and got down on one knee, listening. For a second I thought I had imagined the sound, then I heard it again—a quick scuffle, maybe the sound of feet padding over the nearby dirt.

"Hokum?" I said, loud enough to be heard nearby, I hoped. But not quite loud enough for my voice to carry very far.

There was no answer.

"Khan?"

I studied the ground in front of the hut, trying to find a shadow or anything that might let me know if someone was out there, and where they were.

I heard the sound again. It was definitely footsteps, moving stealthily, and in my direction. I straightened, then flattened myself against the wall, figuring at this point my best bet was to wait.

22

RANIKAY TANZAY, AFGHANISTAN, FIVE YEARS BEFORE

THE second time Merc saved my life, we were working an area about twenty miles to the east of the buildings where I found the skeletons, on the other side of a range of mountains. We'd been dropped by helicopter two days before; we were scouting for a group of Afghan army and special forces soldiers who'd set up a hammer-and-anvil sweep through the valley.

The idea was that they were going to chase the terrorists into an ambush at the far end of a five-mile-long valley. Our job was, first, to make sure they didn't have reinforcements lurking down there, and then to watch them as they fled, just in case they stopped somewhere along the way. If they did stop, we'd call in an air strike to take them out. And it would be a *serious* air strike—two B-52s were somewhere to our south, ready to turn mountains into dust on our word.

There were three of us. A guy we called "Joker" was the third member of the team. His real name was Sydney Greenberg; he was a Jew from Long Island, a fact he liked to point out at every opportunity. As in: "Even a Jew from Long Island knows this is bullshit." And: "I want to show those ragheads that a Jew from Long Island ain't gonna take it." Or: "Where can a Jew from Long Island get some red meat chow?"

The funny thing about Joker was that although he kept mentioning his religion, he admitted he didn't believe in God. There's an old saying to the effect that there are no atheists in foxholes. Joker was proof that it isn't true. I've never heard anyone talk about religion or atheism as matter-of-factly as Joker, who could go on at great lengths about why God couldn't exist. Usually, though, his explanations came in short sentences when he'd point to something horrific, like a bombed-out house or a corpse or an IED, and say, "See?"

Most of us don't spend a lot of time working out what we believe before we get into the army, or before we become adults for that matter. We kind of go with the flow of whatever made sense to us when we were seven or eight, before our hormones kicked in and we stopped thinking about anything that didn't have to do with sex. But Joker had spent a lot of time pondering it. He could go head to toe with anybody, even quote back Bible verses at them. I saw him wear down a couple of evangelicals at base camp who tried double-teaming him a few days before our mission. I saw one of them burning his Bible the next morning, swearing off God for good.

The night we went out we were dropped off around 0100, two klicks from our first lookout spot. Things went real well; the night was dark but with our night-vision gear we had no trouble seeing. The maps were old—the same 1:100,000s the Russians had used—but they were accurate here and we had GPS gear with us to help. We made our objective inside a half hour. There was no Taliban, and no anyone, as far as we could see up and down the valley. We dug in and waited.

The following night we got a message that the operation was being delayed forty-eight hours. We were supposed to stay in place. In theory this was doable; we had food and water for ten days, and our mission was only supposed to last for four. So you throw two more days on top of that and we still had a good margin for error.

Joker, though, got antsy. It was the tail end of winter and pretty damn cold, even when the sun came out. He started pushing to do a recon around the far side of the ridge, a good two and a half miles away, arguing that the Taliban might be sneaking up on us.

It was possible, I guess, theoretically possible—though my feeling at the time was that no one was going to be sneaking around anywhere. I doubted there were any fighters for the Afghan soldiers to find farther west, let alone around here. Merc was in charge of the team, though, and he thought it was a good idea. Joker set out around dusk, skipping across the slope like a monkey who's just stolen a banana.

He was supposed to go for exactly one hour, then report back. If anything happened—he saw something, the radio didn't work—he was supposed to turn tail and come back.

He didn't check in. Given the topography, though, we didn't get too upset. When we hadn't heard from him four hours later, we figured something was up. But a storm was moving in, a quick-hitting blast of sleet, which came down to the accompaniment of thunder.

"I screwed up letting him go, huh?" said Merc as we huddled under the tarp shelter we'd set up.

"I dunno," I said. It seemed to me smarter to lie; no sense laying guilt on him. Joker *had* wanted to go, and it *was* possible we could be ambushed, and even though he hadn't come back yet, most likely he was on his way back and had taken shelter somewhere because of the weather.

"I'll stay up," Merc told me. "You catch some sleep."

I got my usual two hours before Merc kicked my leg and told me we had traffic in the valley. I crawled out to the ridge and peered down on the world's largest collection of mules. Donkeys were everywhere, flooding through the valley, south to north. Maybe one or two out of every five had gear tied to their backs; the rest were packless. At least fifty men, all armed with Kalashnikovs, were accompanying them.

"Taliban or tribesmen?" I asked.

"There's a difference?" said Merc. He wanted to call a strike in, figuring it made more sense to get the slow-moving animals and their human companions here and now than to wait for an operation that hadn't even begun yet.

"What do we do about Joker?" I asked.

"What do you mean?"

"If he's in the valley, he's going to get flattened."

"He's not in the valley," said Merc. He said it with the dead certainty you'd use if you were talking about something you'd known your whole life, like your mother's name.

"I know he wasn't *planning* on going into the valley," I said. "But—"

"There's no but, Jack. If we don't call a strike in now, these guys get away. Besides, Joker'll know to get out as soon he sees them. If he has any sense."

"If he had any sense he'd be back here."

Merc called it in. At just over a mile from the target area, we were close enough to hear the whistle of the first bombs as they came down. The sound was remarkably similar to what you hear in the movies. Most of war's not like that—movies, TV, books: there's no way to duplicate the way sounds grab you in the throat and change your voice, the way the smell gets in behind your skull and becomes part of your skin. But the bomb drop was right out of an old War World II movie.

What followed wasn't. The explosions were so intense I fell from my knees. Part of the opposite cliff gave way with an enormous roar. Above the thunderous tumult rose a scream—one solid wail, the cry of a huge, wounded beast, echoing through the valley.

"Wow," said Merc. "Wow."

It probably took an hour for the dust to settle enough for us to use the night gear effectively. There were rocks and bits of animal and men everywhere. We couldn't go down and put anybody out of their misery—we were still holding a covert position—so we sat there and watched while dozens of animals and at least ten men writhed and moaned themselves to death. A couple of mules picked their way out of the rocks, going back in the direction they'd come. If there were any men among the survivors, I didn't see them.

The problem now was finding Joker. We hoped he'd taken cover during the bombing and was just waiting until there was a bit more light to make his way back. We had breakfast, called in a report on the bombing, and then flipped a coin to see who would go and look for him. I won, and twenty minutes later I was scrambling across a pile of bowling-ball-sized rocks about a mile away. The rocks filled a crevice below a cliff wall I thought was too perilous to climb across. Something caught my eye at the extreme right, a long straight line standing out in an ocean of circles. I stopped, stared at it, waited for my brain to process the image into something it could identify.

Rifle.

I went forward a bit, making sure I wasn't walking into an ambush, then circled back. The gun was an M4 automatic rifle. One M4's about the same as another if it's not yours, I guess, but I knew when I saw it that it had to be Joker's; there was no one else around for it to belong to.

I crouched over the spot, then started sweeping my eyes in a semicircle, looking for its owner.

I didn't see him until I stood up. Something lay among the dirty yellow rocks about ten yards below me. As I got closer, the gray turned to a blotchy brown camo, and I realized I was looking at part of a uniform.

Joker had been buried under an avalanche of rocks, one to two layers deep. I started pulling them off, even though it was pretty obvious he was dead. Most of the rocks were between thirty and forty pounds, but a few were considerably more, far too heavy to lift or even roll without help. I got close enough to the back of his head to stick my hand on his neck and make sure he didn't have a pulse. Then I replaced the rocks I'd removed, took a GPS reading, and went back to Merc.

"They have a new spot for us to check out," he told me as soon as I got back. "They want us there by nightfall. It's fifteen miles from here."

"What about Joker?"

"I'll tell them later."

"But—"

"They've already started the operation. They won't be able to spare any forces to pick him up right now anyway."

"Well, that sucks."

"He's dead, Jacky. What do you want?"

THERE was no way of knowing whether Joker had died before, during, or after the air strike. Any of those possibilities was plausible. He might have been on the rocks when the bombs started hitting, or he might have fallen from the cliff I'd skirted well beforehand. He could have been crushed hours earlier or later, when the side of the hill gave way. But it was hard not to make a connection between his death and the bombing.

If it bothered Merc, he didn't mention it. He just tore down the hide we'd constructed and moved on.

Without Joker, we had more gear to carry, so it was dark by the time we found the spot they wanted us to scout from. It overlooked a fork in a valley, not quite as narrow as the pass they'd had us watching before.

There was one other crucial difference—seven huts stood on the north side of the fork, in the shadow of the hill. There were no guards or defenses that we could spot, but there were animals—more donkeys, as it happened—and we saw a total of three or four people tend to them or pass in front of the windows of the nearest houses.

We called for instructions. It was funny at first; whoever Merc was talking to on the other side of the line didn't want to believe him when he said there was a village there. Finally we were told we must be in the wrong place. Three GPS readings later, we were ordered to sit tight and wait for further instructions.

Meanwhile, we heard action back to the northeast, a heavy bomb strike. The explosions were so far away it sounded like a train passing in the distance.

"Looks like they're following the game plan," said Merc. "Oughta be down here by tomorrow."

"You figure this village is on their side, or ours?"

"They're on whatever side has the guns at the moment," he told me. "You want to call in the air strike?"

"We're supposed to wait for instructions."

"That's what they're going to tell us to do. Hit the village."

"How can they? These people are civilians."

"I doubt it."

"I don't." I said that even though I had no proof of anything.

"Why would you think they're not on the Taliban's side? Where do you think the guys with the donkeys were going?"

"Not here, necessarily."

"You had no problem hitting them."

"They had to be Taliban. They were moving at night."

"That's not very good logic, Jacky."

"You think they were civilians?"

"No way."

"Then what's wrong with my logic? Those people are staying put at night, not going out fighting or running over to Pakistan."

"You think the people down there have signs that say which side they're on?" said Merc. "We can go down and ask them, but they'll look at our weapons and they'll tell us they're on our side."

"I'm not calling in an air strike."

Merc scratched the stubble on the side of his face. We hadn't let our beards grow to blend in with the tribesmen, like the Special Forces who worked directly with them did. We just didn't want to spare the water to shave.

"I'm not calling it in," I told him.

"I know, Jacky. I will. If it comes to that."

WE still hadn't received any instructions by 0600 when a figure appeared at the eastern end of the pass. He was on foot, alone, with an AK47 slung over his shoulder. He took the southern fork, the one on the right from our vantage point, walking at a good but not panicked pace. The fact that he was carrying a rifle meant nothing here; after twentysome years of civil war, rifles were as commonplace as pens or pocketknives, tools you carried to work with you every day, no matter what your profession. I lost him after a mile or so, the view obscured by the twists in the pass.

In the meantime, the hamlet woke up. Three women had appeared, doing various chores, and a pair of older men had set up on stools in front of one of the houses. Merc radioed this all back in. The response was basically thanks for the info, continue to hold.

Around 0730 the guy who had passed down the right fork came back up it. He was moving a little faster, but remained nonchalant enough to keep his rifle on its strap at his shoulder. He made his way up around the bend and back in the direction he'd originally come from. Twenty minutes later, he was back—this time with two dozen friends. These guys were definitely fighters; not only did they have AKs but a few were carrying grenade launchers and belts for a machine gun.

Merc got on the horn and gave an update while I watched the troops. I expected them to go down the fork like their scout had. Instead, they went to the village. I was still trying to figure it out when one of them started firing at the old men in front of the hut. In the next instant, they were raking the houses with riflefire. Without thinking, I zeroed my gun on the bastard who'd started it all, and began firing.

Merc started cursing and grabbed his M4, firing as well. In the space of maybe ninety seconds, we'd both burned two mags of bullets and dropped at least eighteen of their guys. The six that were left retreated beyond the buildings, off to our right and out of view.

"We can flank them by going over that ridge there," said Merc, pointing to a rock outcropping about thirty yards away. "Otherwise they get away and warn their friends. Or come for us."

"Yeah," I grunted, already moving in that direction.

We'd had a serious advantage, catching them by surprise and firing from above. But now the survivors were in a better position; they outnumbered us and presumably knew the terrain far better than we did. By all rights we should've stayed put.

No, by all rights, I never should have fired. That was a screwup. It was instinctual, but it was still a screwup.

Even so, I'd probably do it again the same way, without hesitating or thinking.

WHEN I got to the ridge I saw that at least three of them were hunkered down on a ledge about seventy-five yards away and a good four hundred feet below me. I can tell you they didn't beat the Russians with tactics like that. Pumping a grenade into their spot was easier than sinking a wad of paper in the office wastebasket.

"Do another," said Merc, after the first one exploded.

I put the second into the dust that was still rising. When the smoke cleared, we could see three bodies from where we were. Of course, we didn't know how many had been there in the first place, or if there were others around in the area we hadn't seen. So we made our way down really slowly, stopping and watching, stopping and watching.

It took about two hours before we were finally at that spot. There were five dead men in the crevice, and another two who'd been wounded earlier lay a few yards away. One had bled to death; the other had maybe an hour to go. He looked up at me, wanting to be put out of his misery. I pointed my rifle down but Merc stopped me before I could fire.

"We don't want to tell anyone we're here just yet," he said.

Then he dropped to his knees and slit the poor guy's throat.

I moved on to the buildings, about fifty yards away. Two animals had died in the crossfire, and there were two bodies of fighters nearby, but no one alive.

The rest of the Taliban fighters had been cut down in front of the houses. All but one were dead. The lone exception had crawled into the rocks, trying to get away; he left a trail of blood. Merc followed the trail while I flanked around to cover him. The Taliban fighter was hiding beneath a small bush, still alive, but just barely; Merc killed him the same way he'd killed the other, with his knife.

I walked back to the house. The two old villagers who'd been outside when the gunmen began shooting lay in the dust, crumpled, long gone. I could see a woman's leg inside the door of the first hut as I approached. I stepped over her shot-up body inside, and searched the place—not that there was much to search. The hut consisted of one room, and had nothing in it we would call furniture.

The next two houses were empty.

There were bullet holes all across the front of the third house, but the wood door was intact. I pushed it open, and saw someone huddled near a mattress on the floor to the left.

At least I'd saved one person, I thought to myself, starting in.

"Jacky!"

As long as I live, I'll remember the way Merc screamed my name. He was right behind me. As I jerked back I saw what he saw—the woman who'd been hunkered down had a pistol at her bosom and her hand was on the trigger.

The gun flashed. I thought to myself: *Goddamn you, bitch. I just saved your life.* Then the next thing I knew I was rolling around outside, and smoke was pouring from the building.

I started patting myself for the bullet hole.

"She missed you, right?" said Merc. He was crouched next to me, sipping water.

"What the hell?"

"She had a gun and a grenade," he told me. "You don't remember?"

I didn't. I still don't. I remember the look in her eyes, though; she was going to kill me.

"I shot her," added Merc.

"And the grenade went off?"

"Don't you think?"

"But we were on her side," I said. "I saved her life."

He just stared at me, like I was out of my mind. And maybe I was.

23

THE CITY OF THE DEAD

I STOOD inside the door of the clay hut underneath the cliff, waiting for whoever was walking toward me to come in. The steps dragged through the ground outside, scuffling, as if they were pushing away little mounds of dirt in front of them.

I glanced across the room and saw the skeletons watching me.

As a shadow filled the doorway I sprang, hitting the person in the neck with the butt end of my gun. His rifle clattered to the ground and he fell back. I spun, ready for his backup—but it was just Diss, sprawled on the ground beneath me, trying to grab his breath back.

"What the hell are you doing?" I told him.

"Looking for you, Sarge." He was choking.

"Next time, announce yourself, or you'll join the skeletons."

"What skeletons?"

His eyes bugged out when he went into the first building, literally bulging from their sockets.

"This is what I mean," he said.

"What do you mean, what?"

"This is what I mean."

That was the most coherent thing out of his mouth for the next half hour. We searched the place, making damn sure there were only dead people here. Finally satisfied, and more than a little spooked, Diss and I went back to the others up near the road.

KHAN had no explanation for the skeletons or the village. He swore there was no such place as this in modern Afghanistan; we must have stumbled on a prehistoric site.

"Unless the Russians did it," he added, glancing toward Hokum.

Hokum stared back. He pulled out a small CD player and plugged his earphones in one at a time, eyes steadied on Khan.

"You oughta be careful not to insult him," Diss said to Khan when Hokum finally turned on the music and walked away.

Later on, Khan and I sat watching the road, talking about how long it would take us to get to Gomal, and what we'd find there. I let him talk; I was a little worried he might be thinking this was as far as he was going to go. Somehow, he segued from the little hamlet near the dried-up river we would aim at in the morning, and began talking about the skeletons I'd seen. Obviously a prehistoric site, he said, not the remains of a more recent massacre. Without even having seen the village himself, he spun theories about what life there had been like.

In Khan's cosmology, people and dinosaurs roamed the earth together. And so did all sorts of wild animals and spirits. It was as if he took all of earth's history and compressed it into a decade or so, pushed the different biomes together. Jungles were next to mountains, snow-capped peaks were over Grand Canyon–like valleys.

I could see how someone from Afghanistan would arrange things in their mind that way. The peaks and valleys are right next to each other, or close enough that you can see one from the heart of the other. High desert and tundra mix together. If it weren't for the last decade of drought, the juxtapositions would probably be even more extreme. Khan was old enough to remember prosperous farms in the north of the country, farms that he said would make a rich man weep.

And a weeping man, rich. It was some sort of saying.

Then, without a noticeable or logical segue, he started talking about leopards. Snow leopards had once roamed this entire territory, up and down the different mountain ranges and well south and east into Pakistan. They were solitary hunters, working the crags in the rocks, moving up and down the cliffs they liked to use to spring on their prey. A good-sized leopard might weigh a hundred and twenty-five pounds. He'd have short forelimbs and big hind legs that would help him jump and scramble after prey. His chest would be enormous, adapted to the thin air and the cold of the higher elevations.

In spring, the young would roam down into the valleys, seeking mates and new territory. Maybe that's what had killed the people in the huts, Khan theorized; a hungry leopard.

I didn't argue with him, I just listened as he went on about the big cats, whom he called perfect hunters, well-bred killers. A snow leopard could kill an animal three times its size. It wanted to do that; the bigger the better: a large animal would provide food for days, and it was easier to chase birds and other carrion feeders away than find a decent-sized meal. The lust for big blood and difficult kills was an adaptation to the environment, just like the legs and chest, the intricate color of the rosettes on his fur. Violence was an adaptation to the environment, bred into the leopard over millennia.

The same with us.

"No leopards here tonight," said Khan finally, getting up. "I sleep tonight. Tomorrow, we find your friend."

THERE was a time, before Sharon, when making love was taking a sledgehammer to the woman's body, when it was punishment, and pain—not so much physical, not bruises and blood, but pain still, enough hurt to make me feel. Pain because all it was was sex, pushing, no urging, no kissing, just pushing.

I told myself it was the army that did that to me but it wasn't the army at all. The army was the only place I felt alive, and this was the opposite of being alive, a substitute for death.

Had it gotten that way with Sharon at the end?

It was desperate in its own way.

What did she think? Some nights she'd lie there, just close her eyes and lie there.

Maybe she imagined herself with other lovers. Maybe she

thought of the places where she would go, the dresses, the car, the big house—the consolations, the payoff for sledgehammer sex.

Why would it matter to me if she had other lovers? Especially now.

She'd seen me as a money machine, and she'd made me look at the world that way, too. If she was sleeping with someone else—it was almost a relief. It meant I wasn't the only sucker.

WE got going just after dawn, driving a little more slowly so we could do a better job avoiding the ruts and saving our tires. By midmorning, we were across the border into the Gomal district. The road roughly paralleled a river to our right as we drove east. About three miles from the point where the river and road would intersect, we saw the wreckage of a truck blocking the way.

I had Khan stop about two hundred yards from it. The terrain around the truck dropped off sharply, but going around it wasn't the biggest problem. There were plenty of places for ambushers to be hiding nearby.

"What do you think?" I asked Hokum after climbing on the back of the truck with him.

"We don't sit here."

At least he was thinking the obvious, I guess.

I jumped down to the road and told Khan to wait for my signal. Then I slid down along the steeper side of the roadway and trotted in the direction of the truck, checking to make sure we could use the embankment to get by. I reasoned that, if this was a blockade for an ambush, whoever had set it up would count on their victim taking the easier path. I watched the ground for IEDs—improvised explosive devices, also known as bombs.

The Iraqi Sunnis have elevated IEDs to an exotic art form, making use of all manner of weapons left over from their hero Sadaam. An Iraqi IED could include a five-hundred-pound bomb and a shaped-charge; calling it improvised is almost an insult.

In Afghanistan, IEDs tended to be much smaller and more prosaic. Often they were warheads from unexploded rockets or rocket-propelled grenades, sometimes mortar shells, rigged with crude devices to make them explode on command. They didn't always go off, but that didn't make them easier to be around if they did.

The truck was an old Russian vehicle, very possibly dating from the 1950s. It had been burned to a dark black, and not one piece of recognizable cloth or plastic remained. The stones beneath the tires looked as if they had erupted themselves.

How long had it been there? More than a day, certainly, but I doubted it had been there *too* much longer than that; the major back at Urgun would have known about it and, even if he didn't do something about it—unlikely, I thought—he would have at least mentioned it, since I told him the route I was taking.

Five yards beyond the front of the truck, I started to climb back onto the road. I was just about to fire a burst to signal Khan to come ahead, when somebody else did it for me—someone up on the hill, and clearly not friendly.

I threw myself down, rolling across the embankment as bullets flew down. Huge chunks of dirt and stone shot around me. There was no question of firing back effectively; I stayed as close to the ground as I could, sliding down the hill until I was out of range of whatever the hell was chewing up the road. Then I ran forward, hoping to get some sort of angle and drop a grenade on the machine-gunner—assuming I could find him.

Khan, Hokum, and the others didn't wait. Khan floored the gas and Hokum laid on the machine gun, pouring lead into the hillside where the gun was. By the time I started back up the hill they were already barreling across the embankment, dust flying and bullets sailing in every direction. I aimed the grenade launcher in the general direction of the machine-gunner, and fired. Where the grenade hit or whether it even exploded I have no idea; I was too busy scrambling to get out of the way of the pickup truck to pay any attention.

The slope had to be a good thirty degrees, and if it was forty-five or even sixty I wouldn't have been surprised. The pickup held on to the terrain pretty well, however, and while it bounced precariously once or twice, enough of the tires stayed on the ground for it to make it back up to the road surface. One moment I was trying to jump to the right and not get whacked by its side; the next second I was humping with all my might to get into it.

Hokum tore through the end of the belt as the truck reached the road. Instead of trying to reload he picked up his 416 and fired a grenade round, then emptied the magazine. By that time I'd jumped up into the truck bed and begun firing myself. I probably burned through the magazine in three or four seconds, but I kept pressing the trigger for another thirty. Finally I realized nothing was coming out, and went to reload. Our other truck cleared the smoke near the blockade. I saw the nose veer up toward the road; then all of a sudden the truck spun back and flipped, rolling over itself three times before stopping on its rooftop.

The Dushka machine gun that had been spitting at us stopped firing. I half jumped, half fell from the pickup, stumbling and falling flat on my face before managing to get to the embankment and run down to the other truck.

Bajaar hung half out the window. The angle of his head didn't look all that good. I lifted him on my back and ran toward the first truck. I put him down as gently as I could in the back, trying hard not to drop him. Then I ran back to get Diss. He'd crawled about ten feet from the pickup when I got there. Before I could reach down to pull him to his feet the road above us exploded, the gunner on the hill zeroing in on the truck. I was all reaction now, jerking Diss onto my right shoulder, running with him, pulling and maybe firing my gun, though if I did there was no way I aimed it at anything, and there was no likelihood at all that I hit anything. Diss finally got his legs under him and we ran together to the other truck, which was already moving, though at a walker's pace. Hokum laid on the machine gun, and in a few minutes, we were far enough away that I could breathe without being choked by the dust from the exploding terrain.

I'D saved a dead man. Not only had Bajaar had his neck snapped in the crash, but the machine gun had splintered bits of the truck and gear into his body; there were so many holes that if his broken neck hadn't killed him he would have bled to death in seconds anyway.

Diss, who'd claimed to be a medic, had trouble even looking at the body, let alone doing anything. I was the one who felt for his pulse, and realized he was gone.

We picked out a spot to bury the kid off the road about a quarter mile, a place marked by a triangular rock jutting from an otherwise flat stretch, making it easy to find even without a GPS device. Khan said there wouldn't be anyone coming to look, though; according to him, Bajaar had been orphaned shortly after birth, his parents killed by the Taliban in the endless war.

"That is the saddest thing," said Khan. "No one will mourn his passing."

I LEFT Diss by the truck as sentry while the rest of us went about digging a grave. We were down to one shovel and a tire iron as digging implements; the parched ground didn't give way easily. Hokum and I worked until we got the grave about three and a half feet deep, then Khan said some prayers in Arabic, and fired off Bajaar's AK47 as a sendoff. We shoveled and kicked the dirt back, covering the top with a layer of rocks.

The work made me thirsty. I stopped and took a swig of water, then two of bourbon. With the loss of the other truck, the half-filled flask in my hand represented my entire stock. For about the hundredth time since we left Kabul, I told myself I'd have to parcel it out in smaller doses and longer stretches. And for the millionth time since leaving Kabul, I told myself I didn't need it, even as I took another sip.

We were just topping off the grave when a single shot creased the air. I turned and saw two men ten yards away. One had a light machine gun pointed in our direction, the other an AK.

Reluctantly, I raised my hands, and told the others to do the same.

24

NEAR AMAKHEL (2)

THE guys who got the drop on us knew what they were doing. For one thing, they had us looking almost directly into the sun, which made it hard to focus on them. They were on a rise which gave them an advantage, both geographically and psychologically. And when they started toward us they remained spread out, with one guy flanking almost in a semicircle.

They wore the long shirts and loose trousers—salwar kameez—common among tribesmen, and had what looked like wrapped scarves on their heads. The man on the left was holding an American M249, also called a "SAW" or squad automatic weapon. The light machine guns were not readily available out here, and it was unlikely to have been given up without a serious fight.

"Tell them we're under the protection of Muhammad Mayden," I told Khan.

He glanced at me sideways. Mayden was a powerful warlord who played both sides of the fight; if anything, he was closer to the Taliban than to the central government.

"A lie here would be a death sentence," he warned.

"It's not a lie," I told him. "Say it."

Khan rattled something off. One of the men responded in Pashto that we should keep our hands up.

It was pretty lousy Pashto, thank God. We'd been ambushed not by Taliban, but by American soldiers.

"I'm an American," I told them, careful to keep my hands up.

"My name is Jack Pilgrim. I'm on my way to Gomal. I talked to your major back at Urgun. He said you guys were out here, but he had you farther east."

The man on the right with the AK laughed. The other continued to stare us down. Both guns were still pointed at our chests.

"We ran into some trouble a few miles back. Taliban has the road blocked with an old truck. We gave 'em hell but they got one of my vehicles, killed my man. We stopped to bury him."

"Jack Pilgrim," said the man who had laughed. "You da man, Jack. Is Pilgrim a real name, or a mission?"

"It's real. Been mine all my life."

"You left a dope for a guard, Jack Pilgrim. You have to be more careful out here."

"Good advice."

Hokum started to move. The man with the machine gun drew a line in the dirt with bullets about five feet in front of him. I was amazed none of the ricochets hit anyone.

"It's all right, Richie. I think we can trust them. Right, Jack Pilgrim?"

"Yeah, that's right," I told him. "We're on the same side."

"That's probably a lie, Jack. But we'll let you get away with that one. For now."

WE found Diss back under the truck, his hands and feet trussed and his mouth stuffed with his shirt. I had half a mind to leave him like that, and as soon as he started offering excuses I threatened to regag him. But it was my mistake, really, leaving him back there to stand guard. Hokum wouldn't have been surprised like he was, and I doubt two soldiers, even two Special Forces soldiers, could have taken him without using their weapons.

In that case, of course, the outcome might have been even worse.

There was another soldier, watching over the others from a vantage on the hill roughly a half mile away. We couldn't see him, but the SF guys who had grabbed us spoke to him through their radios. They called him "Vulture." The quiet guy with the machine gun was Dog. The talker was Man, as in "you da man," a phrase he used every ten minutes or so, like it was on a timer. It could be an insult: *You da man, Jack; you tell us which way to go.* It could be a compliment: *You got booze? You da man, Jack.* It could be just another expletive in a long string of curse words.

Diss and Khan got in the cab with me. Everybody else rode in the back. Man told me he'd tap on the roof when it was time to turn; until then, I was supposed to stick to the road.

"And drive as fast as you can, no stopping for anything. You da man."

I DIDN'T see the turnoff until we were right on top of it, and I didn't see their camp until after we parked and hiked around a pair of bends to find it. There were no buildings, just a pair of clearings, rocks, and three different caves, all shallow and unconnected, though there was enough of a natural trench in the terrain between them so a man could get from one to another and remain under cover.

They had a small cooking stove, utensils, and a large satellite dish and radio, but nothing in the way of furniture or anything like amenities. I got the impression that they moved constantly, using a slew of hides all through this area, each one stocked with provisions, ammo, and weapons. They wore native clothes and beards to blend in. From a distance they definitely looked like tribesmen. Up close it'd be a different story—their skin didn't have the parched look of someone who'd lived here all his life—but my guess is that by then it wouldn't matter. You only got that close if they wanted you to, or if you were dead.

Man was the NCO in charge. It was getting late and he told us we'd want to stay the night; traveling at dark was dangerous not because of the Taliban, but because air patrols would assume that anyone on the road after dark was Taliban, and we'd be fair game.

"Then we'd have to go scrape you up in the morning, which would be a pain."

"We'll stay."

"You da man, Jack. You da man."

According to Man, the people who'd set up the roadblock were probably not active Taliban guerrillas. More likely they were simply thieves, and inexperienced ones at that.

"Experienced thieves would've killed you, Jack Pilgrim." Man grinned. "Put a couple of bullets through your fancy tac vest. Twelve point seven round goes through everything."

Hokum made a face, but I've learned that criticism, even when harsh, can have its benefits.

"How do I avoid the experienced ones?" I asked.

"Don't drive on the road, number one. Number two, when you do, go fast."

"Number two cost me a pair of tires and almost got half of my team killed."

"You da man. Heads you lose, tails you lose."

This was apparently so funny to him that he bent over and nearly split his loose pants laughing. When he calmed down, I told him I was going to the district capital at Gomal, which according to my map was another ten kilometers away.

"There any way to get there without taking the road?" I asked.

"You're fucked, Jack Pilgrim. You gotta take the road. If you're goin' there."

"Why are you going there?" asked Vulture. It was the first thing he'd said since he came into the camp, changing places with Richie, whose turn it was to act as sentry.

"I have to talk to the police chief there."

"No police chief there," said Vulture.

"What happened to him?" I asked.

Vulture seemed vaguely familiar, but I couldn't say for sure that I'd met him. He was a black guy with a round, chubby face, though his body was skinnier than Bajaar's had been. He stood about five ten, and was somewhere in his late twenties or early thirties.

"Ran off. You don't remember me, do you, Sarge? I was a rigger when you were on temporary duty at Fort Bragg."

"I'm sorry, I guess I didn't recognize you." I still didn't, but I held out my hand to shake his. Truth is, I didn't even remember which assignment he was talking about. And all I could think of was Diss's claim that he'd been a rigger, too.

"You're out here looking for Merc Conrad, aren't you?"

"You know where he is?"

Vulture shook his head. "No. I wouldn't bother looking, either."

"We're talking about Merc Conrad, huh?" said Man. "Why are you looking for him?"

"He's my partner," I told him.

"And?"

"If he's in trouble, I got to help him."

"You da man." He rolled his eyes.

"Merc's gone crazy," said Vulture. "He recruited a bunch of Afghans from the security force, some stragglers from their army, a couple of other nuts, and he's looking for bin Laden's treasure."

Man laughed.

"I don't quite get the joke, I'm sorry. What sort of treasure?"

"Weapons, Jack Pilgrim. Weapons," said Man. "The great terrorist emperor bin Laden has a secret stash of weapons in eastern Paktika, and your friend—your *partner*—is trying to get them."

"He thinks bin Laden will go for the weapons as we withdraw. The idea is that it'll help put him back in power," Vulture explained.

"What are we talking about? Rifles?"

"Bigger than that," said Vulture. "Missiles. Maybe a nuke."

"If he'd had a nuke, he would have used it on us on nine/eleven, or right after."

Vulture shrugged.

"Fifty mil if he gets bin Laden. Good reason to go, in any event," said Man.

"Merc's not that crazy."

Vulture looked at me like I'd just sworn the world was flat.

I CAN'T say that I'd never heard any rumors about bin Laden and secret weapons in the border area. On the contrary, I'd heard plenty of rumors—bin Laden's got a nuke, bin Laden's got bio weapons, bin

Laden has anthrax from Russia, radioactive waste from China, some weird strain of measles from France: there was a rumor for every possible calamity, matched to a dozen different hiding places in every province along the border and others a hundred miles away. Merc heard those rumors, too. He wouldn't have believed them. And as for the fifty-million-dollar reward that the government had posted for bin Laden's capture—well, someone like Diss might be motivated by it, to the extent that they were motivated by any idea that belonged in the rational world. But Merc knew he could get money much more easily through Iron Rock. As bad as our finances were, jetting off to grab bin Laden wasn't a logical solution to them.

Of course, I was assuming Merc was being logical. Out here that wasn't a particularly good assumption.

25

NEAR AMAKHEL (2)

DISS kept trying to make excuses about how he knew the "Green Beret dudes" were on our side all the time, and just grabbed him before he could explain what the story was. Vulture thought this was pretty funny, and egged him on, asking him at exactly what point he spotted them.

Man was on watch—they didn't trust us to take a turn—and Khan and Richie were sleeping in one of the caves.

Finally, Diss had enough of the smirks and Hokum's stares, and went off to bed. By way of making conversation, Vulture asked Hokum if he was Russian; Hokum grunted. Maybe it was my booze—we were passing it around—but in a few minutes he was talking about some of his time here.

HOKUM had been with a special Russian unit when the command ordered a retreat from Kabul. His squad leader was handed a list of names and a mission—eliminate the people on the list. They were all supposed to be supporters of the rebel movement against the government, and the Russians decided to give them a going-away present.

The squad piled in a Russian truck and set out. It was pretty much open season on Russian military vehicles by then, and they took small-arms fire all the way up to their first objective, which was a villa about a mile out of the town center. A machine gun opened up on them as they drove up; before half of the squad could get out of the truck, a grenade hit it and blew it apart.

Hokum and the other survivors pressed the attack against what proved to be three dozen mujahideen rebels. An hour later, the villa was on fire. Dead Afghans were scattered along the outskirts of the building and its walls. There were eight Russians left, but only two, counting Hokum, had escaped injury. Even so, all of the wounded men decided to move on to the next objective.

They took two cars from a nearby house for transport. Target two was the same deal as number one, but on a slightly smaller scale. This time, two Russians were killed, and another injured so badly they drove him to a unit that was bugging out. Then Hokum, his commander, and a third guy went to the last house on the list.

When they pulled up, there was no opposition, no guards, no gunfire. Hokum took the back of the house; the commander and the other man took the front. The back door wasn't even locked. Hokum figured the place was empty; by now the mujahideen must have known what was up and fled. But as soon as he stepped through the door, he heard voices. He went through the place quick, real textbooklike; the only people inside were an older woman, her daughter, and the daughter's two children. He had them sit in the living room, hands on head, while he continued the search.

Hokum was just getting back from searching the upstairs when his squad leader took out his pistol and threatened the old woman, telling her he would kill her if she didn't reveal where her son-in-law was. The old woman clearly didn't understand Russian, and none of the three soldiers understood whatever language she was using. In frustration, the commander grabbed one of the kids and pointed his pistol to her head. Hokum felt his heart jump, but words spewed from the old lady's mouth, and among them was something that sounded like an address three blocks away. The squad leader threw the child down and turned to Hokum.

"Shoot them all," he told him.

Hokum looked at his squad leader. He'd never been given an order like that—to shoot women and children.

"Under other circumstances, it might have been possible," Hokum told us. He paused for a long time, staring blankly into the distance; I imagine he was thinking of the circumstances. "But not that day."

The commander repeated his order. Hokum turned and saw that the old woman had dropped to her knees and was bowing, in the style a Muslim used when praying.

"Shoot them!" demanded the squad leader.

Hokum glanced at the other soldier, who if anything was more horrified by the order.

"Then I will," said the commander.

Hokum shot him through the head as he raised his pistol. The other soldier stared at him for a moment, and then finally nodded. They fled together, deserting the army on that day.

FOR the next decade or so, Hokum lived as an outcast in Soviet Georgia. He became a mercenary there, selling his services to the highest bidder as a kind of political hatchet man, something like the Blackshirt bullies Mussolini employed in Italy during the twenties and thirties. Eventually he found his way to Somalia, and the Congo, and back to Afghanistan.

"Here I will die. No further," he told us. And for the first time since we'd met, he took a swig from my flask.

"I DIDN'T recognize you at first, Sarge," said Vulture after Hokum had gone to one of the caves to get some rest. "You gained weight."

"Hard living." I laughed.

"Face looks softer, too. You don't have the stare anymore."

"Stare?"

"You had this way of staring at people, like you wanted them to come at you, like you were praying they would. Like you lived just for the chance to beat them to a pulp."

"Aw, I couldn't have been that bad."

"No, that was good. People knew you weren't bs'in' around. I mean, it was just training and all, but I guarantee, anybody around, they would've followed you to hell and back."

I remembered Vulture, a little. He had been a rigger, which is an important job—basically, every time you go out of an airplane you put your body and soul in his hands. But it wasn't a front-line combat job; it was a support role, with a different attitude attached. I'm not being disrespectful, either. You really wouldn't want most combat guys packing a parachute; they're just not going to pay attention to it long enough, day after day, jump after jump; the danger's too abstract.

The army is a massive corporation, with different jobs for every type of person. Combat guys cop attitudes—I sure did—but where would they be if the private in charge of loading their bullets on the supply truck put cotton balls there instead?

Vulture had been heavier when I knew him. He'd lost a lot more weight than I'd put on.

"You were one of the reasons I decided to shape up for the Q course," Vulture told me, referring to the qualification ordeal prospective Special Forces soldiers pass through to get in. "You talked me into it."

"I must've been drunk that night."

He laughed. "Me, too. But I'm glad I took your advice. It's real out here, Jack. Real. No bullshit. Real. We go out on a patrol, right. It's me and Man and Richie. We know exactly what we're doing. We find these small groups of Taliban bastards moving up and down the valley—they're all over, Jack, like fleas you can't get rid of. They never see us. We wipe 'em out any way we can. We have a dozen different ways. Ambush, IEDs, avalanches. You name it, we've done it."

His eyes were wide, as if I were the one telling the story and he couldn't believe it.

"You can tell the Taliban, because around here, they only move in very small groups," he added. "And they're always moving. Ambush like you ran into? That wasn't Taliban. Not worth the effort. They're gathering strength, setting up an infrastructure, you know? When we leave, that's when they'll make their big move."

"When are they pulling you guys in?"

"Haven't said. Could be any day. I wish they wouldn't. Some days I want to stay out here forever."

26

GOMAL

WE went to Gomal despite what Vulture had said about the police chief, passing through the village of Amakhel 2 (it was one of three Amakhels in the province) and a couple of other little towns along the way. Even though it was the district capital, Gomal was a small place, a couple of storefronts lining the main street. The village elders told Khan that the police chief had gone to Kabul for a meeting a few weeks before. That was an easy excuse for any public official who wanted to disappear—people legitimately traveled to Kabul and didn't come back for months, even lifetimes.

The man the chief had left in his place told Khan he'd never heard of Merc, but it was quite obvious that he was lying. I had Khan tell him that I was Merc's brother—a stronger connection than friend in the tribal culture here. He took a step back, but didn't give us any information.

As we were leaving, I spotted a hand-written poster on the wall in English and Pashto announcing a "security meeting." The featured speaker: *Mercury Conrad, warrior.*

It had been held six weeks before. I pulled it down, and stuffed it into my pocket.

WE bought some food, some replacement tools, and a handful of blankets in the village. What we could have used was more gasoline. We were down to ten five-gallon tanks, not counting the truck's full load. Under normal driving conditions, fifty gallons might be good enough for more than a thousand miles, but there was no such thing as normal driving in Afghanistan. So far, we'd gotten about fourteen miles to the gallon—ridiculously good. At that rate, we had almost twice what we'd need to get out to Gayan and get back over to Urgun, where I could take advantage of Colonel Armstrong's offer of a helicopter ride if something happened to Khattak. But our mileage was bound to get worse, and there was always the possibility of losing gas to things like bullets.

I had been thinking of buying some donkeys, but at this point they'd be more trouble than they were worth. Besides, I knew I could get some in Barmal, our next destination.

The farther we went, the more I was convinced I'd find Merc in an area around the borders of Barmal and Gayan, Paktika's far eastern districts. Or, more likely, inside a triangle of Pakistan wedged between them. We'd spent a lot of time there during the war; if he did have an army, it'd be a good place to train it.

Partly because of the gas situation, and partly because of what Man and Vulture had told us, I decided we'd take a riverbed trail in Barmal district, rather than going the long way around via the road. I'd been that way before; there were only two spots where I thought we'd have trouble drivingwise, and in all honesty they were no worse than some of the ripped-up sections of road we'd already crossed to get here. Hokum was for it, after he gave his usual grouse about my "lousy" maps.

Khan and I shared the cab, while Diss rode up top with Hokum. The Russian still hadn't forgiven him for allowing himself to be manhandled by the Special Forces guys, so Diss sulked in a corner. He looked so forlorn when we stopped for a pee that I told him he'd be paid like a regular employee.

"Well, I expected that," he said indignantly.

"You volunteered."

"Hell, no, I was looking for a job," insisted Diss. "I oughta get a bonus, just like Hokum."

"Hokum's not getting a bonus."

"How much you payin' him?"

"Same as you."

"How much is that?"

"Two hundred a day."

"That sucks."

"Just be thankful I didn't dock your pay for screwing up back there," I told him, getting back in the truck.

THERE it was, a big fat lie, and it was probably written all over my face. I should've told him the truth: Hokum was worth twenty of him, not just two and a half.

I didn't, though. I took the easy way out, breaking a rule I'd learned as a sergeant: never ever lie to the people you work with. Never lie in general, but especially not to the people you're going to depend on to save your neck when the metal starts flying through the air.

Even if they're certifiable crazoid nutjobs.

I'd broken that rule a hundred times with Iron Rock. Not at first—at first I'd been scrupulously honest, with clients, with employees, with myself. But then I started hedging. First to clients: we've done plenty of threat analyses on truck depots. Then the employees: great job. You'll be in line for a bonus at the end of the year.

Then to Sharon: I love you more than ever.

And finally to myself. Though by that time I couldn't quite tell where the line between truth and fiction was.

I almost hopped out of the truck and told Diss the real story. But I didn't. I guess I hadn't hit rock bottom yet.

"YOU know Muhammed Mayden?" asked Khan about an hour after we'd started again.

"Yeah. Sure do." I was behind the wheel, driving a relatively easy stretch of the trail.

"Important man. But dangerous."

"Yeah."

"The rumor is—"

"He plays both sides. The Taliban don't really trust him. They tried to have him killed five years ago."

"To say you are under his protection—"

"I saved his life. I was with him at an ambush, and I shot someone running at him with a sword."

Khan was silent for a long time. Finally he said, "You think that has earned you anything?"

It sounded more like a statement than a question, so I didn't bother answering.

THE riverbed ended about two miles before the map said it was supposed to, and a mile earlier than I thought it would. That might not have been a problem if it hadn't dead-ended in a canyon, which wasn't marked anywhere on the map, and didn't appear anywhere in my memory.

For the first time since we'd started, I felt seriously disoriented. On the one hand I knew it was important for the others that I remain completely confident; on the other hand, I'd made a mistake somewhere along the way, and I had to figure it out real quick or we were in big trouble.

"I gotta get out and look around," I told Khan when I spotted the wall ahead. "Hang tight for a minute."

I hopped out and trotted up a shallow rise to the right. Obviously the river flow had changed since I'd been there. I took a GPS reading and studied the paper; we were about two miles north of where we should be.

I preferred not to backtrack. Besides the lost time, it wasn't going to be easy to find the old path; otherwise I would have realized my mistake much earlier.

We needed only another mile and a half before we'd hit the road we were aiming at. I studied the landscape, working my binoculars back and forth. Go here, or go back? I couldn't make up my mind.

"What's it going to be, Jack?"

The voice took me so much by surprise, I dropped the binoculars. It was my wife's.

OF course she wasn't there.

I twisted around as I bent to scoop the glasses up, expecting that it was Diss or maybe Hokum, and the wind or my mind had played some sort of trick. But it was no one, just my imagination.

What's it going to be, Jack?

She used to ask me that all the time. "What's it going to be Jack, spaghetti or roast beef?" "What's it going to be Jack, Cancún or Jamaica?" "What's it going to be Jack, left or right?"

I was the one who was making the decisions. I was the one who'd gravitated toward the flash and bling. What she'd said to me that afternoon in the bar in New York was true. She didn't care, at least not the way I had.

The border of the Gomal district in Paktika was a ridiculous place to have reached such an obvious conclusion, but there it was. I couldn't blame Sharon for anything; she wasn't Eve, handing me the apple, or some Siren leading me astray. The big house, the fancy hotels, the trips, the cars, the jewelry—she didn't ask for that, she didn't even hint. She liked it all; no question about that. But I'd been the one calling the shots. If I'd gone astray, I'd been the one holding the map.

I COULD see where the road was, or at least ought to be—the hard-packed dirt blended in with the landscape.

"We have to go off over there," I said loudly as I walked back to the truck. "The road we want to pick up is dead ahead."

We were less than a half mile from the road when we hit a soft spot in the ground too wide and too long to simply drive through. I felt the front start to slide right and tried riding it out, but within a few feet I was spitting dirt. The others scrambled out of the truck and we went to work, rocking and prodding. After ten minutes of getting nowhere I called a break and got out to survey the situation.

The pickup had lodged itself in a liver-shaped sand trap about fifty feet long. Rocking back and forth wasn't going to get us out; we'd be better off pulling it from the firm ground ahead. I had a block and tackle, but there weren't any trees or big rocks nearby to use for leverage. So we started unloading the pickup, figuring it would be lighter and easier to push that way. That took nearly an hour, and it was another two before the Toyota was free and repacked. I had Diss walk ahead of me until we got to the road so we wouldn't get stuck again.

Just as we reached the roadbed—easy to follow because it was a little higher than the surrounding ground—the air cracked with the sound of a rifle being fired from a good distance away. The bullet made a sharp *tek-chew* as it flew through the air and slapped against the rocks nearby.

Another followed. I stepped on the gas. The ground ahead erupted into a sand geyser. Whoever'd been watching us had detonated an IED.

Fortunately, he was a bit premature—though only a bit. The front window blew out, crumbling into tiny pebbles of glass. The right tire went flat, as well, but I was able to keep up enough momentum to get past the dust cloud and continue on the road. Hokum unleashed machine-gun fire from the rear long after we were clear.

Khan hadn't said a word the whole time, and when I finally looked in his direction I half expected to see him slumped against the door. But he was sitting there, just silent, staring straight ahead.

"You all right?" I asked when we stopped.

"Yes," he said.

I could tell from the way he said it that the next time we stopped in a place big enough to disappear in, he would.

THOSE WHO SEE THE FUTURE

27

BARMAL DISTRICT

THAT night, my bourbon ran out.

It wasn't the only crisis, but it was the most severe. We'd replaced the tire and continued on. Either the IED or some bullets had ruptured two of the gas cans, reducing our reserve. More ominously, all of the hamlets we passed through had been burned, flattened, and emptied. We made camp at one of them, maybe ten miles southwest of the district capital.

"How long ago do you think the village was burned?" asked Khan.

"At least a few days. But my guess is not too much longer than two or three weeks. Why would the Taliban do this?"

Khan shook his head. The road ran through a ridgeline about a third of the way up a row of mountains. Above and below us the fields were scorched. They'd been set on fire with kerosene or some other liquid. The smell, a burnt, green smell, hung over the area. Here and there a few islands of plants remained; they'd been poppies.

"Price of heroin's goin' up this year," said Diss, hopping off the truck.

We needed to post a lookout above while we set up camp. Given Diss's dismal performance so far, the only choice was Hokum. He frowned—his first outward show of displeasure with me since we started—then took one of the British light machine guns with him and set off. The radio worked fine here, and I could hear him grunting as he checked in every few minutes.

"This gonna hurt your business?" Diss asked Khan as I lit the camp stove to heat up a little dinner.

"I am not a poppy dealer."

"You ship drugs, though, no?"

"No."

"Hey Diss. Knock it off," I said.

"No sweat."

"I sell supplies to people in need," insisted Khan. "Different supplies."

"Like the bomb that almost blew us up?" asked Diss.

Khan didn't answer. If he hadn't sold those exact explosives, he'd probably sold some just like them.

"You hanging in until Gayan?" I asked him, squatting in front of the pot. I had some lentils cooking. We needed a rib-sticking meal.

"Yes," he said, but without the conviction he'd used earlier, and certainly without the emotion he'd shown when denying that he was involved in the drug trade.

"Business been okay so far?"

He shrugged. "Takes time."

"Why are you here, Khan?" asked Diss.

"Why are you?"

"Oh, this is the place." Diss held out his hands and practically twirled, like he was playing an orphan in a thirties movie and had just been adopted. "This is the place to be for a guy like me. Getting shot at—makes you feel alive."

"You don't shoot back," said Khan.

"Sure I did. Sure I did. Jack—didn't I shoot back?"

"Sure," I said, though I'd've been willing to bet good money the other way.

"So why are you here?" Diss asked Khan.

"I'm the translator."

"And?"

"I have business."

KHAN gave me another reason later that night. I'd taken Hokum's place on the hill. For the first night since we'd started our trip I saw a gunfight involving an AC-130 Spectre gunship in the distance, to the southeast of where we were. Cannonfire spewed from the sky, as if God were pointing his finger at the ground and eliminating whatever mortal had crossed him.

An hour later, I saw another, this time to the southeast, somewhere in Gomal, where we were going.

Khan came up the hill a short time later. The climb had taxed Hokum and left me reeling for a good twenty minutes, a dramatic reminder of how out of shape I was. But Khan came over the crest of the hill as nonchalantly as if he were turning a corner in Kabul.

"Couldn't sleep?" I asked him.

"There are times in a man's life when it does not pay to sleep," he said, turning his attention to the skyline.

"You're quite a philosopher for a salesman."

He smiled but didn't turn toward me.

"Firefight," I said, pointing. "You can see the gunship."

"Ferocious."

"Wouldn't want to be on the wrong side of it, that's for sure."

"I was born out there," he said.

"In Gayan?"

"Yes." He stared some more, then added, "My mother gave me to relatives to raise. It was a very good arrangement for me. I would never have been educated otherwise. In Afghanistan, I am a well-off man. I could not have done better if I stayed. Most likely, I would be dead."

I handed him the night glasses, though we were way too far to see what the AC-130 was shooting at.

"You came with me to look for your mother?" I asked, finally realizing what his true motivation was.

He took the glasses without answering, and watched for a while. When he was ready, he spoke again.

"My father was killed by the Taliban. They were not called the Taliban then. We knew them as freedom fighters."

"Your father worked for the Russians?"

"No." He turned quickly, flashing anger. Then he held out the glasses to me and said no again, gently this time. "My father followed Muhammad Mayden's brother. He was a trusted man. But my father and some others were betrayed."

The word "betrayed" came out after a long pause, as if he'd had to push it from his mouth.

"There were two sides, rivals for power, in the village and the surrounding settlements. The conflict began before I was born, before my father. All that remained was the anger, not the reason. They fought each other as readily as they fought the Russians, and gave less quarter. Muhammad Mayden's brother headed one faction, a man named Asaan led the other.

"My father was a captain. One day the group he headed, along with two others, were sent to a mountain pass to prepare an ambush. Except that when they got there, they were ambushed themselves. Muhammed Mayden's brother was among those killed. It is said that someone within their organization wanted the leader out of the way."

"Who?"

"Muhammed Mayden took over."

Out of habit, and trying to fill the silence with something to do, I reached for my flask. As I unscrewed the top, I realized he was watching me.

"Here," I told him.

He surprised me by taking it. When he gave it back, there was exactly one half-mouthful left. I thought about it, then drained it.

IN the morning, I called Khattak, not just to check on the helicopter arrangements, but to see if he'd heard anything about fighting in the Gayan area. He hadn't. According to the news, the U.S. had pushed up its timetable for withdrawal from the country. The troops were already being pulled out; the FOB at Urgun was going to be evacuated by the middle of next week.

So what did that mean for me? For one thing, I probably had until the middle of the week to get back to Urgun, if not Kabul. For another, maybe Uncle would consider the missing two million dollars small change, and let bygones be bygones.

Probably not.

And it wouldn't have changed much, either. Even if Race or the CIA station chief air-surfed down in front of me right now and said "all's forgiven," I'd still keep going, trying to find Merc. Because he'd sunk deep into a hole and needed my help. Whether he'd gone crazy or gone native or what, he needed me.

And I, for reasons I couldn't explain, I needed him, too.

WE were treated like gods at the first village we came to that morning. Children ran out to the truck, flooding the street between the small buildings, their arms up, their faces smiling as if it were Christmas and we were playing Santa Claus. I laughed and honked my horn at them; Hokum threw candy from the back.

We were about halfway through the village when I realized that the only people I'd seen were children. It wasn't unusual in a rural area for the kids to run up around you, but usually—always—you'd see some adults standing nearby, watching carefully. The young guys would pretend they didn't notice, and the women would watch from behind veils, but they'd be there. No adults were in this village at all.

Khan noticed it, too. I saw the worried expression, but he didn't say anything. I thought it best to drive on.

ACCORDING to my map, and my memory, the high valley we were driving through was filled with villages, tiny hamlets of six or eight houses, punctuated by larger settlements. Most were gone—some recently burned down, others just gone with no trace. The crops that the villagers would have been tending—poppies for the most part, with maybe grain close to the road for the occasional inspectors to save face by noting—were gone, too.

Barmal, the district capital, had swollen to several times its original size, which still left it small compared to any sort of county seat I was familiar with back in the States. The most prominent building was a mosque, a yellow-brick building which sat at the center of town. I found the village elders there, or two of them anyway, after discovering that the police station no longer existed. It wasn't that it had been blown up or knocked down or even taken over; it had simply ceased to be there, according to everyone Khan asked about it.

I'd spent a good amount of time in Barmal during the war, coming in and out. The people whom I'd known here seemed to be all gone. The local police and army detachment, the interior ministry representative—the interim government's spy and spy handler—the merchant who'd supplied me with everything from vegetables to blankets, even the old lady who used to sell me tea cheap, all gone.

"To Kabul," people told Khan when we asked after them.

Even the village elders were different. The two we met professed not to know me, and I certainly didn't recognize them. They were both at least seventy, though their exact ages were impossible to determine. They had long beards like most older men in Paktika, and wore the brimless caps common in tribal Afghanistan. Their hats were red, not white. Until now I'd thought white was the universal color, and I never got a chance to ask why theirs were different.

Their faces were round and large, full of color, but their arms looked very thin and frail, and their hands were blue with veins. They greeted us warmly, welcoming us as tribesman often did in remote Afghanistan, insisting on finding us some tea and making us comfortable. We were brought outside, to a small veranda shaded by the portico of the mosque. One of the old men found some sugar cubes as a treat for us, and we thanked him profusely for his generosity. The small cubes were the equivalent of caviar and champagne in America.

I had Khan explain that I had been here during the war. The men thanked me, and praised the U.S.; they said they remembered the brave actions of the Americans, and were happy to welcome me back. The fact that their words followed a formula used for all visitors made them no less sincere. I asked after all of the men I could remember. All, they said, had gone to Kabul, the black hole at the center of their universe. It sucked the most ambitious and productive people away.

The elders had heard of Merc. They claimed he was east—Pakistan—or maybe north—Gayan district.

"Does he have an army with him?" I asked through Khan.

The answer was ambiguous, but shaded toward a no.

"Are there Afghans with him?"

"Some."

"Why?" I asked.

The elders stared at me. Finally one asked through Khan, "You are his brother, aren't you?"

"He means, you should know, not him," explained Khan.

"Yeah, I got that. Ask them about the Taliban. Where are they?"

Khan raised his eyebrows, but turned to the old men and began a long conversation, which he didn't bother to translate until they were finished.

"What you call Taliban, they refer to by the names of the different leaders," relayed Khan. "They are said to be strong again, and picking up strength, but they are not seen here."

"Did they burn the villages to the east?"

Khan seemed to think the question was somehow impertinent, but he asked it anyway. The answer—again it came in the form of a very long conversation—was that Taliban bands must be responsible. Or the government.

"I doubt it was the government," I told Khan.

"Well, I think you are right, but saying that would not be wise. They are being diplomatic, and so must we."

"Ask them where Muhammed Mayden is."

The elders said he stayed to the southeast—Pakistan—and named a number of villages where they thought I might find him, including a place called Mana Krieger which I knew fairly well. He had apparently suffered a loss in prestige since I had been here last, but was still powerful.

One of the elders added that Mayden was not among the leaders allied with the Taliban, but he was not liked by the Afghan army, either. This apparently accounted for his being in Pakistan, though the elder didn't say this.

"I don't see the army in Barmal," I said. "Where are they?"

The elders nodded as Khan began to translate. The army apparently came through on sweeps every so often, but stayed mostly to the north and west.

"They don't like the Taliban," said Khan after we left them. "They will tolerate them if they have to, but they would prefer to be left alone. They used positive words to describe your friend," he added. "They called him the warrior of darkness, a scourge to enemies."

"That's positive?"

Khan nodded solemnly. "But they spoke of him as if he were a ghost, far away. There are legends of a dark spirit from before humans, like an old God that was banished by the Prophet Muhammad because he could not pray properly, but who still roamed the world meting out justice, very violent justice. They compared your friend to him."

"Dark spirit—sounds like Satan."

Khan nodded again, just as solemnly.

WITHOUT bourbon to take the edge off, it was hard to fall asleep. We'd taken a room in a house belonging to a relative of one of the elders; strict tribal custom protected us, but given everything we'd seen and heard I wouldn't have dreamed of not posting a guard. After an hour of turning over and over on my third of the small mat, I got up and went out to relieve Hokum. No use two of us missing sleep, I told him. He got up slowly and without saying a word went inside.

To reach the room we were in, you walked down a narrow hall, through an empty room and then into ours. I stood guard in the hall, leaning against the wall, one of the Gimpy light machine guns in my lap and the 416 to my left. Basically I was going to destroy the house if anybody tried to attack us, because the British machine gun's bullets would tear the flimsy wooden walls to toothpicks.

The thirst started in my mouth and throat, then worked down to my chest and finally my gut. It felt like a pair of hands, clawing at me from inside. Sweat poured down the back of my neck, soaking my shirt. It was cold—we were in the mountains, there was no heat in the house, and I doubt the temperature was over fifty—but I was hot, burning. Snatches of things I remembered from the last time I'd been in this part of Afghanistan crept into my mind, and every time I turned my head I thought I saw a shadow of something lurking at the edge of the room or hall. I got up and walked around, but the shadows grew, the fringe of darkness closing in.

The first time you're in combat, fear's a thrill. You don't experience it as fear, though. Or maybe I should say that if you experience it as fear then you're unlikely to come through in one piece.

You experience it as your heart thumping, as everything around you flattening out, the unimportant things disappearing. Your vision gets better, and your ears can hear things you'd never hear under any other circumstance.

Afterward, you're exhausted but high. That's the vulnerable time. That's the time when you relax—not a sleeping kind of relaxing, not ease, because your body is still hyped on adrenaline. But your attention relaxes, your focus softens. That's when you can get creamed.

For some guys, the initial thrill is a drug they want to take again and again. I was like that. I wanted, even needed, to go out on that edge. Merc, too.

Some people say there's no time like the first time, but I never felt that way. Maybe it was just the adrenaline or the sleep deprivation, but it was always sharp, intense in different ways.

But the longer you stay on the edge, the harder it is to get back. The edge is a different world, or another dimension, a place without colors, where you have white and black and every shade in between, but that's all there is. If you stay there long enough, you'll never see color again.

Worse, at some point you'll realize you like it that way. Once that happens, you don't get out—you burrow down into it. Your hungers become primitive hungers. You're all instinct, living in the now. You lose yourself on the edge of what man was, and what he became.

If you stay there long enough, you'll never come back.

That's why I was here. I'd come to rescue Merc not from physical danger, but from the darkness that he'd plunged back into. He was in a place beyond fear, where hope was a foreign concept.

He'd saved my life, now I was supposed to save his. The money was beside the point, irrelevant, though infinitely easier to talk about.

The real question, though, wasn't whether I could save him. The question was, could I save myself?

28

BARMAL

SOMEWHERE before dawn, I nodded off while on guard. It may have been for an hour; it may have been for a few seconds. When I opened my eyes, I heard Hokum's lumbering footsteps coming from the room behind me. I got up, nodded to him, then went in to get the others.

Khan had left while I'd slept. While I told the others he'd gone on business, I knew in my heart that he wasn't coming back. Whatever motivated him to come—business probably, or the desire to see his past and the future he'd never had—he couldn't stomach what he found here, and what he expected to find farther on. The real surprise was that he'd lasted this long. He'd go back to Kabul and sell his weapons and "supplies" in a place where he didn't have to confront the results. Khan, like most of us, would soon forget about where he came from; it was easier that way. You just closed your eyes and walked through life, hollow but alive, numbed but safe.

My head pounded, and none of the local concoctions or the coffee I made from our dwindling supply cured it. Every muscle in my upper back had cramped, and parts of both legs were tingling, the nerves pulled taut against my spine.

There were two donkeys tied to the rear of the pickup when I went out. They were Khan's way of saying good-bye, a magnanimous gesture really, since the animals would not have been cheap.

"What the hell are we going to do with those?" said Diss when he saw them. "Ride them?"

"If we have to," I said.

"They'll slow us down," said Hokum.

"We're not going to be moving that fast anyway," I said.

His eyes told me he didn't like that answer.

"We go off the road about five miles northeast of here," I explained. "There's a trail that cuts through the mountain pass that knocks off a dozen miles into the next district. I've been on it before. A lot."

Hokum frowned, then shrugged. "I'll go."

Diss had no clue where we were. He was all hyper, ready to hit the road, ready to "shoot them up," whoever "them" were. The fact that so far he hadn't measured up to his notion of whatever he thought he was didn't seem to faze him. In fact, it didn't even register. I wouldn't be able to trust him much in a serious firefight, but I'd never counted on him anyway.

One of the village elders came to the truck as we were getting ready to go. He said something in Pashto that I didn't understand, then pressed a folded piece of paper in my hand. It was a poster similar to the one I'd found in Gomal, for a meeting that had taken place two and a half months before. This one described what Merc was going to talk about.

"Fight the evil," it said. "Join us."

And at the very bottom: "We have their weapons. We will not be defeated."

THE pass ran through Pakistan. It connected to a trail, another road, and a series of streambeds that formed a semicircle back to Gayan, Afghanistan. Though the area was technically in Pakistan's Federally Administered Tribal Territory, it was so remote that it was essentially a no-man's-land. The elders' remarks, along with my earlier suspicions, convinced me that if I was going to find Merc anywhere, it would be in one of the little settlements that lay near the semicircle. There were about a half-dozen places I thought were the most likely possibilities.

I called Khattak when we reached the turnoff from the main

road. I arranged for him to meet us in Gayan in five days, unless I called and changed plans. If I wasn't there, I gave him three GPS points to fly over to look for me. The spots were all in Pakistan, but he just grunted without pointing it out.

Along this stretch of the border, there are no fences to mark the boundary. There are no checkpoints, no guards. Unlike the better known and wider passes, which have been used for centuries, there are no settlements or roads. You literally have no idea where you are at any given moment. One second you're in a valley twenty yards wide that's definitely in Afghanistan; the next you're climbing a wide hill in Pakistan. The maps that agree on where the line is don't agree on what the land looks like there, and vice versa. The two countries have never actually drawn the border here; the maps use the line some British clerk in Bombay decided would facilitate paperwork back in the nineteenth century.

We've been told in America that Pakistan's leaders are on our side, but that's not true. They don't all believe what the Taliban believes in, but that doesn't put them on our side by a long shot. Even if it did, the mountains of northern and eastern Pakistan are a world away from Karachi and Islamabad. If the government cared about stamping out the Taliban, sending enough troops there to chase them would leave the border with India exposed, and as far as they're concerned, India is a much graver threat.

But the fact of the matter is, they don't care. On the contrary, the Taliban is extremely useful, a reason for the U.S. to give weapons and support, to not press certain issues, like nuclear disarmament, that Pakistanis don't want pressed. The Taliban keeps the U.S. from getting too close to India, Pakistan's traditional rival. The Taliban's puritanical ways make Pakistan look liberal and modern by contrast.

Pakistan's leader, General Pervez Mushrarraf, hasn't kept bin Laden alive, and I doubt very much it was within his power to kill him if he wanted. But Mushrarraf isn't really our friend, just a convenient ally. And in the part of Pakistan where we were going, he was as irrelevant as the president of the United States. Even moreso.

WE were probably about a half mile over the border when the rain came. If I'd been a farmer, or maybe a heroin smuggler, I'd've welcomed it, since the ground was parched. But I wasn't either of those things. The rain made it difficult to control the truck down the narrow trail we were driving. Even with the four-wheel drive in low I was slipping and sliding, and finally I had to untie the donkeys and have Hokum lead them behind us. About twenty minutes later, I smacked the tail end of the truck pretty bad against a rock outcropping. Something in the back seemed to crack and give way, but I kept moving, working my way down to level ground. Water had already started to flow along the trail. The runoff was a good two or three inches up the side of the tires and that was just a start. We had to get up higher, or we'd risk being flooded out if the rain continued.

I checked the side of the truck while I waited for Hokum and the animals. When I hit the rock, I'd knocked the fender into the tire, screwed up the exhaust, and whacked the gas tank off-kilter. I pulled out the tire iron and bent the fender back. The entire side of the truck hung low. The spring at the rear had been either broken or misaligned, and there was nothing I was going to do about it. The gas tank looked solid at least. As for the exhaust pipe, since it wasn't touching the tires I let it be. I didn't really care if it fell off. The Pakistani DMV was unlikely to be handing tickets out for exhaust noise.

The donkeys were giving Hokum fits, complaining loudly about moving in what was now a rising stream. We rehitched them to the pickup and started up again, slipping a bit in the rain and mud but still moving steadily. As we started to climb, the rain let up slightly, and while we were still pushing aside a good torrent the tires gripped decently.

THE rain swept in another memory, or half-memory, as we drove.

We were on a yacht in Baltimore, a year before. It was early evening, midsummer. Sharon wore a sundress, a gold wisp of silk that caressed her body. Out of nowhere, a downpour washed us off the deck into the cabin. We squeezed around a cluster of silver-haired wannabe-yachtsmen and their lemon-tart eye candy, grabbing new drinks and pretending to be interested in conversations about Bermuda and polo. Merc was there, too, standing near the caviar with his latest hood ornament, Thera or Thelma or Theona. He was working his way through the alphabet that year, and had reached *T*.

The original plan was just to show the flag, stop by, grab a drink, stay long enough that the clients saw us, then split. Despite the rain, I wanted to stick to the agenda, and after a few minutes when the storm let up I nodded at Sharon to follow me toward the exit.

She shook her head no.

"Have another drink, Jack," said Merc, sliding around one of the serving tables and putting his arm on my shoulder. "Don't be in a rush."

As I turned toward him, I realized he wasn't looking at me, but at Sharon. And she was looking back.

"You don't have to leave, Jack," Merc said. "Stick around. Have another drink."

The memory of that night, the instant of that glance, drifted back like a ghost sifting through a wall. Her eyes, the tilt of her head, the slight flicker of her lashes as she focused—not on me, but on Merc.

This time, it wasn't a dream or a misapprehension. It was a memory of something that had really happened, something I must have suppressed at the time. I saw it as the rain slammed off the windshield. She'd been looking at him, not me.

It was real. I knew it was real.

DRIVING up the twisting mountain road was like coming home. Even in the rain, I recognized the crags opposite us. I'd walked along this road with a group of local militiamen hunting Taliban guerrillas several times; twice I'd taken shelter near the cave we were heading for, calling air strikes in when we'd found ourselves outnumbered. Some of the puddles we were driving through had no doubt been created by the bombs I called in.

Without a front windshield in the truck, the rain poured into my lap. I had to put the glasses on to see. Hokum held one of the British machine guns out the opening, peering through, bending to spot lookouts on the ridge line that ran to our left.

"Ain't nobody gonna be out in this storm, Ruskie," said Diss.

No sooner had Diss started to laugh, than a burst of bullets flew through the top of the truck.

29

FEDERALLY ADMINISTERED TRIBAL AREA, PAKISTAN

BLOOD, rain, and sweat flew around the cab as I jammed the gas. One of the wheels spun and we spurted forward, the tires sliding and then gripping, sliding and gripping, over and over in the space of thirty or sixty seconds. I got up the ravine and saw the cave next to the open field. We skidded next to it, animals screeching behind us. I threw open the door, and pulled Diss out, leading him to the shelter.

I figured Hokum would follow. But he didn't. I ran back and saw that a handful of bullets had gone through his skull, drilling holes like a farmer's augur in a field ripe for planting. I grabbed his gun, but left him in the truck, circling around the side of the cave to a narrow path I knew cut to the top. I groped my way up quickly in the rain, half expecting I would meet our ambushers on the way. When I got to the top, I had a view of the crags where they had been. No one was there.

I squatted, hunkered over my gun to protect it, and waited for the rain to pass or become so intense I wouldn't have to worry about being attacked. The water soaked the beard I'd been growing, lubricating it, making it less itchy. My back was tight again, and my neck hurt, but my headache was gone, and the terrible thirst I'd had the night before, the thirst that had gradually grown over the past five years, had disappeared.

The weight of the gun in my arms was perfect. There were no

questions now, no thinking to interfere with what I did. If someone, anyone, appeared on the ridge in front of me, they were dead. I would shoot them, and kill them, and be ready for the next.

The rain turned into an imperceptible mist about midafternoon. I waited a little while longer, then climbed down. Diss was exactly where I left him in the cave, his 416 next to him, not even in his hands. I walked to it, picked it up, and gave it to him.

"This is yours. You need it. You have to have it with you every second here. Every instant."

His eyes were the eyes of a ghost. Together we took Hokum from the truck and put him into a corner of the cave.

He would have wanted me to say a prayer. He thought I was religious, after all; seeing me in church was what made him decide to come with me.

No. More likely that was the excuse he gave himself. Hearing where I was going, he must have realized it was his chance, the chance he'd been looking for since he'd come to Afghanistan. He'd die on his own terms: with the gun in his hands, and without harming children. That was his line, and he'd managed to stay on the right side of it, not an easy accomplishment.

"Our Father, who art in heaven, hallowed be thy name," I started, after we'd wrapped his oversized body in plastic. "Thy kingdom come. Thy will be done, on earth as it is in heaven."

I stopped. I'd forgotten the rest of the words.

"Deliver us from evil," prompted Diss.

"Yeah," I said. "Deliver us from evil."

I couldn't, for the life of me, remember anything else, and so I left it at that.

THE bullets had killed one of the burros, but the other was standing placidly behind the truck, head down, wondering what came next. I cut away his companion and pulled him as far down the road as I could, dragging the body through a stream of muddy water to the start of a ravine. I gave it a push and the poor dead beast tumbled away.

When I got back to the truck, the other donkey gave me a puzzled expression, his large eyes blinking. I got some of the fodder we'd bought for him; he ate hungrily but not greedily, leaving exactly half.

"Diss! Mount up, let's go," I called.

Diss walked out of the cave, a shell-shocked look on his face.

"I—I—I don't know," he stuttered.

"Too late for that now," I told him. "We're here. Come on."

"Jack."

I walked to him, and grabbed him by the front of his shirt. "You wanted to see this, right? You wanted to be on the edge? You wanted to hunt bin Laden, go after the Taliban? Well, that's where the fuck we are. You're stuck now. So you have two choices, Disney—you can walk back into that cave, sit down next to Hokum, take out your gun and blow your fucking brains out. Or you can come with me. Which is it?"

He got in the truck. By the time I got behind the wheel, he'd summoned his courage and was trying to sound cheerful.

"Where we goin', Sarge?" He unfolded one of Hokum's maps.

"Place called Mana Krieger. It's about a half mile above the road, near a spot where the road intersects with a stream. We won't be able to get across the stream until tomorrow, because of the rain, and even then it'll be dicey, so we'll stay in Mana overnight."

"Yeah? Good place to sleep?"

"There are worse."

"I can't seem to find it on the map."

"It's not on the map. But it's there."

MANA wasn't on the map, but I knew where it was by heart. If we'd been walking, it would have taken three hours to get there. The truck was in such poor shape and the road so wet that it took almost twice that.

I had to keep stopping to make sure the water wasn't too deep for us or the donkey to pass. Twice I led the animal across streams that had opened in the road and had Diss hold him until I could drive across.

Before the rain, I hadn't planned on staying there at all—Merc wouldn't go there. He didn't like Muhammed Mayden and Mayden didn't owe him anything. And even before Khan had told me what had happened to his father, I knew trusting Mayden would be foolish.

But with someone on our trail, and the road blocked by the stream, Mayden offered a better chance than simply sitting here and waiting to be surrounded. If he wasn't in the village, there were others who might help. I remembered three people there who spoke English the last time I'd been through. I could trust any one of them to tell me what they knew. Assuming, of course, they were still alive.

I saw the village from about a half mile off. It sat in the middle of a field of poppies, and I imagine the farmers were pretty happy about the rain. We could smell fires and food cooking as we drove up; saliva was just about coming from Diss's mouth.

A hundred yards from the village, two men appeared from the side of the road, both with AK47s.

"Keep calm, Diss."

"Easy for you to say. They're pointing them right at me."

"I got one pointing at me, too. They won't shoot us."

"Why? Because we're, like, visitors?"

"Absolutely."

It was bullshit—they sure as hell *could* shoot us. Hospitality toward visitors was a greatly exaggerated local trait. Humor was also said to be a tribal quality, and these guys didn't look like they'd start feeding us one-liners.

"You sure these guys aren't Taliban, Sarge?" asked Diss as the men approached the truck.

"Yeah, I'm sure," I lied.

I slowed down even further, but let the truck creep along as the gunmen came up.

"I am a friend of Muhammad Mayden," I told the man who came to my side of the truck, using Pashto and then repeating what I said in English. "I have come from Barmal and am traveling eastward."

He said something in Pashto which I couldn't understand, but then added Muhammad Mayden's name.

"Friend," I said. I clasped my hands. "A brothers' bond."

Apparently that was the wrong answer, for he pulled his rifle up and put it against the side of my head.

30

MANA

THE metal at the business end of a rifle feels like no other substance in the world, especially when it's against the side of your skull. Generally, it's cold, but through some sort of alchemy its ice burns hot when it touches the thin skin at your temple.

I kept my hands on the wheel, waiting for the man with the gun to decide whether to blow my brains out or let me through. There was no sense flooring the gas; even if I'd managed to avoid him I'd never get far enough to pick up my own gun. Besides, I was cold, wet, and tired. If I'd made a miscalculation about who the village belonged to, I'd rather pay the consequences sooner rather than later.

"Out," said the man with the rifle. He pulled the door open.

"Muhammad Mayden," I repeated, not moving.

"What are we going to do?" asked Diss, his voice a full octave higher than normal.

"We're going to wait until they tell us to do something we want to do," I said. "Or we're going to get shot."

"Out!" demanded the man again.

"Muhammad Mayden."

The men started talking among themselves in Pashto. The gunman wasn't watching me now, and it's possible that I could have pulled the gun out of his hand. But I still wouldn't have gotten very far. Finally the men came to some sort of decision—while the others jumped on the hood and back of the truck, the one with the gun pulled open the door and tried to shove in behind the wheel.

"Go around. I'm driving," I told him, using English and gesturing because I didn't know the words in Pashto. I pointed adamantly, and finally he got the idea. I wasn't just being stubborn; the odds were that he'd never driven before.

"I thought you said these guys were our friends," said Diss.

"I didn't say they were our friends. I said they weren't Taliban."

"Man."

"You have to be cool, Diss. I've been through all of this before. Plenty of times. Just play it the way it goes."

"I can't be cool. They gonna kill us?"

"I wouldn't have come here if I thought they would."

"You're crazy, man. You're crazy."

I guess I could've said something like, takes one to know one, but I didn't think of it at the time.

THEY led us along the row of small huts that formed the center of town to one slightly larger than the others. I was surprised to be brought here rather than the dull brown stone structure behind the houses, which served as a mosque and the de facto administrative center of town. Made of wood, the house was a story and a half high, with a tin roof and a bit of a porch in front. The street was paved with solid blocks of gray stone, each twenty inches square. An additional layer of these stones formed the floor of the porch and the house behind it.

As I got out of the truck, the men surrounded me. I held my hands out and let them take the weapons, ignoring their pokes and prods as best I could. But when they started to push me inside, I resisted, yelling, "Hey!" and pushing them off before continuing. They kept Diss out on the porch, which was fine with me.

The building was larger than it seemed from outside. A single lamp lit the long, narrow interior. Three figures sat at the far end, cross-legged on the floor, talking with each other. One of my escorts ran forward and, I guess, explained the situation. Two of the men got up and went out with most of the guards, while I was prodded toward the remaining figure, who was dressed in thick wool salwar kameez.

It was Mayden. Older—his beard, an almond red when I'd last seen him, was now whiter than Santa Claus. But he had the same odd-shaped ears sticking almost straight out from the side of his skull, and the scar that ran along the top of his forehead, where one of his lieutenants had tried to scalp him, apparently for a reward. Either the man thought he could get the money without actually killing his leader, or miscalculated the effect the wound would have; his effort had been unsuccessful and was rewarded with a stoning, after his own scalping.

"Sergeant Pilgrim," said Mayden. He pointed at me. He could speak English reasonably well, though his accent sometimes distorted his words. "Why are you here?"

"I'm looking for an old friend of mine, Mercury Conrad."

Mayden shook his head. "I know who you're looking for. I know."

"Can you help me find him?"

"Why?"

"I have to talk to him."

"I would not help a man to his death. Even an American unbeliever."

"I don't think Merc's gonna kill me. If he was interested in killing me, he could have done it a long time ago."

Mayden folded his arms in front of him. "You Americans. You come, you stir things up, and you leave. What do you think will happen when you are gone?"

I wasn't meant to actually answer the question, so I didn't.

"You think you are the center of the universe, the powerful angels? Of course you are not. You are weak—little children who must break everything they touch."

He was silent for a while. I tried changing the subject.

"Why are you in Pakistan, not up across the border?"

He frowned at me.

"This village has always been friendly to me."

"But—"

"There is a dispute over the poppies. Here, I cannot be bothered."

Again, a silence. Finally I asked, "Do you know where Merc is?"

"Find the Taliban, and you will find him."

Mayden started to get up, but I grabbed his arm. "Where exactly is he?"

The warlord gave me a ferocious look, but I didn't loosen my grip. We stared into each other's eyes. He was roughly my age, but he'd lived at the edge all his life, and it had made him an old man.

I was looking at myself, at the person I'd become if I stayed out here too long.

"Go south along the stream from Nezamkhel." His eyes remained locked with mine. "He will find you in the canyons there."

"Thank you."

I let him go. He rose, and so did I. But as he started to leave he stopped, and asked me a question: "Why did you tell the guard you were my friend?"

"You are."

He narrowed his eyes, as if by doing so he might be able to see inside my skull. Perhaps he was remembering the incident when I had saved his life; more likely he was thinking what I had just realized, that we were the same basic impulse, our fates transposed by circumstance.

"You may stay in the village for tonight," he told me. "Then you will leave. If I see you again, I will not be hospitable."

MAYDEN'S blessing, such as it was, allowed us to move freely in the village. Diss seemed relieved to be alive. The wild look he'd had in his eyes had been replaced with the stunned expression of an animal winded and cornered after a long chase.

"Just follow along and be quiet," I told him. "Everything will work out."

I found one of the people I knew here, a craftsman who repaired shoes and clothes and different sorts of gear used by farmers. He'd fixed some belts for us that we used for animals that last time I'd been here. When I walked into his shop he looked up at me with the same smile he'd used five years before to indicate our gear was ready. His hair was grayer and the lines deeper around his eyes, but the grin was exactly the same.

"Sergeant Pilgrim," he said.

"Ahmed." I hadn't remembered his name until that moment. "I hope you're well."

"Very good, thankee." His accent was just as bad as Mayden's, but I was getting used to it now. I was understanding more Pashto, as well, though long sentences still tended to baffle me. "You need belt?"

"Come look at my mule," I told him. "See if you make better."

"Make better. Yes."

The job was a pretense to talk to him. I waited until he was done examining the belts and had proposed two replacements before asking about the Taliban and what was going on in the area nearby. We went back to his shop, where his wife had brewed tea. Over the next two hours he told me about the raids that were made nightly all through the valley and well up into Afghanistan. The Taliban were active again, and in Ahmed's mind there was no question that they would be back in full force once the Americans were gone. Mayden's village was safe—he was, as usual, "riding both halves of the camel" and playing the Afghans and Taliban off each other. My presence was a threat to his neutrality, though; if the Taliban heard of it, they would conclude he was more against them than for them, and attack.

"Sooner or later, they'll attack anyway," I told Ahmed. "They won't accept neutrality in the end. You should leave before that happens."

"If I were going to leave, I would have left long ago," he said. "I'm an old man, now, no? Too old to leave."

"How old are you?"

"Thirty-five. An old man."

THERE was one hope for the villagers who did not want to join the Taliban. A dark beast had been preying on them over the past few months, raiding Taliban strongholds, burning them out as they burned out others. There were many men in the beast's army, though Ahmed didn't know how many exactly. Nor did he know that the dark beast was Merc.

"Where is the beast?"

Ahmed had trouble explaining, even when I showed him my map. The area he indicated was in the east, in the direction I was going. It wasn't far away—but it was impenetrable, Ahmed claimed. The beast lived in the rock and could not be attacked by man.

"The Taliban have earned his wrath with their pride," said Ahmed. "The beast has great weapons, invincible weapons."

"What kind of weapons?"

"Fire and lightning."

Reality, rumor, and myth were tangled together, and there was no separating them. I paid him for the belts and left him to do his work, promising to pick them up before I left in the morning.

THE attack that had killed Hokum had also cost us five of our gas cans. Worse, a good portion of our food had also been mutilated and spoiled by the gunfire and leaking gas. I tried buying what I could, but Mana didn't have much for itself, let alone surplus to sell to outsiders. The best I could do was a few loaves of bread and a roasted pigeon, or what looked like a pigeon, for dinner. My stomach had tightened a bit, but I still felt hunger, and my legs were dead tired. At least the headache was gone.

Diss didn't complain about the food. I took that as a bad sign. He also let water spill out of the side of his mouth, wasting it. I let it slide. It'd been a long day, far longer for him than for me. Diss had finally gotten to the edge and realized he didn't want to be there. But it was too late to go back.

THE idea that Sharon had cheated on me with Merc was like the poison from a snake bite, relentlessly seeping through my body. Jealousy overwhelmed the wall between imagination and memory. The more I resisted—the harder I told myself that it hadn't happened, that Sharon would never have slept with Merc, and that even if she had wanted to, Merc wouldn't have done that to me—the larger the thought became, crowding out everything else. I saw them together in places they couldn't have been, remembered whisperings that had never happened.

Driving again, moving up through the jagged mountain trail, I tried to focus on the land before us, the possibility of ambush, but the external dangers paled beside the internal wrath of my envy. I looked for tracks near a rock outcropping, and thought of Sharon's lips pressing toward his. I saw a ravine that would cover an approach, and saw Merc's fingers slipping around her breast.

Finally, I couldn't take it anymore. "Stop!" I screamed. "Stop! Stop! Stop!"

It was only then that I realized I was still in the village. I was sleeping.

Stiff, cold, I pulled the thin blanket around my neck and huddled against the dark, trying as best I could to keep my mind blank, as if emptiness were the only protection against fear.

WE left at dawn. About two miles out of the village, I got a bad surprise. The gas tank had sprung a leak. It was now less than half full, with a trail behind me. The leak looked to be coming from a split seam about midway up. Below that, it didn't seem to leak, but finding that out had cost about ten gallons of gas.

The stream that had blocked the road the day before was still there, though not as high or swift. I waded out to the middle; it reached almost to my waist—too high for the truck. The only alternative to waiting here for a few days was to try to find another spot to ford. I drove up the stream bank, going about a quarter mile at a time before stopping and checking. Finally I found a spot where the water was only ankle deep. Diss led the donkey across. I backed up a bit, then floored it. My front wheels slipped into a deep rut halfway across, but the back still gripped, and I managed to slide out on the other side. We backtracked down to the road.

There were two villages immediately to the east of the road, but I could see from a distance they were both burned out.

"You okay with that?" I asked Diss as we drove. He was holding the Gimpy light machine gun against the dashboard, but my question was really to try and keep him in the game. His eyes were glazed and he was far off, though God knows where.

"Gun," he told me.

"Yeah." At least he could still identify basic objects.

"Gun."

"So where'd you grow up, Diss?"

"Jersey."

"Jersey?" I think this was his third or fourth version of his life.

"Nobody ever picked me for the basketball team," he said.

It was such a non sequitur that I laughed. He looked at me like he wanted to kill me.

"I wasn't much of a basketball player myself," I told him.

When he didn't answer, I gave up trying to make conversation.

WE stopped around midday to eat and make sure we were in good shape. We were within sight of a small settlement, maybe two dozen houses, all perched in a line on a hillside to the right of the trail. It wasn't a hamlet I remembered from the war and I didn't intend on stopping there. The stream Muhammad Mayden had spoken of was only twenty miles away; at our present pace we'd reach it well before dark. I'd camp there, and we'd start down toward the canyons in the morning.

At some point we were going to have to abandon the truck. The streambed was narrow in several spots, and it would be wiser to get off it anyway and pick through the high ground. The donkey could easily handle our gear.

"I want you to sit on the top of the truck with the machine gun," I told Diss when we finished eating. "We're going to go past that settlement up ahead, and they're much less likely to bother us if they see someone with the big gun."

"I can drive."

"I know the road better. It makes more sense for me to drive."

Diss nodded, but I had to physically lead him to the rear of the truck, practically pushing him into place.

"Don't fire unless I tell you to," I said.

He pushed down behind the gun, swinging it around a little.

"You got me, Diss? Don't fire unless I tell you to."

"Yeah. Okay."

We got past the settlement with no problem, without even seeing anyone. The trail flattened into a road nearly two lanes wide; there were shoulders even, or at least ground sturdy and smooth enough to hold the truck. We came upon a knot of men with camels, transporting something up out of Pakistan.

There were six men; four were dusky faced, non-Pashtuns. That didn't automatically mean they weren't Taliban, but it was a good bet.

"Easy, Diss," I yelled up to him as we drove. "We just sail right by these guys."

He didn't answer, or if he did it was lost in the rumble of the truck. I had my 416 in my lap, with the grenade launcher ready to go. I'd fire and step on the gas if something went wrong.

The men looked at us warily, but they didn't take defensive positions. I imagine they were working things out just as I was. The rule here was live and let live, except when it was shoot first. The trick was knowing which one to follow.

I drove by slowly but steadily, keeping as far to the side as I dared, but giving the camels enough room so I didn't provoke them. As I passed the end of the caravan, my hands tightened on the wheel and my heart started to pump hard. This was our most vulnerable point; it would be all up to Diss if something happened.

The truck jerked as the front tire hit a rock. I steadied it, staying on the road. Then we were past them.

For the next hour, we drove downhill, going at the rate of about twelve miles an hour. This was great time, and if the trail had been in a straight line, we'd've reached the stream easily. But the trail followed the geography of the land, rising and falling and ducking away as it picked through the high ridge. It had gotten cold, and I had the heater on. I could see snow on a nearby mountaintop, and I thought of the snow leopards Khan had talked about.

To live out here, to survive, they had to be pure. They stalked, they killed, they ate. That was their day. On rare occasions, they would come together to have sex. Then it was back to the basics. Stalk. Kill.

Had our ancestors been like that? They must have been. And if they were, we were, too. Deep down. And at the edge.

WE were no more than three miles from the stream, but I realized we had to find a spot to stay the night before we got there. I was tired, tremendously tired, and beyond the stream there were settlements and I couldn't trust myself to focus properly without more rest.

I'd just spotted a fair place a few hundred yards off the road at the base of a small plateau when I heard the heavy stutter of a big machine gun.

"What the hell are you doing, Diss?" I screamed.

Then I realized he wasn't firing; someone else was. At us.

31

BEYOND MANA

I HAD my foot to the floor as we fishtailed down the side of the trail, up over a short rise and then through a patch of whitish sand, so fine it could have been ash. The back of the truck seemed to disintegrate behind me. Dust enveloped us, and I couldn't see where we were going. I hit something and the vehicle began moving sideways, skidding down a four- or five-foot hill and slamming against a row of boulders. I grabbed my rifle and one of my rucksacks, then climbed out the open windshield. Diss had fallen from the back and landed facedown near the bumper. I grabbed at his shirt. Fortunately he started to move and all I had to do was lead him with me as I ran for the rocky crevices I'd seen earlier.

Whoever had been firing at us had probably stopped by then, the gunner's view blocked by the smoke if not the terrain, but I was too dazed to tell. I didn't even know where the gunfire had come from.

We scrambled up the side of the plateau about twelve yards, until we came to a wall of fallen rocks. I stopped there, pushing Diss down, and tried to get my bearings.

My side hurt and I was out of breath. All that working out in the gym back home hadn't been nearly enough. Pushing weights, running in place—bullshit compared to this. I could rev myself to some ideal heart rate for thirty or forty minutes at a time, but it wasn't nearly enough.

"Who?" said Diss.

"Doesn't matter who. The question is where."

I'd left my binoculars in the truck, but there was no question of going back; they just weren't worth the risk.

We were on the high ground. There was a ridge a bit higher than us a mile away. In between there was a plain, with ravines and scattered rocks.

If the machine gunner had been on the opposite ridge, then he would have been able to fire at us now. Logically—though admittedly logic might not have anything to do with it—he had to be on the plain. This also made sense given how far the ridge had been; while the machine gun's bullets could easily reach that far, in my experience it took a closer distance for a gunner to lay down such accurate fire.

I scanned the area but couldn't find the position. There were dozens of possibilities.

The truck was to our right. The donkey lay in the dirt thirty yards behind it, rolling its head but not getting up. I guessed that its legs had been broken or it had been shot.

"Everything we got's in that truck," said Diss. "Ammo, food, water, everything."

"Yeah, but it's going to stay there for a while."

I glanced behind me, starting to get paranoid. I knew the machine gunner hadn't been here, because otherwise he would have taken out the front of the truck—not to mention us as we ran uphill. But I couldn't quite make the logic calm my adrenaline.

"Let's try getting up higher, behind that second set of rocks up there," I told Diss.

As I rose, the machine gun started again. A half-dozen bullets exploded in the rocks just below me. I got back down before his aim improved.

WHEN machine guns were first used in meaningful numbers during World War I, they changed the way men fought. Massed formations and orchestrated charges over open ground became obsolete. At first, the weapon was so fearful that armies resorted to trench warfare, a bloody stagnation winnable only if one side was able and willing to lose an obscene amount of men, which then made it vulnerable to counterattack.

Eventually, tanks and airplanes as well as new tactics changed the equation, but the heavy machine gun remains ferocious. Logically, it should make no difference to a dead man whether his life was ended with a slim bullet from an M4 or a monster-sized round from a Ma Deuce or a Dushka. There is not *so* much difference in the speed or the size of the bullets as they fly through the air; the smaller caliber, if it hits in the right spot, is just as deadly. But the volume of the violence as it spits at you, as the bullets fill the air beside your head—hunkering against the dirt, you would give anything not to hear that sound, not to feel the metal smell as the bullets burn the oxygen out of the air. Flattened against the ground, you feel as if the earth had begun throwing bits of herself at you, magma from her core. To be shot then by a small gun would seem a relief.

SEVERAL times over the next few minutes I started up the hill, only to be beaten back by an onslaught of machine-gun fire. Our enemy was hunkered down in a ravine about thirty yards from the trail we'd been following, and maybe a hundred and fifty from where we were. That sounds like far away, a football field and a half. But it was pretty close for that gun.

It was also close enough for my grenade launcher, and once I knew precisely where he was, I tried to take him out. My first shot sailed a bit far, but I pumped two more almost on top of him, and all I got in response was more machine-gun fire. He had some sort of natural pillbox out there; I couldn't even see his head. With only three grenades left, I decided to save them for a better strategy.

So long as we stayed near the rocks, he didn't bother firing. I was worried there was a reason for that beyond conserving ammo. The gunner's companions—surely he wouldn't be alone out here—might be flanking us. I had a decent view of the approach, though, and I didn't see anyone. The only possibility was an attack from the rear, which at the moment I couldn't do much about.

Night came on slowly. "As soon as it's dark," I told Diss, "we'll get the hell out of here."

He didn't answer.

"We can swing around and come up behind him," I said. "We'll have to go up toward that ridge there. It'll take a few hours, but we can get behind him before daybreak."

Still no answer.

"You with me, Diss?"

"There's a million of them out there."

"There's only one, Diss. Just relax."

"A million."

The plan wasn't the most brilliant one I'd ever dreamed up. If I'd had more faith in Diss I would have left him there and snuck around myself. If I'd been there with Hokum instead, I'd've gone straight up the side in the dark, let Hokum cover me if anything happened. But Hokum wasn't here.

A smarter plan might have been just to run. But that meant leaving the rest of our supplies, and that I didn't want to do. I had my flask and one small canteen of water. Diss had a metal bottle. We had no food.

Running would also leave this guy behind us, either tracking and following, or just sitting here and blocking our way if we had to go back.

What I couldn't figure out was why our persecutor would be alone. And yet that seemed to be the case. If he'd been working with someone, they'd have had more than enough time to come up behind us by now.

STARING at the same landscape for hours mesmerized me. At some point my mind slipped from the present to the past, and then beyond that, into a dreamscape. Sharon was next to me. I reached to kiss her, but she turned away, walking down the hill. It turned from sand and rock to grass, the lolling lawn of some business associates I'd visited or maybe I'd dreamed I'd visited in Westchester.

Then Merc was there, kissing her.

I reached out and grabbed him. Somehow they were right next to me. I took him by the throat and punched hard, hit him square in the face.

Pain brought me back to the present, and reality. I'd fallen asleep, and in my nightmare had punched the rock next to me. My fingers were bruised and scraped, and the knuckles ached, though not as bad as the silvery hole that had opened in the center of my chest.

DOES fear always take a metaphorical as well as physical form? If we can't deal with what is immediately in front of us, do we have to find something more manageable to confront?

Or is it that fear doesn't spring from the external at all? Is it something that's always with us, and that simply takes temporary forms and shapes from whatever material happens to be convenient? Is the awful truth that it's not death we fear, but living?

FINALLY it was dark enough to move around. I nudged Diss to follow me as I started moving around the right side of the ledge. I got about ten feet before the machine gun fire started again. The bullets went over our heads, but as we scrambled forward they came lower and we found ourselves pinned down again, this time with only eight or nine inches of headroom.

"What now?" said Diss. He started to sob.

"We wait some more."

I started to crawl back to rocks where we'd been, but there was an open spot, and the bullets started dancing through it as soon as I pushed forward. Caught by surprise, I ducked back.

"Son of a bitch has a nightscope," I told Diss. "We'll figure something else out."

"What are we going to do?"

"I'm going to cover you, and you're going to get around to the higher spot over there," I told him, pointing upward. "Then you cover me."

I hadn't suggested this before because frankly, I doubted Diss would be in any shape to draw the fire away and cover me. But it seemed like a better idea than waiting now.

"I can't," said Diss.

"I'm not asking you to do anything tough," I told him. "You gotta run thirty yards, that's it. Five seconds. Thirty yards. Wait a full minute, then start to fire."

"I can't!"

"Well, you better damn well try," I said, picking up my gun. "On three. One, two, three—"

I launched a grenade, then started firing, doling out several bursts and drawing a fusillade in return. When I looked to the left, Diss was gone.

"I made it!" he yelled from the rocks.

"All right, cover me," I told him, reloading.

"Wait! Let me catch my breath."

While I waited, the machine gun started again, raking the rocks where I was. Grit and chips of stone rained down on me. I stuffed another grenade into the launcher.

"You ready?" I yelled.

Diss didn't answer.

"Diss?"

"I'm not ready!"

"Well, get ready!"

I'd never been in combat with someone I couldn't rely on one hundred percent. Merc—when we were in Afghanistan, we were parts of the same body, right leg left leg. We'd have had that machine gunner's head by now. It wasn't just execution. It was knowing that the other guy was going to do everything, everything he could. Just like you would.

"Let's go, Diss! On three. One, two, three!"

I fired the grenade and ran for it just as it hit. The machine gunner began spraying the rocks a second later. I threw myself over the boulder, pummeled by pebbles and stone chips but untouched by bullets.

Diss didn't start firing until I was almost at his side, but once he started, he worked through the entire box, dropped it, then reloaded and fired again. The machine gun continued to bark all along.

"Now what?" asked Diss when we ran through the second mag.

"Now we circle around."

"How?"

I looked back. The way was blocked by a sheer cliff and a sharp ravine; there was no way we were climbing up or down.

"Why the hell didn't you tell me there was a problem?" I asked Diss.

"I thought you had a plan."

WE were trapped again. The only way out was to go up or to go down. Up was out of the question; down involved a fifty-foot slide to a tumble of rocks. We'd be in his sights the whole time.

I tried thinking of something else, but my brain was stuck. All I could come up with was hanging out until the machine gunner got tired. It wasn't much of a plan, but rolling down the hill was pretty extreme, and going back to the spot where we'd been didn't make much sense.

Every half hour or so I raised the stock of my rifle or pushed my arm up. Always I drew fire. Eventually it got to be a kind of game, the machine gunner toying with me, waiting to see how far I'd go before he'd fire.

"We gotta get outta here," Diss kept mumbling. "There's millions of them."

"We'll get out of here," I told him. "We just have to be patient. Eventually he's going to get tired, or run out of ammo."

"His friends'll kill us first."

"If he had friends, they'd already be here," I told Diss. "Relax."

"I can't relax!"

"All right, then don't relax."

"It's not all right! I can't relax! I can't!"

And with that, Diss jumped up and started running back to the rocks where we'd been.

32

BEYOND MANA

I LEAPED up and started firing as soon as the machine gunner did. Even though it was dark, I could see Diss running. I saw him get hit, the bullets blowing his head apart as if it were a water balloon.

The second I saw that, I went over the side.

I didn't think about it consciously, I just did what I had to. I slid down the ravine on my butt and back, against the sand and rocks. I managed to keep my legs out until I hit, then crumpled hard against the rocks.

The machine gunner must've been too focused on making sure he'd really gotten Diss to see me. I lay on the ground for a long while, barely conscious except for the pain in my legs and my head, and the pounding on the right side of my chest. When the machine gun stopped, it was eerily quiet. I heard the donkey braying in agony, his screams dulled by his fatigue as his life slowly ebbed away.

I might have been on the ground on my back for only a few seconds, or I may have been there for hours. I kept telling myself that I had to get up, that I had to move, but my legs just wouldn't do it.

The sky, which had been cloudy earlier, cleared. I could see the stars. I stared at them as if I were a kid again, bored at night on a beach, counting them and wondering what it would be like to go up to them.

Finally my knees started to work on their own, pushing me over. I bent upward. My rifle was near me, but I couldn't find my pack. I crawled up on top of the rocks and finally saw it lying about ten yards away.

The machine gunner saw it, too, and then he saw me. I rolled back, falling behind the rocks. The gunfire stopped, then started again. There was a loud explosion, and the night turned red. He'd turned his attention to the truck, and one of his bullets had set it on fire. Ammunition began cooking off, hissing and snapping. Between the pops I heard the donkey howling its misery.

There was no reason not to run now. I grabbed my gun, backed away along the rocks, then, as the last gas cans in the truck exploded, I got up and stumbled away.

I WALKED until it was light. Sometimes I managed to move relatively quickly, but most of the time I was just barely making headway, tired and hurting, dragging my right leg with me through the dark. Had anyone stopped me then, I would have given up, surrendered, just let them shoot me. It would have taken a light prod to beat me. In a way I was beaten already. Several times I stumbled to the ground and it took an enormous burst of energy just to get up.

I made my way along the side of a jagged set of hills at the foot of one of the snow-covered mountains I'd seen from the distance earlier. I was going in the general direction of the stream Mayden had told me about, but I wasn't sure precisely where it was. I thought the ground should be going downhill, but most of what I was doing was climbing. Still, I pushed on, knowing I had to find someplace safe where I could rest. Sleep was what I needed, all I needed for now—sleep.

About a half-hour after daybreak I saw the mouth of a cave about ten yards up an incline ahead. Even though the hill wasn't steep at all, I went up on my hands and knees, dragging myself inside the shelter. I hunkered against the side. When I put my head down in the dirt, I fell asleep.

WHY are you looking for me?

The voice was Merc's, but I knew it was an illusion. I was dreaming, or more accurately, in a state between nightmare and insanity.

"I'm coming to help you, man," I told him. "I'll be there."

Well, get moving then.

MY mouth was full of dirt when I woke. I started to spit it out, then began coughing. When I managed to stop I wiped at my mouth, but I couldn't make enough saliva to get the dirt out. I had to grope for my water and washed the caked grit away. Finally I got my mouth clear and sat back, gathering my wits.

The cave was in shadows, but it was light outside. Besides the smell of the dirt, I could smell something like musk, an animal. But I saw none; the scent could well have been part of my dream.

Hunched over at the mouth of the cave, I was amazed that I had gotten here in the dark. Cracked and jagged, the ground was a collection of boulders and piles of smaller rocks.

According to my watch it was nearly four P.M. I was hungry. I had two Pop-Tarts—officially they were called something else, but that's what they were, wrapped in a silver-colored plastic bag. I also had a dried stick of beef jerky, and two energy bars. I went with the beef, then washed it down with a gulp of water. My flask was now less than a quarter full, and it was the only water I had.

The GPS locator had been in the backpack. I still had the sat phone, though. I stared at it, debating whether to call Khattak and have him come and pick me up.

What was there to debate? I'd been heavily battered and nearly killed. Was Merc worth this?

Yes.

Even if he'd slept with Sharon?

Yes.

More importantly, I was. If I gave up now, I'd consider myself a failure. It was too soon.

What would it take then, to give up?

Death. Not even that.

Even though I'd been ready to quit hours ago, now I wasn't. I'd give it one more day, see how I did.

I could always quit. Always.

Until I did. Then I'd never be able to quit again.

THE third time Merc saved my life, we'd been cut off from the militia detachment we were working with and chased by a group of Taliban into the upper reaches of a mountain a few miles from where I was now. We'd been in a hell of a firefight, and Merc had been shot twice in the right arm. One of the bullets had just grazed the top of his shoulder, but the other sailed through his bicep. It was a clean, relatively small wound, ugly to look at and painful as all hell, I'm sure, but not fatal, which meant minor in the context of things. We dressed it, and he did his best to try and forget it.

It was the tail end of winter, and it was really cold. There was still snow on the ground, even at the lower elevations. Our long-range satcom radio had taken a direct hit in the firefight we'd escaped from, and was out. We had a GPS locator with us, at least, and we knew where we had to go to get help.

The way Merc figured it, we had a day and a half of walking before we'd reach an outpost set up by other Special Forces soldiers and some of the locals. The way I figured it, we had three. By day four, we were still on the mountain and the base was nowhere in sight. One of the problems was the map we were using, based on an old Russian piece of fantasy. Nothing was where the paper said it should be, and every time we found something close we couldn't reconcile it with the GPS points.

Finally we saw a road we thought we knew a few miles in the distance and began making our way down toward it. After about an hour, we came to a narrow ledge along the side of a ravine. It ran about fifty feet, and looked like the only way down.

Merc went first. With his right arm injured, he leaned close to the wall, going sideways in spots. I followed, getting closer and closer, worried that he was going to slip. He stumbled once or twice and I dropped to my knee, ready to grab him.

But it was me who slipped, almost three-quarters of the way across. I felt my left foot starting to go and tried to drop the rest of my body to the ledge, but on the way I hit something and bounced the wrong way. I grabbed at the edge of the ledge as I went over, my fingers digging into the dirt. I didn't have enough of a grip, however, and I could feel myself starting to slide. I tried to jerk my leg up and over, but that made it worse; my right hand went off and that was it—I was falling into the rocks below and there was nothing I was going to do about.

Except I didn't. Something grabbed my left arm and locked the rest of my body in place, dangling over the edge.

"Go slow," said Merc in my ear. He'd thrown himself down flat, his left arm hooked around a crag and his right, his wounded arm, holding me.

I could see his face from the corner of my eye. The pain must have been excruciating, but he didn't moan or complain. I put my head against the side of the ledge, then with a loud scream got my right leg over and barreled onto the ledge, rolling over him and dragging him with me.

"What'd you think? You were an angel and you could fly, asshole?" he said when he finally caught his breath.

"Yeah, that'd be the day. Me an angel."

He laughed, but then he added very seriously, "Don't be too hard on yourself, Jacky. I could see you as an angel. Not Gabriel. But an angel."

He was dead serious. From there, we got into our one and only discussion about religion. He was a Protestant, Episcopalian I think, not that he actually went to services. He believed in God and in angels, but they existed in a dimension we couldn't see.

"I didn't think you believed in God, let alone angels," I told him.

"Oh, you gotta believe in something, Jacky. You do. I do. But that's—you see, that's the thing of it. God's not this kind old man sitting back in an easy chair in heaven somewhere. God's the bastard inside you, driving you on. God hates you. It's the only explanation for the world, don't you think?"

"No."

"We came from animals, right?"

"I don't know what you're getting at, Merc. What's that got to do with God?"

"Animals are instinct. They're unforgiving. A wild animal, a leopard, a lion, kills for food. They kill, they live, they die. That's God's plan. Man screwed it up. Man evolved into this thinking being, this being that makes excuses, gets away from the original idea. God's not happy with that."

"Maybe He made man evolve in the first place. Maybe he didn't want man to kill," I said. "That's what Christianity's all about."

"An eye for an eye is Christian, Jack. That's at the root of religion. That's justice. We've gotten away from that. We've gotten away from nature, and we have to pay."

"What's that got to do with angels?"

Merc laughed, then got up. "Let's go find that road, huh? I'm getting hungry."

I HAD one of my Pop-Tarts for dinner. When it was dark, I moved out. Air patrols wouldn't attack a man like they would a truck; they might not even see him. I'd left my night goggles in the truck, but I had the night scope for the gun, and every so often I stopped and used it to scout ahead.

I reached the streambed a little after midnight. The water that had been so plentiful less than twenty-four hours ago and maybe ten miles away had seeped and evaporated into a thick layer of mud. The flask had only a few fingers' worth left. I took enough water in my mouth to wet it, sloshed it all around and swallowed. Then I started walking down the dried-up stream, looking for a place where I could hole up. A nest of boulders on a rise about fifteen feet above the creekbed was the best I could do. It was hardly ideal, but it was better than sleeping out in the open. I put my head against the rock and fell off, my mind wandering while my body collapsed in complete exhaustion.

Some hours later, voices entered the dream I was having, foreign voices that snapped and hissed at each other. Instantly I realized that the voices were not part of the dream, but it took forever for my body to catch up to my mind. I forced my eyes open, remembered where I was, then looked over the side of the rocks to see a half-dozen men in tribal clothing carrying AK47s and walking down the dried streambed in my direction.

33

PAKISTAN, SOMEWHERE SOUTHEAST OF NEZAMKHEL

How do you know if a man is your enemy if he's not wearing a uniform announcing it? If you can't tell from his language or some other sign?

Had the men below me been coming from the south, out of Pakistan, I probably would have assumed they were a Taliban raiding party. But in this case I couldn't be sure. I wanted to think they were a local militia hunting Taliban, or maybe even a security force allied with Merc. I wanted to believe it, but I couldn't allow myself to do so.

I wouldn't have attacked them, even if I'd been convinced that they were Taliban. Even if I managed to kill them all—and with only one grenade and my rifle, that was far from guaranteed—there was a good possibility another group would be nearby.

If I'd been sure they were on my side, I wouldn't have shown myself, either. It would have been hard to convince them that I was friendly. Even if I managed it, there was no telling what they might do; an American alone out here might strike them as something to be investigated, and they might take me back to wherever they'd come from.

But knowing for sure one way or the other—I wanted that knowledge. It was a hunger, as bad as the physical hunger I felt in my stomach, a thirst almost as bad as the one in my throat.

They took their time passing. Their voices were kids' voices, quietly joking. I suppressed the urge to run down and join them—a wild fantasy, a death wish almost.

When they were gone, I rose slowly, rechecking the area to make sure I'd picked well. Then I sat back down, and fell asleep again.

DISS came to me while I slept, his body riddled with bullets, his hair flowing back as if a wind blew at his face. His eyes bulged with the same craziness I'd recognized that first day at the Kabul airport. I knew it was a dream, but I couldn't stop it.

There's millions of them out here, Jack Pilgrim! Millions of them! All around you! They're marching! Millions, Jack Pilgrim! Millions!

WHEN I woke again I was freezing. My teeth chattered together. I got up and started moving around. It was three in the afternoon, and the sun was almost directly on me, but I was freezing. I walked down the streambed, hopping around, looking to see if the men who had passed had left anything, but they hadn't. I took a swig of water—one more left—then climbed up on the rocks to pee.

You can tell how dehydrated you are by the color of your urine. Clear, not dehydrated at all. Mine was almost green. It stunk, and it stung.

I walked down the dried-up streambed for about two hours, stopping every so often to dig my fingers into the mud, hoping I might come up with some water. I kept a lookout ahead; I expected that the men I'd seen had made camp ahead. I figured I'd sneak into their camp at night, see what I could find that would be useful.

By five-thirty it had started to get dark, and I hadn't come across them yet. My eyes were burning holes in my head, cold, jagged holes. And I was thirsty. Very thirsty. The hunger was nothing compared to that. I saw a cave at the side of the streambed and walked to it slowly. I told myself I was just going to check it out, but once I was in it momentum took over; I lay down and fell asleep.

WHERE are you, Jack?

"I'm over the border in Pakistan, Sharon."

Why?

"I'm lost."

You always knew what you were doing. How could you be lost?

"I'm lost . . . Sharon?"

What, Jack?

"Did you sleep with Merc?"

You're not there yet, Jack.

"Not where?"

Where you're going. You're not there.

"Are you there?"

You're not there yet.

"Did you sleep with him? Sharon, answer me—did you sleep with him? Are you with him now?"

You're not there yet, Jack.

How many layers of betrayal are there? If you cheat on your wife or your husband, are you just betraying them, or does it go deeper than that? Do you betray yourself?

If your best friend takes your money, your success, your fame, is that the ultimate betrayal? Is it the worst?

If he sleeps with your wife, as well, is that the worst?

Of if it turns out that you never had any of those things, if those things—money and success and love—were illusions all along, were you the one who broke your trust? If you took those things and placed them above what you should have believed in, were *you* the real sinner?

Whatever they'd done or not done paled beside what I'd done to myself. I wasn't exonerating them. I wasn't even sure what, if anything, they'd done. I was simply realizing that what I had to do had nothing to do with Sharon, and not even, in the end, with Merc.

It was light when I woke up. Six A.M. I pulled myself together, took stock of my supplies. I ate the last Pop-Tart and set out.

Walking was hard. I kept telling myself Merc was going to find me. Mayden had said as much. It was just a matter of walking until he found me. I pushed to keep going.

Somewhere around noon, the sun got so hot that I had to take my last gulp of water. I just had to. I drained the flask, holding it upside down over my mouth. There was a tiny bit more than I expected, and the excess made me feel as if I were drunk. I held it in my mouth a long while before I swallowed.

Once I swallowed, everything fell apart. I realized what a fool I'd been to come here looking for Merc. Mayden had been lying—he'd sent me this way to get me away from him. Probably he'd sent the band that had passed me the day before to find and kill me.

I was dead meat, an offering, payment for something I knew nothing about. And Merc—Merc was gone, long gone, beyond the edge of the universe, back in some primordial existence at the edge of the human soul. Gone.

I changed direction. I walked for maybe an hour before finally realizing that I still had the sat phone. I stopped and took it out of my pocket. I looked at it.

Was it really a phone? If I called Khattak, would he really come for me? Would he?

I punched the number I'd preset. It rang once, then twice, then three times. He wasn't going to answer—of course he wasn't going to answer.

"Yah?"

"Khattak?"

"Jack Pilgrim?"

"I need you to pick me up."

"Where the bloody hell are you?"

"There's a streambed that runs from the village of Nezamkhel. It's in Barmal District in Paktika. Follow it into Pakistan. The stream's dry where I am, just mud, but you should be able to see it from the sky. There's no one around. I'm okay. Come in at night."

"You have flares?"

Did I have flares?

I didn't. But I did have chemsticks in the vest, chemical light sticks that would show him where I was.

"Don't break it open until you hear me," he said. "Keep your phone ready. If I don't see you, I'll call you."

"Yeah," I told him. "Yeah."

34

PAKISTAN, SOMEWHERE SOUTHEAST OF NEZAMKHEL

ALL it took was a phone call. Imagine being behind the lines at the Battle of the Bulge, dialing for help. In the middle of the Bataan March, in Stalingrad, at Shiloh. Standing before Charon, the boatman of hell. Punch the buttons and get out.

I MOVED westward along the streambed, looking for a good place for Khattak to land. I found a fairly flat stretch, maybe a quarter mile long. Then I sat down to wait.

I'd failed. Worse, I'd given up.

All of the pains I'd felt in the past several days came back, throbbing. My head felt as if it were going to split horizontally. My legs were so strained, the ligaments so twisted, I had trouble standing again. And my stomach—my stomach was an ember roasting in a cook's fire, churned and fanned to encourage the flame.

An ordeal doesn't ennoble you. Surviving doesn't make you better. It doesn't erase what you did in the first place. I'd brought myself here, out of pride and foolishness. My illusions had been as bad as Diss's in the end. I'd spent the last few years closing my eyes to what was going on, taking the money people threw at me, salving my insides with fake finery. I got so blind I let Merc rip me off and steal from the feds, and all I did was thank him for it. And then I'd charged off to make it all right, like some superman, some knight in shining armor who could fix the world.

Surviving the past few days didn't change that. So when finally, late into the night, deep into the pitch-black shadows of the night, when I heard the helicopter coming toward me, flying well above first to make sure it was safe before descending, I didn't leap for joy. I didn't jump and shout and yell, "Thank God!" I didn't think of my wife, or of trying to make things right back home.

I wasn't grateful. I was resigned. I broke the chemical sticks and set them out.

I sighted the chopper through the night scope on the rifle. It was a Hind, all right. It was Khattak, and he was coming to get me.

The big bird banked to the left. I lit my last stick and stood close enough for him to see me as he came down. The Hind circled completely around me, dropping cautiously. It slid north, then came back in a hurry, descending through two thousand feet, coming on fast.

When he was about five hundred feet away, I heard a pop and a whistle, like the loud hiss a bottle of warm champagne makes as its cork is released. In the next second, a shoulder-launched missile struck the helicopter, and instantly it turned to flame.

35

PAKISTAN, SOMEWHERE SOUTHEAST OF NEZAMKHEL

THIS is the measure of my despair: I didn't move as the helicopter spiraled down in front of me.

I stood frozen as it hit the ground and exploded. The fuel burst into a fireball almost straight up, and ammo inside the aircraft began cooking off. I stood there, close enough to the heat for it to bring sweat pouring from my skin, squeezing the last liquid from my body.

It wasn't that I could have saved Khattak if I'd run to the chopper. It was far too late for that. The helo went nose in and the crash alone would have killed him. I didn't make the attempt even to save myself. If the Hind had come even five yards closer, I would have been caught in the fireball. I stood there, completely drained, uncaring about my fate, about the world around me, about anything.

Sharon brought me back.

It wasn't a hallucination or a dream or a nightmare, a mirage or a vision. It was a memory: her lying in bed, sleeping, eyes closed, hair splayed on the pillow—perfect beauty. It was a specific night, the night I left her in the Vegas hotel, but it could have been a dozen other nights, a dozen other times. I could have been lying next to her, or walking, or talking like we used to do.

It wasn't lust or a desire to see her again. It was all memory, simply memory—memory of who I was, attached to that glimpse of beauty.

To surrender now, like this, to give up, meant renouncing that glimpse. Though I'd wandered away from who I was, though I'd been lost and seduced by money and easy times, the core of me was still there, just as the primitive part that lived at the edge was. I could perceive and long for beauty. I could feel it move me from across the room. I could remember it, even when I stood at the pit of ugliness.

I snapped out of the depression I'd fallen into.

As I did I realized there were three people coming up behind me, three guerrillas, the Taliban fighters who'd shot down the chopper. I didn't know this the way a student knows his spelling words, or the way an intelligence officer analyzes the enemy position, or even the way a skilled Special Forces sergeant knows how to attack a dug-in enemy. I knew it the way a leopard would know it, instinctually, without any sort of higher brain intervention, without the interference of the frontal lobe. I knew it the way a leopard knows to turn his eyes, to tense his body, to leap, to bite, to hold on until the last death rattle signifies victory.

I leaped to the side and with a scream I fired, pouring lead into the men, who'd either missed me in the flames of the inferno or mistaken me for the hollowed-out victim I had nearly become.

It felt good to stand there screaming, my finger pressed hard on the trigger. It felt incredibly good. It was rage, pure rage. I screamed and I fired and I fired and I screamed. My finger may have been on the trigger for a good five minutes after I'd burned through the magazine. It didn't matter. It didn't matter if I killed anyone, it surely didn't matter if I were killed. I would have gladly traded death for that long instant of black rage, that moment of recognition, that taste.

I'd go back for it. I'd trade anything for it. You would, too.

And then, when it was spent, when I finally realized the box was empty, I turned back into the person I'd been looking for since that night in Vegas. I was still deep in the blackness beyond the edge, deep in the primordial hell mankind had fought so hard to escape thousands of years before. But I was myself again. I was Jack Pilgrim. And from now on there would be no going back.

36

PAKISTAN, SOMEWHERE SOUTHEAST OF NEZAMKHEL

THE guerrillas had strapped Korans to their chests in place of body armor. Three across. I'd scored bull's-eyes on all of them.

I took one of their AK47s and all of the ammo I could find. What I really wanted was water. At that point I would've drunk whatever they had, even the bacteria-laced local crap. But there wasn't any. Nor was there food.

I found the missile launcher—an American Stinger, left over from the campaign against the Soviets.

I waited for others to show themselves, but none did. With the fire finally out, I reversed course again, setting back in the direction Mayden had told me Merc was. Even if Merc wasn't there, it was the way I had to go—sneak east, then south until I found a Pakistan army detachment. Anybody looking for me would expect me to go the other way, toward Afghanistan, and they'd be waiting.

BY daybreak, I'd passed the point where I'd turned around earlier, and found a small group of bushes and trees to rest in. I was out-of-my-mind thirsty. The vegetation meant there must be some water around, but I couldn't see it. I decided I'd sleep a while, then look for it. I sucked some of the leaves, but they were more a tease than a thirst quencher. My throat felt as if it were cracked and my lips were so parched they hurt. Finally I pulled the leaves out of my mouth and curled down to sleep.

An hour or so later I woke up and started moving again. Gradually I realized I was being watched from a hill about a quarter mile away. Stalked. I looked through the scope of the 416 but I couldn't see him. He blended in, or ducked down. But he was there. I knew he was there. And he was good.

So good, I thought it might be Merc. I stopped, waited and stared, but he didn't show himself. An hour, two hours, nothing. I waited so long without seeing anything that I thought it must be my imagination. I crawled away through the brush, moving to a set of rocks nearby. I stayed there for another hour. I didn't see him. Finally I got up, ready to fire if anything moved. But there was nothing.

I walked backward for a few yards, then crouched, watched again. Still nothing.

It wasn't my imagination, though. There was something—I caught an odd glint of light as I turned. I couldn't see the glasses he was using to watch me, but I knew he was there.

It must be Merc, I thought. Merc *was* this good, this patient. He must be watching, trying to make sure it was me.

He'd know it was me. It didn't make sense that he wouldn't come forward.

Walking steadily again, I moved parallel to the streambed, working my way southeastward with it. There were a few clouds in the sky, but it didn't look like it was going to rain anytime soon.

My stalker followed. I caught a glint of light once as I turned. A half hour later, I heard a rock kicking along the ground far in the distance.

The valley the now-dry stream had once flowed through had widened, and the farther I went, the harder it would be for him to stay close without being seen. So I picked up my pace.

I wanted it to be Merc. But I had to guard against my desire. I couldn't let it dictate what I did.

It got hotter as the morning went on. My head felt as if it were pressing toward the ground. I could hear odd sounds in the distance. The landscape at times would start to waver. Without sleep and water, your senses begin to recede. Mine were pulled into a fantasy realm where dream and nightmare mixed. I kept walking, just walking.

Then at noon, my stalker slipped. I heard him fall behind me, not a hundred yards across on the other side of the stream. I spun, and saw him splayed on the ground, lying there, staring at me.

I saw Merc's face.

And then I realized, it wasn't Merc at all. It was a Pashtun face, rounder than Merc's, darker than his would be, with a longer beard. As I watched, he pulled a rifle up from beneath his body where it had fallen, placed it out on the ground in front of him, peered through the scope. It was a bolt-action gun, an ancient but honest weapon, and I watched him put his right hand to the metal, watched him as he prepared to kill me.

And just before he went to squeeze the trigger, I fired my 416, shot right from the hip, spraying bullets around and across and through him, firing until the magazine was empty.

HE was slumped over the rifle, an old M1942 Soviet sniper gun. I bent and pushed him over. For a second, the face I saw was Merc's. But then my eyes came back from the dream state they'd retreated to and I saw it was just a Taliban guerrilla, another of the devoted brotherhood who strapped the Word of God to his chest to protect him from the infidel.

I pulled up the string of Korans and realized that one of the books had indeed stopped a bullet. The slug was caught in the pages, misshapen, as if it had melted when it was fired. I slipped it into my breast pocket, bullet and all, then went back to searching him for something useful, like water. But he had none.

It occurred to me, as I stared at the blood oozing from his body, that I could suck that.

The idea revolted me. But my thirst was incredible, and in the end I knelt and drank my enemy's blood until it ran down my lips and covered my chest.

A HALF hour later, my stomach revolted. I dropped to my knees and retched, convulsing as my stomach emptied. Finally, I collapsed, drained of energy and desire, emptied of everything, ready finally to meet my fate.

HYPOCRITES & THIEVES

37

TRIBAL BORDERLANDS

BLOODSHOT eyes stared at me. Millions of them, as if I were in the middle of Diss's nightmare.

Laughter.

Why did you come, Jacky? What were you hoping to prove?

More laughter.

If you screw this up, Pilgrim, you're going to lose everything. Everything. Your house, your car, the fancy watch on your wrist, your wife, your life. Everything.

Blood soaking everywhere.

I REGAIN consciousness. I smell dirt, then a fire, then something cooking like flesh.

In my memory of what happened next, my body is passed hand to hand over a thousand miles. The stars are overhead. The night has become very still, and also very cold. The pain I've felt, and the thirst, are gone.

Merc appears, his face blackened. His eyes are bloodshot, and I realize they are the eyes I'd seen earlier, the millions of eyes staring at me.

Then I sleep, deeply, without dreams, for what seems like forever.

38

TRIBAL BORDERLANDS

YOU'RE a mess, Jacky. Why'd you let yourself go so badly? You're out of shape, mentally as well as physically. Emotionally—forget about it. When I knew you, you'd never have lost your whole team, or been so reckless. You were a planner, Jack. Here you let yourself get bushwhacked and turned all around, confused. What gives?"

"Merc."

I open my eyes and see Merc sitting across from me. He wears gray native clothes, a long shirt and baggy pants. His beard is thick, though from its length I guess it's only about six weeks old. There's a fire between us, and his face is red from the glowing embers. We're in a cave, and the smell of smoke is so thick that I think I'm on fire.

Is this a dream? I'm not sure at first. I blink my eyes, trying to figure it out as Merc continues.

"I know the agency sent you. They're pissed. They think I stole their money, when all I did was put it to use."

"Merc."

"It's me, Jacky. You're alive. Ran out of water, huh? You never took enough." He shook his head and got up, walking toward the mouth of the cave behind him. "You slipped, man. You just went totally to seed."

"How'd you find me?"

"I knew you'd come. Eventually. They'd send you to find me. They've been trailing you every step of the way, I'm sure."

"Is Sharon here?"

"Sharon?" Merc laughed. "Your wife? Sharon?"

"Did you sleep with her?"

He laughed again, this time longer and louder. "Jacky, why the hell would I sleep with your wife?"

His surprise shamed me, and I couldn't speak.

"She's a beautiful woman, Jack. Don't get me wrong. But she's not the kind of woman you just have sex with, right? You know that."

"Yeah." It was an effort just to mumble the word.

"Besides, she wouldn't screw you like that. I would." He laughed again. "I sure would. Right?"

"You wouldn't."

"Don't be so sure, Jacky. Don't be so sure. Out here . . ."

He let his voice trail off.

I was wrapped in a blanket. My shoulders and neck were sore and my legs numb, but I wasn't tied down or restrained in any way. I rocked forward to get up but my head felt dizzy and I settled back.

"You've been here two days," said Merc, as if answering a question I hadn't asked. "That was Khattak's helicopter that the Taliban shot down, wasn't it? Bastards. But he always knew he was going to go like that. Sooner or later we all will. That's why we're here."

"Why didn't you tell me what was going on?"

Merc turned around. "What was that?" he snapped, his tone suddenly sharp and aggressive.

"You didn't tell me about any of this."

"No shit. What would you have done?" He shook his head. He looked the way he looked when we were busting gut in the Q course, figuring out what torture our instructors would propose next. He looked young. "I'll tell you what you would have done—you would have tried to stop me, right?"

"I don't know."

"Come on, Jacky."

"You lied to me, man. And our money—"

Merc came over and leaned down into my face, grinning. "You accusing me of being a thief?"

"The accounts are all screwed up, Merc. I had to use my own money to make payroll."

"There's more important things than money. A lot more important. You really don't understand, do you?"

He turned and walked from the cave.

A FEW minutes after Merc left, two veiled women entered the cave with a bowl of stew and a cup of water. I grabbed for the water, practically drowning myself as I gulped it down. Then I tried taking the soup but they pushed my arms down gently, as if I were a child. I was so weak my hands just went right down. One of them began feeding me.

When they left, I was alone again. I could see through the mouth of the cave that it was night. I was too weak to get up, and eventually I just leaned down and went back to sleep. This time I had vivid dreams, dreams of Sharon dancing naked before me, dreams of driving with her in the BMW on the Taconic Parkway in New York, speeding through a warm Indian summer afternoon, the trees a violent profusion of color.

When I woke up again, it was daytime. There was a plate of food, bread and olives, along with water nearby. I pushed over to it, got to my knees, and drank. I was still eating the bread when Merc came into the cave.

"Hey, Jack. Good to see you up and around. I've got something you'll like. Coffee! *Coffee, Jack.* Real friggin' coffee. Here."

He held out a cup. I took it gingerly. The smell had already begun to perk up my senses, tingling my nose and loosening my sinuses. Merc smiled at me, then sat nearby. He had his own cup.

"You have to have some vices, even here," he said as he sipped it. "Sorry it's black. Not too easy to get cow's milk out here. And I never was much for dairy creamer."

The coffee threw all sorts of electrical switches in my brain. I could feel my heart jump, and blood rush to my face.

"Good, huh?" said Merc. "You still drinking bourbon, Jack?"

"I stopped."

"Good idea. I saw you had the flask with you, though."

"I put water in it."

He nodded solemnly. "Liquor dulls the senses. Almost as bad as the poppy juice. Kind of ironic, don't you think? The Taliban use our addictions to fund their war. It's beautiful. It makes perfect sense. A lot of the things they do make no sense at all—they're psycho crazy fucks, I'll tell you. But that—that's genius. That's real genius. We're our own worst enemies, and they know it. If it weren't for us, they'd be nowhere."

He laughed.

"What happens now?" I asked.

"To who? Me? You? I can't see the future, Jack. You know that. Whatever happens, happens."

"You told me the CIA was following me."

"They are."

"Are they here?"

"Not yet. They're still trying to figure it all out. It may take them quite a while. They may totally miss it, or just give up. Hard to tell."

"Where are we?"

"Where do you think, Jack?"

"Pakistan."

"Or Afghanistan. Depending on where the line is drawn. Does it matter? We could be in China."

"What about the Taliban?"

Jack got to his feet without answering the question. "Come on and take a look at us. Look at what we got here. You'll be surprised."

He reached down and helped me up. My feet were wobbly, but I stutter-stepped along, letting my blanket go along the way.

The cave was near the summit of a hill dotted with similar openings, connected by a series of narrow ramps and ledges. The paths gradually widened toward the bottom of the hill, where a shallow stream flowed. Opposite, less than fifty yards away, was another hill, this one steeper and without as many caves. Two rope bridges connected them at the southern end. People moved around, not just armed men, but what seemed to be workers and even children. I saw a group of kids ushered into the clearing between the two hills, where three women in burkas began addressing them, apparently giving a school lesson.

"We have an entire tribe," Merc said proudly. "Our own tribe. Three hundred and seventy-six people. Just under half are warriors. Growing every day, Jack, in ones, twos. We're a nation, Jacky. A regular stinking tribe, every bit as legitimate as the tribes over the border or the others to our south and east. This is our land now."

"Uncle—"

"Uncle what, Jack? Uncle isn't going to like this? Well, Uncle shouldn't have come in the first place then, right? Why did he come? To kick out the Taliban. Well, all right, I can buy that—revenge. That makes sense. Eye for an eye. But somewhere along the way, somebody forgot the equation. Somebody forgot to total up the score. Because they let Osama go. They let him go, Jack. You know, and I know, and every soldier in our unit knows, and the generals know, which means to me that the president knows. Why? Because they're not serious? Because it helps them? Because, at the end of the day too many people didn't have the balls to do what needed to be done?"

"And you do."

"Damn straight I do. So do you. You've been out here. You know."

"You think the CIA is going to let you stay here?"

Merc laughed, but didn't answer.

"There's rumors all over the place that you have a secret army," I told him. "And that you have secret weapons."

"Not much of a secret if everybody knows about it, huh?"

"Are the weapons?"

He smiled at me, and then he nodded. But I'd seen that grin on his face before. He used to use it to bluff people.

"What sort of weapons?" I asked.

"Jacky, I keep telling you—it's no secret if people know about it, right?" He laughed. "We have to take care of the Taliban, Jack. No more innocent victims. No more nine/elevens. We get them this time. Completely."

"I agree we should but—"

"There's no buts, Jacky. None. You know it."

I SPENT the rest of the day wandering around the camp. The people eyed me suspiciously, but I seemed to have the run of the place. My sat phone was missing; I assumed Merc or his people had taken it, along with my weapons and the flask. The only thing they'd left me with, besides my clothes, was the wounded Koran I'd taken off my stalker.

There were several hundred people in the village, as Merc said. Most but not all were Afghans. I saw at least eight Europeans, and a couple of Asians, possibly Chinese, though I didn't get close enough to ask.

There was a village at the foot of the other hill. People appeared to be going out to it and working on building houses there, carrying rocks and working with lumber that had been delivered some time ago, if the brownish color of the wood was any indication. They were also digging a shaft in the ground, a defensive trench back to the caves, I thought. There were rat holes for machine gunners and trenches just beyond the village, between the settlement and the open plain that led away from it to another pass in the mountains.

The double hill formation was being turned into a fortress. Attackers, or anyone else for that matter, could only get inside from the east. The western hill sat in the shadow of a mountain with steep crags too difficult to scale in an attack, and to the north and south were deep ravines where raiders could be easily picked off.

Toward midafternoon, the workers in the village began cleaning up, apparently hiding their work so that it wouldn't be seen by observers above. I guessed that Merc knew what the surveillance schedules were, and planned accordingly. Well before dusk, everyone was back in the caves, including myself. Merc had sent a bald, clean-shaven man to bring me back. He had a quiet, unassuming nature, and spoke English in a soft, retiring voice. His accent sounded Midwestern, and after he led me back, I asked if he was American.

"From Canada, originally," he said. "You could tell from my voice."

"I couldn't place it, exactly."

"Amir Conrad is wonderful, isn't he?"

"Amir?"

"Leader. He prefers English, but the Afghans tend to use Pashto since it's their native language. They call him Amir."

I sat down next to the now cold fire. "How did you get here?"

"The Amir found me. I was doing missionary work in Kabul. But I didn't know what I was talking about. One night, he and I met by chance in a cafe. I didn't have money to pay a bill, and he took pity on me. We began talking. Soon I realized he understood everything that I didn't."

"About what?"

"God, Mr. Pilgrim. The angry God who is our father." He bowed his head. "Excuse me now. I have chores to see to. The women will bring you food shortly. When the time is right, they will start your fire."

DINNER was a mush of rice and some sort of grain, with bits of a grilled meat mixed in. It wasn't a lot, but it was filling. I felt my strength coming back.

The women came around eight to light the fire. I sat and watched as they worked. They were a team, one stirring the ashes, the other carrying the kindling and wood in small bundles. It was a machine-like coordination built over many repetitions. When they left, I stared at the flames, trying to sort out what to do next.

Clearly I wasn't going to talk Merc into leaving with me. And maybe he shouldn't. What he had going here wasn't going to meet Uncle's approval, nor would the Afghans like it. But he wasn't hurting them, either. He'd created a new world on the edge, one that didn't accept their realities but was too far away to make much difference to them.

The fact that he was this deep into Pakistan would protect him from the Afghans. The Paks weren't likely to come up here after him, either. His only real problem was the Taliban.

I hadn't asked him why, but I didn't need to. I knew why. He'd gone through the same thing I'd gone through, but at the critical point, he'd turned one way and I'd gone the other. He'd decided to stay on the edge, or maybe beyond it, back in the place where the primeval ruled. I'd turned toward something else.

I was going back. I'd turn the corporation over to the feds and walk away. I'd get my wife, and start over. If she'd come. If not, I'd go without her.

"You have a real village here," I told Merc when he came in about a half hour after the fire had been started.

"That's what I been tellin' you, Jack. A real village. This is where it starts. Eden."

"Doesn't look much like a paradise to me. Nothing grows here."

"It will. That stream is only a start."

"How do you get your food?"

He gave me one of those smirks again. But it was a serious question, and he knew it.

"We have food. We're careful. We have wells. We'll have irrigation ditches by the summer. We'll grow wheat, other vegetables. It's a step-by-step thing."

"You sure you can grow wheat up here?"

"You're a worrier, Jack. You should relax. Food comes. You got here, right?"

"I'm not food."

Merc laughed. "We're not cannibals, Jacky. Don't worry. You're the one that drank the blood. But I like that. Drink your enemy's blood. Kind of a baptism."

Had Merc been watching all along? Was the man who had stalked me Taliban, or one of Merc's followers? And what about the men who'd shot down the chopper?

"You're one of us, Jack. You'll see. I'm glad you're here." Merc got up. "What do you need, Jacky? What's going to make you happy?"

"Nothing."

"We all need things, Jack. That's what makes us human."

AN hour later, a girl in a veil and a long, thick dress came to the cave. I realized as soon as she walked in that Merc had sent her—she was the "need" he'd referred to. I watched as she shed the long coatlike dress that she wore over another, lighter garment. It wasn't an overly sexual gesture and yet it filled me with lust. She began slowly to unbutton the next layer, her fingers moving smoothly from top to bottom, each push, each gentle tug a gesture of seduction. And then finally she was naked, except for her veil.

It was only then that I found the strength to put up my hand and say no, shaking my head gently.

The girl didn't believe me. She knelt toward me, her breasts swaying slowly, then let the veil drop.

"I can't," I said. "No, thank you."

She leaned and kissed me, a gentle touch on my cheek, then another on my neck. When she put her hands to my shirt, I folded my fingers around them, then eased hers away.

"No."

Dejection came to her face, then tears, slowly coming down her cheek.

That was the moment I was most vulnerable, when the pit opened in my chest and I had to fight against falling in. I motioned that she should go and closed my eyes. I held them closed and waited. When I opened them, she was gone.

39

TRIBAL BORDERLANDS

So if my wife hadn't been a temptress or a cheater, a thief or heretic, hadn't been a guide or a savior, what had she been? Who was the beautiful woman who was more than a quick fuck, to put it the way Merc might have. What did she really want, if not bling and fancy cars?

I heard the sound of thunder in the distance, rain pounding on the earth. They reminded me of a rainstorm I'd driven through with Sharon a year before in upstate New York; in an instant I was back there, lost with her, hunting for a friend's summer house. The rain fell in fistfuls, slamming against the windshield; I couldn't see and finally I pulled off.

The day before she'd been to a doctor, a specialist who told her that there was no hope that she'd ever get pregnant. She wanted a child. We both did; she was still shell-shocked from the revelation. The doctor had told her we could adopt, or even try finding a surrogate for my sperm. He intended those alternatives to be encouraging, I'm sure, but they'd only left her feeling more numb.

"You really wanted a kid, didn't you?" she said as the rain pounded down on us.

I did, but I hesitated to say that. I didn't want to hurt her.

"I know you did, Jack. I know."

"It's okay," I told her.

"Would you want to adopt?"

"No." The word flew out of my mouth before I could stop it, before I could think about what I wanted to say.

She didn't answer. I turned and saw that she was looking straight ahead, staring at the rain, her face now hardened into the mask a pioneer woman would have used facing the endless prairie.

I should have said something like, "we can if it's important to you." Or, "what do you want?" Or even, "I really haven't thought of it all that much, maybe I should."

But I didn't. Her silence had become a wall I couldn't climb over.

We sat there for another fifteen minutes while the rain pounded the car, both of us silent. Finally, the massive downpour lightened to a steady spray, and we moved on. We found her friends' house and ended up having a pretty good time, a great weekend really.

After that we never talked about adoption or having children again. And the silences and impenetrable walls grew more frequent.

It wasn't just the kid she wanted. She wanted me to reach across, and I hadn't.

Love.

As easy as that.

But the easy things had become impossibly difficult.

The thunder grew louder and I saw her again, saw her next to me on the bed, sleeping. I rolled toward her but she slipped farther away, just out of reach. I reached for her and the rain flooded around us, thunder and lightning. We were in an ocean, sinking. I clung to her, grabbing desperately as the rain fell harder and harder, the drops so large they roiled the water.

40

TRIBAL BORDERLANDS

NOT rain, not thunder—the sound of a helicopter.

In an instant I knew it wasn't part of a dream. I leaped up. The sound grew louder. There were several choppers, four or five at least. They were big Chinooks, their distinctive double-bladed slaps pounding the mountain.

Chinooks are heavy-duty aircraft, capable of carrying more than forty troops depending on their gear and the chopper's configuration. Special Forces units use them for ferrying teams behind enemy lines.

I went to the cave entrance. A man squatted there, a grenade launcher in his lap. He put his hand out, gesturing that I should stay inside. I dropped to my knees beside him, listening and debating what I would do if the helicopters landed.

The first thing, the most obvious thing, was to grab the launcher from the man here. It wouldn't be an easy fight, though—he was as big as I was, and his bare forearms were thickly muscled.

The noise of the helicopter rotors grew steadily louder, the ground reverberating with the deep bass of the churning blades. For a moment, the pounding was so loud it seemed as if judgment day had come. And then, gradually, inexorably, the sound began to recede. The guard and I remained motionless, listening until all we could hear was a vague whisper in the distance.

MERC wouldn't talk about the helicopters the next day. I asked him where he thought they were going but he ignored the question. Instead, he wanted to talk about a Taliban village on the next ridge over, three miles as the crow flew, but about eight if you were walking.

"The whole village is their camp," he said. "It's their base of operations for the attacks into the Paktika districts. They come up out of there, hit a couple of isolated hamlets, then retreat. It's part of their strategy."

"Is that where the Chinooks were going last night?" I asked.

"We call them Taliban but that's not really who they are. Al Qaeda—they're ten times worse than al Qaeda was when we were here, Jack, worse than the old Taliban. They've gone completely back to their roots, completely hard-core. I haven't wanted to attack their village until now, because it'd be too tough a fight. But now that you're here, we can get it. You and me can do it together."

"The Chinooks—they would have been us, not the Paks. They came out of the west."

"What we do is flank them," continued Merc, as if I hadn't said a word. He paced around my cave, nodding to himself and gesturing with his hands. "They have lookout posts on a ridge above the village. That area is very similar to ours, two hills, V-shaped, a little tighter wedge than us. They have caves, but they don't live in them like we do. They've gotten just a little too fat, just a little. They have huts in between, on the flatland. That's where they live. So we go up on the southern hill, we take their lookout posts, on the far eastern end, then sneak down the path right into the heart of the place. There are irrigation ditches—those are going to be the main problem, I think, because they can fall back into them. The fields are to the north of the buildings, so if we're not fast enough they can use them for cover and make their way to the caves. If they're in the caves, it'll be a hell of a fight. These buggers will make us pay for every inch."

"Merc, you're not listening to me."

"The place will be booby-trapped. They've had enough time to do that. They were gone for a long time. They only came back recently, a few months, but long enough. I haven't wanted to attack, but now that you're here, we can do it."

"Because I'm here, or because you figure the CIA is coming?"

Finally, Merc stopped and looked at me. It was as if he'd finally heard something I'd said.

"You're getting better, Jack. I can tell. You're more yourself. You got rid of the poisons. That's good."

"What kind of weapons do they have?" I asked him. "I heard rumors when I was in Barmal and Mana."

"Unsel didn't tell you?"

"Unsel told me you stole money from Uncle and they wanted it back. That's all he said. He didn't even tell me what Leopard was. He didn't say anything about this, and nothing about weapons. I didn't even hear about the weapons in Kabul."

"You think they want their money back? The amount of money they're talking about—what, the whole program? Leopard? Two million dollars? Give me a break. That's nothing to them. God, they spend more than that buying flowers for graves. They want the weapons, Jack. They want Osama and his followers. They know I know where they are, but they don't trust me. So they sent you to keep an eye on me. You follow me, they follow you. All right. So we'll play it their way. Tomorrow, we go."

"How do you know that's what they have in mind, Merc?"

He'd gradually worked his way over to me and we were now less than two feet apart. He grabbed me by the shoulders.

"Osama's out there, Jacky. I can smell him. He wants his weapons. There are caves on the other side of the village—they set it up just like the way I set it up here. That's where I got the idea. Osama, Jacky. The devil's there and we're going to get him."

Merc was crazy. I don't mean that he wasn't sane. The truth was, what he said made perfect sense. But it had nothing to do with the world outside. He'd lost all touch with everything beyond this valley, beyond the edge. He'd sunk so deep in it that he was never coming back.

There was no way to tell him that, though. The only thing I could do was go with him and see what happened. We'd take the Taliban village—I didn't think there'd be any question of that. Then, if he was right and all the CIA wanted was to find those weapons, there'd be an easy way out. I'd bring them to them, or show them where they were. I'd have Merc use my sat phone and call them.

Or I'd find an opportunity to slip away. Another day and I'd be strong enough to leave on my own.

"We'll attack tomorrow," Merc told me. "We push off at dawn, surround the place, and get them in midafternoon, when they're returning from the fields getting ready for dinner. It's their most vulnerable time. Be ready."

I would have been. But that night, just after dusk, the Chinooks came back. And this time they didn't just pass overhead.

41

TRIBAL BORDERLANDS

THE way I knew it was real was the stream of shells that exploded all along the face of the caves. Big howitzer shells, exploding from the jaw of an AC-130 Hercules gunship. The thing just opened up without warning, with the helicopters still too far to be heard. The shells peppered the side of the hill, sending us deeper into the caves. I'd never been on the receiving end of Spectre attack before. It was relentless, and yet somehow random, as if lightning were striking across a field again and again and again. There'd be rumbles and bursts, punctuated by stillness, then the roar of the earth being torn apart, and the *thud-thud-thud* of shells slamming into dirt and stone nearby.

The choppers came in maybe ten seconds after it stopped. It was the best-coordinated assault I'd ever seen, and I'd been part of a few good ones.

Even so, the village put up a damn good defense. The bombardment by the gunship kept them back in the caves but hadn't taken much of a toll, and when it eased for the choppers to come in, Merc's people were ready. They got one of the Chinooks, tearing it apart with missiles or rocket-propelled grenades. The fire lit the night, silhouetting the soldiers as they made their assault.

In some ways, it was a replay of the attack on Tora Bora, though the space and scale were much smaller. But this time, the American commanders had learned their lesson. They were serious—they didn't send a handful of Americans to lead Afghan soldiers. They sent Rangers and Delta people, several hundred of them in an endless, relentless stream. They broadcast warnings to surrender, and followed them up with rocket attacks on each cave, working their up slowly and relentlessly. When one man went down, two more took their place. This was the way they should have gone after bin Laden. This was how they would have gotten Satan if they'd tried.

I didn't have a weapon. Going out of the cave would have been suicidal. I hunkered near the entrance, crouched down by the rocks. Merc's warriors ran back and forth, moving very deliberately, as if they'd practiced this a dozen times.

I felt torn. I didn't want them killing Americans. On the other hand, they were under attack for no good reason that I could see. Merc might be crazy, but these people weren't on the enemy's side. They wanted to eliminate the Taliban, Afghanistan's enemy, and the West's. It was a mistake to attack them, especially since they would fight to the end. I could tell they would, by the way they moved.

From the corner of the cave, I watched a group of Rangers take on a machine gunner maybe thirty yards away and well below me. The Rangers started by tossing grenades at him. His shelter had been designed so that only a direct hit would get him. Otherwise all he had to do was duck down and the rocks around him kept the blast and shrapnel from reaching.

It took the Americans a few throws to realize they had a better chance of tossing an apple into a chimney from a hundred yards than of getting a grenade in the exact spot needed to kill him. They moved to flank him, and got pinned down by crossfire.

Another team took up the fight, this time with mortars. Again, it was like trying to land a basket from outside the arena. Finally they used the attack to cover an advance, and got close enough to hit him with a flamethrower.

They had every weapon imaginable—more firepower than I'd seen in my days here—and still it was tooth and nail.

Gradually, the fighting moved upward, the Americans pressing on relentlessly. The other hilltop fell. Soldiers began raining machine-gun fire and shoulder-launched missiles at the caves. Then there was a massive explosion, and smoke and flames enveloped the top of the opposite hill.

"They're out of their minds, Jacky," said Merc, rushing into my cave with two of his soldiers. He'd changed into black fatigues. They were stained with blood and dirt. Sweat soaked the top of the collar beneath his bulletproof vest, which had tears in the fabric, front and back.

"Out of their fucking minds," he repeated.

"We have to surrender, Merc. It's the only hope."

"They want the Taliban. That's who they should be gunning for."

A grenade exploded near the mouth of the cave. The Rangers had gone back up on the other hillside. Merc and I were at the side, huddled together; his men were sprawled at the front of the cave, not firing, waiting until they had solid targets. One man had an AK47, the other a grenade launcher.

"Where are the Taliban, Merc? Where the hell are they?"

"Next valley over. I told you. We were going there tomorrow."

"If that's true, why didn't Americans attack them, not you?"

"You tell me, Jack. They're insane. I mean, maybe they missed it. Maybe they think we're the Taliban. Who knows what Uncle thinks?"

The gunfire suddenly let up. A loudspeaker boomed, telling us again to surrender, the message repeated in both English and Pashto. Merc made a face.

"You think they'd let us go after this?" he told me. "They got us right where they want us. This is to assuage their consciences."

I thought he was crazy. Hell, I *knew* he was crazy. It must have showed in my face.

"You still don't believe me," he said matter-of-factly. "You think I lied to you."

"You *have* lied to me, Merc."

"Not about this. Not about anything important."

"The company wasn't important?"

"That was just money, Jack. You know that's bullshit. You know it."

The gunfire stoked up again.

"You led them to me, Jacky," he said. "Were you in on it, or just a fool?"

"I wasn't in on it."

He nodded. "Yeah. You were always a little naïve, especially when you were drinking. That was the problem."

"I wanted to help you—you saved my life three times. Four times, now. Let me save yours. Let's give up."

The idea that I'd come because he'd saved my life took him by surprise somehow. The tough, almost maniacal mask that had held his face in check dropped, and I saw sadness, incredible sadness.

"It balances out, doesn't it?" he said. "Somehow."

A missile or maybe a rocket-propelled grenade landed just below the mouth of the cave, shaking the walls so violently dirt fell from the roof. The soldiers at the front began firing their weapons.

"Time to get the hell out of here, Jack." Merc pointed to the back of the cave, at the wall. "Take the sledgehammer. The wall was bricked up, but you can get through it. Once you're through, you climb down to the shaft. Then run. Just go. Get away. Get far away."

I looked into his eyes. The mask was back. He grinned. "Like what you see?"

"Well, let's go then," I told him.

"I'm not going, Jack. It's me they want. They can't deal with me—they want to get me because I'm more of a threat than the Taliban. Crazy, huh? Because I know what the truth is—because I can face it and they can't. I know what has to be done, and I know that they're too weak to do it." Merc started to laugh. "The Taliban's the enemy. Me, I'm one of them. If they leave me behind, leave me here, they know I'll succeed. They're afraid of what I'll become."

"You destroyed the villages in Afghanistan," I said, suddenly realizing what should have been obvious all along. "You destroyed them. You burned them to the ground. Not the Taliban."

"They had to be destroyed, Jacky. Otherwise the Taliban would have moved right in. They're getting ready to do that now. They have big weapons hidden in the mountains. Big ones."

"Jesus, Merc—how many people did you kill?"

"This is war, Jack. You don't keep track. You look at your objectives. It's the way it has to be. It's the way God designed us."

Flames lit the opening of the cave. One of Merc's soldiers rose, started firing his gun, emptying the magazine. As he did, I saw three rectangles beneath his shirt. At first glance I thought they were boxes of ammo, and wondered why he would keep them where it was hard to reach. Then I realized they weren't boxes at all, but books—the Koran vest the men who had shot down the helicopter had worn.

Flames from the darkness outside engulfed him. He screamed, then threw himself forward, still firing his gun at the enemy as he died.

I grabbed Merc's arm. "Let's go."

He pushed me away, pulling a pistol from his belt.

"Go and find the camp where the Taliban's weapons are," Merc said. "There are missiles there. Go. You were always stronger than me. Naïve and stupid. But strong. That's worth something."

"I was never stronger than you, Merc."

"Braver, too," said Merc. He pulled the gun up and pointed it at me. "Remember the time with the kids, Jack? The first mission here. When those children found us on the recce? Out here, farther north"

"Yeah, I remember."

"I really blew it, didn't I?"

"You didn't blow it. How did you blow it?"

"I should've killed them, Jack. Should've grabbed them and killed them."

"No. You did the right thing."

He looked into my eyes. "You got to be hard, Jack. You gotta be really hard."

And with the word "hard" still on his lips, he pulled the gun back, opened his mouth, and blew his brains out.

SATAN

42

TRIBAL BORDERLANDS

THE firing outside had begun to subside. At some point while Merc and I had been talking, the other solider had left, very possibly to join his comrade in death.

I got down on my knees, looking at Merc. The bullet had blown away the back of his head as it exited, but his face was intact. He had a smirk, his last smirk, but something else was in his eyes, as if he'd seen something at that last moment that had reassured him he was right.

I took the gun from his hand and then, before I could get up, I heard a sat phone ringing—my sat phone.

It was in the right leg pocket of his fatigues. I pulled it out and held it up to my ear.

"Yeah?"

"Jack. How are you, Jack?"

"Race? Captain?"

"Jacky, listen to me. We don't want. To harm you. There's been more than enough. Bloodshed. Just give up. You've done your duty. Identify yourself. To the Rangers and you will not be harmed."

"You set this whole thing up?"

"Jack, you're going to have to work with me here. Or you're going to get killed. With the rest of them. Now I need you to tell me. Where is Conrad, okay? That's step number one. Then, tell me where you are. So we can get you out."

"Merc says there's a Taliban village not far from here. They have weapons—missiles. There were all sorts of rumors—"

"Jack, you know he's off his rocker. Right? He's psycho. Your friend's a murderer, Jack. He's been burning down villages. On both sides of the border. A whacko."

"He says they have weapons."

"He's a madman. We've searched for weapons. Now where the hell are you?"

"How'd you follow me here?"

"We're working against time, Jack. Sooner or later, they're going to find you. If they don't know it's you, they'll kill you. Now tell me where you are. And tell me where Mercury Conrad is. I don't want you getting hurt."

It must have been the phone—they must have used it somehow to track me. I threw it against the wall, shattering it.

I jumped up and ran to the back wall, looking for the sledgehammer Merc had mentioned. It wasn't anywhere I could see. There was nothing here but dirt and rocks.

The dirt was loose sand, not the hard-packed surface at the front of the cave. I kicked at it, then dropped to my knees and clawed at the ground. Within seconds I felt a piece of wood. I pulled it up, and took a swing at the wall.

Nothing happened. I swung again. Flames appeared at the mouth of the cave again, spreading farther inward.

The wall seemed to give a bit.

I heard a machine gun, very close. I swung again and broke through the wall.

More gunfire. The flames pulled the oxygen out of the air, sucking my lungs inside out. I swung, and as I swung a surge of energy took hold and I went crazy, wailing against the wall as it gave way. There was an explosion very close to the cave entrance. I dove headfirst into the hole, rolling down a shaft and tumbling into the darkness.

When I stopped, I found myself in a circle of blue shimmering light. I smelled dampness. I rose, and discovered I was at the edge of a very shallow pool of water, no deeper than ankle high. I walked through as quietly as I could, toward the edge of light ahead.

The hill above me groaned with explosions as Merc's people made their final stand. This was more a tunnel than a cave, a long shaft built into the side of the hill and used, apparently, to store water. The far end was a narrow slit in the side of the mountain, facing the moon, which had sent its beams to show me the way out.

I pushed aside some of the rocks, ducked as a bit of the top gave way, and stepped out into the valley on the other side of Merc's village.

I'd taken no more than two steps when the moon darkened. I looked up and saw the big hull of the gunship passing above. Tracers erupted from one of its guns. It looked like a vampire or devil passing by.

When it was gone, I began walking southeastward, following a tumble of rocks into a mountainside crevice. After thirty yards, I was on my hands and knees, crawling upward. I must have gone more than a mile that way, and then suddenly the ground leveled to my right, and I saw a broad path leading southward in the direction Merc had said the Taliban village lay.

A few minutes after I started down it, I heard the echoes of the Chinook helicopters returning on the other side of ridge. I hunkered down near the road, listening, making sure they weren't coming for me. Only when the last reverberation had faded in the distance, did I start walking again.

Twenty minutes later, the ground shook with a violent, earthquakelike roll. Planes had been sent to bomb the last vestiges of Merc's village into dust, erasing all trace of him. From high overhead, B-52s dropped stick after stick, raining explosives down on his remains. I must've been more than three miles away by that time, and still the thuds were strong enough to shake me back to my knees.

MY plan was to head east and find one of the larger Pakistani villages in the Federally Administrated Tribal Area, and from there to get to Peshawar, the largest city in this part of Pakistan. I figured that, as the crow flew, I was no more than twenty-five miles from Bannu or maybe Tank, both places where I ought to be able to get a bus to Peshawar. I was maybe ten miles, most likely much less, from a road that would take me to either. There were villages all along the road where I could find food and water, and where I'd also be able to buy another weapon. As long as I kept moving and presented no obvious threat to the locals, I would more than likely be left alone.

The problem was that Uncle might tell the Pakistani secret service to look for me. They'd arrest me if not assassinate me. That might not be a problem in Bannu or even Peshawar, even though I'd stick out; the local service chiefs had their own agendas and I was confident I could fly under the radar if I left quickly. Peshawar was probably a different story, as was Islamabad, where I'd have to go to get anywhere beyond Pakistan.

I'd been in Peshawar once, and I knew I could catch a bus from there to Islamabad, the capital maybe a hundred and fifty miles away. We had run a security job there, and I might be able to contact some of our old workers. Uncle and the Paks might be watching, but unless I thought of something better in the meantime, I'd have to take the chance. Even if the plan wasn't the best I'd ever thought of, it was certainly better than the one that had gotten me here in the first place.

By the morning, I'd concluded that Race was right, that Merc was just deranged about the Taliban or, maybe more likely, had invented their village to keep me from trying to flee. So when I came around the corner of a cliff on a narrow trail just after dawn and saw it lying at the foot of a pair of hills pockmarked with cave openings, I was shocked. I dropped to my knees, scanning the nearby countryside for a better vantage point.

As I did, I heard something coming up the path toward me. I threw myself over the side of the trail, scrambling for a place to hide.

43

NORTHWEST OF MAROBI RAGHZA, PAKISTAN

A SMALL herd of goats clomped up the path, heading toward one of the small pastures that were tucked into the hills I'd just passed. They were wearing bells, which clanged lightly back and forth as they passed. I couldn't see them from where I was, and didn't dare raise my head, worried that the herder might see me and alert the Taliban village.

I waited until I couldn't hear them anymore, then crawled out slowly, looking for stragglers, human or animal. When none appeared after ten minutes, I got up and started down the path, walking very slowly. Nearly an hour later, I reached the turnoff to the village where the goats had come up from.

There was some scrub vegetation around, and it took me quite a while to make sure a lookout post wasn't hidden somewhere nearby. Finally, I circled farther south and climbed back to the path, looking for a spot to look at the village where I wouldn't be seen. I had to climb up over another ridge, watching the whole time to make sure that I didn't stumble on a guard post designed to keep someone from doing exactly what I was doing. It must have been after midday by the time I finally reached a good vantage point.

Just as Merc said, the hills that sheltered the village made a V, with the path running through a gully across the open end. I could see one or two roofs in the distance, but I didn't have a good enough angle to see beyond them. It was clear, though, that anyone coming into the village could be easily spotted from either side of the surrounding highlands, as well as the village itself.

The easiest thing to do, and by far the smartest, was to bypass the village completely. The path to the southeast was open and would be easy to follow. And yet, running away never occurred to me. I had no illusion that I was going to single-handedly take on a Taliban stronghold. But I wanted to make sure that's what this was. I couldn't leave without doing that. It was the last thing I owed Merc, some affirmation—to me, to no one else—that he wasn't as insane as Race and Uncle had claimed.

Merc's plan called for an attack up the southern side. Presumably he'd wanted to do that because it was more lightly guarded than the northern. So I worked my way there, crossing a barren hillside and then coming onto a small, cultivated plain. The poppies there were already shin-high. When I reached them, I sat down and waited for the sun to set, feeling it would be easier to avoid being seen in the dark.

I heard the goats come back around dusk, the sound of their bells carrying on the wind. I waited another two hours, the darkness growing, the moon slowly mounting the nearby hill.

There were two paths up from the field. I didn't take either, instead climbing up a series of large rocks to the east of the second path, closest to the vertex of the V had the hills been a letter of the alphabet. From a distance, the rocks looked bowling-ball smooth, but up close they were anything but. Nature had left them gnarled, with many crevices and easy handholds, and though the moon was ducking in and out of clouds, I had an easy time seeing where the climb would be simplest.

If I had been posting defenders, I would have had sentries at the top of each path, with a lookout between, and another even higher at the vertex. I made my way up accordingly, slithering through some brush until I reached a patch of rock that could not be crossed without exposing myself to someone at the intersection of the two hills.

As I'd climbed, I decided that all I had to do was spot a sentry to confirm what Merc said was true; the villages on this side of the border had no reason to post night guards on their perimeters. So I stared in the direction I believed a guard would be, waiting for some movement, even a shadow, to confirm someone was there.

I waited an hour. More. Finally, I crept forward. Ten more minutes passed. Fifteen. I took a pebble and tossed it. Nothing.

I backed down to the edge of the hill and worked my way toward the path until I could see where it came up. There was a log there, clearly something that had to have been placed by man. But no one was on it, or immediately behind it.

Crawling forward must have taken me twenty minutes, perhaps more. The position must have been a watch post, for there was a circle of rocks nearby with the ashes of a fire. But the ashes were cold and the spot was unmanned.

Slowly and carefully I crawled around the top of the hill, scrambling behind what little cover there was. It was almost morning before I was sure that there were no guards on the hill, and if there were guards on the other they were sleeping. I settled down to rest for a few moments; as I did, my eyes grew so heavy I drifted off to sleep.

WHY aren't you with me, Jack?

"I want to be, Sharon. I do."

Why aren't you here?

"I got lost."

You always knew what you were doing. How could you be lost?

"I didn't know what I was doing. I got suckered in. I got soft and I was swayed by things that weren't important. Bling—junk that didn't matter, on the surface. It wasn't who I was. I wasn't rich."

I never thought you were rich, Jack. It wasn't your money that made me love you.

"What was it?"

You seemed to know the way.

"I know. But I got lost. I closed my eyes to where I was going, to what was really going on. I tried to become something I wasn't. I was fooled by people who were more out of touch than I was. My own fault. I forgot who I was."

Why aren't you with me, Jack?

"I will be. I have something to do first."

When?

"As soon as I can. I promise."

THE tinkle of the bells from the herd of goats woke me from the dream. I flattened myself on the ground, and caught a glimpse of them leaving the village.

An hour or more must have passed as I watched the huts, gradually becoming more and more aggressive about showing myself. There were no breakfast fires, no smoke. I told myself that didn't mean anything; a poor village might start its day without a warm meal or tea. But little by little as the sun rose, I realized that the only explanation for the lack of activity was that the village had been abandoned.

And it had been abandoned in haste, as I saw as soon as I looked in the huts. Bedclothes were scattered around on the floor.

How long did they plan on staying away? A day? Two days? I went from hut to hut, looking for clues, but life here was so simple that it was impossible to know. There were plenty of possessions left in each of the three dozen houses. Several had primitive cellars, hiding places beneath thin slats of wood and rugs that had been removed. There were weapons in two, and ammo in several others. I took an AK and as many magazines as I could slip into my pants.

A complex of caves lined both facing walls at the sides of the village. They proved conclusively that Merc was right—this had been a Taliban stronghold. Some of the caves may have been natural, but all were deepened and in many cases connected with elaborate ladders and twisting tunnels just wide enough for an armed man to pass through. There were generators and electric lights, an elaborate ventilation system, jugs of water stored along the walls and even a set of plastic pipes. Wires ran through the place. And there were pictures of Osama bin Laden all over the place.

I ripped one down to take back with me. When I did, I saw that there was a niche behind it in the wall. I reached in and pulled out what looked like an old-fashioned flotation belt. It took me a few seconds to realize it was a suicide bomb kit, complete with a button to take you straight to paradise.

THERE were too many caves to look in, and besides, I'd found what I came for. But as I started to trot down the ramp in front of the entrances on the southern side of the village, I realized that one of the cave mouths at the foot of the opposite hill was much wider than any of the others. I also saw what looked like a set of steel rails buried in the dirt at its mouth.

They weren't steel rails; they were made of wood. But that was just as interesting.

All of the other caves I'd entered narrowed and turned after the opening, but this one didn't. I walked in slowly, staying to the side, the AK ready. About ten yards in I stopped, unable to see anymore. I went back to one of the houses where I'd seen a kerosene lamp, then stayed there a while and ate some of their stale bread. By the time I got back to the cave, it was almost three. I was less cautious now, moving quickly because I figured whoever they'd left behind to herd the goats would be returning in a couple of hours.

The cave ended in a pile of rocks thirty yards from the entrance. I climbed up to the top, and began throwing them down. There was clearly something behind them. I worked like a madman for more than an hour until finally I could see into the passage.

The space beyond the rocks looked like a garage or a warehouse, with a smooth cement floor. A rail ran down the center. The space was immense. In it sat three large cylinders, which even with my dim light I knew had to be Scud-sized missiles.

I was still staring at them when I heard the goats approaching the mouth of the cave.

44

NORTHWEST OF MAROBI RAGHZA

I DOUSED the lamp, picked up the rifle, and slipped down the pile of rocks, moving as quietly as I could.

The goats began to bleat loudly. My eyes adjusted to the darkness, and I could see shadows moving maybe a few yards away in the gray dusk of the cave.

So where was the herder?

It might just be a boy, no more than seven or eight. But would they trust someone like that to guard the flock all alone here for days? More likely there'd be a pair of guards, trusted veterans.

If it was a kid, could I kill him?

If it came to that. If it was me versus him, and he had a gun, and a real chance to get me, then I'd kill him. But I didn't agree with what Merc had told me at the end. What he'd said, about how hard you had to be—that was true at the abyss, on the edge—it was gospel for him, but not for me. I was beyond that, and I wouldn't kill except to avoid being killed myself. There was a distinction, and that distinction made all the difference.

The goats kept coming toward me, baaing like sheep. I edged toward the mouth of the cave, looking for their masters. Finally I was close enough to see eyes—but they were all red eyes, waist high. Goat eyes.

The animals flocked around me, nudging me as if I were their friend, or maybe their savior. As they came with me to the cave entrance, I ducked down, using them for cover. They licked at me, nuzzling even, happy to see me, happy to see any human.

Their herder wasn't waiting near the mouth of the cave. He wasn't in one of the houses nearby, or even the caves. He'd fled with the rest of the village, leaving the goats to fend for themselves until he got back.

I PACKED three of the suicide belts on each of the missiles, and rigged wire I'd ripped from the caves so that I could be outside when I detonated them. It took me more than five hours to get it all set up, and when I was done, I wasn't sure it would work.

It did, though. My God, did it. The explosion gutted the mountain, sending a thick layer of dirt all over, and causing a small avalanche. The goats, who'd hung around me as I worked, fled in terror. I ran, too, unsure of how far the tumult might continue. I ran until the wind cut my face. I ran until the stars were bright above me. I ran and I ran, and when I finally collapsed at the side of the road, I was many miles away.

45

PAKISTAN

I GOT to Peshawar three days later. Compared to everything that had happened over the past two weeks, the trip was placid, a vacation. I was a curiosity, regarded probably as a CIA spy, but so wild-looking that no one who came near me could be sure. The aura of insanity is a great protection in the wide world; it's seen as an infectious disease, a hint that the primordial is not that far off. People gave me space wherever I went. I was grateful, and careful not to test their generosity, or intentions.

In Peshawar, I bought a cheap cassette player and made several tapes detailing what had happened to me, where, and when. I made up envelopes, and sent several out, addressed to our New York office, our Kabul mail stop, a P.O. box we used in Germany, my house, and Merc's. I kept two tapes, and threw five away. I found an Internet cafe, where one of the machines had a microphone for recording MP3 files. I played the tape, recording a file, then sent it via e-mail to our office in New York, to my e-mail address, and to Unsel's. Then I boarded a bus to Islamabad, the capital of Pakistan.

Two guys from the embassy were waiting when the bus pulled in. They said they were from the embassy, but they were clearly CIA. They took me to a house outside the city, let me get cleaned up, even brought me new clothes. The next morning, a woman whom I gathered was some sort of deputy station chief, not the top honcho but close, came to talk to me. She knew about the e-mails, and the tapes I mailed.

"You're going to jail for a long time, Mr. Pilgrim," she told me, brushing some imaginary lint off the legs of her smart powder-blue pantsuit. "There are more than three dozen charges we can file against you. The Afghans have charges, and the Pakistanis have charges. That's not counting civil actions against your firm. You are in a lot of trouble. A whole mess of trouble."

"I don't think so."

"Well, clearly we have a difference of opinion." She got up. I think she might have been pretty if she'd worn just a little more makeup. "If I were you, I would start thinking of ways to make sure you stay in American custody, rather than Pakistani."

"Have you listened to the files?"

"What? The ravings you sent via e-mail? Who would believe them?"

"I sent tapes, as well."

"We've intercepted them all," she said.

I pulled out the package the cassette tapes had come in and gave it to her.

"Twelve tapes. I have two. When you've found all of the others, hand me over to the Pakistani government. Or better yet, give me to the Taliban. I'm sure they'd like to have retribution for blowing up their missiles."

IT took a few days, but we worked something out. They probably figured I was bluffing, but couldn't be absolutely sure. By then they would have verified what I said about the missiles, so maybe someone in the hierarchy realized I was on their side and it would be insane to kill me.

Actually, I doubt that. But I suppose it's a possibility.

I did some research later on, and from what I can tell, the missiles were larger than normal Scuds. They may have been improved versions, which the Soviets were using toward the end of the war there—over a thousand missiles were fired at enemy villages during the war, something we never heard too much about in the West. I thought they looked a lot like an early-generation Pakistani missile, the same one originally designed to carry nukes against India, but since I didn't take any pictures, I can only rely on memory. And memory, except when it's recalling beauty, is always a faulty thing.

My deal with Uncle was that I would have free passage to a place in South America, where I'd keep my mouth shut. They'd take over Iron Rock. Now that it was a shell of its former self, it could be very useful to them.

I get a small sum every few months as payout. It's really their way of keeping tabs on where I am, but that's okay. If I need to, I can disappear.

My journey back to Afghanistan, through hell, had brought me back to life. Before it, I'd been dead and didn't know it. I'd been seduced, like we can all be seduced, by money and power and glitz, by comfort and ease, by everything associated with living in the twenty-first century, far from the jungle's edge. Along the way, I'd numbed myself to the world, and to myself; worse, I'd forgotten who I was, and what was real.

When I left Islamabad, I knew who I wasn't: I wasn't some wannabe-rich guy on the make, numbing his insides with booze so he could ignore the bullshit he nodded his head to. I wasn't somebody who cared what I was driving or how fine my suit was cut, how good my watch looked or whose head turned in my direction. I wasn't someone who spent time thinking about the stock market, or what the Fed was up to. I didn't have to rub elbows with anybody I didn't like, or tell tales of what I had done with my life to pay for dinner.

Saying who I was, though, that was harder. I was a guy who'd seen the very edge of human existence: the deep rage at our core, the beast of ourselves we escaped when we evolved out of the jungle. I was a guy who not only had been tempted but had succumbed to temptation, who'd been fooled and schooled, used in the worst ways possible.

My experiences hadn't ennobled me, nor had they, as the saying went, made me stronger. They were just bits of the stored memory, guideposts I could touch in my brain when I needed to examine the way forward.

And Sharon.

I'd been wrong about her, wrong about her cheating, and even more wrong to blame her as the source of my woes, the temptress in the Garden. She was just another soul who wandered by and thought I knew the way out of the woods. I'd led her astray, not the other way around.

When I flew out of Islamabad, I knew I wanted her, but I also knew she had to come of her own free will, without me fighting for her. When the plane from Islamabad landed in Delhi, I bought her a ticket from JFK in New York for my final destination. I arranged for it to be sent via courier to our house, then left a message on our machine, telling her it would be there, and she could come if she wanted. Or not. I called when I knew she wouldn't be home, when I knew I'd have no chance to persuade her.

She came.

The day I met her at the airport, I pressed the Koran that had stopped the bullet into her hands and said someday I'd explain everything I saw, but I wouldn't speak of it until she felt she had to know everything.

That day has not yet arrived.